MURDER
ON THE
MARMORA

Also by Conrad Allen

MURDER
ON THE
MARMORA

Conrad Allen

ST. MARTIN'S MINOTAUR NEW YORK

www.minotaurbooks.com

Library of Congress Cataloging-in-Publication Data

Allen, Conrad, 1940–
    Murder on the Marmora / Conrad Allen.—1st ed.
        p. cm.
    ISBN 0-312-30791-8
    1. Dillman, George Porter (Fictitious character)—Fiction. 2. Masefield, Genevieve (Fictitious character)—Fiction. 3. Private investigators—Fiction. 4. Cruise ships—Fiction. 5. Ocean travel—Fiction. 6. Nobility—Fiction. 7. Egypt—Fiction. I. Title.

PR6063.I3175M886 2004
823'.914—dc22

                                                                        2003058551

First Edition: January 2004

10 9 8 7 6 5 4 3 2 1

To my beloved granddaughter, Carys Ellen, in the hope that she may one day read this book.

MURDER
ON THE
MARMORA

ONE

She was a disappointment. The first time that he saw her, George Porter Dillman felt as if he had somehow been let down. After the Cunard liners on which he had regularly crossed the Atlantic, the *Marmora* looked curiously small and unimpressive. Built in 1903, she was the first P&O vessel to exceed ten thousand gross tons but that meant she was still only a third of the size of the *Lusitania* and the *Mauretania,* so beloved by Dillman, who had been fortunate enough to sail on the maiden voyages of both ships. While the two massive Cunarders each carried over three thousand people aboard, the *Marmora* had little more than nine hundred. Nor could the P&O ship hope to match them for pace. The greyhounds of the seas could achieve a maximum speed of over twenty-six knots. At full pelt, the *Marmora* could only edge above eighteen knots and was more comfortable at an unhurried fourteen or fifteen.

It was, Dillman realized, unfair to measure the smaller ship against two giants of oceanic travel. He was not comparing like

1

with like. The *Marmora* was no transatlantic liner, built to power its way through the most dangerous waters on the globe. It was an elegant vessel that cruised halfway around the world, taking its passengers on a more leisurely and varied route, filled with visual interest. For that reason, Dillman was looking forward to his first voyage with his new employer, P&O—or, to give the line its full name, the Peninsular and Oriental Steam Navigation Company. Since they were setting sail in December, he would be spending Christmas at sea, and that would be a novel experience for him.

When he went up the gangway at Tilbury, therefore, he did so with alacrity. The *Marmora* posed a new challenge and it was one that he was eager to accept. Like everyone else streaming onto the ship, he was wrapped up warmly against the cold weather. Dillman wore a heavy overcoat, a homburg hat, scarf, and gloves but his luggage contained clothing for much warmer climes. The festive season would be celebrated in blazing sunshine.

As soon as he had been shown to his cabin, he unpacked his things then went off to report to the purser, Brian Kilhendry. He was invited into an office that had an overwhelming sense of order about it. Documents and papers on the desk were stacked in neat piles, and even the artificial flowers in a vase on the wooden filing cabinet had been arranged in the tidiest positions. As a private detective, Dillman worked very closely with the ship's purser and he had always enjoyed a cordial relationship with those holding the office on Cunard ships. They had been courteous, efficient, and extremely helpful.

From the moment he met Brian Kilhendry, however, he had the feeling that this purser would be the exception to the rule. The Irishman was a stocky man of middle height with curly ginger hair that was starting to thin rapidly. Now in his thirties, Kilhendry, a striking figure in a spotless uniform, had the face of a professional boxer. The broken nose lent him a strange charm. He gave Dillman a brisk handshake before waving him to a chair.

"So," said Kilhendry, eyeing him shrewdly through narrowed lids, "you're the famous George Dillman, are you?"

"I don't lay any claims to fame, Mr. Kilhendry," replied Dillman.

"You're far too modest."

"Am I?"

"Apparently," said the purser with the tiniest hint of mockery in his voice. "I've a friend who works for Cunard and he tells me that you're a one-man law enforcement agency. You solve crimes almost as soon as they're committed."

"If only that were true. But I'm afraid it isn't."

"No?"

"To begin with," said Dillman, "I'm not a one-man operation. I work in tandem with my partner, Genevieve Masefield. She deserves as much credit as I do for any success that we've enjoyed."

"Oh, yes. I know. My friend told me lots of things about Miss Masefield."

"Complimentary things, I hope."

"For the most part."

Dillman did not like the smirk that accompanied Kilhendry's remark. There was an implied criticism of his partner to which he strongly objected. The purser's manner was annoying him. Dillman concealed his irritation behind a bland smile.

"On which ship does your friend sail?" he asked.

"He's second officer on the *Caronia*."

"She's a trim vessel. We made four crossings in her."

"Arresting people right, left, and center, from what I hear."

"Only when they deserved it, Mr. Kilhendry."

"You even solved a murder on the *Caronia*," the purser noted.

"We did what we were paid to do," Dillman said quietly, "and we'll endeavor to provide the same service on the *Marmora*."

"I doubt very much if it will be needed."

"All passenger lists tend to have a small criminal element in them."

"Yes," Kilhendry said airily. "We do have the occasional thief, pickpocket, and cardsharp aboard but I pride myself on being able to spot them before too long. I've a nose for villains, Mr. Dillman, and so does my deputy, Martin Grandage. There's not much that gets past us, I promise you."

"How do you know?"

The purser was checked. "What do you mean?"

"Well," said Dillman, "how can you be sure that dozens of crimes have not taken place on board that you and your deputy simply failed to detect? Anyone can spot the obvious crooks, but some are very sophisticated these days. They plan things with great care and know how to cover their tracks."

"Not on the *Marmora*," boasted Kilhendry. "I run a clean ship."

"That remains to be seen."

"I know this vessel, Mr. Dillman—you don't."

"Granted," said the detective. "But even you don't have an intimate knowledge of every passenger on this voyage. There'll be over four hundred and fifty of them in all. Your nose will have to be ubiquitous to sniff its way through that lot."

The purser's eyes flashed. "Don't you get clever with me!" he warned. "I'm just trying to let you know where we stand."

"Oh, I've worked that out, Mr. Kilhendry. You don't really want us here."

"What I don't want is to have anyone treading on my toes."

"In other words, you're marking out your territory."

"The *Marmora* is my ship."

"Captain Langbourne might dispute that," Dillman said wryly. "So might P and O. However possessive you may feel about it, the ship is owned by the company. They hire all of us to sail in her with specific duties. And I may as well tell you now," he added, rising to his feet, "that we intend to earn our wages from P and O, even if that means treading on a few toes."

"I can see we're not going to get on," said Kilhendry, curling a lip.

"You'd decided that before I even came in here."

"With good reason, Mr. Dillman. I don't like Americans."

"Ah," sighed the other. "So that's what you have against me: my accent."

"No—your attitude. Americans always seem to think they own the world."

"It's not a delusion from which I've ever suffered," said Dillman with a grin. "Beware of generalizations, Mr. Kilhendry. They're always misleading. For instance, I've heard that all Irishmen are pugnacious yet you are the soul of restraint."

The purser's body tensed and his eyes flashed again but he quickly regained his composure. Reaching for some papers on the desk, he handed them to Dillman and became businesslike.

"Here are the passenger lists for first and second class," he explained. "As you know, we have no third class or steerage. Unlike Cunard, who pack their liners with emigrants, we only cater to people who can afford some luxury."

"Then they're entitled to get what they pay for," said Dillman.

"I've also given you a diagram of the ship. The *Marmora* has only five passenger decks. I'm sure that you'll soon find your way around each one of them."

"We will, Mr. Kilhendry."

"Make yourself known to my deputy."

"Mr. Grandage?"

"Yes," said the purser. "We have royalty aboard until we reach Port Said. That means that I'll have my hands full. I don't want you bothering me every five minutes to tell me you caught someone stealing a handkerchief or that you think a certain passenger is cheating at poker. Report to Martin Grandage instead."

"What if a serious crime is involved?"

"We don't have serious crimes on P and O ships, Mr. Dillman. At least, not on the ones where I'm the purser. I told you before. I run a clean ship."

"There's always someone who'll try to dirty it for you."

"That's where you and Miss Masefield come in," said Kilhendry with a touch of disdain. "Wipe up the mess before I even see it. Do you think that you can manage that?"

"We'll do our best."

"Good." He gave a cold smile. "Welcome aboard, Mr. Dillman!"

Genevieve Masefield had done it so many times before that it had become a matter of course. She traveled to the port with the other passengers, befriended a number of them on the way, then slipped aboard as part of a small group. On this occasion, she had a choice of companions. The Cheriton family, who had met her on the way to Tilbury, were more than ready to adopt her but Genevieve chose instead to board the ship with Myra and Lilian Cathcart, whom she had rescued from the attentions of an overzealous customs officer. In the space of a few minutes, Genevieve had got to know and like the two women. All three of them came out of the customs shed and paused to take a first approving look at the *Marmora* with her sleek lines, her two tall funnels, and her distinctive P&O flag, fluttering at the masthead. Genevieve saw her as a refreshing change from the Cunard liners to which she had become accustomed.

"You've obviously been abroad before, Miss Masefield," observed Myra with admiration. "I could see it from the way you handled that bossy individual in the customs shed. Have you sailed on a ship as big as this before?"

"Oh, yes," said Genevieve.

"We've only been to France on a ferry from Dover. This is the first time we've been farther afield and we're so terribly excited about it." She turned to her daughter. "Aren't we, Lilian?"

"Yes, Mother," said Lilian with a diffident smile.

"My husband hated to travel," Myra continued. "That's why we always spent our holidays somewhere in England. It was an effort to get Herbert to take us anywhere. Wasn't it, Lilian?"

"Yes, Mother."

"That's not a complaint, mark you. I was happily married for twenty-four years and I have the fondest memories of my husband. But I do wish he'd been a little more adventurous with regard to travel. Don't you, Lilian?"

"Yes, Mother," her daughter agreed obediently.

Myra Cathcart was a tall, slim, handsome woman in her late forties with a zest about her that was not muffled by the thick fur coat and hat she was wearing. She seemed to exude vitality. While Lilian had inherited her mother's classical features, she had nothing like the same spirit. Shy and self-deprecating, she glanced around nervously as if expecting someone to tap her on the shoulder and accuse her of some nameless transgression. She looked so young and hesitant that it was difficult to believe that she was twenty-two years of age. Having mourned her late husband for a decent interval, Myra was embarking on the cruise of a lifetime with real enthusiasm. Lilian, by contrast, gave the impression that she was being dragged reluctantly along.

"Well," said Myra, nudging her daughter, "what do you think of the *Marmora*?"

"Very big," replied Lilian.

"It will take us all the way to Egypt."

"But it's such a long way to go, Mother. Will we be safe?"

"Of course."

"P and O has an excellent safety record," said Genevieve, trying to reassure Lilian. "Have no fears about the *Marmora*. She's done the trip a number of times without the slightest mishap."

"Lilian is a worrier by nature," said Myra. "She'll feel better once we're aboard."

Her daughter was doubtful. "Will I, Mother?"

"You know that you will, dear. Come along."

The trio joined the other passengers who were walking toward the ship. Myra Cathcart moved forward with a confident step but

Genevieve noticed how wary the daughter was. The closer they got to the vessel, the more unsettled Lilian became. Without warning, she came to a sudden halt, as if having second thoughts about the whole enterprise. The other women stopped beside her.

"What's wrong, Lilian?" asked her mother.

"I don't know."

"This is a special moment for us. Savor it."

"I wish that I could, Mother," said Lilian with a shiver, "but I'm frightened."

"Of what? Of whom?"

"Of everything."

"That's perfectly normal," said Genevieve, taking over. "The first time I was about to cross the Atlantic, I was quietly terrified. I imagined all kinds of disasters taking place. In the event, it was a very smooth voyage with no problems at all."

It was not exactly true, but Genevieve was certainly not going to tell her new friends about the murder that took place on board the maiden voyage of the *Lusitania*, or describe the way she had become involved in helping to catch the killer. Lilian needed to be soothed, not further alarmed by the story of a gruesome crime at sea. Genevieve felt great sympathy for her. She put a comforting hand on Lilian's arm.

"Think of the tales you'll be able to tell your friends when you get back to England," she said. "They'll be green with envy when they hear that you rubbed shoulders with royalty."

"Yes," said Myra, smiling at her daughter. "The Princess Royal and her husband will be traveling with us. I wonder if she'll wear a crown for dinner. It will be such fun to find out, Lilian, won't it?"

"I suppose so," murmured her daughter.

Myra became concerned. "What is *wrong* with you?"

"Do you feel unwell?" asked Genevieve. "They have a doctor aboard, you know."

Lilian shook her head.

8

"Why are you holding back like this?" asked Myra.

"I keep thinking about that other ship," said Lilian.

"What other ship, dear?" wondered her mother.

"The one that I read about in the newspaper last year. It was called the *Mervinian*. I'll never forget that name because of what happened to the crew. It was a cargo vessel that foundered in the Bay of Biscay." Lilian gave an involuntary shudder. "Six of the crew were drowned. After a week in an open boat, the survivors were picked up by our very own ship, the *Marmora*. They were in a terrible state."

"I'm sorry to hear that," said Myra, "but it has nothing to do with us."

"It has, Mother. We'll be sailing past the Bay of Biscay."

"But in a much larger vessel than the cargo ship," Genevieve pointed out. "The *Marmora* is big enough to handle rough seas. She's been built for that purpose. You'll be surprised how stable she is, Lilian."

"It won't help me to forget the six men who drowned."

Myra clicked her tongue. "Why do you always remember bad news?" she said. "It's morbid, Lilian. I'm taking you on this voyage so that you can enjoy yourself, not brood on other people's tragedies." She took her daughter firmly by the arm. "Now, let's not detain Miss Masefield any longer. What will she think of us?"

The three of them set off again then took their place in the queue at the gangway. When they finally stepped on board, Myra Cathcart laughed with an almost childlike glee but her daughter remained withdrawn and fearful. Lilian had an inner sadness that showed in her face and manner. Genevieve wondered how that sadness had come about in the first place. Like her friends, she was traveling first class and followed a steward when her cabin was assigned to her. Myra was thrilled to discover that their cabin was only four doors away and they were, in effect, neighbors. Genevieve was not quite so pleased about the proximity of the Cathcarts. While she

9

found them pleasant company, she did not wish to be monopolized by them or it would hamper her work as a detective.

She had an early illustration of the danger. Before she had even had time to unpack her trunk, there was a tap on the door. Genevieve opened it to admit a beaming Myra Cathcart. The older woman had shed her fur coat, revealing that she was wearing a Zouave jacket and an intricately embroidered skirt that brushed the floor. Her fur hat was still firmly in place.

"You must come and see our cabin, Miss Masefield," she insisted. "It's perfect for our needs. Even Lilian was impressed by the clever way it's been designed. It's similar to this one," she went on, looking around, "but somewhat larger. Do come and see it."

"I'd like to, Mrs. Cathcart," said Genevieve, taking some more items from the trunk. "When I've finished hanging everything up."

"I'm far too excited to unpack. There's plenty of time for that."

"I hate things to get creased."

"What a gorgeous dress!" remarked the other as Genevieve hung a blue evening gown in the wardrobe. "Oh, I do wish Lilian had the courage to wear something like that! But I'm afraid she only chooses clothes that she can hide behind. Whereas you," she said, indicating the smart two-piece suit Genevieve was wearing, "know exactly how an attractive young woman should dress."

"Thank you, Mrs. Cathcart." Genevieve had also removed her topcoat to give herself freedom of movement and placed her wide-brimmed hat with its ostrich feather on the little table.

Now that she was able to see her properly, Myra realized how poised and beautiful Genevieve was; she had a natural grace that made the visitor sigh with envy.

"If only Lilian were as brave as you!"

"There's nothing brave about unpacking a trunk."

"I was thinking about this voyage," said Myra. "You're traveling alone without the slightest qualms, but Lilian is in a state of anxiety even though I'm there to hold her hand. You have such a wonderful air of independence."

"It's something I've had to cultivate, Mrs. Cathcart."

"Do tell my daughter how you did it. She needs instruction."

"I'm sure that this voyage will be an education in itself."

"I hope so. It's one of the reasons I decided to come on this cruise." Myra gave a confiding smile. "The main reason, of course, is that I've always wanted to see the world and I finally have the opportunity to indulge my fantasies. Is that why you're sailing on the *Marmora*?"

"To some extent," replied Genevieve.

After hovering for another minute, her visitor pressed her to join them in their cabin, then let herself out. Myra Cathcart was going to be a problem. Genevieve had the feeling that she had been identified as the daughter Myra wished she had in place of the timid and melancholy Lilian. She was afraid that the older woman would soon make a habit of popping along the passageway to speak to her. When she finished unpacking, Genevieve waited for a quarter of an hour before she finally went to find the others. There was no need to knock on the door. Myra Cathcart, obligingly, had left it open. At the very moment when she got there, Genevieve saw someone emerge from a cabin farther down the passageway and walk away from her. Though she only caught the briefest glimpse of the man, it was enough to make her gasp in surprise. The shock of recognition caused her face to turn white.

Myra Cathcart swooped down on her then saw the apprehension in her eyes.

"What's the matter?" she asked. "You look as if you've just seen a ghost."

TWO

Martin Grandage was a tall, strapping, dark-haired Englishman in his early thirties who was beginning to run to fat. His chubby face was lit by an almost permanent smile and he was unfailingly polite and friendly. When Dillman first saw the deputy purser, Grandage was helping an elderly female passenger out onto the main deck. The detective waited until the man was free before he introduced himself.

"Mr. Grandage?" he said, offering his hand. "My name is George Dillman. I was told to make myself known to you."

"How do you do, Mr. Dillman?" said Grandage, shaking his hand warmly. "This is a real privilege for me. Your reputation goes before you."

"That's what Mr. Kilhendry said."

"You've spoken to Brian, then?"

"Not exactly," replied Dillman. "I spent most of the time listening to him."

Grandage laughed. "Brian is like that. He has to let you know that he's in charge. But he's a first-rate purser and his bark is far worse than his bite. The problem is, I fear, that he has something of a phobia about Americans."

"Isn't that a handicap?"

"In what way?"

"Well, he must meet scores of my fellow countrymen in the course of his work. Does he ignore them or just give them all the evil eye?"

"Neither," said Grandage. "He turns on that Irish charm of his."

"I can't say I saw any sign of it."

"That's the other problem you need to know about, Mr. Dillman. You're at something of a disadvantage. Brian Kilhendry sees you as a Cunard man. An outsider. He's fiercely loyal to P and O. As far as he's concerned, you're an interloper."

"I'm glad you don't seem to share that opinion, Mr. Grandage."

"Not at all," the other said earnestly. "I'm looking forward to working alongside you and Miss Masefield. I'm hoping to pick up a few tips."

"Don't watch us too closely," advised Dillman, "or you'll draw attention to us. We like to blend in with the other passengers. Invisibility is our main weapon."

"It's the opposite with us. That's why they put us into these uniforms. People can see at a glance who we are and what we do." He patted his chest. "These gold buttons are supposed to impress people. I hope they work. I had to sew them on myself." Grandage gave a chuckle then regarded the detective with interest. "What brought you into this line of work, Mr. Dillman?"

Dillman gave a shrug. "Pure accident, I guess. I set out to be an actor but I spent most of my time auditioning for parts that I never actually got. In order to feed and clothe myself, I became a Pinkerton man and discovered that my acting skills were of immense value. I played far more parts for the Pinkerton Agency than I ever did onstage."

"But what enticed you into the nautical world?"

"An offer that I couldn't refuse," explained Dillman. "The sea is in my blood, Mr. Grandage. I come from a family that builds oceangoing yachts. My formative years were spent afloat. Whenever I step on a ship, I feel at home."

"So do I," said Grandage. "With all its faults, I love this job."

"Then you're a man after my own heart."

Dillman warmed to him immediately. After his abrasive interview with the purser, he was relieved to find the deputy so friendly and cooperative. Dillman was glad that he would be dealing for the most part with Martin Grandage, and he knew his partner would feel the same. Unlike Kilhendry, the deputy purser was on their side.

"This is not the best place to talk," said Grandage, as more passengers came out to swell the numbers on the main deck. "I'd appreciate a proper chat with you and Miss Masefield later on."

"Where will we find you?"

"My office is very close to Brian Kilhendry's."

"Right," said Dillman. "We'll choose a quiet moment."

Grandage chuckled. "There *are* no quiet moments on the *Marmora*, I'm afraid." A buzz of curiosity came from the crowd that was gathering at the rail. "It looks as if the royal party is just arriving. I'll have to go."

"Nice to have met you, Mr. Grandage."

"The pleasure is all mine." He shook Dillman's hand again. "Welcome aboard!"

He sounded as if he really meant it.

Genevieve Masefield decided she had been mistaken. The man she had glimpsed in the passageway could not possibly be the person she feared he might be. It was too great a coincidence. She had seen him only in profile for a fleeting second, and that was not nearly long enough for her to make a positive identification.

Her sense of guilt had got the better of her. By the time she finished admiring the cabin occupied by Myra and Lilian Cathcart, she had dismissed the incident from her mind. Like her friends, she was keen to be on deck at the moment of departure. After retrieving her coat and hat, she led the way to the exit. Their cabins were on the promenade deck, and most of the other passengers accommodated there were already at the rail.

Genevieve and the Cathcarts got there in time to witness the arrival of the Princess Royal and her family. They were getting out of the gleaming car that had driven right up to the ship. Two other vehicles were heavily laden with trunks and valises for the royal party. Porters descended on them at once and started to unload them.

"I don't think *they* had to bother with customs," Myra said enviously. "That man who questioned me was so disagreeable—I mean to say, do I look like a smuggler?"

"Of course not, Mrs. Cathcart," said Genevieve. "You were very unlucky."

"Until you came to my aid. You really put him in his place."

"I knew the ropes, that's all."

They leaned over the rail to watch the royal party coming on board. Members of the crew formed in two lines below and, at the top of the gangway, Captain Langbourne was waiting to greet his special guests. The two children came first, followed by their parents. All four of them were dressed in winter wear.

Lilian came to life for the first time and gave a breathless commentary. "That's Lady Alexandra on the left," she said, pointing a gloved finger. "She's seventeen. Lady Maud is only fourteen. They're such lovely girls. Doesn't the Princess Royal look stately? You can tell that she has royal blood. Her husband is the Duke of Fife. He was only an earl when he met his future wife but he was created a duke upon their marriage in 1889."

"You seem very well informed," said Genevieve.

"Lilian has a passionate interest in the royal family," Myra told her. "She has a scrapbook filled with cuttings from the newspapers. There's nothing that Lilian doesn't know about even minor royalty."

"I think they're wonderful, Mother."

"So do we all, dear."

"The Duke is so handsome, isn't he?" continued Lilian, staring at the tall figure in the top hat. "He's eighteen years older than the Princess Royal. That means he's only eight years younger than the King himself, but it makes no difference. They're very happily married. You can see that even from here."

Genevieve could see nothing because the newcomers had gone up the gangway and stepped aboard. She was pleased to see Lilian so animated. It proved she was not as coy and submissive as she had first appeared. Genevieve looked forward to learning more about Lilian Cathcart.

It was Myra who took up the conversation, however. "An eighteen-year gap in ages," she said. "That's far too much, in my opinion."

Lilian became defensive. "They're ideally suited, Mother."

"But they belong to different generations."

"That doesn't matter."

"I believe it does, Lilian. Marriage is about common interests."

"They love each other," asserted her daughter. "Isn't that enough?"

"I'm sure that it is," said Genevieve. "I've known cases where the husband and wife have been separated by twenty years or more, yet they've been very contented. By the same token, I've met married couples of similar ages who hate each other. Children make a huge difference, of course. They help to bind a family together."

"Would you like to have children, Miss Masefield?" asked Myra.

"It's not something I've ever thought about, to be honest."

"But you're bound to marry one day. You must have dozens of admirers."

"Admirers don't always think in terms of proposals of marriage," Genevieve said with a smile. "That's why one has to be so careful."

"What sort of man *would* you choose, Miss Masefield?" said Lilian.

"One that I could love and trust."

"And one that could support you properly," added Myra, as if giving a note to her daughter. "Love, trust, and a reliable income are the bedrock of a happy marriage."

"I don't agree," said Genevieve. "If money is a prime factor, then the whole business becomes a trifle mercenary. I think I'd prefer a poor husband, whom I adored, than a rich one I could never trust."

"How would you pay the bills?"

"Together."

Myra was shocked. "Surely, you'd not expect to work after marriage?"

"Why not?"

"Looking after a husband is a full-time occupation."

"That depends on the husband, Mrs. Cathcart."

"Mine would have been horrified if I'd even contemplated taking a job."

"Father was horrified at most things," Lilian said sadly. "Change of any kind frightened him. He felt that women were simply there as a form of decoration."

"Lilian!" Myra exclaimed.

"It's true, Mother. I revere his memory but I also remember that he spent all his time stopping me from doing things I wanted to do."

"Only because they were inappropriate. I'm ashamed of you for giving Miss Masefield the wrong idea about your father. He doted on you. Show some gratitude," she urged. "It's only because he left us so well provided-for that we can afford this cruise."

"What did your husband do?" asked Genevieve.

"He sold shoes," Myra said proudly. "Herbert owned two factories and a chain of shoe shops in the Midlands. 'A nation walks on its feet'—that's what he always said. He made sure that anyone in Cathcart Shoes walked comfortably." She smiled fondly. "He was a remarkable man in his own way. He worked so hard for us. Too hard, in fact."

Lilian bit her lip. "Please don't talk about that," she said. "It only upsets me."

"Then let's have no more unkind remarks about your father."

"I wasn't being unkind, only honest." Myra quelled her with a glare and Lilian shrank back into her shell. "I'm sorry, Mother. I won't do it again."

"So I should hope."

"We should be off soon," said Genevieve, peering over the rail. "They're hauling the gangway in. This time tomorrow, we'll be a long way from London."

"That's what worries me," Lilian confessed.

"It's what excites me," said Myra. She grasped Genevieve's hand. "Oh, I'm so glad that we met you, Miss Masefield. And I'm overjoyed that you're going all the way to Australia, just like us."

"Are you, Mrs. Cathcart?"

"Yes. It will give us chance to get to know you properly."

Genevieve quailed inwardly. The remark sounded like a threat.

In spite of the cold wind, the majority of passengers ventured out on deck to share the moment of departure and to wave to all the friends and well-wishers still ashore. George Porter Dillman took the opportunity to familiarize himself with the interior of the vessel, walking down empty corridors and inspecting deserted public rooms. First-class passengers, over 350 in number, were berthed amidships on the promenade, hurricane, spar, and main decks.

The 170 second-class passengers had cabins on the main deck. Public rooms for both classes were on the hurricane deck and Dillman was impressed with what he saw. Efforts had been made to ensure both comfort and visual interest in the lounges, dining rooms, smoke rooms, and music rooms. He was particularly struck by the ornate woodcarvings.

When he inspected the promenade deck, he made a point of going to Genevieve's cabin. Knowing she would not be there, he slipped a note under the door, asking her to call on him at her convenience. The distant sound of cheers told him that the *Marmora* had cast off and he soon felt the vessel tilt and ride. Engine noise built up but it was not overly intrusive. The ship had five double-ended boilers and two single-ended ones. While the passengers waved their farewells, Dillman knew that trimmers and stokers would be working hard to keep the boilers fed with coal. In his opinion, they were the unsung heroes of the shipping companies.

Having gained a rough working knowledge of the layout of the ship, he went back to his first-class cabin on the main deck. It was not long before Genevieve joined him. As he let her in, he ducked under her hat to give her a kiss on the cheek. She was delighted to see him. They had arrived separately and agreed that they would not be seen together in public. Operating independently, they had found, enabled them to cover far more ground than would have been the case if they presented themselves as a couple. It made their occasional meetings in private all the more precious.

"Well," said Dillman, "what's your first impression of the *Marmora*?"

"A good one," she replied, removing her hat and undoing the buttons on her coat. "She's compact and well appointed. What about you, George?"

"I was disappointed at first," he admitted. "Working for Cunard has spoiled me. I expected the *Marmora* to be bigger somehow.

Now that I've taken a closer look at her, I withdraw my reservations. She's well designed and ideal for her purpose. And, of course, having a much smaller number of passengers will make our job so much easier."

"Easier in one way, harder in another."

"What do you mean?"

"It will be much more difficult to escape. We can't lose ourselves in a crowd."

"Do you feel that you need to, Genevieve?"

"Oh, yes. I've heard the alarm bells already."

She told him about her meeting with Myra and Lilian Cathcart, people she liked but who somehow had to be kept at arm's length. Genevieve was not sure which of them would be the more dependent on her. Myra's geniality would enable to her to make other friends aboard, but Lilian would not mix easily.

"I suspect that the daughter will be the real headache," she decided. "And the last thing I want is to have Lilian hanging on to me like a drowning sailor clinging to a piece of wreckage."

"A very beautiful piece of wreckage," he said gallantly.

"It could be a drawback, George."

"You've coped with that problem many times before."

"But only on much larger ships with two or three times as many passengers." She relaxed and gave an appeasing smile. "I'm sorry to trot out a complaint the moment we meet," she said. "Myra Cathcart may even turn out to be a boon. If my guess is right, she's something of a merry widow. Myra will attract a lot of people around her and I'll get to know them without having the trouble of making their acquaintances on my own."

"That's all part of our job," Dillman reminded her. "Merging with the passengers and befriending as many of them as we can. There's no better way to gather intelligence."

"I know, George." She glanced around. "You have a very nice cabin, I must say."

"It's a long voyage. Comfort is essential. What's your accommodation like?"

"Too close to the Cathcarts."

"I could always arrange to have you moved."

"No, no. They'd be terribly offended. I'll stay put."

"Fair enough."

"Have you met the purser yet?"

"Yes," said Dillman, with a slight grimace. "Mr. Kilhendry is not the most sociable fellow. He told me to my face that he's not an admirer of the American nation and he resents the both of us because we worked for Cunard. He views us as intruders."

"Even though we're here to solve any crimes that are committed aboard?"

"Mr. Kilhendry believes that he can police the ship on his own."

She was alarmed. "But we need to work hand in glove with him."

"Not in this case, Genevieve."

"How on earth are we going to manage?" she wondered.

"By dealing almost exclusively with his deputy, Martin Grandage. I took to him at once," said Dillman. "He's a much more affable character. Mr. Grandage wants to see the pair of us later on so that he can give us a few pointers."

"Perhaps he can tell us why the purser is being so awkward."

"It's in his nature. He's very territorial."

"I look forward to meeting him," she said through gritted teeth. "We're sailing all the way to Australia, George. I don't relish the idea of doing that when the man in the best position to help is actually trying to hinder us."

"There's one way to solve that problem."

"Is there?"

"Yes, win him over."

"How do we do that?"

"By showing him he needs us on this ship."

"That's easier said than done," she said. "If there are criminals aboard—and I'm sure we'll have the usual smattering—they'll be used to operating on a lengthy cruise. We've never done that, George. Our villains have always been hit-and-run merchants on a five-day Atlantic crossing. We're up against a different enemy."

"That's what makes it so interesting."

"I'd feel happier if we had the purser's full backing."

"Then woo him over, Genevieve. I can't do it. As soon as I open my mouth, I set off all his prejudices about Americans. I always thought we had an affinity with the Irish, but not in Mr. Kilhendry's case. He thinks we're too arrogant."

"You're the least arrogant person I've ever met."

"Try telling that to the purser."

"I most certainly will," she promised. "Do we have any special orders?"

"Only to keep out of his way."

"I was thinking of the royal party."

"Oh, Mr. Kilhendry has taken personal responsibility for them," said Dillman. "I doubt if we'll get anywhere near the Princess Royal and her family. Apparently, they're traveling to Egypt for health reasons. They want to escape the English winter."

"I can sympathize with that."

"Did you watch them come aboard?"

"Yes," said Genevieve. "It was the one and only time Lilian Cathcart showed any spirit. She worships the royal family. Lilian did everything but wave a Union Jack. According to her, the Duke of Fife is eighteen years older than his wife."

"I'm not sure I'd embark on a marriage with that age difference."

"You never know, George. Love can make such things seem meaningless."

"Do you speak from experience?" he teased.

She grinned. "Ask me again at the end of the voyage."

"You're on this ship to work, Miss Masefield. Not to go hunting for romance."

"It has a nasty habit of hunting *me*, George."

They shared a laugh and their eyes locked for a full minute. He realized how much he had missed her during the time they had been apart. Dillman fought off the impulse to reach out for her, and became serious. He picked up the papers that lay on the table between them.

"We'll see Mr. Grandage together," he said, "but I think you ought to show your face to the purser as well. I can't promise that it will be the most pleasant experience of the day for you. However," he went on, holding up the papers, "Mr. Kilhendry needs to know who you are and to give you a copy of these."

"What are they?"

"The passenger lists and a diagram of the ship. They're very useful. That's how I knew which cabin you were in," he explained. "I simply checked the first-class list."

Genevieve's ears pricked up. Recalling the shock she had been given earlier, she saw that she now had a way of expelling any lingering fears that a certain person was aboard. She could put her mind at rest.

"May I see the first-class list, please?" she asked.

"Of course," he replied, handing it over. "Are you looking for someone?"

"No, George. Nobody in particular."

It was a lie. Genevieve was searching for reassurance. She ran a finger down the list, confident that she would be able to relieve her mind of its vestigial anxiety. But there was no relief at all. One name suddenly jumped off the page and made her start. She felt as if she had just been punched hard in the stomach.

THREE

As befitted members of the royal family, the Duke and Duchess of Fife, and their children, had been given the cabins that could best lay claim to be considered staterooms. They were large, plush, and superbly furnished. Other passengers had to unpack their own luggage but the royal couple was traveling with a small retinue of servants to take care of any menial tasks. While the ship made its way along the Thames estuary, Fife remained in his cabin with his wife. He was a tall, broad-shouldered man of almost sixty years, with a military bearing. His high, domed forehead and clear-cut features gave him an air of distinction but the full mustache, now peppered with gray, hinted at a more raffish side to his character. Accounted something of a rake in younger days, Fife had been redeemed by marriage and dedicated himself to being a family man and to running his vast estates in Scotland.

"How do you feel now, my dear?" he asked solicitously.

"I'm fine, Alex," replied his wife, reclining in a chair. "A little tired, perhaps, but there was so much to do before we could set off."

"This will be the first Christmas we've spent abroad. Do you mind that?"

"Not in the least. I'm rather looking forward to it. If we stay in England, we always seem to end up eating and drinking far too much. Father has such a remarkable appetite. The last time we spent Christmas Day at Sandringham, he insisted on having twelve courses."

"It was something of a challenge," Fife agreed with a smile. "It will be interesting to see what sort of fare we get in Egypt. Some of their dishes are very exotic."

"I'm going there for the warm weather rather than the food."

"And for some sightseeing, Louise. Egypt is positively filled with ancient relics." He gave a quiet chuckle. "Just like your family."

"Alex!"

"I was only joking, my dear."

It was not a joke that she appreciated because it had such a strong element of truth in it. From the time she was born, Princess Louise Victoria Alexandra Dagmar had been surrounded by people who were substantially older than her. Queen Victoria, her grandmother, who had dominated the family in every way, had survived until her eighties and her spirit lived on. Other people in her circle were also long-lived and Princess Louise wondered if it was because she was so accustomed to being with older people that she had married a man who was almost twenty years her senior. It did not matter. She had never regretted her choice. Fife had been a devoted husband.

"How long will it take us to get to Port Said?" she asked.

"Eleven days, if all goes well."

She was worried. "Is there any reason why it shouldn't?"

"No, my dear," said Fife with a consoling hand on her shoulder. "The *Marmora* is an excellent vessel and Captain Langbourne is an experienced sailor. The only thing that might slow us down is bad weather."

"That's what I'm afraid of, Alex. I don't want the children to be seasick."

"They're young, healthy, and full of life. Have no qualms about them."

"I was once horribly seasick when I was Maud's age."

Though she was the eldest of the King's three daughters, Princess Louise had always been rather shy and self-effacing. She was a slim, pale woman in dark attire. Marriage had helped her to blossom a little but she was still nervous and hesitant at times. The prospect of spending eleven days afloat was not one that appealed very much to her.

"I hope that we will be able to maintain our privacy on board," she said.

"We can't stay in our cabin throughout the whole voyage, Louise. Sea air is bracing. We need to get our fair share of it."

"Yes, I know, but I don't want to spend too much time in the public eye."

"Noblesse oblige."

"I've never enjoyed being stared at by all and sundry."

"Then you certainly don't take after your father," he observed with a grin. "If the King were here now, he'd probably be chatting in the engine room with the chief engineer or standing on the bridge to give the captain advice on how to sail the ship. He had to wait such a long time to succeed to the throne that he's determined to enjoy every moment of it, and to meet as many of his subjects as he can."

"Father thrives on public occasions. I hate them."

"You prefer hearth and home, dear, and I love you for it."

"Thank you, Alex." She looked around. "Where are the girls?"

"Still glued to the porthole in their cabin, I expect."

She was about to rise. "Do you think that we should check on them?"

"No," he said, easing her gently back into her seat. "They can look after themselves. They're terribly excited about the whole trip. Maud, especially. She can't wait to see the Pyramids. Try to relax, Louise. When they remember that they have parents, they'll come looking for us in their own good time."

She sat back in her chair. "You're probably right."

"I'm always right. That's why I married you."

Princess Louise smiled for the first time since they had come aboard. She reached out to take his hand and gave it an affectionate squeeze. He smiled back at her. A moment later, there was a knock on the door then it burst open. Their two teenage daughters came bounding into the cabin. Fife raised an eyebrow in amusement and turned to his wife.

"What did I tell you?" he said.

When she handed the passenger list back to him, it took Dillman only a second to pick out the name that had startled her. He did his best to reassure Genevieve but she was only half listening to what he said. Staring ahead of her, she tried to work out the implications of what she had discovered.

"You may be worrying unnecessarily," he said.

"I don't think so, George."

"It may not even be him."

"It is. I'm certain of it. I saw him earlier."

"You *thought* you saw him, Genevieve. Appearances can be deceptive."

"Not in this case," she said ruefully. "Look at the number of his cabin. It's on the same deck as my own. He was coming out of it when I caught sight of him."

"Maybe it's another man with the same name and a similar build."

"It was Nigel. There's no question of that now. He's not only on the same ship as me, his cabin is actually in the same passageway as mine. That frightens me."

"Why?"

"I'm not sure," she replied, rubbing her hands together. "I just know that it does."

"It's not like you to be frightened by anything."

"This is different, George."

"Is it?" he asked, taking her by the shoulder and leading her to a chair. "Sit down for a moment," he advised. She lowered herself into the chair and he crouched in front of her. "That's better. Now, let's try to get to the bottom of this, shall we? What is it that's upset you so much?"

"Somebody from my past whom I'd rather not meet."

"That could cut both ways, Genevieve."

"What do you mean?"

"Mr. Wilmshurst must have his own share of guilt about what happened."

"Don't you believe it!" she said with vehemence. "Nigel doesn't know what guilt is. He's completely amoral. He never accepts that he's to blame for anything."

"Yet, in this case, he certainly was."

"Up to a point."

"That's not the way you explained it to me," he said. "According to you, he did something that you felt was unforgivable and so you broke off your engagement to him. Isn't that what happened?"

"Yes, George."

"Then he was at fault. You've no reason to have a conscience about it."

"Yet I still do," she confessed. "I suppose it was because I *wanted* the engagement to come to an end. When he provided me with an excuse, I jumped at it."

"You have no regrets about that, surely?"

"None at all. I liked Nigel a lot at first. There was even a point when I believed that I actually loved him. But I was far too dazzled by his social position to look at him objectively. When his father dies, he inherits the title and becomes Lord Wilmshurst. The notion of being a 'Lady' is very tempting to someone who comes from my background."

"You *are* a lady, Genevieve," he told her. "In every way."

"A title means so much in English society."

"Is that why you were rattled? Because you were reminded of what you missed?"

"No, George," she returned. "It's a source of relief to me now. I'd never have fitted into that world. I can look the part but that's all that I could have done. Besides, I'm much happier doing what I'm doing now."

"Watching out for pickpockets on a P and O ship?"

"Working alongside someone I can respect."

"Thank you." He rose to his feet. "So what do you think is going to happen?"

"Sooner or later, I'll have an embarrassing meeting with Nigel."

"Embarrassing for you or for him?"

"Oh, only for me," she said. "He'll probably think it's hilarious. Nigel has never been embarrassed in his life. You'll see. He's a law unto himself."

"I'm only concerned about his effect on you, Genevieve. It may hamper your work, and that's worrying. Let's face it, there's no way that you can avoid him unless you transfer to second class. Would you prefer to do that?" She shook her head. "Are you certain about that?"

"I'm not running away, George," she promised. "I'm not going to hide in second class simply because I don't wish to bump into Nigel. No," she went on, "I'll just have to take a deep breath and get on with it. But I know one thing. From now on, the *Marmora* is going to seem even smaller."

"Are you afraid he might bother you?"

"Nigel is doing that already and I haven't even come face-to-face with him."

"What I meant was whether or not you were afraid he might harass you."

"I wouldn't rule that out. Knowing him, I think he might take a delight in it."

"Then I can offer you some relief on that score," he said, reaching for the passenger list again. "You were so shaken to see Nigel Wilmshurst in here that you didn't notice the name directly beneath his."

"Who is it?"

"Someone called Araminta Wilmshurst. It looks as if he's married, Genevieve."

"Married?"

"Yes, you'll be perfectly safe from him now."

Nigel Wilmshurst brushed a speck of dust from the sleeve of his jacket then admired himself in the mirror. Tall, thin, suave, and self-regarding, he was meticulous about his appearance. His dark hair was brushed neatly back and his mustache carefully trimmed. Watching him from the other side of the cabin, his wife giggled with amusement.

"You spend more time in front of a mirror than I do," she complained.

"It's important to look one's best, Araminta." He turned to grin at her. "Until the light goes out at night, that is. Then it's important to *do* one's best." She giggled again. "You are going to have a wonderful time, Mrs. Wilmshurst."

"I hope that you will as well, darling."

"Oh, there's no doubt about that. I have plans."

"Do they include me?"

"You, me, and lots of champagne," Nigel said, crossing over to her. "Happy?"

"Deliriously."

"Did I surprise you?"

"Completely," she admitted. "When you told me we were going away for our honeymoon, I thought that meant the Isle of Wight or even Scotland. I never dreamed that I'd be spending the first month of married life in Egypt."

He kissed her on the lips. "The honeymoon begins here. On the *Marmora*."

"Do you think people will notice?"

"Why? Would it trouble you if they did?"

"A little. I don't want everyone to stare at us."

"They'll be too busy goggling at the royal party. Talking of which," he went on, "I meant what I said about arranging to dine with them at some stage."

"Oh, Nigel!" she cried with excitement. "Do you think that you could?"

"It's one of the many occasions when Father's name comes in useful. The Duke is bound to remember Lord Wilmshurst. They've been on many shooting parties together."

"What did they shoot?"

"Confounded socialists, for the most part."

Araminta Wilmshurst went off into a fit of giggles. She was a short, shapely young woman with an almost doll-like prettiness. Her auburn hair was parted in the middle, puffed out at the sides, and collected into a bun at the nape of her neck. Her two-piece suit of blue satin was tailored to perfection. She still had the bloom on her that she had possessed when she walked down the aisle with her husband. Nigel Wilmshurst ran a finger softly down her cheek and admired her afresh.

"Who is the most gorgeous woman aboard this ship?" he asked.

31

"The Princess Royal."

He laughed with scorn. "The Princess Royal?"

"I think she's beautiful."

"Her mother is, I grant you," he said. "Queen Alexandra is still a very handsome woman. But her three daughters are as plain as pikestaffs."

"Nigel! That's a dreadful thing to say."

"Well, I'm not the only one who says it. The rumor is that the three sisters used to be known as 'the Hags.' And some people had even worse names for them. I respect the Princess Royal as much as the next man but I'd be lying if I called her beautiful."

"She has such dignity," argued his wife.

"It doesn't make her face any more appealing to look at."

"Don't be so ungentlemanly!"

"I'm sorry," he said. "I didn't mean to be boorish. Nobody could mistake her for anything but a member of the royal family. However, in my humble opinion, she does not even begin to compare with a certain Mrs. Nigel Wilmshurst."

"Do you mean that?"

"Why else do you think I was waiting at the altar for you?"

She went into his arms. "You can be so sweet to me sometimes."

"I intend to make a habit of it."

"Make sure that you're sweet to the Princess Royal as well."

"I'll be exquisitely charming toward her and the rest of the family."

"Is it true that she's taken up salmon fishing?"

"What else is there to do in the Scottish Highlands?" he asked mischievously. "She can't toss the caber or go out and shoot game so she's settled for catching a salmon or two. Good for her, I say. It shows a sense of enterprise."

Araminta shook her head. "Fishing seems so, well . . . unladylike."

"You were ladylike enough when you went fishing for me."

"Stop teasing," she said, playfully pushing him away.

"Do you deny that you set your cap at me?"

"I won't have it compared with salmon fishing."

"But I still have the hook in my mouth," Nigel said, embracing her again. "And I'm so glad I took the bait. I just wish that I'd done so much sooner."

"We only met six months ago."

"That's what I mean. All those empty, pointless, wasted years!"

"They couldn't have been all that empty," she noted. "Your sister told me you'd been engaged once before. Is that right?"

"Yes and no."

"It's either right or it isn't, Nigel."

"Maybe, but it's not the kind of thing I want to discuss at this moment."

"Does that mean you're ashamed of it?"

"No," he said, holding her by the shoulders. "It means that what happened in the past was a foolish mistake. The lady in question could not even hold a candle to you, Araminta. I've forgotten all about her."

"Who was she?"

"I can't even remember her name," he lied. "The past is dead and buried. It's foolish to dwell on it. Especially when we have so many things to look forward to. You'll love Egypt. It's so full of magic and mystery."

She smiled. "And there was I, thinking it would be the Isle of Wight."

"Only the best is good enough for my wife." He was about to kiss her again when there was a tap on the door. He eased her away and turned around. "Come in!"

The door opened and a steward brought in a bottle of champagne in an ice bucket. Setting it down, he stepped out to collect some champagne glasses from his trolley. Nigel Wilmshurst took them from him and sent the steward on his way with a tip. After locking the door behind him, Nigel uncorked the bottle with a flourish and poured out the champagne. He offered a glass to his wife then clinked it with his own.

"As I told you," he reminded her. "The honeymoon begins here!"

When he had finished his official duties, Brian Kilhendry went off to find his deputy so they could compare notes. They were still discussing the arrangements for the captain's table that evening when the visitors arrived. Genevieve Masefield came first, introducing herself to both men and gaining admiring glances from each of them. Once the niceties had been disposed of, she turned to confront the purser.

"I gather that you don't have a great deal of confidence in us, Mr. Kilhendry."

"That's not exactly my position," he replied.

"Then what is?"

"You and Mr. Dillman will only be duplicating what Martin and I can do."

"Many hands make light work," said Grandage. "I'm all in favor of that."

"As long as we don't get in each other's way," added Kilhendry. "Our stewards act as our eyes and ears, you see. They are our intelligence network. If we're not careful, we'll have too many detectives and not enough villains."

Genevieve shrugged. "Isn't that a good thing? Prevention is always better than the cure. If the villains realize they're outnumbered, they may think twice."

"It doesn't work that way, Miss Masefield."

"Then how *does* it work, Mr. Kilhendry?" she pressed.

Before the purser could answer, Dillman appeared, having delayed his arrival so that he would not be seen with his partner. After a few brief exchanges, Kilhendry took the opportunity to slip out and leave them alone with his deputy. Grandage held a chair so that Genevieve could sit down. Dillman took the other chair in the office.

"Before we start," said Grandage, taking some papers from the desk, "I was told to give these to you, Miss Masefield. Mr. Dillman already has a set."

"The passenger lists?" she asked, taking them from him.

"And a diagram of the ship until you get your bearings."

"Thank you, Mr. Grandage."

"Look," said Grandage with a warm smile, "I know that Brian—Mr. Kilhendry—asked you to report to me, but I don't want to restrict you in any way. I'm only too delighted to have you both aboard. I know what you did for Cunard. As far as I'm concerned, you have a completely free hand."

"That's encouraging to hear," said Dillman.

"Yes," Genevieve agreed. "We don't want anyone looking over our shoulder all the time. It would only inhibit us."

"I can understand that," said Grandage. "Just come to me if you need any help."

"We will," said Dillman. "I went on a quick tour of the ship while everyone else was on deck. It seemed the best time to explore the nooks and crannies."

"Unfortunately, you were not the only person who thought that."

"I don't follow."

"We've had our first theft, Mr. Dillman."

"Already?"

"The thief knew when to strike. He got away with some money and jewelry."

"Where was the cabin?"

"Second class."

"Then he may not be a professional," said Dillman. "There'd be much richer pickings in first class. Most thieves would start there."

"Not in every case," argued Grandage. "The more wealth people have, the more care they take to protect it. Our safe is packed

35

with valuables that have been put there by first-class passengers. No, this was an opportunist theft by someone who knew exactly where to go. Mrs. Prendergast is heartbroken."

"Mrs. Prendergast?" echoed Genevieve.

"The victim. When she discovered what had happened, she was mortified."

"Have you looked into the case, Mr. Grandage?"

"I was hoping you'd do that," said the other. "Calming down distraught women has never been my forte. Besides, I think you'd get more out of her than I managed. All that Mrs. Prendergast did when I was there was to burst into tears."

"I'll go and see her as soon as we've finished here."

"Thank you, Miss Masefield. You'll find her cabin number on the list."

"I'm surprised the purser doesn't want to keep this crime to himself," said Dillman. "He gave me the impression that he only had to wave a magic wand and culprits would rush forward to confess."

Grandage chuckled. "I wish that it *did* happen that way."

"At least we now have a reason to be on the *Marmora*."

"You have over four hundred and fifty reasons, Mr. Dillman, because that's the number of passengers aboard and they all deserve to be safeguarded. Some, of course, need an even greater degree of protection."

"The royal party?"

"Yes," said Grandage.

"But I understood that Mr. Kilhendry was looking after them."

"There's a limit to how much time he can spend on guard. I don't need to tell you how busy a purser is during a voyage. You're at the mercy of everyone. It's a twenty-four-hour nightmare. Brian Kilhendry is tireless, but even he can't be in two places at the same time. We need to have contingency plans."

"What sort of contingency plans?" said Genevieve.

"I'm looking at them," replied Grandage, shifting his gaze from one to the other. "I want you to keep a special eye on the royal party. It won't be too onerous a job. The Princess Royal is known to be reserved. She likes to keep herself to herself."

"They must come on deck at some time," said Dillman. "They have two teenage daughters. I can't believe they'd do without daily exercise."

"I'm sure they won't, Mr. Dillman. They'll have a regular routine. The Duke has promised to let me know what that routine is so that you have some forewarning."

Genevieve was puzzled. "But why? Surely they're not in danger?"

"We can't be certain of that. Like me, I daresay you hold the royal family in the highest esteem. We're true patriots, as are many of the people aboard. But we are also carrying a number of foreign nationals."

"I'm one of them," Dillman volunteered with a grin. "An arrogant American."

"You don't pose any threat," said Grandage, "and it may be that nobody else on the *Marmora* does, either. But we can't take that risk. The British monarchy may be respected at home but it's reviled in some countries. It's not beyond the bounds of possibility that someone might want to strike a blow against it. A symbolic act, if you like, whether out of envy, spite, or political conviction."

"What are you asking us to do, Mr. Grandage?" said Genevieve.

"Take on the role of unofficial bodyguards," replied the other. "Look after the royal party. I have a strange feeling that your expertise will be needed."

FOUR

Mabel Prendergast was a big, heavy woman in her sixties with silver hair that was brushed severely back and held in a bun. Her shoulders were hunched, her head held down, and her knees bent, as if she were apologizing for her size by trying to appear slightly smaller. Tears were still moistening the old woman's eyes when Genevieve Masefield called on her. Mrs. Prendergast was amazed to learn that her visitor was a detective but she burst out crying again the moment Genevieve asked her to explain what had happened.

It was several minutes before she managed to control herself. "I'm sorry, Miss Masefield," she said, dabbing at her eyes with a handkerchief. "I never thought that anything like this would happen."

"We'll do our best to recover whatever was stolen."

"My cabin was locked. How on earth did the thief get in here?"

"That's what we'll need to find out."

"It's not the loss of the money that upset me," explained Mrs. Prendergast. "It was the theft of the jewelry. Some of those pieces had great sentimental value. They were gifts from my husband. He'll be terribly hurt when he hears about this."

"Isn't your husband traveling with you?"

"I'm afraid not. His health would never permit it. He's very frail. No," she went on, "I decided to make the effort while I'm still able to do so. Our son works in Cairo, you see, and his wife has just presented us with a first grandchild."

"A boy or a girl?"

"A baby girl. I simply had to go out to see her."

"Of course," said Genevieve.

"To be honest, we never thought that David, our son, would ever marry. He seemed to be wedded to his career in the diplomatic service. Then, about eighteen months ago, he found himself a wife at last and he's now become a father." She wrung her hands. "David will be so shocked by this. I mean, you don't expect it on the P and O."

"Every shipping company has the same problem, I'm afraid. When people go on our cruise, they tend to relax and lower their guard. That's when a thief will move in."

"But I was only out of my cabin for about twenty minutes."

"Two minutes would have been long enough, Mrs. Prendergast," said Genevieve. "Where were the stolen items kept?"

"The jewelry was in a box. I hadn't even unpacked it from my trunk."

"But the trunk was unlocked?"

"Oh, yes," replied the other, glancing across at the large wooden trunk in the corner. "My clothing was scattered all over the floor. That's what shook me most, I think. The idea that someone had been rummaging through my belongings. It's disgusting!"

"I know."

"I felt as if I'd been invaded, Miss Masefield."

"P and O recommend that passengers have anything of value locked in a safe."

"That's where I'd intended to put it as soon as I took the jewelry box out of the trunk. It was tucked away right at the bottom. The thief had to burrow for it."

"What about the money?"

The old woman looked a trifle shamefaced. "It was in my handbag," she admitted, "and I left that lying on the table. Yes, I know that it was stupid of me," she said, cowering defensively, "but I thought that it would be perfectly safe in here."

"How much was taken?"

"Well over a hundred pounds."

"Oh dear!" sighed Genevieve. "That's a real blow. Was anything else stolen from your handbag? Your passport, for instance?"

"No, Miss Masefield. That's still here. So is my train ticket to Cairo."

"That's some consolation, anyway."

"I don't feel very consoled."

"Now," said Genevieve, taking a notebook and pencil from her pocket, "the first thing I'll need is a list of the items stolen from your jewelry box. If any of them are distinctive in any way—engraved with your name, perhaps—make sure that you tell me. Have you met anyone on the way here or since you came aboard?"

"Yes, lots of people."

"I'll need their names, if you can remember them."

"But they were so nice and friendly. You surely can't suspect any of them."

"We have to explore every avenue, Mrs. Prendergast. What's very clear to me is that you were deliberately chosen as a target. No other passengers in second class have reported a theft."

"Why me?" the old woman asked in dismay.

"For two reasons," said Miss Masefield. "If, by chance, you'd caught the thief in the act, you'd pose no threat to him. He'd know he could push you aside and make his escape. The other reason is more obvious, I'm afraid," she continued, using her pencil to point at the items she mentioned. "That's a beautiful brooch you're wearing, and those diamond earrings are even more eye-catching. A thief would be bound to notice that gorgeous ruby ring and that lovely watch of yours as well. Since you have a certain amount of expensive jewelry on display, there was a fair chance you'd have brought more with you."

"I did. A whole box of it."

"Let's start there, shall we?"

"If you wish," murmured Mrs. Prendergast.

"What was the most important item in the jewelry box?"

"My mother's wedding ring."

Dinner on the first evening afloat was informal though some of the passengers decided to dress up for the occasion. A few full-length evening gowns made their appearance and there was an occasional man in white tie and tails amid the prevailing suits. George Porter Dillman sided with the majority and looked elegant in a navy-blue three-piece suit that emphasized his slim build. When he entered the first-class dining room, he did not need to search for a seat. A place had already been reserved for him by some fellow passengers he had met on the way to Tilbury.

"Come and join us, Mr. Dillman!" invited Morton Goss, rising to his feet.

"Thank you," the detective said.

"We were hoping to be able to grab you."

"Yes," said Rebecca Goss. "We Bostonians must stick together."

Dillman took a seat at the long table being shared by the Goss family with a dozen other people. The chairs were bolted to the floor but swiveled easily to allow access. Morton Goss was a short, stooping man of fifty with a bald head that was covered with a fine cobweb of hair and large eyes that gleamed behind his spectacles. An Egyptologist with an international reputation, Goss had a true zealot's passion for his subject. His wife, Rebecca, by contrast, was a small birdlike creature with no interest in archaeology of any kind but with an abiding interest in people. While her husband collected relics from ancient Egypt, Rebecca Goss preferred to make new friends.

"We haven't seen you since we came aboard," she complained with a good-natured smile. "Have you been hiding from us, Mr. Dillman?"

"Not at all, Mrs. Goss. My cabin is on the main deck. Where are you?"

"On the promenade deck."

"That explains it, then," said Dillman.

"Not really. Polly went looking for you and couldn't find you anywhere." She switched her gaze to her daughter, who was seated beside Dillman. "Could you, Polly?"

"No, Mother," said the girl.

"Did you search the main deck?"

"Yes, I did. Twice."

It was disturbing news. Dillman did not like the notion that someone was on his tail, especially when she happened to be an impressionable seventeen-year-old girl. Polly Goss was taller than both her parents, and, though still rather gauche, was both attractive and personable. When Dillman turned to her, she gave him a smile of frank admiration.

"Did you enjoy your trip to London, Miss Goss?" he asked.

"Very much. It was wonderful."

"What did you do?"

"Mother and I saw all the sights and we went shopping. Oh, and we saw a play one evening. Father, of course," she added, glancing across at him, "spent most of his time at the British Museum or at the university."

"What play did you see?"

"*Major Barbara*," replied Rebecca. "Do you know it?"

"Yes," said Dillman. "I'm very fond of George Bernard Shaw's work."

"It was so funny," said Polly. "I've never seen anything quite like it before."

"I managed to catch that production myself and enjoyed it hugely. The problem was that I went into the theater to see Major Barbara but I came out remembering her father."

"That's odd. So did we."

"It's the way that Underwood's part is written, Miss Goss. He's a villain who's made to sound like a hero. I think that Shaw was making the point that the devil always has the best tunes." He looked over at Goss. "Do you agree?"

"Don't ask me, Mr. Dillman. I slept through the last act."

"Morton!" scolded his wife. "You always do that."

"I get tired, Rebecca. And I don't have the same interest in theater as you."

The first course arrived and they suspended the conversation while they were being served. Dillman found the Goss family pleasant companions. Rebecca Goss hailed from Boston and her husband had been born only forty miles away. At their first encounter with Dillman, they had been able to trade comments about the city and its people. Goss was on his way to Cairo to return some relics that had been loaned to the museum in Boston. Since his wife and daughter had come with him, he had decided to visit London en route to Egypt. After a first spoonful of soup, he peered over his glasses at Dillman.

"You never did tell us what you're doing on this cruise," he said.

"Exactly the same as everyone else, Mr. Goss," said Dillman. "Enjoying myself. As you may recall, I worked in the family business for some years, designing and constructing yachts. I decided that it was time I saw what steam-powered vessels could do. Sailing with P and O gives me the ideal opportunity to do that."

Rebecca beamed at him. "I'll bet you didn't expect to do so with royalty."

"No, Mrs. Goss. That's an added bonus."

"I was hoping that we'd see them in here this evening but they must be dining in their own cabin. We simply must catch sight of them before we get to Egypt. It will be something to boast about when we get back to Boston."

"Yes," said Polly. "I never thought I'd travel with members of a royal family."

"But that's exactly what you did on the voyage to England," said her father.

"No, it wasn't. We had no princesses aboard the *Saxonia*."

"You had something far better, Polly."

"Did I?"

"Of course," said Goss. "What's more, you got much closer to them than you'll ever get to the royal party on the *Marmora*. You sailed in the company of two pharoahs of ancient Egypt—or, at least, with treasures from their respective reigns. They had far more power than a mere princess. Amenemhet was founder of the great eleventh dynasty and Rameses I founded the nineteenth dynasty. These men were like gods in their day."

"But all they left behind," said Polly, "was a handful of carved stones."

"Wait till you get to Egypt. You'll see some of the greatest monuments ever built by men with supreme power over a civilization. A handful of stones?" Morton Goss gave a dry laugh. "That's not how I'd describe the Pyramids or the Sphinx."

"How many times have you been to Egypt?" asked Dillman.

"Too many," replied Rebecca.

"Now, that's unfair," her husband protested. "In my dreams, Mr. Dillman, I've been a hundred times. In actuality, alas, I've only made five trips."

"Five extremely long trips, Morton," his wife reminded him.

"It's a requirement of my job, Rebecca. You understood that."

"I didn't understand how lonely Boston could be while you were away."

"That's why I brought you with me this time, my love," he said, trying to appease her. "And I included a visit to England so that you could see what the Old Country was like. Except that, compared to Egypt, of course, England is not really old."

"Don't start again, Father," begged his daughter. "Please!"

"I can see that you're not going to follow in your father's footsteps," observed Dillman. "Does archaeology hold no interest for you, Miss Goss?"

"Not really, Mr. Dillman."

"Polly's talents are musical," Rebecca explained. "She plays the flute."

"I *try* to play it, Mother," said the girl.

"And you do it very well. She's won competitions, Mr. Dillman."

"Congratulations!" Dillman said with sincerity. "I know how difficult it is to play a wind instrument. When I was a boy, my parents bought me a horn and they lived to regret it. I produced the most dreadful sounds from it. You have to be able to do so much with your mouth." Polly's eyes ignited in agreement but she said nothing. "In the end, they sent me off to have piano lessons instead. That was kinder on their eardrums."

"You must hear Polly play sometime," announced Rebecca.

"No, Mother!" said the girl, though the prospect clearly thrilled her. "You can't inflict me on Mr. Dillman like that."

"It would be a pleasure to hear you," Dillman said graciously. "We have a small orchestra on board so you'll have ample opportunity to enjoy live music. However," he went on, looking at Goss before swallowing a mouthful of soup, "I'd like to come back to these relics you're returning to Cairo. They must be very valuable."

"Priceless."

"Then I hope that you've had them locked away in a safe."

"The larger items, yes," said Goss, "but I like to keep some of the smaller ones with me so I can gloat over them like a miser with his hoard of gold."

"What happens if you lose them?"

"They're quite irreplaceable, Mr. Dillman."

"Then I'd suggest you have them put in a safe, as well."

"That's what I've been telling him," said Rebecca, "but he won't listen to me."

"You should, Mr. Goss," said Dillman. "The relics might be stolen."

"Come now, Mr. Dillman. That's hardly likely, is it? Secrecy is the best protection for anything valuable. That's why I've been careful to say nothing to anyone else. Apart from us, the only person who knows about them is the purser, and he's not going to sneak into our cabin when we're not there, is he?" Goss waved a dismissive hand. "Even if a thief were to stumble on them, he'd never recognize what they are. He'd take the same view as Polly here—that I collect little stones with strange carvings on them. There's no danger, believe me. They're as safe as if I had them on a string around my neck."

It was ironic. When her engagement was broken off, Genevieve Masefield had sailed on the maiden voyage of the *Lusitania* with the intention of starting a new life on the other side of the Atlantic. She had been eager to get away from the man she was to have married and liberate herself from all the many associations with him. In the event, she had met Dillman and finished up working in harness with him. It meant that she had not escaped Nigel Wilmshurst at all. Having tried to flee from him on one ship, she was now trapped with him on another. The irony had a cruel edge to it.

After delaying her arrival in the dining room until the last moment, she took the vacant seat that had been kept for her between Myra and Lilian Cathcart, feeling that, under the circumstances, the women might act as a useful camouflage. But she did not need them. When she finally plucked up the courage to survey the room, Genevieve saw no sign of her ex-fiancé. She started to relax. By the time the main course was served, she even began to enjoy the meal.

Myra Cathcart was at her most voluble, joining in every conversation with gusto and scattering her opinions freely. Lilian was more subdued but even she was making a conscious effort to take part in the exchanges. Now that they were afloat, she seemed to have shed her earlier fears about the ship's safety. Disappointed that the royal party was not dining in public, she shifted her attention to Genevieve instead.

"It's nothing like I ever imagined," she confessed. "There are moments when it feels more like being in a hotel than sailing at sea."

"That's what the best cruise ships are," said Genevieve. "Floating hotels."

"Filled with delightful ladies," ventured the man on the opposite side of the table, sharing a benign smile among the three of them. "I could not have chosen a better seat."

"Thank you, Mr. Dugdale," Myra said sweetly. "Though I don't pretend that I can compete either with Miss Masefield or with my daughter."

"Oh, but you do, Mrs. Cathcart. Mature beauty is without compare."

Myra laughed gaily and Lilian blushed—unused to coping with compliments herself, she found it even more difficult to handle those paid to her mother. Genevieve was interested to see how the two women reacted. She found Walter Dugdale, who had made the comment, to be amusing company. He was clearly a man of eccentricities. He was the only man in the room who wore a Norfolk jacket, and his beard was so long and pointed that it made him look like a sorcerer. Genevieve put him in his mid-fifties but he could well have been much older. He sat directly opposite Myra. A native of Chicago, the thin, almost emaciated Dugdale had the easy manner of a veteran traveler.

"What a pity I'm to lose you and your daughter in Egypt!" he sighed.

"There's a long time before we get there, Mr. Dugdale," said Myra.

"I know, and I'm going to make the most of every second of it."

"You sound very decisive."

"I'm the sort of man who can make up his mind quickly, Mrs. Cathcart."

"Have you sailed on P and O ships before?" asked Genevieve.

"Oh, sure," he replied, "Many times. I ought to buy shares in the company. I might get back some of the money I've spent on them over the years. I love the experience of a cruise. Nothing to beat it, in my view."

"And you're going all the way to Australia?" said Lilian. "It will take you ages."

"That's the attraction, Miss Cathcart. Where better to be than in a floating hotel with no sense of rush and no pressure of work?"

"Does that mean you're retired?" Myra probed.

"More or less," said Dugdale, stroking his beard. "More or less."

The American was attentive to both Genevieve and Lilian but his real interest seemed to be in Myra. He kept fishing gently for bits of personal information about her, and she was doing the same with him. Genevieve tried to strike up a conversation with the man opposite her but it was difficult. Stiff and solemn, Karl-Jurgen Lenz was a taciturn German in his fifties, with a quiet intensity. He limited himself to curt replies but listened carefully to what was being said. Like Dugdale, his gaze drifted most often to Myra Cathcart. A photographer by trade, Lenz was on his way to Egypt.

They were halfway through the main course before Genevieve finally managed a word with the young Englishman who sat on the other side of Lilian. He had been too busy talking to the elderly couple opposite him to pay much attention to those beside him, and Lilian was too shy to initiate a conversation with a stranger. When Genevieve leaned forward to eat, she could see him out of the corner of her eye. He was slim, fair-haired, and had an almost boyish face. His voice was educated and his manner open. Genevieve was glad when she eventually had the chance to speak to him. She introduced herself and Lilian Cathcart, then waited to hear his name.

"Delighted to meet you both," he said with a smile. "I'm Roland Pountney."

Genevieve was jolted without quite knowing why. Then she remembered where she had heard the name before. It was on the list of shipboard acquaintances that had been given to her by Mrs. Prendergast. The man was a suspect.

Nigel and Araminta Wilmshurst dined together in the privacy of their cabin. They wanted nobody else to intrude on their wedding night. When they retired to bed, the ship was dipping and rising gently over the waves. The bride had had far too much champagne to feel nervous and she yielded up her virginity to the man she loved with a mixture of innocence and urgency. Afterward, cradled in his arms, she purred with contentment. The evening was everything she had hoped it might be.

"Have you ever done that before, darling?" she whispered.

"No, of course not," he lied.

"You seemed to know exactly what to do."

"Only because you helped me, Araminta."

"My brother did it before he was married," she confided. "I wasn't supposed to know about it but one of his friends told me. They took Tony off to this place and paid a woman to . . ." Her voice trailed off. "I thought it was the most shameful thing to do, but, apparently, it's not unusual. I just hope that his wife never finds out about it."

"I trust you'll have more sense than to tell her."

"I wouldn't dream of it, Nigel. She'd be cut to the quick. I can imagine how I'd feel if anyone told me something as revolting as that about you."

"Well, they're not going to," he said, "because there's nothing to tell."

"I'm so glad." She kissed him. "What will we do tomorrow?"

"Exactly the same."

"Nigel!" she said with a giggle.

"Isn't that what a honeymoon is for? It gives us the chance to get to know each other properly, and I certainly want to know my wife a lot better. If it was left to me, I'd spend the whole voyage in bed with you."

"That's ridiculous!"

He pretended to be hurt. "Are you tired of me already?"

"Don't be silly!"

"You'd rather we slept apart?"

"Never!" she cried, clinging tightly to him. "But I would like to see something of the ship. And you did say we'd dine with the royal party at some stage. We can hardly do that if we stay in here all the time."

"Are you saying that you prefer the Duke of Fife's company to mine?" he teased.

"Why can't I have both?"

He grinned indulgently. "You shall, Araminta. You shall."

"You're so good to me, darling. Thank you."

She kissed him on the lips and he responded with ardor. It was some time before he let his head roll back on the pillow. His wife nestled up against him.

"Nigel . . ."

"Yes?"

"That other woman you were engaged to once—"

"This is hardly the moment to talk about her," he said with irritation.

"I just want to ask you something. You did say that we'd have no secrets, and I'm bound to wonder. I simply want to know the truth then put it firmly behind us."

He was brusque. "You know all there is to know, Araminta. I made a ghastly error and drew back, the moment I realized it. I've been grateful ever since."

"But you must have got close to her at one point," she persisted. "Close enough to want to do with her what you and I just did as husband and wife. There must have been some love and tenderness between you."

"Well, there wasn't," he said, sitting up. "Now, please, let's drop the subject."

"Just answer me this."

"Araminta—"

"One last question, I promise you. Supposing you met her again . . ."

"There's very little chance of that happening."

"But suppose that you did, Nigel. How do you think you'd feel?"

"I know damn well how I'd feel," he said harshly. "My stomach would turn at the very sight of her. See her again? I'd run a mile!"

FIVE

On their first night afloat, the royal party found the *Marmora* surprisingly comfortable. Once they had grown accustomed to the pulsing rhythm of the engines and the undulations of the vessel, they slept soundly in their beds. Over breakfast next morning, served in the salon that connected their two cabins, they were full of praise for the vessel. Lady Maud, in particular, was anxious to explore it further.

"Can we go out on deck now?" she asked, swallowing a last piece of toast.

"Don't be so hasty, Maud," said her mother.

"But I'm dying to see the ship properly. So is Alex."

"Yes," said Lady Alexandra. "We've been cooped up in here far too long."

"There's so much to *see*, Mother, and we're missing it all."

"Not if you look through the porthole in your cabin," said the Princess Royal.

Maud pouted. "That's not the same."

The two daughters were pretty girls but they had inherited too many of their mother's features to be judged truly beautiful. They had long, pale faces and large eyes. At seventeen, Alexandra had already acquired something of her mother's dignity and solemnity. Three years younger, Maud was still excitable. She turned to her father as a court of appeal.

"May we go on deck soon?" she pleaded.

"Of course," he said with an indulgent smile, "but only when we are all ready to venture out. We are not ordinary passengers, Maud. We cannot go wandering about the vessel at will. Decorum has to be observed. As soon as we step outside our cabins, every eye will be upon us. That imposes responsibilities."

"I know, Father."

"Then curb your impatience. We'll go out as a family."

Maud nodded obediently. "May we get down from the table?"

"If you've had enough breakfast."

"Thank you, Father," said Alexandra.

"We'll call you in due course," promised Fife.

"Clean your teeth then look for some warm clothing," their mother advised. "It will be quite chilly on deck at this time of year."

"Yes, Mother," said Maud.

The two girls got down from the table and went into their own cabin. Princess Louise watched them go. Fife drained the last of his coffee and addressed himself to the small pile of correspondence at his elbow.

"I'm not sure that I'm ready for a stroll just yet," Louise said.

"You must have a morning constitutional, my dear."

"Later on, perhaps."

"We can't keep the girls waiting too long," he said, reading an invitation card before setting it aside, "or we'll have mutiny on our hands."

"Maud seems to think that we're on the royal yacht, where she can go on deck whenever she chooses. We're only four among hundreds of passengers this time. The rules have changed."

"I think that our daughters appreciate that, Louise."

"I hope so." She glanced at the little pile of envelopes. "Anything interesting?"

"Invitations, for the most part," he said, glancing at a note on P and O stationery. "This one is from Sir Marcus Arundel, suggesting that we might join them in their cabin for drinks one evening."

"Oh dear!"

"We have to be sociable, Louise."

"Yes," she sighed resignedly. "I suppose so."

"You're becoming too reclusive, my dear. If we're not careful, we'll end up being called 'the Hermits of Mar Lodge.' "

"I love Mar Lodge. It's so wonderfully private."

"Almost as private as you," he teased before slitting open another envelope. "Ah, yet one more invitation. Lord Wilmshurst's son."

"Do we know him?"

"No," he replied, "but I was closely acquainted with his father at one time. Lord Wilmshurst was the best shot I've ever seen. And he had an extraordinary fund of sporting anecdotes. Interesting to see if the son takes after his father."

"I don't share your passion for anecdotes."

"This young fellow won't bore you with anything like that, Louise."

"How do you know?"

"Because he and his wife are on honeymoon."

She was startled. "Honeymoon? Yet they seek the company of others?"

"Mr. Wilmshurst sounds like a gregarious bridegroom. He doesn't just want us there for drinks; he's suggesting that we dine with them." Fife saw the mild disapproval in her face. "Don't worry," he said. "I won't commit us to a meal until I've had a chance to meet the chap. But I do owe it to his father to be congenial.

Besides, the girls will expect some company while we're aboard. It's such an agreeable way to pass the time."

After speaking to Roland Pountney for two minutes, Genevieve Masefield knew that she could cross his name off the list of possible suspects. Whoever had stolen the money and jewelry from Mabel Prendergast's cabin, it was most certainly not this young man. During dinner on the previous evening, it had been impossible to have a proper conversation with him, especially with Lilian Cathcart sitting between them, so Genevieve was pleased to bump into him when she took a stroll around the deck. Pountney displayed a row of perfect teeth and politely touched his hat. After exchanging a few remarks about the weather with him, she asked him where he had been when the ship set sail.

"Up here on deck, of course," he replied. "Weren't you, Miss Masefield?"

"Yes, Mr. Pountney."

"It's always a unique moment. I never miss it."

"Nor me."

"The only problem was that I had to share it with that gloomy German."

"Herr Lenz?"

"That's right. He stood beside me and had the gall to tell me that German liners were superior to any built in our shipyards. Apparently, he was commissioned to photograph ships from the Hamburg-Amerika Line so he feels that he's an expert on maritime travel."

"He hardly said a word to me all evening."

"When we stood at the rail, I couldn't stop him talking."

"Perhaps he's shy in female company."

"Oh, I don't think that's the case," said Pountney, "I had the feeling he revels in it. Herr Lenz is one of those strong, silent, watchful types. He seemed to be enchanted by the lady beside you."

"Mrs. Cathcart? Yes, she managed to attract a lot of attention."
His eyes twinkled. "So did you, Miss Masefield."

Genevieve acknowledged the compliment with a smile. Roland
Pountney was an affable young man with an air of quiet prosperity
about him. Everyone promenading on the first-class decks was well
dressed, but Pountney was immaculate in his overcoat and hat.
Even his black leather gloves were of exceptional quality. Clearly, he
was not the man who had broken into Mrs. Prendergast's cabin.
When the ship left Tilbury, he had stayed on deck for some time.

"You said last night that you were traveling on business," she
recalled.

"In the world of finance, alas, one always travels on business."

"And you're going to Egypt?"

"First of all," he said. "I don't believe in buying a pig in a poke.
I like to see where my money is going. I'm investing rather a lot of
it in a project in Cairo."

"It's very sensible of you to carry out an inspection, Mr. Pountney."

"It doesn't pay to be too trusting, Miss Masefield, especially
where foreigners are concerned. Not that I have any prejudices
against them, mark you," he added. "Most of my investments
have been abroad. That's why I've prospered so much."

"I'm glad to hear it."

"The world is my oyster." He laughed softly. "I'm a seeker after
pearls. But tell me a little about Mrs. Cathcart, if you will, please."

"Myra? Why?"

"Because she sounded like an interesting lady. I only caught
snatches of what she was saying but she had far more life about
her than that daughter of hers."

"Lilian is inclined to be reticent."

"It's not a problem that troubles her mother. Mrs. Cathcart
talked and laughed her way through the entire meal. I could see
the effect she was having on the two men opposite. The American

gentleman was entranced with her," Mr. Pountney said.

"His name is Walter Dugdale."

"He was even more taken with the lady than Herr Lenz. I know that it's very early to make such a judgment, but I think your friend may have made a conquest—if not two of them."

"Hardly!" said Genevieve. "That's the first time she's met either of them. Myra Cathcart might be amused at the notion that she'd caught Mr. Dugdale's eye but I doubt if she'd be pleased to hear that Herr Lenz had taken an interest in her. She made an impression on both of them, I grant you, but that's as far as it goes. Mr. Dugdale was excessively polite, that's all."

"He's a rich American bachelor."

"How do you know?"

"I saw no sign of a Mrs. Dugdale. Did you?"

"No," said Genevieve, "but my guess is that he has been married."

"More than once, probably," Mr. Pountney agreed. "They make a hobby of it over there."

Genevieve laughed.

"I didn't mean that to sound quite so flippant, and I might be wrong about Mr. Dugdale, but he—and Lenz, for that matter—were doing something that few men in their position would have done."

"What was that, Mr. Pountney?"

"Paying far more attention to Mrs. Cathcart than to you."

"I was not exactly ignored."

"No," he agreed, "but you didn't collect the sly glances that your friend was getting from both men. They must have been blind, Miss Masefield," he continued, touching his hat again. "Had I been sitting opposite you, I wouldn't have noticed any other woman at the table. Good day to you."

After bestowing an admiring smile on her, he strolled off along the deck.

When he saw the man in action, George Porter Dillman was forced to revise his opinion of the purser. Brian Kilhendry oozed professional charm. The blunt Irishman who had given Dillman such a tepid welcome was now chatting happily to passengers in the first-class lounge. He seemed to have mastered some of their names already and dealt with their various requests with practiced ease. Kilhendry was relaxed yet supremely in control. After glancing at his watch, the purser excused himself and headed for the door.

"Good morning," said Dillman, intercepting him.

"Good morning, Mr. Dillman," said Kilhendry. "Did you sleep well?"

"Extremely well."

"We can hold our own against the Cunard Line, you know."

"I never doubted it for a second, Mr. Kilhendry. But I'm glad of a quiet word."

"I'm busy, I'm afraid. Save it for Martin Grandage."

"This won't take a moment," said Dillman. "It's something that your deputy might not even know about. I gather that you took possession of some Egyptian relics."

"That's correct," the purser admitted crisply. "Several of them are locked away in our largest safe. I know nothing about such things, but Professor Goss, the gentleman who entrusted them to me, tells me they're highly valuable."

"I know. I had dinner with him and his family."

"Oh, of course. The professor is American."

"I was more interested in the security of his property than his nationality, Mr. Kilhendry. While the major items were lodged with you, many smaller ones were not. Mr. Goss—he prefers to be called that rather than 'Professor'—has kept some of the relics in his cabin. I think that you should persuade him to let you put them under lock and key."

"Why?"

"Because it eliminates the risk of theft."

"Who would want to steal a handful of ancient stones?"

"Who would want to rob a harmless old lady in second class?" asked Dillman. "Yet that's precisely what happened while the ship was leaving her berth. Even your famed nose has not been able to pick up the scent yet. Those ancient stones in Mr. Goss's cabin are worth a great deal, in the right hands."

"They're in the right hands, Mr. Dillman. Those of your fellow countryman."

"What happens if they go astray?"

"I should imagine the professor—or Mr. Goss—will be rather upset."

"Don't you think you should make sure that eventuality will not occur?"

"I can see that you've never been a purser," Kilhendry said tartly. "We don't *compel* our passengers on the P and O. We give them fair warning and leave it at that. If they wish to keep items of value in their cabins, that's their decision. Most of the property is insured before they even step on board. It's yet another safeguard that we offer on P and O Lines. Excuse me, Mr. Dillman," he went on, "but I have important work to do. Take your next unnecessary fear to Martin Grandage."

He stalked off and left the detective both annoyed and pensive. Irritated by the purser's abrupt manner, Dillman wondered yet again what had provoked it. How could a man who was so effortlessly pleasant to the passengers aboard the ship, be so offhand with one of his colleagues? Something more than mere dislike of the Cunard Line was involved. Dillman resolved to find out what it was. In the meantime, a more immediate problem confronted him. Polly Goss was bearing down on him with a mixture of nervousness and bravado. Her smile was tense.

"Hello, Mr. Dillman," she said.

"Good morning, Miss Goss."

"I just wanted to apologize for my father. He does go on, I'm afraid. You must have been bored rigid over dinner."

"Not at all. I was fascinated by what he was saying."

"He treats everyone as if they were students in class."

"Well, I was only too grateful to be taught by him. Your father is obviously a leading expert on his subject."

"Yes," she conceded, "but that subject is so frightfully dull."

"Not to anyone who's interested in Egyptian civilization."

"I'm not, Mr. Dillman."

"You may change your mind when you actually get to Cairo," he said. "I envy you the opportunity. It's something I've always wanted to do, myself. Before that, of course, you have the voyage to enjoy. There seem to be lots of young people aboard. I'm sure you'll soon make new friends."

She grinned at him. "I'd like to think that you're one of them."

"Of course. That goes without saying."

"And I will play the flute for you—if you wish, that is."

"Yes," he said with feigned enthusiasm, "that would be very nice."

"Do you want to fix a time?"

"Let's wait a day or two, shall we? Then we can get used to the routine on board and find out when the music room is likely to be empty."

"We don't have to go there," she said, blurting out the suggestion. "We could always find somewhere more private than the music room."

"I'm sure your parents will want to be there to hear you."

"They've heard my repertoire dozens of times. I'd be playing for you."

"I see."

There was an awkward pause. "Are you glad that you left Boston?" she said.

"Sometimes."

"I couldn't wait to get away," she confided. "It's so predictable. I knew exactly what I'd be doing every day of every week. There were no surprises. And the worst of it was that it's terribly conventional. There's a way of doings things that you simply have to follow. I'd never dream of talking as freely as this to anyone in Boston."

"Why not?"

"Because we've only just met, Mr. Dillman. You're a stranger."

"I'm quite harmless when you get to know me."

"But that's the point," she stressed. "Back in Boston, it would take months to get to know you. We'd have to go through all those ridiculous social rituals first. Go to the right places, meet at the right times, say the right things."

"Some people find those rituals very comforting."

"Well, I'm not one of them. And I suspect that you're not, either."

"No, Miss Goss. I'm not."

She grinned again. "Then why do you still conform to the rules?"

"Rules?"

"Why do you call me 'Miss Goss' when you know that my name is Polly?"

He hunched his shoulders. "Courtesy, I guess."

"But I hate being 'Miss Goss.' It's exasperating."

"May I call you Polly, then?"

"Of course," she said, grasping his arm. "We're friends now, aren't we?"

She saw him first. He was alone. Genevieve found it remarkably easy to avoid being seen by him. Wearing a long coat and a large, wide-brimmed hat, she merged with all the other ladies on deck who were similarly attired. Genevieve simply had to turn her head and the brim of her hat obscured her face completely. Nigel Wilmshurst walked within a yard of her without even knowing she was there. He looked older. When she'd first met him, she had been dazzled by his youthful zest and appearance. That seemed to have faded somewhat, though she did not subject him to any real appraisal. All she allowed herself was a glance at him as he strode past. He still exuded the confidence that had once impressed her. She could see it in his expression and in his bold step. But she felt no lingering affection for the man to whom she had once been engaged. If anything, she felt a mild repulsion. Too many unpleasant memories had surfaced.

Wilmshurst had not seen her but Walter Dugdale recognized her immediately.

"Ah!" he said with a throaty chuckle. "There you are, Miss Masefield."

"Hello, Mr. Dugdale."

Wearing a fur-collared cape and a hat with a tall crown, he looked even more like an amiable wizard. He raised his hat to her then stepped in closer so that she could hear him clearly above the tumult of the engines and the excited chatter from the passengers on deck. Closing one eye, he studied her through the other.

"Remarkable!" he concluded. "Quite remarkable."

"What is, Mr. Dugdale?"

"You are, Miss Masefield. So is Myra—Mrs. Cathcart, that is. And so, to some degree, is her daughter though she, poor girl, chooses to hide her light under a bushel. All three of you are English roses."

"Roses at this time of year? That's rather perverse gardening."

"I was speaking metaphorically," he said with a smile. "It's something to do with the shape of the face and the tilt of the head. There's an endearing Englishness about all three of you. It's such a pity that Lilian does her best to conceal it."

"I don't think she does it deliberately, Mr. Dugdale."

"Maybe not, but the result is the same."

"I'm sure that Lilian will mellow as the cruise progresses."

"I do hope so," he said, adjusting his cape around his shoulders. "She's old enough to stand on her own feet yet she still relies too completely on her mother. I had tea with them earlier. To be honest, I'd planned on being alone with Mrs. Cathcart but the daughter invited herself along as well. It was almost as if she were a chaperone."

"I don't think Myra Cathcart needs a chaperone."

"Nor do I."

"She has such amazing vitality."

He beamed at her. "Do you think I hadn't noticed that? It's a shame she can't spare any of it for Lilian. That daughter of hers could do with it."

"Don't underestimate Lilian," said Genevieve. "She can be aroused by her passions. I was with her when the royal party came aboard. Lilian was a different person. She suddenly came alive and showed some of her mother's exuberance."

"I'm reassured to hear that."

"Give her time, Mr. Dugdale. Her light may shine forth yet."

"Unfortunately, my time is limited. In ten days' time, we arrive in Port Said."

"We're stopping at Marseilles before that, to refuel."

"If only we could bring more members of the royal family on board as well."

"Why?"

"Didn't you say that the monarchy was Lilian's obsession? They'd be a useful diversion. That way, I might even get to speak to her mother alone." His expression hardened. "Before *he* does, that is."

"Who?"

"Karl-Jurgen Lenz. That brooding German. Don't tell me you didn't notice how hypnotized he was by Myra Cathcart. Quite rightly, of course," he went on. "She's a most striking lady. So open and so . . . unexpected."

"In what way, Mr. Dugdale?"

"You only have to look at her to see that. She's *genuine*, Miss Masefield. She's not one of those gold-diggers who come on cruises like this in pursuit of a rich catch. Goodness!" he exclaimed. "She'd not have her daughter in tow, if she were. A real adventuress would never even admit to *having* a grown-up daughter. That's why Myra Cathcart is so unusual. She attracts men without even trying."

"It's a problem many women have to cope with, I fear."

He cackled. "That's a fair comment! But you take my meaning."

"I'm more intrigued by your opinion of Herr Lenz," she said. "You're the second person this morning who's told me that he was unduly interested in Myra Cathcart. He was such a sullen dinner companion."

"I sympathized with you for having to sit opposite him."

"I felt rather sorry for him, Mr. Dugdale. He seemed so lonely."

"Didn't I look lonely as well?"

"No," replied Genevieve. "You are such an accomplished traveler that you'd mix easily in any surroundings. That was the difference between the two of you. Herr Lenz stuck out like a sore thumb. You blended in perfectly."

"I take that as a compliment."

"It was intended as one, Mr. Dugdale."

"There is, unfortunately, another difference between the two of us."

"Is there?"

"Yes, Miss Masefield," he explained. "Karl-Jurgen Lenz is going to Egypt and I'm not. That gives him an advantage. On the other hand," he continued with a broad grin, "we still have ten days at sea. That gives *me* an advantage."

Cackling to himself, he went up the stairs that led to the boat deck. Genevieve was glad he had spoken to her. She liked Walter Dugdale and was happy to be his confidante. What she expected to happen between him and Myra Cathcart, she did not know, but she had no fears for the latter. Dugdale was kind, urbane, and intelligent. He would be a good friend to Myra and that would make her less reliant on Genevieve. The pleasant and easygoing man from Chicago was a much more appealing individual than the grim photographer from Germany. Genevieve refused to believe that Lenz had a serious interest in Myra Cathcart. He seemed too intense and self-absorbed.

Genevieve was struck by a sobering thought. Speculating on the curiosity that her friend had sparked off in two dinner companions had taken her mind completely off the subject of Nigel Wilmshurst. Perhaps he would not be the problem she had envisaged. As a married man, his attitude toward her would have undergone a profound change. Instead of fearing a confrontation, she simply had to ignore him. He did, after all, have reason enough to avoid her. Genevieve felt a sense of freedom again. It did not last.

"I've been looking for you everywhere," said Lilian Cathcart, swooping down on her with patent relief. "Can we go somewhere to talk?"

"What's wrong with talking here, Miss Cathcart?"

"It's not private enough. I need your advice, Miss Masefield."

"Then let's adjourn to the lounge," suggested Genevieve, leading the way. "You look as if it's something serious."

"It is," said Lilian, hard on her heels.

When they got to the first-class lounge, they found a quiet corner from which Genevieve could see without being seen. Lilian Cathcart was evidently upset, faced with a situation that was new and troubling. She launched into an explanation.

"I'm worried about Mother," she began. "Something has happened to her."

"What do you mean?"

"She's changed. Mother is doing things that I find rather unseemly."

"Showing an interest in a certain man?"

"It's worse than that, Miss Masefield," said Lilian, chewing a lip. "Mother has always been very friendly, but it's gone beyond that stage now. She's encouraging him. It's so blatant. I blushed when I heard some of the things she said."

"Perhaps you weren't meant to hear them," Genevieve said tactfully.

"I don't follow."

"Your mother is an adult. Like you, she can do whatever she chooses."

"I'd never embarrass her in that way. It was hurtful."

"I'm sure that Mrs. Cathcart didn't mean it to be," said Genevieve. "Besides, one of the pleasures of a voyage like this is to explore new friendships. That's all your mother is doing. Have no worries about Mr. Dugdale. He strikes me as a thoroughly decent man in every way."

Lilian's face went blank. "It's not Mr. Dugdale that I'm talking about," she said.

"No?"

"It's that German gentleman. Herr Lenz."

Genevieve was taken aback. "*Really?*"

"He had the audacity to ask her right in front of me."

"Ask her what, Miss Cathcart?"

"He wants to photograph Mother," said Lilian, quivering with indignation. "He invited her to go to his cabin one day and—I just couldn't believe this—Mother *agreed*."

SIX

Martin Grandage watched carefully through the window. Having warned both Dillman and Genevieve that the royal party was about to have its first public outing, the deputy purser made sure that he himself was on hand. A portion of the promenade deck was cleared so that the Duke and Duchess of Fife could emerge with their daughters into the light of day. Curiosity had brought a sizable crowd to view the newcomers but they saw little and heard even less. Standing at the rail, Fife was pointing to the French coastline and explaining something to his wife. The two girls were so glad to be out in the fresh air at last, they inhaled it with the relish of liberated prisoners. Since they were all wearing large hats and long overcoats, the royal party looked very much like any of the other first-class passengers aboard, except that their bearing was decidedly more formal.

"The novelty will soon wear off," said Grandage, glancing at the onlookers. "Some of these people don't even have cabins on this deck. As soon as they heard that royalty was showing its face, they came flocking. After a few days, interest will flag; everyone will be so used to having the Duke and Duchess aboard, they'll take little notice of them."

"I'm sure the royal party will be grateful," observed Dillman, standing beside him. "At the moment, they must feel as if they're in a cage at the zoo. Look at the faces in the crowd. Somebody will start throwing buns in a moment."

Grandage laughed. "No feeding the animals!"

"How often are they likely to come out on deck?"

"Twice a day, at least, Mr. Dillman. I had a word with one of their aides. They'll be out for half an hour or so every morning and afternoon. When we get farther south, of course, and the weather is much warmer, we'll see even more of them."

"So there'll be a set routine?"

"That's the idea. Makes things easier for us."

"Who's that fellow in a bowler hat?" asked Dillman, indicating a thickset man on the far side of the royal party. "Is he with them?"

"Yes," replied Grandage. "That's Mr. Jellings. I'm not certain what his official title is but his job obviously includes keeping an eye on them. He's there to prevent anyone lunging forward to ask for autographs."

"What if someone wants more than an autograph?"

"That's when you and Miss Masefield take over."

"Let's hope it's not necessary," said Dillman. "I suggest that we split up now. We don't want to be seen together too often in public."

"Not that anyone is looking at us when they've got a Duke and Duchess to stare at. But it's a wise precaution," agreed Grandage. "Excuse me."

He moved away and left Dillman to step out on deck and merge with the crowd. As time passed, feeling they had seen enough, some of the spectators drifted slowly away. One of them recognized Dillman and came over to him.

"Hello there," said Morton Goss. "What do you think of the performance?"

"Is that what it is?"

"You were an actor, Mr. Dillman. You should know. We're the audience and they're the members of the cast, going through a well-rehearsed domestic drama."

"All I can see are four people enjoying a breath of fresh air."

"But not in the relaxed way that you or I might do so. They're on duty. They're conscious of being watched. They have to play their parts."

"I take it that you're not too impressed," said Dillman.

"I was, for a short while," Goss told him. "My wife and daughter are engrossed. They'll stay in the front row until the whole family disappears. I've got more important things to do than stand out here in the cold. Work calls, Mr. Dillman."

"Work? On a pleasure cruise like this?"

"I'm not just returning the items to the museum, you see. I have to give a series of lectures while I'm there. They take time to prepare."

"What are you talking on, Mr. Goss?"

"Oh, the dynasty that obsesses me." He jerked a thumb over his shoulder. "I don't mean the one to which these folk belong. No, Rameses XI is my hero. Sometimes known as Ozymandias."

"Ozymandias, 'king of kings'? The one in Shelley's poem?"

"That's the guy," said Goss, "though I think Shelley was a bit unkind to him. His architectural achievements were breathtaking. Rameses XI excavated the rock temples at Abu Simbel, completed the magnificent great hall of Karnak, built the temple at Abydos, and added the first court and pylon at Luxor. Unfortunately, he picked a quarrel with the Hittites and the long war left Egypt impoverished, or there would have been even more astounding monuments in his reign."

"When did Rameses XI rule?"

"From 1304 to 1237 B.C. Yet some of his work is still standing."

"I can't see any modern architecture surviving for that length of time."

"It doesn't *deserve* to, Mr. Dillman."

"Didn't you say you had some relics from the dynasty of Rameses?"

"Yes, but that's Rameses I. He only reigned for two years. Still, I've got one of two items from his brief period in power. They're among the things I keep in my cabin. If you're interested, I'd be happy to show them to you."

"I'd appreciate that, Mr. Goss."

"Sometime this afternoon, perhaps?"

"Early evening," Dillman suggested, wanting to be back on deck for the second outing of the royal party. "If that's convenient for you. Half an hour before dinner?"

"That's fine with me."

Goss patted him on the shoulder before moving away. Dillman was grateful for the invitation. He was interested to see the relics and even more curious to see where they were kept, hoping that he might be able to persuade Morton Goss to have them put in the safe with the larger objects. Even when he was chatting with the Egyptologist, his gaze had not left the royal party for long. Someone else now joined them, clearly enjoying the privileged position that allowed him to converse with the Duke and Duchess. It was Brian Kilhendry and he seemed to be putting some sort of request to them. Dillman wondered why he was doing so in public rather than in the privacy of the royal cabin.

Though she had nothing to report, Genevieve Masefield paid a courtesy visit to the old lady to assure her that the investigation was continuing. Mrs. Prendergast was as tearful as ever. After a sleepless night, she had been unable to eat any breakfast and was now too afraid to stir from her cabin in case someone else might break in. Genevieve did her best to give the other woman some peace of mind but it was difficult.

"No thief would be foolish enough to strike twice in the same place," she said. "He took all that he wanted from here, Mrs. Prendergast. You're quite safe."

"I don't feel it, Miss Masefield."

"Try to overcome your fears. Get out and meet people."

"I'm wary of doing that after what you told me," said Mrs. Prendergast. "I was shocked at the thought that the thief might be one of the passengers I'd talked to earlier."

"Well, I can reassure you on that point. I've spoken to all the people whose names you gave me and they each have an alibi. None of them was the culprit, I'm sure."

"Then who was? One of the staff?"

"That's highly unlikely," decided Genevieve. "P and O is very careful whom they employ. As it happens, I checked on the stewardess who looks after your cabin and she was with the chief steward at the time when the theft took place. No, Mrs. Prendergast," she said, "I think we're looking for a professional thief. Someone who knows what he wants and where to get it."

"Does that mean he has another victim in view?"

"Probably."

"Then I feel sorry for them. It's a hideous experience."

"You have to get over it," Genevieve said softly. "I know it was distressing but it's wrong to let something like this spoil the whole voyage. Luncheon will be served in half an hour. Make sure you get a good meal inside you."

"I will, Miss Masefield. Thank you for your help."

"You know where to find me, if you need me. As long as you remember what I told you yesterday. Don't mention my involvement in this case to anyone. A ship's detective can work far more effectively if he or she is completely anonymous."

"I understand." Mrs. Prendergast followed her to the door. "Is there any hope at all that you'll recover the jewelry that was taken?"

"We'll get it back for you," said Genevieve. "Eventually."

She let herself out and made her way back to her own cabin, wishing it was not on the same deck as the one belonging to Nigel Wilmshurst and his wife. He was, however, nowhere to be seen. Genevieve went swiftly into the cabin and gratefully closed the door behind her. A minute later, she was opening it again in response to a rapping on the woodwork. Myra Cathcart stepped into the cabin, her face glowing.

"I'm so glad that I've caught you before luncheon," she said.

"Why?"

"I thought you ought to be aware of a rather amusing situation." Myra gave a laugh of disbelief. "I wouldn't have thought it possible. I mean, I only met the two of them over dinner last night. It's not as if I'm in the first full flush of youth."

"You have admirers," said Genevieve. "Mr. Dugdale and Herr Lenz."

"How did you know?"

"I sat opposite them, remember?"

"Was it as obvious as that?"

"Well, it was easy to see that Mr. Dugdale found you enchanting. I wasn't so sure about Herr Lenz. He seemed very preoccupied. But he did keeping glancing at you."

"He told me that I had the perfect face for his camera," explained Myra. "He wants to photograph me and, before I knew what I was saying, I agreed that he could. Now, of course, I'm having second thoughts."

"Don't you like him?"

"In a way, Miss Masefield. I just find him rather earnest."

"What about Mr. Dugdale?"

"Oh, he's charming. Walter—he insists I call him that—is a real gentleman. And I do like the fact that he's from Chicago. I don't know why, but I've always had a soft spot for Americans. They always seem so much more cosmopolitan than we do."

"Mr. Dugdale is certainly cosmopolitan," said Genevieve.

"When I listen to him, I feel like a real stay-at-home. Walter's been *everywhere*. That's why I find it so hard to believe he's taken such an interest in me."

Genevieve smiled. "Does it worry you?"

"Not in the least. I'm very flattered." Myra frowned slightly. "It's Herr Lenz's interest that unsettles me a little. When I look in Walter's eyes, I know exactly what he's thinking. Herr Lenz is more enigmatic." Myra grinned. "It's ridiculous, isn't it? I came on this cruise because I'd always wanted to see Egypt. In the back of my mind, I suppose, I did hope that Lilian might find it stimulating, perhaps even meet a young man who could pay her some attention. Instead, *I'm* the one who's attracted the attention. It's taken me completely by surprise, Miss Masefield."

"I'm not surprised. You're a very handsome woman."

"Thank you. That's what Walter told me. I had the feeling he'd tell me a lot more but, unfortunately, Lilian was there at the time. She thinks I'm being scandalous."

"Have you tried to discuss it with her?"

"There's no point. My daughter is very old-fashioned. It's one of the reasons she's never managed to have a proper friendship with a man, let alone a romance. Lilian still sees me as a wife and mother. She feels that I'm betraying my husband."

"You're entitled to a life of your own, Mrs. Cathcart."

"How can I do that when I have Lilian at my elbow all the time?"

"Tell her that you need a little more freedom."

"I've tried," Myra said sadly, "but she only accuses me of deserting her. Lilian has so little self-confidence. That's why she rarely strays away from me. Look," she continued, putting a gentle hand

73

on Genevieve's arm, "I don't suppose that I could ask a favor of you, could I?"

"What sort of favor, Mrs. Cathcart?"

"Oh, do please call me Myra. We've surely got to that point now."

"Very well," said Genevieve. "How can I help you, Myra?"

"I feel so dreadful even asking you this," said the older woman, turning away. "It's almost as if I want you to conspire with me against my own daughter. But it's for Lilian's good as much as my own." She faced Genevieve again. "She'll be spared so much embarrassment. I hate to see her writhing with discomfort like that."

"Where do I come in?" asked Genevieve.

"As a distraction. I need someone to occupy Lilian for a while."

"Won't she realize she's being kept deliberately out of the way?"

"Not if it's you, Genevieve," said Myra. "I may call you that, mayn't I?"

Genevieve nodded.

"She thinks the world of you. I know how desperate she is to show you her scrapbook devoted to the royal family. And there are lots of other ways you could divert her without arousing her suspicions." She pursed her lips in dismay. "Heavens! This must sound so awful. Do you think I'm being a dreadful mother?"

"No, Myra. I think that you're taking practical steps to enjoy this voyage."

"Does that mean you'll help me?"

"Well," said Genevieve, "I hate the idea of deceiving your daughter like this. At her age, she ought to be able to cope with the fact that it's only natural for her mother to attract admirers. With your permission, I'd like to put that to her."

"Of course."

"If I can persuade her to give you more elbow room, there won't be any need to lure her away under false pretenses. All of us would benefit, then. I'd prefer it that way."

"So would I, Genevieve," said Myra, nodding with enthusiasm. "Knowing my daughter, it will be an uphill task. But if anyone can bring Lilian round, it's you."

Dillman had underestimated Morton Goss. When he called on the latter that evening, he discovered the academic did not, after all, take a cavalier attitude toward the safety of his property. The relics from ancient Egypt that had been entrusted to him were kept in a strongbox that had no less than three heavy padlocks on it. Dillman was impressed. He was also touched by the care with which Goss handled the exhibits. After unlocking the box, the Egyptologist extracted each item as if it were very delicate, peeling off the cotton wool in which it nestled before placing it gently on the table.

"I'd be grateful if you didn't actually touch anything, Mr. Dillman."

"I don't think I'd dare to. How old are these things?"

"Some go back almost four thousand years," said Goss, putting more stone fragments on display. "Each one has its own special story to tell."

Dillman bent over to peer at the largest of the fragments. A series of symbols had been chiseled neatly into the stone. He tried to make out what they represented.

"Are these hieroglyphics, Mr. Goss?"

"That's right. Aren't they beautiful?"

"Beautiful but quite mystifying."

"It's a pity we have only this fragment left," said Goss. "It's from an Egyptian obelisk. The inscription is easy to read," he went on, pointing to the symbols he identified. "This squiggly line stands for 'water.' This bird is an owl. This item here is a tethering rope, and I think that's probably a pool, even though only half of the symbol is left. Don't you think it's fascinating?"

"What fascinates me is how you can tell so much from so little."

"It's a trick that takes years to master."

"How can you be so accurate in dating these remains?"

"We can't," admitted Goss. "We have to rely on educated guess-work."

Dillman was puzzled. "But didn't you tell me earlier that some of these things came from the reign of Rameses I?" he said. "If he was on the throne for only two years, how on earth can you be certain the relics come from so precise a date?"

"Because he was kind enough to leave me a clue, Mr. Dillman."

"A clue?"

"Rameses I had his name put on these," Goss said with a grin, indicating two of the fragments. "You'd have to be an expert in transliteration to know that, of course, so you'll have to take my word for it."

"Where are they from?"

"One is part of an inscription from a statue of Rameses I. There's a much larger section of the statue locked away on board. And the other," he said, nodding at the second fragment of stone, "is probably from a sarcophagus that was built by a talented mason. Time and effort went into this."

"You should have been a detective, Mr. Goss."

The other man smiled. "That's exactly what I am, I suppose."

He showed off every item, saying a few words about each before wrapping it carefully in cotton wool and putting it back in the strongbox. Dillman was intrigued. He had only ever seen such relics in a glass cabinet in a museum. To get so close to them in the company of an acknowledged expert was quite thrilling. He was sorry when the three padlocks were clicked back into place. Goss put the strongbox into the wardrobe and locked the door before removing the key.

"As you see, Mr. Dillman, I do take certain precautions."

"Very sensible of you, Mr. Goss."

The door to the adjoining cabin opened and Rebecca Goss

came in with her daughter. Both women were dressed in their finery for dinner but it was Polly who was the more striking. She wore a full-length evening dress of black velvet with hoops of red velvet from the hem to the shin. Its plunging neckline was softened by lace. Around her neck was a gold chain with an opal pendant. What made her look so arresting was the fact that she had used cosmetics for the first time. They had been so artfully applied that Dillman suspected some help from the mother. Polly Goss seemed years older. She reveled in Dillman's scrutiny of her.

Formal wear was not compulsory, but both men wore white tie and tails though with differing success. Dillman looked even more elegant but Goss was faintly incongruous. His sleeves were too long for him and his trousers too short, but it did not trouble him. When he had his beloved relics beside him, nothing else mattered.

"We waited until we heard you finish in here," explained Rebecca Goss.

Her husband blinked. "You were eavesdropping?"

"Not exactly, Morton."

"Mr. Dillman and I were having a private conversation."

"We had to know when we could come in."

"Yes," said Polly. "We were afraid to interrupt you but we didn't wish to be late for dinner." She smiled at their guest. "You look very smart, Mr. Dillman."

"And you look very fetching," he replied. "So does your mother."

"Thank you," said Rebecca, pleased with the compliment. "I wish that my husband had your build. He's the bane of every tailor in Boston. Though it's not really the way his clothes are made. It's the way that Morton wears them."

Goss shrugged. "I prefer comfort over everything else, Rebecca."

"A little concern for your appearance would not come amiss.

Talking of which," she went on, "has anyone else seen that strange gentleman from Chicago? The one who was wearing a Norfolk jacket?"

"His name is Mr. Dugdale," said Polly. "We met him in the lounge earlier."

"He has this pointed beard and bushy eyebrows. They make him look almost satanic," said Rebecca, "but he seems the nicest man. He kept us amused for hours."

"That's an achievement!" Goss said under his breath,

"Mr. Dugdale speaks fluent French."

"How do you know that, Mrs. Goss?" asked Dillman.

"Because we heard him, didn't we, Polly?"

"Yes, Mother," replied her daughter. "He put that odious Frenchman in his place."

Goss was baffled. " 'Odious Frenchman'?"

"His name was Monsieur Vivet. He kissed my hand and kept leering at me."

"He's the sort of person who kisses *every* woman's hand," Rebecca added with disapproval. "I admire Gallic charm in small doses but Monsieur Vivet tried to drown us in it. He came very close to being offensive."

"Who is this fellow?" wondered Dillman.

"A famous chef, apparently."

Polly scowled. "Famous for kissing your hand when you don't want it kissed."

"Be fair to him," said her mother. "Monsieur Vivet is a man of international repute. I just wish that he didn't keep boasting about it. If Mr. Dugdale hadn't been there, the little Frenchman would have talked our ears off."

"Do you see what happens when I let my wife off the leash, Mr. Dillman?" said Goss with a chuckle. "She rounds up some of the oddest characters on the ship."

"Walter Dugdale may have been odd; Claude Vivet was simply intolerable."

"Why was that, Rebecca?"

"Because he kept talking about himself."

"According to him," said Polly, "he's going to prepare a meal for the royal party. Not that he's been invited to do so yet but he was certain they'd jump at the offer once they realized they had him aboard."

"Did he say anything about the food on the *Marmora*?" asked Dillman.

"He thought it was abominable."

"I can see that he's determined to win friends in the kitchens."

"He was revolting, Mr. Dillman," declared Rebecca. "Luckily, Mr. Dugdale was there to help us out. I don't know what he said, because I don't speak French, but it finally got rid of Monsieur Vivet. We owe him our thanks."

"Well," said Dillman, glancing at his watch, "time to go and force ourselves to eat what he considers to be abominable food. Personally, I think it's delicious." He opened the door. "You've given me a timely warning, Mrs. Goss. I'll steer clear of this fellow. If there's one thing I hate, it's having my hand kissed by a stranger."

The women laughed, then Rebecca glanced in the mirror to make a few final adjustments to her appearance. When she had finished, she went out on her husband's arm. Polly smiled meaningfully at Dillman. He offered his arm and she clutched it as if she had spent the whole day waiting for that particular moment. Dillman could smell her perfume. It had been liberally applied. He led her politely out of the cabin.

Dinner was a sustained ordeal for Genevieve Masefield. No sooner had she taken her seat between Myra and Lilian Cathcart than she saw a familiar figure coming into the dining room. Attired in white tie and tails, Nigel Wilmshurst was escorting a slim and attractive young woman in a white satin dress. Even from that distance, Genevieve could see that his wife was wearing the most gorgeous jewelry. To her relief, the couple sat on the other side of the room with their backs to Genevieve, but she remained on edge in case Wilmshurst happened to glance over his shoulder. It made her a nervous conversationalist. Even the phlegmatic German noticed she was ill at ease.

"You feel unwell, Miss Masefield?" he asked.

"Not at all, Herr Lenz," she replied. "I'm a little tired, that's all."

"Then you need—how do you say it?—the early night."

"I'll rally in due course."

"Good. I like that."

"Are you enjoying the voyage, Herr Lenz?"

"*Ja.* I am." He shot a glance at Myra Cathcart. "Very much."

Genevieve felt Lilian Cathcart stiffen beside her. She was enjoying the meal even less than Genevieve. Her mother was once again basking in the attention of two men and the rivalry between them was more open. Walter Dugdale had seized the initiative by telling Myra about his house in Chicago. He was evidently a man of means. Karl-Jurgen Lenz, not to be outdone, talked about his recent photographic exhibition in Berlin and asked Myra if she would like to visit Germany one day. Genevieve felt very sorry for Lilian. Unable to develop a friendship herself, she was horrified at the ease with which her own mother was handling two potential suitors. It left her feeling tetchy.

"I knew I shouldn't have come on this cruise," she said.

"It's too soon to decide that yet," remarked Genevieve. "Besides, your mother hardly could have gone on her own, could she?"

"To all intents and purposes, that's what she has done."

"I think you're exaggerating a little, Miss Cathcart."

"Am I?" said Lilian, as the two men tried to talk to Myra at the same time. "I might as well not be here, Miss Masefield."

"Well, I'm very glad that you are. You're my guide to the royal family. I knew next to nothing about the Princess Royal and her husband until you filled in the details. You made me see them as real people. I'm grateful to you for that."

"Oh. I was only saying what everyone knows."

"But we *don't* know, Miss Cathcart. Because we don't care as much as you do."

Lilian's face shone. "I love the royal family and every aspect of it. I can't think of anything nicer than working at Buckingham Palace or Windsor or Sandringham."

"Have you ever tried to pursue that ambition?"

"My parents put a stop to that. Father wouldn't even entertain the idea that a daughter of his would be in service, even if I were employed by the royal family. He said I should aim higher than that." She grimaced. "Left to him, I'd have married the general manager at one of his factories."

"Is that what your mother wanted as well?"

"It's not what *I* wanted, Miss Masefield." Lilian retreated into a hurt silence and watched the two men vying for her mother's attention.

Still in his Norfolk jacket, Walter Dugdale paid Myra gracious compliments and continued to find out more about her background and interests. Lenz, by contrast, wore white tie and tails with some style. He was more talkative than hitherto but he was not holding his own against the American. Genevieve noticed a hint of frustration in the German's eye. It eventually gave way to a quiet malevolence as he tried to score points off his rival. The more they were drawn to Myra Cathcart, the less the two men liked each other. Dugdale managed to conceal his enmity beneath a bland smile but Lenz did not have the same social skills. His hostility became more open.

When the meal came to an end, the rivals were still engaged in a verbal joust so they could impress Myra. Her daughter was disgusted by it all and turned away. Genevieve, however, was mesmerized by the way Myra coped with the battle for her affections. The older woman laughed merrily as if it were a situation to which she was accustomed. Yet she had been married to the same man for many years and never had been on a cruise before. Unlike her daughter, she had a natural aptitude for the pleasures of shipboard life.

Genevieve was so enthralled by the little triangular drama being played out in front of her that she forgot all about Nigel Wilmshurst. When she happened to glance across the room, she was given a severe jolt. Rising from his chair, Wilmshurst turned around and saw her for the first time. Genevieve contrived a pale smile of recognition but it was not acknowledged. Wilmshurst turned his back on her with contempt and quickly took his wife out of the room. Genevieve did not know whether to be insulted or relieved. He had cut her dead.

SEVEN

George Porter Dillman recognized him immediately. The description he had been given of Walter Dugdale was so accurate that he had no difficulty in identifying him. Seated alone at a table, Dugdale wore his distinctive Norfolk jacket and stroked his beard as he contemplated the boiled egg on the plate in front of him. A mere handful of people had made their way to the dining room for an early breakfast. Dillman had planned to eat alone but curiosity took him across to his fellow American.

"May I join you?" he asked.

"Please do, my friend," said Dugdale, indicating the seat opposite. "There's nothing quite so joyless as eating alone—unless, of course, it's solitary drinking." He extended a bony hand. "Walter Dugdale."

Dillman shook his hand before sitting down. "George Dillman," he said. "But I already knew who you were, Mr. Dugdale. Your name was mentioned in dispatches."

"Oh?"

"Apparently, you went to the aid of two ladies in distress."

"That sounds like me," Dugdale said with a grin. "Who were they?"

"Mrs. Goss and her daughter."

"Ah, yes. The ladies from Boston, They were set upon by this overeager little Frenchman: Claude Vivet, master chef. At least, that's what he would have us believe. I could see that he was bothering them so I suggested he take his culinary skills elsewhere."

"Were those your exact words?"

"No," admitted Dugdale. "I favored a more direct approach. French is a language that lends itself to confrontation. I suppose that's not surprising in a country that's been seasoned by revolution."

Dillman took an instant liking to the man. He found him wry, quirky, and genial. Dugdale talked freely about his career in business and, in return, Dillman explained how he came from a family that designed and made oceangoing craft. His companion studied him shrewdly.

"I thought there was a hint of the sailor about you, Mr. Dillman."

"I was born less than a mile from the sea."

"I was born close to Lake Michigan but that didn't make me want to become a yachtsman. On the contrary, I came to hate water. Never even learned to swim."

"Neither did a lot of sailors," said Dillman. "Curious, isn't it?"

"I'd say that was a case of tempting Providence. Do you swim?"

"Oh, yes. My father taught me at a very early age."

Dillman ate a frugal breakfast but lingered over it because he was enjoying the conversation so much. Walter Dugdale was clearly savoring the detective's company. He could sense that he was talking to an experienced traveler.

"May I ask why you wear a Norfolk jacket?" said Dillman.

"Is there any reason why I shouldn't?"

"None at all. But it did rather set you apart during dinner last night."

Dugdale grinned. "That was the idea, Mr. Dillman," he confided. "One of my blessings is that I don't possess the herd instinct. I like to stand out. If every other man in here had dined in a Norfolk jacket, I'd probably have turned up in white tie and tails. Call it perversity, if you wish. Or call it a blow struck in the name of individuality."

"That takes a certain amount of bravery," Dillman said with admiration.

"Bravery or folly? The two are often interchangeable." Dugdale fingered his jacket. "As for this," he went on, "it's warm, hard-wearing, and good enough for the King of England. Those are three excellent reasons to choose it. It's the best possible souvenir of the Old Country."

"Do you visit England often?"

"Whenever I can, Mr. Dillman. I'm a confirmed Anglophile."

"So am I," confessed Dillman. "London is so refreshingly different from any American city. I spent hours just wandering around its streets. There's so much to see."

"The sights I most enjoy in London tend to wear lovely dresses and have exquisite manners. The English lady is beyond compare, in my view," announced Dugdale, with the air of a man who had made a special study of the subject. "You only have to look at some of the divine creatures who have graced this voyage with their presence. Nothing can touch a true English rose. Don't you agree?"

Dillman thought about Genevieve. "I believe that I do, Mr. Dugdale."

"I mean no disrespect to American women. They have their virtues, as I should know. I married two of them," he said with a cackle. "But there's something about their English counterparts that makes them effortlessly superior."

"Breeding? Class?"

"It goes deeper than that, my friend."

"Does it?"

"Oh, yes. When I find out the secret, I'll let you know."

Dillman smiled. "I think I'd prefer to look for that secret myself."

"What better way to employ our leisure hours on the *Marmora*?"

Walter Dugdale's eyes lit up as he saw Myra and Lilian Cathcart coming into the room. Gulping down the last of his coffee, he wiped his mouth with a napkin and rose from his seat with an apologetic smile.

"Do excuse me, Mr. Dillman," he said, "but I have to continue my research."

Nigel and Araminta Wilmshurst had breakfast in their cabin. Facing each other across the table, they were still in their dressing gowns as they picked their way through the generous spread before them. While the young bride was still bubbling with happiness, her husband seemed rather distracted.

"What's the matter?" she asked.

"Nothing, Araminta."

"You're not listening to a word I'm saying."

"Yes, I am."

"Then what was I talking about?"

"Your parents."

"That was five minutes ago, Nigel," she said with mild reproof. "You see? You're not listening at all. You were miles away."

He blew her a kiss. "I'm sorry, darling. I promise to concentrate from now on."

"Is there something on your mind?"

"Yes," he said, squeezing her hand. "Pleasing my wife."

"You haven't been yourself since we left the dining room last night."

"I ate something that disagreed with me, that's all."

"Really?" she said with anxiety. "Why didn't you tell me? Have you taken anything for it? There's a doctor on board, you know."

"It wasn't that serious, Araminta. Some minor tummy trouble."

"Then you should complain. The food is supposed to be of the highest standard."

"It is," he said, indicating his empty plate. "You can see that from the way I tucked into my breakfast. I'm fine now. The problem came and went very quickly."

"Are you sure? You've been acting so strangely."

"I'm taking a little time to get used to the idea of being married."

She giggled. "I'm not. I'm loving every minute of it."

"So am I, Araminta." He smiled warmly. "What would you like to do today?"

"Keep my husband's attention."

"You'll have no difficulty doing that, I promise you. In fact, you may have to beat me off to get rid of me. Now," he went on, setting his napkin aside, "I've got two nice surprises for you."

"Wonderful! I adore surprises."

"Sir Marcus Arundel has invited us for drinks this evening. It turns out the royal party will be there, so you'll have the chance to meet them sooner than you thought. If we're on our best behavior, I'm sure that the Duke and Duchess will be bound to accept the invitation to dine with us."

"That's marvelous, Nigel!"

"I strive to give you pleasure."

"But you said there were two nice surprises."

"I've discovered that there's a photographer on the ship," he said. "A German fellow who had an exhibition of his work in England, so he must be good. I thought it would be fun if I asked him to photograph us."

"Oh, yes. It would be a lovely souvenir."

"Only one of many that you'll have on this trip."

"Thank you, Nigel."

"I haven't asked him yet, mind you. He may refuse."

"Nobody could refuse you a thing," she said fondly, "because you're the most gorgeous man in the world and I love you dearly. Who else would have thought of arranging a honeymoon like this?"

"I take all my wives to Egypt," he teased. "Force of habit."

Araminta giggled. She had forgotten how preoccupied her husband had been earlier on. He was hers again now, and that was all that mattered. When she finished her breakfast, she got up to give him a kiss then went off into the bathroom. A few minutes later, the steward arrived. Wilmshurst waited until the man had loaded everything onto his trolley before sidling across to him. He kept his voice low so that there was no danger of being overheard by his wife.

"I need a favor," he said, taking some coins from his pocket to slip into the steward's hand. "There's a friend of mine aboard and I need to know the number of her cabin. Can you find it out for me, please?"

"Of course, sir. What was the name?"

"Masefield. Miss Genevieve Masefield."

The man smirked. "Leave it to me, sir."

Genevieve was in a quandary. If she had breakfast in the dining room, she risked the possibility of another brush with Nigel Wilmshurt; yet, if she stayed in her cabin, she was a sitting target for Myra and Lilian Cathcart, both of whom had tried to engage her as an ally. On balance, she preferred another rebuff from her former fiancé to being cornered by a mother and daughter who each sought her help. Accordingly, she braced herself and went off for a late breakfast. Genevieve was in luck. The Cathcarts were just leaving as she arrived, and neither Wilmshurst nor his wife was in the dining room. She was able to enjoy a meal with the Cheritons, a family of three—father, mother, and son—whom she had met on her way to Tilbury. Ill health was taking them to Egypt for the winter but they made light of their disabilities. Genevieve was struck by the kindness of Alfred Cheriton, the son, an unmarried man in his forties, who was escorting his elderly parents to a country that would be kinder on their weak lungs. Whenever one of his parents wheezed, he looked at them with mingled concern and affection.

They were interested to hear that Genevieve was going all the way to Australia, and accepted without query her plausible explanation for the visit. The Cheritons could not believe that a young woman would choose to travel all that way on her own.

"It's very courageous of you, Miss Masefield," said the son.

"Why?"

"I don't think that I'd be able to do it alone."

"But I'm not doing it alone, Mr. Cheriton," said Genevieve. "I have people like you and your parents to make the journey a painless one. On a cruise like this, nobody is allowed to be lonely. We become one big family."

"There's some truth in that," he conceded. "Everyone is so friendly."

Genevieve would have been happy to go on talking to the Cheritons but she had work to do. Excusing herself from the table, she went off in search of the deputy purser. Martin Grandage had asked her to keep him informed of any progress she made in the search for the thief who had robbed Mabel Prendergast and, though she had no suspect in mind as yet, she felt that it was time to give him a report. Grandage was busy when she got to his office and she had to wait a few minutes until he had placated an angry passenger who was complaining about the noise from the engines. When the man stalked off with a set of earplugs in his hand, Grandage invited her in and told her about the complaint.

"What did he expect?" he asked. "There's no such thing as silent engines. As it is, his cabin is about as far away from them as it could be. If he wants the ship to sail, he's going to have to put up with a modicum of noise."

"You soon get used to it," said Genevieve.

"That's what I told him. The earplugs should help. I just wish I'd had the sense to wear a pair myself before he came charging in here."

"I could hear his raised voice through the door."

"He wasn't the loudest today, Miss Masefield."

"Then who was?"

"Your next customer. Frau Zumpe."

"Does that mean we've had another theft, Mr. Grandage?"

"We've had the crime of the century," he said with a smile. "Frau Zumpe insists that we solve it immediately or she's threatening to sue the P and O. She's not a dear old lady like Mrs. Prendergast, who wouldn't say boo to a goose—Frau Zumpe would wring its neck with her bare hands if it so much as honked at her."

"Who is she?" asked Genevieve.

"A fearsome lady in first class. She's like something out of a Wagnerian opera. Frau Zumpe doesn't actually wear body armor but you feel that she might. She's a female warrior with a voice like a foghorn."

"I think I'd prefer Mrs. Prendergast."

"So would I, Miss Masefield, but we have no choice in the matter." He waved her to a seat but remained on his feet. "Have you made any headway yet?"

"Not exactly," said Genevieve. "I'm still eliminating possibilities."

"'Possibilities'?"

"People Mrs. Prendergast met on her journey to Tilbury. Or acquaintances she made on the ship itself. Whoever went into her cabin knew that she was safely out of the way on deck. I thought it might be someone who'd met her and noticed her expensive jewelry. That could still be the case," she concluded. "Thieves often size up their victims by what they're wearing."

"That's not what happened with Frau Zumpe."

"How do you know?"

"Because she doesn't wear jewelry of any kind. She's such an incendiary lady that it would probably melt. What she had taken from her cabin was money," he said. "A substantial amount of it. I didn't dare point out that she should have given it to us to look after. Had I done that, I think she might have attacked me. Frau Zumpe was already in a foul temper."

"Why?"

"Because she felt that she was being palmed off with the deputy purser."

"How will she react to a female detective?"

"I dread to think, Miss Masefield."

"You could always send George Dillman along instead of me."

"No," he decided. "I'm afraid it has to be you. My guess is that one man is responsible for both thefts. There are similarities between both cases. Since you're looking after Mrs. Prendergast, you'll have to take on Frau Zumpe as well."

"As you wish, Mr. Grandage. I'll do my best to pour oil on troubled waters."

"There's only one way to do that."

"Is there?"

"Get her money back at once," he said. "With interest."

The royal party confined itself that morning to a small area of the promenade deck. When they emerged in the afternoon, however, the Duke and Duchess took their children for a walk so that they could investigate the other side of the vessel. Dillman followed at a discreet distance. Curiosity was still intense, though there were fewer people about than on the previous day. One of them caught Dillman's eye at once because there was something faintly sinister about him. He was a tall man in a long coat and flat cap. Dillman remembered seeing him sitting at Genevieve's table on the previous day. As the royal party stood at the rail and watched the dark water being turned to white foam by the thrust of the vessel, the man was setting up a camera on a tripod. Dillman strode across to him and tried to sound casual.

"Excuse me," he said, "but do you have permission to take photographs?"

"No," replied Karl-Jurgen Lenz. "Why should I need it?"

"Because the Duke and the Duchess guard their privacy."

"What harm will it do if I take a few photographs of them?"

"It will be seen as an intrusion."

Lenz stiffened. "Who are you?" he asked. "You have a position on this ship?"

"Only as a passenger," replied Dillman, keen to maintain his cover. "I learned my lesson this morning. I was foolish enough to try to get some autographs from them and I was politely turned away. Members of the royal family do not give autographs to strangers. It's beneath their dignity."

"Photography is different," argued Lenz. "I do them a favor."

"Not unless you get clearance beforehand."

"But I am well known for my work. In Germany, I am quite famous."

"Perhaps you are," said Dillman, "but we're not in your country now."

Lenz was offended. "I had an exhibition in London," he said proudly. "Lots of people came to see it. They say very nice things about my work."

"All that I'm giving you is a friendly warning."

"Well, it is not needed, sir. Perhaps you leave me alone, no?" He continued to adjust his camera. "You are American. You do not understand these things."

"I understand what privacy means."

"My country has special ties with England. King Edward is the uncle of Kaiser Wilhelm. His mother, Queen Victoria, she have the sense to marry a German. That make us all members of one family." He stood back from his camera. "Nobody will object."

"Very well," said Dillman, backing off. "I'll get out of your way."

"Good."

Dillman moved away and took up a vantage point from which he could still watch the royal party. The Duke of Fife was using a finger to indicate another ship that was passing them in the middle distance. His daughters waved to it. Lenz was determined. Having set up his equipment, he asked the people who were standing between him and the royal quartet to get out of his way. As soon as that happened, he was spotted by Mr. Jellings, the thickset man who worked for the Duke and Duchess. Dillman watched with amusement as he hurried across to Lenz with his arms stretched wide. There was a brief altercation between the two of them before the German gathered up his camera and tripod and stormed angrily away.

"There seems to have been a rift in the 'family,'" Dillman said to himself.

He heard someone come up behind him and he turned to see Brian Kilhendry.

"You're not needed here, Mr. Dillman," said the purser. "Everything is under control. I'm sure that you have work elsewhere."

"I do like to come up for fresh air occasionally, Mr. Kilhendry."

"Is that what you did on Cunard?"

"I did my job," said Dillman, "and so did Genevieve Masefield. She's on the trail of a thief at the moment. One that must have eluded that celebrated nose of yours."

Kilhendry scowled. "You're not going to let me forget that, are you?"

"Not while you treat me like a trespasser on this ship."

"But that's exactly what you are, Mr. Dillman. Both you and that partner of yours. The pair of you are trespassing on my property and I don't like it. If I had my wish," he asserted, "I'd have the two of you put ashore at Marseilles. You'd not be missed."

Genevieve Masefield delayed her visit to Frau Zumpe until after luncheon, hoping that it would have given the other woman time to simmer down. The opposite was true. The longer she was kept waiting, the more furious Frau Zumpe became. When Genevieve first stepped into her cabin, she had to endure two whole minutes of abuse. She held up both hands to quell the torrent.

"Thank you, Frau Zumpe," she said firmly. "You've made your point and it's now time for me to make mine. P and O cannot take responsibility for items of value left in cabins. Passengers are advised to place money and valuables in the purser's safe. If you had done that, you would not be in this position now."

The other woman glared. "You say that I am to blame?"

"I'm saying this might have been avoided, that's all."

"I am the victim here, not the thief. He stole my money."

"Only because it was left in a place where he could get at it, Frau Zumpe."

"You think that I want to be robbed?" yelled the other.

"No, no. Of course not."

It took Genevieve a long time to calm her down. Frau Zumpe was a woman with a hot temper. Short, squat, and wearing a plain brown dress, she had a pudgy face framed by close-cropped fair hair. So many lines had been etched into her features that she looked much older than her thirty years; Genevieve found herself feeling sorry for her husband. Frau Zumpe seemed to read her mind.

"If my dear husband were still alive," she announced, "he would insist on talking to the captain. Ernst looked after his wife. He speak up for me."

"I'm sorry to hear that he's no longer with us," said Genevieve, feeling sympathy for her. "But even he would not have been able to talk to the captain. These things are outside his remit, you see. Captain Langbourne is solely concerned with sailing the ship. It's the purser who has responsibility for problems like this."

"Yes," she cried. "I know. But do I see the purser? No, he send me away. I have to tell my story to this other man."

"Mr. Grandage is extremely efficient."

"But he is only a deputy. I wanted to speak to the man in charge."

"Right now, you have a woman in charge, Frau Zumpe. And I assure you that I'll do everything in my power to solve this crime and return your money to you."

Frau Zumpe was skeptical. "You have been a detective for long?"

"Long enough."

"You have caught thieves before?"

"Several of them."

"Where?"

"On Cunard ships," Genevieve explained. "I crossed the Atlantic in both directions many times and there were always some crimes to solve. Including murder."

"Murder?" echoed the other. "You have dealt with such a thing?"

"More than once, unfortunately."

"But I think it safe to travel on a ship."

"Ninety-nine percent of the time, it is. We just have the occasional setback."

"It is more than setback, Miss Masefield," said Frau Zumpe. "I lose—in your money—almost five hundred pounds. You see why I am angry?"

"I do, Frau Zumpe, but nothing will be gained by shouting at Mr. Grandage or me. We're here to help." Genevieve took the notebook and pencil from her pocket. "Let me go through the details with you. I understand the theft occurred last night."

"*Ja*, that is so."

"When did you discover it?"

"This morning. I go straight to the purser. He call in his deputy."

"How can you be certain of the time of the theft?"

"Because the money was there when I leave for dinner," said Frau Zumpe, "and when I go back to my cabin later on to get a shawl. I keep it locked away in a box in the wardrobe. When I open the wardrobe this morning, the box has gone."

"But nothing else?"

"There was nothing else to take. Only my money."

"No signs of forced entry. No clothing thrown about?"

"Nothing like that, Miss Masefield."

"Can you remember the precise time when you got back here last night?"

The other woman shrugged. "It was nearly midnight, I think."

"And where were you until then?"

"That is my business," retorted the other. "I do not have to tell you."

"I didn't mean to pry."

"Then why do you ask?"

"Because it may be relevant," Genevieve said patiently. "In the past, when thefts have occurred, the victim has often made some unguarded remarks to a person he or she has met on board a ship. That person may be the thief himself, or his accomplice. When he finds out there's something of value in a particular cabin, he simply has to work out the best time to break into it."

"But he did not break in. There was no damage to the door."

"That's what worries me. It was the same with Mrs. Prendergast."

"Who?"

"A lady in second class, who's traveling to Egypt. She had money and jewelry stolen from her cabin on the very day we sailed."

Frau Zumpe gasped. "What kind of ship is this?" she demanded.

"A good one."

"When you have a thief preying on women passengers?"

"That's an important clue," said Genevieve. "So far, he's struck twice and picked a lone female on both occasions. I'm fairly certain the same man is behind both crimes. He guessed that Mrs. Prendergast would have valuables in her cabin, and let himself in while she was on deck watching the ship leave the dock."

" 'Let himself in?' " said the other woman. "He has a key?"

"It's the only explanation."

"Then it must be one of the stewards."

"Not necessarily. I'll look into that possibility, of course, but I think it will be in vain. A steward could never expect to get away with such a thing. He'd know that we'd check on the whereabouts of the staff at the time of the theft. No," Genevieve continued, her pencil poised, "I'd prefer to follow a different line of inquiry by working my way through the contacts that you've made."

"Contacts?"

"Friends, dinner companions, acquaintances. Anybody you've talked to for any length of time, Frau Zumpe. I know that you'd never be foolish enough to give away any details about your financial situation," she said, seeing the glint in the other woman's eye, "but a clever thief can make assumptions."

"How would he know the money was in my cabin?"

"He wouldn't," said Genevieve, "but he was tempted to take a look just in case there was something worth stealing. When he opened your wardrobe, he probably couldn't believe his luck."

"Luck! It was not lucky for me, Miss Masefield."

"No, it must have been a terrible shock. But you understand what I'm saying? The thief knew you were otherwise engaged and that he could enter your cabin with impunity. He might even have had an accomplice who was deliberately keeping you away. It often happens like that, I fear."

Frau Zumpe winced. "But he was such a nice man. He would never do such a thing."

"Who?"

"The gentleman I was talking to in the lounge," said Frau Zumpe, suddenly looking vulnerable. "There were six or seven of us at first, then some of them go off to bed. In the end, there were just the two of us. He keep me talking until midnight. He was a gentleman. I think he is being friendly with me, that is all."

"What was his name?"

"Dugdale," said the other. "Walter Dugdale."

The body lay facedown in the middle of the cabin. It was completely lifeless. The blood that had gushed from the head wounds had now started to dry, but it had done its damage. A long red river, with many tributaries, had stained the back of the Norfolk jacket.

EIGHT

When the summons came, Dillman had just finished dressing for dinner. There was an urgency about the knock on his door that made him open it immediately. A steward was standing outside.

"Good evening, sir," the man said politely. "The purser sends his compliments and asks if you can join him in his office."

Dillman was surprised. "The purser? Are you sure it wasn't his deputy?"

"No, sir. It was Mr. Kilhendry. He wishes to see you as soon as possible."

"Of course."

The steward walked away. After checking his appearance in the mirror, Dillman left his cabin and hurried along to the purser's office, wondering why Brian Kilhendry had asked to see him when the purser spent most of his time keeping out of the detective's way. He was soon given an answer. Kilhendry opened the door to admit him and looked at Dillman with an amalgam of resentment and relief.

Martin Grandage, also in the room, was obviously grateful for his arrival. The pleasant smile had, for once, deserted his face. "Thank heavens you've come!" he said. "We've had a disaster."

"Of what kind?" asked Dillman.

"The worst—a murder."

"I'll handle this, Martin," said Kilhendry, taking over. "A gentleman in first class has been battered to death in his cabin," he told Dillman. "His name is Walter Dugdale."

"Dugdale?" repeated Dillman. "But I had breakfast with him this morning."

"You won't be sharing a meal with him again. According to the doctor, he died from a massive brain hemorrhage. His skull had been cracked open by repeated blows from a blunt instrument of some sort."

"Poor devil!" sighed Grandage.

"How was the body discovered?" asked Dillman.

"By a steward," explained Kilhendry. "It seems that Mr. Dugdale was a methodical man. He had a drink brought to his cabin at a precise time every evening while he was dressing for dinner. When the steward got no response to his knock, he assumed that Mr. Dugdale was in his bathroom, so he let himself into the cabin. He got a very nasty shock."

"What did he do?"

"He came running to me. I went straight along to the cabin with Dr. Quaid so that we could see for ourselves. It was pretty gruesome."

"I'll need to view the murder scene," said Dillman. "Who else knows about this?"

"Nobody apart from us and the doctor."

"What about the steward? He must to be sworn to secrecy."

"He has been, Mr. Dillman," Kilhendry said sharply. "We're not that stupid. The fewer people who are aware of this, the better. The captain will have to be told, of course, and the chief steward. But that's it."

"Not quite. My partner will need to be informed. Genevieve will be very upset to hear about this—Walter Dugdale dined at her table. Right," he went on, becoming decisive. "I'd like to see the body straight away and search the cabin."

"I'll come with you, Mr. Dillman."

"Would you like me to go instead?" Grandage volunteered.

"No, Martin," said the purser. "You carry on as usual. Keep a smile on your face and give the impression that everything is perfectly normal."

"It won't be easy, Brian."

"It's something that we all have to do," said Dillman. "We must keep this quiet at all costs. If word gets out, it will have a dreadful effect on the atmosphere aboard."

"That's not going to happen on *my* ship," Kilhendry affirmed.

He opened the door and led Dillman along the passageway to the nearest steps. The moment he was back in the public gaze, the purser's manner changed completely. He beamed at everyone they passed and exchanged a few words with a passenger he recognized. Dillman was impressed with his calm demeanor. Nobody would have guessed that Kilhendry was on his way to view the body of a murder victim. When the two men reached Walter Dugdale's cabin, the purser tapped the door three times. It was inched open and an anxious eye was applied to the slit. Seeing who it was, Dr. Quaid let the two visitors into the room then shut the door behind them.

Dillman was introduced to the doctor but paid him scant attention. His gaze was fixed on the body that still lay, as it had been found, in the middle of the floor. Cause of death was obvious. Dugdale's skull had been smashed open from behind. Until the heart stopped pumping, bleeding had been copious.

"Mr. Kilhendry told me to leave everything as it was until you got here," said Quaid. "Poor chap didn't know what hit him. It would have been over very quickly."

"That's small consolation," Kilhendry said with irritation. "A murder is a murder. The simple fact is that Mr. Dugdale has ended up dead and we have a huge problem on our hands. This has never happened to me before. You're the expert, Mr. Dillman," he added bitterly. "What do we do now?"

"We might begin by showing a little sympathy for the murder victim," Dillman said pointedly. "I don't believe that Mr. Dugdale got himself killed simply in order to annoy you. He's the important person here, Mr. Kilhendry." He turned to Quaid. "Can you give us an idea of the likely time of death?"

"That's easy," replied the doctor. "Within the last couple of hours."

Quaid was a stout man of middle height with a fringe of black curly hair around a gleaming head. He wore glasses and kept pushing them nervously up the bridge of his nose. There was the hint of a Scots accent in his voice.

"I've had fatalities on board before," he said, "but only by natural means. You don't expect to see this kind of thing on a P and O cruise. When you've seen all you need to, Mr. Dillman, I'd like to clean him up so that I can examine the wounds properly."

"He'll need to be moved, as well," said Dillman. "We can't leave him here."

"Where can we put him?"

"Somewhere very private where the body can be left on ice. Is there an empty storeroom or something, Mr. Kilhendry?"

"I'll find a place to hide him," said the purser.

"A good time to move him would be during dinner. Everybody will be out of the way then. I'd be only too happy to help."

"No, Mr. Dillman. Martin Grandage and I will take care of that. You direct all your energies to finding out who did this."

"And *why*." Dillman said thoughtfully. "What was the motive? Mr. Dugdale was a delightful man. Intelligent, sophisticated, and very popular with the ladies. It's difficult to imagine why anyone would want to kill him, especially in so brutal a fashion." He glanced around the cabin. "It's possible he disturbed a thief, of course, but the man would have had no reason to bludgeon him to death when he simply could have knocked him out. And thieves usually leave a place in disarray after they've rummaged through everything. As you see, this cabin is neat and tidy. Also," he added, slipping a hand gently under the corpse to extract a billfold from the inside pocket of the Norfolk jacket, "any self-respecting thief would have taken this."

"I'll leave you to get on with your job," said the purser, wagging a finger, "but I want to be kept informed at every stage. Is that understood, Mr. Dillman?"

"Yes, Mr. Kilhendry."

"We'll be back to move the body when dinner is in full swing."

Dillman was glad when the purser let himself out. At such a sensitive time, he did not want Kilhendry looking over his shoulder. It would inhibit him. Dillman first checked the bathroom to see that everything was in order. He then gave the doctor permission to use the faucet so that the latter could begin to wash the blood from the head wounds on the corpse. Dillman, meanwhile, took a swift inventory of the cabin, opening drawers, looking in the wardrobe, and checking every item that lay on the table. Walter Dugdale, it transpired, had been reading *Nostromo* by Joseph Conrad. A bookmark showed that he was halfway through the novel. Dillman thought it rather heavy reading for a man with such a lighthearted approach to life.

The most interesting item on the table was a leather-bound address book, filled with names of people in a whole variety of countries. Dillman had the feeling it would repay study. Apart from a wad of money, there was little else in the billfold except a sepia photograph of an attractive young woman. Dillman suspected he might be looking at Walter Dugdale's daughter. It was a reminder that the dead man would be sorely missed on board as well as by family members.

"We're going to need to explain his absence, Dr. Quaid," he said. "A lot of people will want to know what's happened to Mr. Dugdale."

"Do you have any suggestions?" asked the doctor, still down on one knee.

"The easiest thing is to say that he's indisposed. We need a medical condition that would incapacitate him and, at the same time, keep visitors away from his bedside. He had such an eye for the ladies that one or two of them are sure to want to see him."

Quaid scratched his head. "Was he a well-traveled man, Mr. Dillman?"

"Exceptionally so. He'd been all over the world."

"Then we ought to give him a tropical disease."

"He told me how much he enjoyed visiting South America," said Dillman, "and he was reading a novel that was set there. Could he have contracted malaria?"

"Easily," replied the doctor, "and it's a disease with a nasty habit of recurring. No malarial victim wants visitors around when he's got the shakes and the sweats. Let's settle for that, Mr. Dillman. We'll pretend he's still alive but suffering from malaria. Mind you, I'm not sure how long that excuse will last."

"It only needs to get us to Marseilles. We stop there to take coal on board. It should be possible to get the body ashore there. P and O will have an agent in the city. He can take care of the formalities."

"Shouldn't the crime be reported to the French police?"

"Not unless you want scores of gendarmes all over the ship. That would really give the game away. No," said Dillman, "this is something that we have to handle entirely on our own. My partner and I are the police force on the *Marmora*."

Myra Cathcart was just about to leave her cabin when her daughter announced that she was not going to have dinner that evening. Folding her arms in defiance, Lilian turned away. Her mother was baffled.

"You must eat, Lilian," she reasoned. "Why spend so much time getting dressed for dinner if you don't actually want it?"

"I can't face another evening of watching you and Mr. Dugdale together."

"Why have you taken against him so violently?"

Lilian spun around to face her. "You know quite well."

"Mr. Dugdale is an acquaintance and nothing more."

"Then why are you leading him on?"

"I'm doing nothing of the kind," Myra said with indignation. "I'm just being friendly toward him. We can't sail on a ship for eleven days without actually speaking to anyone, Lilian. That would be absurd."

"You do more than speak to Mr. Dugdale."

"Lilian!"

"You do, Mother. The worst of it is that you don't realize that you're doing it. But I can see the look in his eyes," she said. "And the same goes for Herr Lenz. You ought to keep your distance a little more."

"I don't think I need any lectures from you on that subject."

"You're ready enough to lecture me."

"Only for your own good."

"I don't make friends as easily as you," Lilian complained, "and it's no use pretending that I do. What I resent is the feeling that I'm being ignored. Whenever Herr Lenz or Mr. Dugdale is around, I might as well not be with you."

"That's because you choose to sit there and say nothing."

"Why spend time with two men like that when we've made friends with someone as nice as Genevieve Masefield? *She* doesn't feel the need to flirt with strangers."

"I do not flirt with anyone!" Myra said angrily.

"Yes, you do, Mother. You encourage them."

"I try to be sociable, that's all. If you could learn to do that, you'd enjoy this voyage far more. Now, come along," she ordered.

"Let's have no more nonsense about missing dinner."

Lilian was obstinate. "I'm staying here."

"That's silly."

"No, it isn't. How can I enjoy a meal when the two men sitting opposite me are ogling my mother? It was even worse last night," argued Lilian, hitting her stride. "Not content with having dinner with Mr. Dugdale and Herr Lenz, you dragged me off to the lounge with them. It was getting on toward midnight before I could pull you away."

"We were having an interesting discussion. You should have joined in."

"I felt too embarrassed by the way you were behaving."

"That's enough!" snapped Myra. "I won't have you talking to me like this, Lilian. If anyone was behaving badly, it was you, glowering at everyone like that. At your age, you should be able to hold your own in conversation."

"I can, when I'm talking to someone I like."

Her mother was torn between anger and sympathy, stung by her daughter's criticism yet realizing how much she must have upset her for it to be made. As a rule, Lilian was a quiet, respectful young woman who almost never raised her voice. Only an inner pain had made her speak out with such uncharacteristic boldness and that filled Myra with regret. Controlling her exasperation, she tried to soothe her daughter.

"I'm sorry that it's come to this," she said, "and I accept my share of the blame."

"It's so unlike you, Mother. You were never like this at home."

"I never had the opportunity to spread my wings, that's why."

"What do you think Father would have said?"

"Your father is no longer here, I'm afraid," Myra said sadly, "and we both know that he didn't believe in foreign holidays. He'd disapprove strongly of both of us for coming on this cruise and yet, at the same time, he would have wanted us to be happy. That's all

I want for *you*, Lilian," she continued, taking the other by the shoulders. "A little happiness and adventure."

"I know, Mother. Thank you."

"Then you'll join me for dinner?"

"Not if I have to endure another evening with Mr. Dugdale and Herr Lenz."

"Genevieve doesn't seem to mind their company. Why should you?"

"Because I'm your daughter. I'm *involved*." Lilian stepped back out of her mother's reach. "We don't have to sit in the same seats every evening," she said. "Other people move around all the time. We should do that as well."

"But I promised Walter—Mr. Dugdale—that we'd see him again at dinner."

Lilian smoldered. "Then you'd better go off to him, hadn't you?"

"Why are you being so difficult?"

"Because I feel that I have a right to be. We came on this trip together but you've let someone come between us. It's time you decided whose company you prefer, Mother," said Lilian, throwing down the challenge: "Walter Dugdale's or mine."

Genevieve Masefield saw his signal clearly. When the meal was over, Dillman rose from his chair and used both hands to adjust his white tie. It told his partner that it was imperative for them to meet as soon as was convenient. By way of a change, Genevieve had dined with the Cheriton family, forsaking her usual place between Myra and Lilian Cathcart in order to enjoy the company of other friends. Sitting with the Cheritons had the advantage of putting her in a remote corner of the room, well away from Nigel and Araminta Wilmshurst. The man to whom she was once engaged did not even spare her a glance this time. He studiously ignored Genevieve. She was content.

After waiting until most of the diners began to disperse, she excused herself from the table and went off to Dillman's cabin. His face was clouded as he let her in.

"Trouble?" she asked.

"I'm afraid so, Genevieve. We've had a murder on board."

"Never!"

"I only heard about it myself just before dinner," he explained, "so there was no time to warn you. A passenger was battered to death in his cabin. Did you notice that a certain person was missing this evening? Someone whom you knew?"

Genevieve frowned as she ran through a series of faces in her mind. She had noticed that somebody, apart from Myra and Lilian Cathcart, was absent from the table where she had sat on previous evenings but she could not at first recall who it was. When she did, she was shaken.

"Surely you don't mean Walter Dugdale?"

"The very same."

"Murdered?" she said, unable to believe it. "But he was such a charming man. He was so friendly. I wouldn't have thought he had an enemy in the world."

"He had at least one, Genevieve, and that person is on the *Marmora*."

"What exactly happened, George?"

Dillman was succinct. He gave her the salient facts without any trimmings. She listened with growing discomfort, understanding the need to keep the crime a secret yet wondering how Myra Cathcart, and others, would react to his disappearance. Genevieve agreed that malaria would be a useful curtain behind which to hide the corpse.

"Do we have any clues?" she said.

"We have a good idea of the time of death," he replied, "and we can assume it was not the work of a thief, caught in the act. As far as I could ascertain, nothing was taken from the cabin. The money in his billfold was untouched."

"What does that leave us as a motive?—hatred? envy? revenge?"

"Who knows, Genevieve? We'll have to keep an open mind."

She gave a shudder. "Walter Dugdale!" she said, shaking her head. "Of all people. I sat opposite him at luncheon and he told me about Australia. He had endless stories about it. Mr. Dugdale was such a talented raconteur."

"He told a different tale when I saw him in his cabin," observed Dillman, "and it was not a pleasant one. What we have to do is to build up a picture of his movements during the last few hours when he was alive. You saw him over luncheon. How did he spend the afternoon? Whom did he meet and what did they talk about? We need to retrace his footsteps, Genevieve."

"I think we should go farther back than that, George."

"Why?"

"Something else has happened. It may be relevant."

Genevieve told him about the theft from Frau Zumpe's cabin and emphasized the fact that the person who had kept the German passenger talking until midnight had been Walter Dugdale. What had begun as a discussion involving six people, had ended up being a chat between only two of them.

"What is so unusual about that?" asked Dillman.

"You haven't met Frau Zumpe," she said. "Mr. Dugdale had such a predilection for the female sex. When there are so many attractive ladies on board, it seems odd that he should stay up late talking to someone as unprepossessing as Frau Zumpe."

"Perhaps she had hidden charms."

"I didn't see any, George. She's a very prickly woman."

"Most people would be prickly if they'd had that amount of money stolen."

"Frau Zumpe even gave Mr. Grandage the shivers."

"Then she must be a handful," he agreed. "Martin Grandage can cope with the most truculent passengers. But let's go back to the point you made to this lady about a decoy. Do you really think that Walter Dugdale kept her talking in the lounge so someone could search her cabin?"

"No," she decided, "but it's a possibility we have to consider."

"Thieves falling out? Haggling over the spoils?"

"That doesn't sound like the Walter Dugdale I knew."

"Who else was in the lounge with him last night?" said Dillman. "Did you get a list of names from Frau Zumpe?"

"Eventually," said Genevieve. "When she'd stopped breathing fire through her nostrils. There were six of them in all. Apart from her and Mr. Dugdale, Myra and Lilian Cathcart were there. So was Karl-Jurgen Lenz. He's a German photographer."

"Yes, I had the misfortune to accost Herr Lenz earlier on when he was trying to take unauthorized photographs of the royal party. I can't say that it was a meeting of true minds. He was quite abrupt with me."

"Herr Lenz does have a softer side."

"Then perhaps Frau Zumpe does as well. You only gave me five names."

"The other person in the group was Roland Pountney," she said. "He's a very affable young man who sat at our table. Mr. Pountney is a financier of sorts. He's on his way to Egypt to get a sighting of a new project in which he's investing. When he told the others about it, Frau Zumpe became very interested. She said that she might have some money to invest if she could know more about the project."

"Now we're getting somewhere," said Dillman. "She showed her hand. Frau Zumpe let it be known she had money. There was no guarantee that it was in her cabin, mind you, but it did mark her out as a potential target. Tell me more about this Roland Pountney. Do you trust him?"

"I've no reason not to, George."

"English? Private education?"

"Harrow, by the sound of it."

"How do you know?"

"Because that's where Nigel went. They have the same vowels, the same gestures, the same unassailable confidence. Mr. Pountney is an old Harrovian, I'm sure of it. In fact," she said, stung by a realization, "he may even have been there when Nigel attended."

"Have you bumped into your former fiancé yet?"

"Not exactly. We exchanged a glance, that's all."

"And?"

"He cut me dead."

"That wasn't very courteous."

"Not everyone who comes out of Harrow is a perfect gentleman," she said with asperity. "Nigel Wilmshurst certainly isn't. He could be very cruel."

"Were you hurt by his rebuff?" said Dillman.

"On the contrary, I was pleased with it."

"Pleased?"

"Yes, George," she said. "It means that he's even less anxious to renew our acquaintance than I am. My fears were groundless. Nigel is not going to be a problem at all. To begin with, he's obviously on his honeymoon. I managed to escape his clutches but someone else didn't, it seems. It means that he has a beautiful wife in tow. Given that," she concluded, "he'll avoid me like the plague."

Nigel Wilmshurst was pleased with himself. At the cocktail party held before dinner by Sir Marcus Arundel, he had gone out of his way to court all four members of the royal contingent. They had clearly warmed to him and he could see that Araminta had made a favorable impression on them as well. The Duke and Duchess of Fife would almost certainly dine with them at some point on the voyage. Accustomed to getting what he wanted, he was well satisfied by the evening's work, especially as it was followed by a sumptuous meal.

Though acutely conscious of her presence, he neither looked in Genevieve's direction nor let her become a distraction in any way. His wife had no reason to scold him. Loving and attentive, he kept her giggling happily throughout the meal. When dinner was over, however, he did notice that Genevieve left the room alone, and he assumed she was returning to her cabin. He had been intrigued to discover that she was sleeping no more than twenty yards from his own suite. The thought excited him.

After escorting Araminta into the lounge with their dinner companions, he waited for fifteen minutes then pretended he had forgotten to bring his cigarette case with him. His wife was now comfortably ensconced and he knew that he could leave her without causing any upset. Wilmshurst excused himself and slipped away on his own. He allowed himself to think about Genevieve Masefield again. It had been such a long time since they had met, and he had forgotten how beautiful she was. Since she had a single cabin, she must be traveling alone. He wondered what her destination was.

When he reached her cabin, he looked up and down the passageway to make sure that he was unobserved. Then he knocked hard on the door and waited.

"Come on, Jenny," he said to himself. "Open up—it's me!"

Over breakfast next morning, Myra Cathcart took the news badly. She was overcome with sympathy and guilt. Her face was puckered with anxiety.

"Walter has been taken ill?" she cried in alarm.

"I'm afraid so," said Genevieve, seated opposite her.

"He looked well enough yesterday afternoon. We had tea together in the lounge. That really upset Lilian. It put her in a strange mood. She insisted that we sit somewhere else last night so that we weren't opposite Walter and Herr Lenz again. The funny thing was, of course, that Walter didn't even turn up for dinner." She put a hand to her throat. "Oh dear!" she exclaimed.

"You don't suppose that he saw us on the other table and took offense? Is that why he wasn't there, Genevieve? Did he simply abandon dinner?"

"No, Myra. It was nothing to do with you."

"How do you know?"

"Because Mr. Dugdale had been struck down by then," said Genevieve. "He is such a convivial man, it seemed peculiar that he should miss dinner. When I bumped into the deputy purser, I mentioned to him that a friend had been unaccountably absent from the meal and he knew the name at once."

"What did he say?"

"That Mr. Dugdale was ill in bed and likely to stay there for days. The ship's doctor is very worried about his condition."

"Why?" asked Myra. "What's wrong with the poor man?"

"He's had an attack of malaria, it seems. He contracted it in South America some years ago and it was never fully cured. It comes back from time to time when he least expects it. Mr. Dugdale is feeling very poorly."

"I must go and see him!"

"No," said Genevieve. "That's out of the question. I wanted to call on him myself but I was told that he's in no state to receive visitors. I'm sorry, Myra. We're going to have to manage without him for a while."

There were tears in the older woman's eyes, as if she were just realizing how fond she was of Walter Dugdale. She pressed for more details, but Genevieve had none to give, following Dillman's advice to say as little as possible. She regretted having to tell Myra a lie but there was no alternative. Upset by the information that a friend was seriously ill, Myra would have been devastated to learn that he had, in fact, been murdered in his cabin. Genevieve felt that it was a kindness to keep the hideous truth from her.

The two women were having breakfast alone together and that made it much easier for Genevieve to break the news. Lilian's presence would have made the situation more awkward, not least because she saw Walter Dugdale as a bad influence on her mother; and, though most likely sorry to hear of his putative suffering, Lilian would be relieved by his sudden disappearance. Genevieve knew that Karl-Jurgen Lenz, too, would spare little sympathy for Dugdale. His rival would be out of the way.

"I must send him something," announced Myra, still fretting. "A letter, perhaps. Or something to cheer him up. What would you suggest?"

"Nothing, at the moment," said Genevieve. "He's in no position to read just yet and simply wishes to be left alone."

"How will I be able to check on his condition?"

"Speak to Mr. Grandage, the deputy purser. He'll know much more than I do."

Myra gave a wan smile. "It's ironic, isn't it?" she said.

"What is?"

"Well, Lilian made me sit at another table because she feels unsettled by Walter's interest in me, but we had a miserable time. Even Lilian admitted that. We found ourselves stuck with an Egyptian lady who could speak almost no English and a French-man who talked our ears off. The worst of it was," said Myra, "that he had the temerity to say some very spiteful things about Walter."

"Why?"

"They fell out over something or other. The Frenchman really hated him."

"Oh?" Genevieve said with interest. "What was his name?"

"Vivet," replied Myra. "Claude Vivet."

NINE

George Porter Dillman had breakfast alone in his cabin so he could pore over the address book that had belonged to Walter Dugdale. It disclosed a large amount of information about the dead man. Dillman learned that Dugdale owned a house on Lake Shore Drive, and he knew enough about Chicago to recognize the location as a prestigious one. Evidently, Dugdale was a wealthy man. He also had a wide circle of friends, most of them in America, but several scattered around the world. There were two problems for the detective. Dugdale's handwriting was something close to a hurried scrawl and he had a habit of using abbreviations throughout.

It meant that Dillman could not always identify the names of people whose addresses were recorded in a squiggly hand. When no abbreviation was used—especially where women were concerned—often only a first name was given. Dillman counted no less than four people named Helen and three called Edith. Presumably, he concluded, the gregarious Dugdale told them apart by their addresses, though the ticks, circles, or tiny question marks against the various names suggested a secret code that would also assist identification. The name and address of one recent female friend was written in full. It was that of Myra Cathcart, from Leicester, England. Beside it was an exclamation mark.

Two items held a particular interest for Dillman because they were jotted on the last page of the address book along with the name of a hotel in London and details of the *Marmora*'s departure from Tilbury. Since both addresses were in Perth, the detective guessed that Dugdale had intended to visit them when he got to Australia. No names were given, only initials. Dillman wondered who "P.B.S." might be, and why "W.A.P." had a circle drawn around it. The two people who were awaiting the arrival of Walter Dugdale would be very disappointed. Since it was impossible to tell whether they represented friends or business contacts, the sets of initials shed no light on the purpose of Dugdale's visit to Australia.

A careful perusal of the address book had taught Dillman a great deal about the character of the man whose murder he was investigating. It also provided a name for the daughter whose photograph he had seen in the billfold. Anna Dugdale, who lived in New York City, was in for a profound shock. Dillman hoped that by the time she was informed of the circumstances of her father's death, the killer might be in custody. Feeling that the book contained clues that he had not yet deciphered, he set it aside for a second look at a later date.

There was a tap on the door and he opened it to see Martin Grandage outside.

"Thank you," the deputy purser said as he was invited in. "I just wanted a quick word with you, Mr. Dillman. You'll recall that I asked you and Miss Masefield to keep an eye on the royal party."

Dillman shut the door. "It may be rather difficult now, I fear."

"That's why I've asked two members of the crew to take over. Being in uniform, they'll be more conspicuous, of course, but it can't be helped. The Duke and Duchess need protection for themselves and their daughters."

"It looked to me as if Mr. Jellings was providing that," said Dillman. "I watched him yesterday, dealing with a photographer who tried to take pictures without permission. Mr. Jellings was polite but forceful."

"I still think that we need additional cover. Especially now."

"What do you mean?"

"We have a killer aboard," said Grandage. "I didn't actually see his handiwork myself but I talked to Dr. Quaid about it. He told me this man is very dangerous."

"There's no question about that."

"Then it behooves us to mount a special guard on our royal passengers."

"I don't believe they're at risk," said Dillman. "It was a vicious crime, I grant you, but Walter Dugdale was murdered for a specific reason. I think it's highly unlikely that the killer will strike again."

"We can't take any chances, Mr. Dillman."

"I agree. Safety precautions are always wise. And I'm grateful that we've been freed to devote all our attention to the hunt for the murderer."

"Do you have anything to go on?"

"Not yet, Mr. Grandage. We're looking into various possibilities. By the way," he said, "the purser asked me to report directly to him on this."

"That's fine with me. Brian will keep me abreast of any developments."

"As long as neither of you expects immediate results."

"Take your time, Mr. Dillman. We want you to get the right man."

"Or men," corrected the other. "More than one person may be involved."

Grandage blinked. "Yes, I suppose that's true. I never thought of that. Listen," he said, taking a step nearer, "there's something else you need to know. I'm sure Miss Masefield has told you about the second theft that occurred."

"From a German passenger. Frau Zumpe."

"Not the most amenable lady."

"I understand that she lost a sizable amount of money."

"She did, Mr. Dillman. That's what I wanted to mention to you. There's been an odd coincidence. At least, I think so. It could be something a little more sinister."

" 'Sinister?' "

"Well, most passengers deposit money and valuables with us at the very start of the voyage then take them out of the safe, as and when they need them. At dinner, for instance, when ladies tend to reclaim pearl necklaces or diamond tiaras."

"Or when gentlemen need a supply of money for cards."

"Exactly," said Grandage. "It's not often that anyone comes to us two or three times in a row to have some cash locked away. Particularly when they leave hundreds of pounds with us on each occasion."

"When was the most recent deposit?"

"First thing this morning. That's what made me sit up and think."

"Why?"

"Because yesterday, the same man gave us three hundred pounds to look after."

"I see," said Dillman. "You're bound to wonder if it might have come from Frau Zumpe's cabin. It is an odd coincidence, Mr. Grandage. What was the passenger's name?"

"Mr. Roland Pountney."

The photographs were excellent. Nigel and Araminta Wilmshurst had nothing but praise for them as they leafed through the collection in their cabin. There were a dozen of them altogether. The composition of each photograph was striking, and the definition remarkable. Karl-Jurgen Lenz was clearly a professional.

"These are first-rate, Herr Lenz," said Wilmshurst. "Congratulations!"

"Thank you," replied the German. "I know my trade."

"I've never seen such lovely portraits," said Araminta, holding a photograph of an elderly lady, seated in a garden. "Could we expect to get the same quality?"

"Of course. All my work is of this standard."

"Where do you do the developing?" asked Wilmshurst.

"In my cabin," said Lenz. "I always travel with my equipment."

"It's just as well, then, because I think that you have two more customers."

"Yes," Araminta agreed eagerly. "We'd love you to photograph us, Herr Lenz."

Lenz inclined his head in a token bow then collected up the examples he had brought of his work. Wilmshurst had a strong distaste for foreigners of all kinds and he was irked by the curt formality of Lenz's matter. But there was no denying the man's talent, and the bridegroom was keen to please his bride.

"How much do you charge, Herr Lenz?" he asked.

"That depends on how many photographs you want, sir. Would you like them taken indoors or on deck? I think maybe we have better light outside."

"Araminta?" said Wilmshurst, inviting her opinion.

"It might be better in private, Nigel," she said. "I don't want to be watched by a crowd of people on deck. They'll guess that we're on honeymoon."

"That little secret was given away the moment you walked into the dining room."

She giggled. "Is it that obvious?"

"Yes," said her husband, "but it's nothing to be ashamed of. I daresay that we're not the only newly married couple on the ship. We don't need to hide away any longer. Now, be honest, darling," he urged. "If you could be photographed anywhere on the *Marmora*, where would it be?"

"Anywhere at all?"

"Anywhere. Standing on the bridge beside the captain, if need be."

"Oh, no," she said. "That's not what I'd choose, Nigel. I'd like a photograph of the two of us in here, of course, but there's something I might want even more. And that's one taken with the Duke and Duchess of Fife."

Lenz was alert. "You *know* them, perhaps?"

"Yes," Wilmshurst said airily. "We had drinks with them only yesterday."

"And you wish me to take a photograph of them with you?"

"It would be such a thrill for me if that happened," Araminta said excitedly.

"Then so it will," her husband assured her. "Now, Herr Lenz. What about cost?"

"There is none," said the other.

"None at all?"

No," replied Lenz, smiling for the first time. "If I take photograph of you with the Duke and Duchess, there is no charge."

Claude Vivet was playing the piano in the music room when Genevieve finally tracked him down. He was a dapper man in his forties with a pencil-thin moustache and dark hair that was combed neatly away from a center parting. His complexion was swarthy and, undeniably, in his younger days, he had been handsome. Vivet played well, and did so with dramatic movements, swaying to and fro over the keyboard and tossing his head back from time to time. The few people who were in the room were clearly enjoying his performance. Genevieve waited until he had finished before she came up behind him.

"Debussy," she noted. "One of his 'Images.'"

He spun round on his seat. *"Oui,"* he said, looking up at her with admiration. "He is my favorite composer."

"You played that piece beautifully."

"Merci." He took her hand and kissed it. *"Merci beaucoup, Mademoiselle."*

Genevieve introduced herself and he jumped off his piano stool at once. Taking a card from his inside pocket, he handed it to her with a flourish. She was impressed with what she read.

"You are the head chef at Le Grand Hotel in Paris?" she asked.

"I was," he replied, inflating his chest. "I make their restaurant the most famous in the city. You know the hotel?"

"Only by reputation."

"I help to make the reputation."

She offered him the card back, but he waved it away.

"No, no. You keep in case you forget my name. I think we will be friends, yes?"

"I'm not likely to forget you or your name, Monsieur Vivet," Genevieve said as she slipped the card into her purse. "Nor will I forget how well you played Debussy."

"You are a pianist as well?"

"Of a kind. But I'm nowhere near as good as you."

"It is a rule in life with me," he explained. "If I do something, I do it properly. Making the food, playing Debussy, or . . ." He broke off with a laugh. "I am a man of many talents, you see. Do you have time to hear about them?"

"Of course. Shall we go into the lounge? They're serving coffee."

"You are English, no? You prefer the tea."

"Not at this time of the morning, *Monsieur.*"

He took her off to the first-class lounge, unworried by the fact that Genevieve was a few inches taller. Claude Vivet strutted across the room then stood behind her chair as she lowered herself into it. He came round to sit opposite her, appraising Genevieve with interest. A waiter glided up to them and coffee was ordered. The man departed.

"You are traveling alone?" he asked in surprise.

"Yes," she replied. "I'm very independent."

"I can see that. How far do you go?"

"All the way to Australia."

"*Mon dieu!* Such a long way. You think, maybe, I persuade you to stay in Egypt with me instead?" he said with a grin. "I go there for *les vacances.* Is very beautiful country. You like it there."

"I'm sure that I would, but I have other plans."

"That is a pity." He looked around. "What you think of the *Marmora*?"

"She's a very comfortable ship. I have no complaints."

"I do," he said, letting his eyebrows shoot up expressively. "The food is so bad I do not touch most of it. I would never dare to put such dishes in front of a customer."

"I think that the meals on board are very good," she said.

"Is because you are English. You are not used to good food there."

"That's a matter of opinion, Monsieur Vivet. We have some very fine chefs in London and they can compete with anyone. Why don't you like the fare on board?"

It was a foolish question because it unleashed a diatribe that went on for the best part of ten minutes. Even the arrival of the coffee did not halt Vivet's flow; indeed, it provoked further disdain as he explained why it was so tasteless. Genevieve let him rant on, observing how quickly he worked himself up into a state of outrage. In the end, he gave a gesture of dismissal.

"The chefs aboard are Italian," he said. "That explains it."

"I'm sorry they don't meet your high standards."

"I show how a meal should be prepared," he boasted, tapping his chest. "One evening, I cook for the Duke and Duchess. They will see why French cuisine is the best."

"Oh?" she said, impressed by his claim. "Have they agreed to let you prepare dinner for them?"

"Not yet, but they will. They see my card. How can they refuse?"

His vanity made him look ridiculous but Genevieve did not mock him. She had sought him out for a reason and worked her way around to the subject of Walter Dugdale.

"I understand that you dined with some friends of mine yesterday," she said.

"The mother and daughter?"

"That's right. Myra and Lilian Cathcart."

"Nice English ladies. The daughter, too shy. She say nothing."

"I think that she took exception to what you were saying, Monsieur Vivet."

He looked surprised. "Me? I hope I not upset them."

"They were a little disconcerted by some remarks you made about an American gentleman." She saw his fists tighten. "His name was Mr. Dugdale."

"I know his name," he retorted, "and I meet him, too. This man is rude to me."

"Really?"

"He insult my cooking. I not stand for that. I despise him."

"Why?"

"Because of the bad things he say. The two ladies, they think him gentleman but they not understand what he call me in my own language. I not forgive that. You keep away from this Walter Dugdale," he advised, his eyes blazing. "He not what he seem."

Roland Pountney was sitting in the first-class smoke room, drawing nonchalantly on a cigarette as he talked to Morton Goss. The Egyptologist preferred a pipe and its tobacco had a pleasing aroma as the smoke curled upward. The room was paneled but its woodwork was less ornate than that in the dining room. Upholstered bench seating ran around the walls and beneath an over-hanging balcony that was supported by pillars. A number of other men were enjoying a smoke, reclining on the benches or sitting at one of the tables in the middle of the room.

When Dillman arrived, he had to peer through a veil of smoke to pick out Roland Pountney. The man had been pointed out to him earlier by the deputy purser, and the detective had bided his time before moving in. The fact that Goss was there made the meeting with Pountney seem accidental. Lighting a cigarette, Dillman drifted casually across to the two men.

"I didn't take you for a pipe man, Mr. Goss," he observed. "Given your interests, I would have thought you'd opt for a hookah."

"It wouldn't fit into my top pocket so easily, Mr. Dillman," said Goss, laughing.

He introduced the newcomer to Pountney and they shook hands. Invited to join them, he took a seat at their table and made polite conversation while he sized up the courteous Englishman. As he listened to the man's distinctive accent, he remembered what Genevieve had told him.

"Excuse me," said Dillman, "but did you, by any chance, go to Harrow?"

Pountney was taken aback. "How on earth did you know that, old chap?"

"It was a guess, really. Though I do flatter myself that I have a good ear for accents, and yours sounds remarkably like that of a friend of mine who went to Harrow."

"What was his name? Perhaps we were there at the same time."

"I doubt it. James Burdock is somewhat older than you," said Dillman, borrowing a name from *Masks and Faces,* a play in which he had once appeared. "He always spoke so fondly of his old school."

"It certainly leaves its mark upon us," admitted Pountney. "Actually, I'm not the only Harrovian on board. I spotted a fellow called Wilmshurst who was a few years ahead of me. We've exchanged a nod or two in passing."

"Don't you want to get together to talk about old times?" asked Goss.

"Not really. To be honest, I never really liked him at school. Nigel Wilmshurst was just not my type, somehow. Besides, I'd be rather in the way at the moment."

"In the way?"

"He's on honeymoon, Mr. Goss. You only have to look at his wife to see that. Attractive filly she is, too. They're clearly off to celebrate the first few weeks of marriage in the sun, so I don't think Wilmshurst would be in the mood to discuss his schooldays." Pountney gave a knowing smile. "He has far better things to do."

"I spent my honeymoon in Niagara Falls," said Goss. "I'd have preferred it to be Cairo but my salary didn't stretch to such luxuries in those days and my wife doesn't have the same obsessive interest in ancient Egypt."

"I'm more concerned with its future," announced Pountney. "There are some exciting commercial developments taking place. Good opportunities for investors."

"Is that what you are?" asked Dillman.

"Yes, I'm always looking for ways to spend money wisely, Mr. Dillman. Not just on my own account, either. I act as a broker for a number of other people. Patriotism is all very well," he argued, "but it does tend to limit one's horizons."

"Does it?"

"Of course," said Pountney. "Most chaps in my line wouldn't dream of investing abroad. They'd rather plow their pennies into British industry and reap what profits they can from that. The real rewards are for investors with the courage to look farther afield." He finished his cigarette and stubbed it out in the ashtray. "That's why I'm heading for Egypt."

"Will you be spending Christmas there?"

"Yes, Mr. Dillman. I have close friends in Luxor."

"Won't you miss being at home with your family?"

"Home is where my latest financial commitment happens to be."

"You're obviously dedicated to your work," said Dillman. "Just like our friend Mr. Goss here. Happy is the man who's found his true métier."

"Is that what you've done?" asked Pountney.

"I think so. Except that, in my case, it was found *for* me. I come from a family that makes its living from the sea, Mr. Pountney. We build yachts. Large ones."

"Like father, like son, eh? What took you to England?"

"Curiosity."

"That's what got me involved in ancient history," admitted Goss.

"Have you ever had cause to regret it?" said Dillman.

"Only when my wife and daughter complain that it takes up all my time. Oh"—he went on as his memory was jogged—"speaking of my daughter, she wants to arrange a time when you can listen to her playing the flute."

"I'll have to let her know," replied Dillman, not wishing to commit himself.

"Polly is eager to show off. She's taken a liking to you, Mr. Dillman."

"Is she a keen musician?" said Pountney.

"Very keen, Mr. Pountney. She practices every day."

"Someone else who's found her mission in life, then." He looked at his watch. "You must excuse me, gentlemen. I promised to meet Sir Alistair Longton at noon and I never keep a prospective business associate waiting. Good to meet you both." Roland Pountney shook hands warmly with both of them before striding off.

"I hope that I didn't interrupt anything, Mr. Goss," said Dillman.

"Heck, no. We were just chatting about Egypt, that's all. Mr. Pountney is an educated man. He may talk about the future of the country but he knows a fair bit about its past as well. He was pleasant company."

"Yes," agreed Dillman. "A model of English charm."

"On the surface, at least," said Goss. "Underneath, I suspect, he's as tough as teak. I guess he'd have to be, in the world of high finance, or he wouldn't survive. Mr. Pountney was very well informed. He had a detailed knowledge of last year's financial crisis back home in the States."

"It was reported in most British newspapers."

"I know, but he actually had investments in the American market. Somehow they turned a good profit, according to him. See what I mean?" asked Goss. "If he can make money while everyone else is losing it in handfuls, Mr. Pountney must be a shrewd man."

The cruise was as much a geography lesson as it was an opportunity to relax in a luxury vessel. After leaving the English Channel, the *Marmora* had made its way south toward the Bay of Biscay, then hugged the coast of northern Spain as it sailed on into the Atlantic. Those who stayed on deck during heavy drizzle could pick out the jagged contours of Portugal and, even though a new day brought rain, wind, and choppy water, almost everyone came out to get a first glimpse of the Rock of Gibraltar, the promontory in the extreme south of Cádiz. Mindful of the fact that it was a British colony, several English passengers set up a cheer when it was conjured out of the driving rain.

The port side of the ship was crammed with spectators, many seeing Gibraltar for the first time and marveling at its dramatic profile. The Duke and Duchess of Fife were among the onlookers, and their younger daughter clapped her hands in jubilation when she saw the Rock. It was not merely a testament to the enduring strength of the British Empire, it was a significant landmark that told them they had now entered the Mediterranean Sea. Warmer weather and quieter waters lay ahead.

Karl-Jurgen Lenz was not deterred by the inclement weather. Long before they got within range of the Strait, he set up his camera so that he could take some photographs of the Rock of Gibraltar as they sailed past. Genevieve Masefield came out on deck in time to see him talking to Frau Zumpe. She noticed how much more animated he became when he was able to use his own language. Wearing a cape and a wide-brimmed hat that was festooned with black ribbon, Frau Zumpe eventually broke away from him. In the open air, she somehow looked less formidable. Genevieve seized the opportunity of a private word with her.

"Good afternoon, Frau Zumpe," she said.

"Ah, is you," returned the other. "You have the good news for me?"

"Not yet. I still have a lot of inquiries to make. But I wanted to check a few facts with you first," said Genevieve. "You mentioned that you were talking with Mr. Dugdale until midnight on the night of the theft."

"So?"

"Did you leave him in the lounge when you went off to bed?"

"I tell you all you need to know."

"Perhaps it was Mr. Dugdale who retired to his cabin first," suggested Genevieve, keen to establish his movements. "Is that what happened, Frau Zumpe?"

The other woman was brusque. "What happened is that someone go into my cabin to steal my money while was I away. You get it back for me, no? What I say to Mr. Dugdale is not important."

"It could be relevant."

"Is no business of yours."

"What about Mr. Pountney?" asked Genevieve, approaching the subject from another angle. "You said that he talked about his investment in an Egyptian company."

"Yes," said Frau Zumpe. "I was interested in what he say. He is very clever and I do not think that of many Englishmen. They are

127

often stupid. Mr. Pountney, he was different. I speak about him to his friend this morning."

"His friend?"

"Sir Alistair Longton. You know him?"

"I'm afraid not," said Genevieve.

"He tells me that Mr. Pountney's venture in Egypt is bound to succeed, so he will put his own money into it. That shows it must be a good investment," said Frau Zumpe. "When you find my money for me, I maybe buy some shares from Mr. Pountney as well."

"What guarantee will you have?"

"The papers, of course."

"Papers?"

"The details of this project in Cairo. Sir Alistair Longton has seen them and he was convinced. I would want to read the documents myself before I make the decision but I think Mr. Pountney is a man to trust."

"Is that what Mr. Dugdale thought?" asked Genevieve.

"Why do you keep talking about him?"

"He must have been there when Mr. Pountney described this venture in which he's involved. As a businessman, Mr. Dugdale must have been interested in it."

"No," said the other woman.

"Why not?"

"He not say."

"He must have expressed an opinion of some sort," insisted Genevieve.

"What does it matter?" Frau Zumpe said testily. "Tell me this, please. You think that Mr. Dugdale was working with the thief who took my money?"

"No, I'm absolutely certain that he wasn't."

"Then we forget him, yes?"

Genevieve could not understand why Frau Zumpe was so

unwilling to reveal what she had been talking to Walter Dugdale about, or to explain which of them had gone off to a cabin first. The woman was being deliberately obstructive but there was no point in pressing her for information that she would not volunteer. Frau Zumpe had calmed down a great deal since Genevieve had first interviewed her and she did not wish to provoke the German woman's anger again. Though they were talking in a quiet corner, the deck was filled with other people who would surely notice if Frau Zumpe exploded again. All Genevieve could do was to thank her for her help and move away.

Gibraltar now became the focal point for everyone. As they sailed through the Strait and took the measure of the Rock, passengers watched with fascination, pointing out certain features to each other and waving cheerily to those ashore. Lenz took a series of photographs and soon became an object of interest himself as some curious children gathered around him. Genevieve was as interested as anyone else to see Gibraltar—for the first time, in her case—but she also observed the reactions of other people. Frau Zumpe was the one who surprised her most. Standing at the rail some yards to the left of Genevieve, she gazed at the passing landmass with a benign smile that took years off her face. Instead of wearing the grim and combative expression that had been there earlier, Frau Zumpe looked almost attractive.

Only when the ship had left Gibraltar in its wake and sailed on into the Mediterranean did the passengers begin to disperse to their cabins or to the public rooms. Genevieve lingered to talk to Lenz as he packed up his equipment.

"Did you get some good photographs, Herr Lenz?" she asked.

"I *always* get good photographs," he said with pride.

"Even in rain like this?"

"Nothing stop me. I work in all conditions." He looked at her with suspicion. "Have you talked to Mrs. Cathcart?"

"Several times. You've seen us dining together."

"Did you speak to her about me?" he said with an accusatory stare. "I wish to take some photographs of her and she agree. Then she change her mind. Why? Did you turn Mrs. Cathcart against me?"

"Of course not, Herr Lenz."

"Somebody did, and you are her best friend."

"We'd never met before we stepped onto the ship."

"Mrs. Cathcart like you. She listen to what you say."

"Well, I did not advise her to change her mind about the photographs," Genevieve said firmly. "It's nothing to do with me. It's between you and Myra Cathcart."

"Mr. Dugdale," he snarled. "If it was not you, it must have been him. He has done this to me. When I see him next," he warned, gathering up his equipment, "I will have something to say to Mr. Walter Dugdale."

Genevieve could not tell him that he would never see Dugdale again. Turning abruptly on his heel, Lenz marched off and left her standing there. It was the second time that afternoon that Genevieve had had some friction with a German passenger. In each case, it had occurred when Walter Dugdale's name had come into the conversation. It was something to ponder.

As the ship altered course to head northeast toward Marseilles, the wind blew the rain in to sweep the decks more purposefully. Genevieve went off to her cabin to get out of her wet coat and hat. As she entered the passageway, however, she found her way blocked by the man who had hitherto ignored her. Nigel Wilmshurst smiled broadly.

"Hello, Jenny," he said, arms wide apart. "We meet at last."

TEN

Genevieve was so shocked by the unexpected confrontation that she was rooted to the spot. Having convinced herself that he would avoid her at all costs, she was now face-to-face with a man who revived some extremely unpleasant memories for her, and it was unsettling. There had been a time when she'd thought she had loved him, but there was not even the most vestigial fondness left. Genevieve disliked him intensely. What made her feel even more uncomfortable in his presence was that, for his part, Wilmshurst seemed delighted to see her.

"Don't I even get a kiss?" he asked, moving toward her.

"No," she said, holding up a hand to stop him. "Stay back, Nigel."

"Why? We're old friends, aren't we?"

"You weren't very friendly when you first saw that I was aboard."

"That's because I was taken aback, Jenny. Dash it all!" he said, running his eyes appreciatively over her. "When a chap comes on his honeymoon, the last person he expects to find on the same ship is the gorgeous woman to whom he was once engaged."

"That's all in the past, Nigel. I suggest that we let it stay there."

"Do I detect a note of bitterness?"

"I'm just being practical," said Genevieve, resenting the boldness of his scrutiny. "We live in different worlds now. You're married to a beautiful woman and I wish you both well. But you and I have nothing to say to each other."

"Oh, but we do," argued Wilmshurst. "We've heaps of things to talk about."

"I don't think so."

"To start with, you can tell me what you're doing on this ship."

"That's my business," she said. "Now, please let me pass."

"Not until you agree to have a proper chat with me sometime."

"In the circumstances, it would hardly be appropriate."

"What do you mean?"

"Well, I don't think that your wife would approve, would she?" said Genevieve. "Have you told her that I'm sailing on the same vessel as you?"

"No," he admitted.

"Does she know that you were engaged to someone else before she met you?"

"Of course—and there's no reason why Araminta should be reminded of it, especially on her honeymoon. That would be bad form. I'm determined to make this an unforgettable experience for my wife."

"How can you do that when you're out here, pestering me?"

"I'm pestering nobody," he said with an appeasing smile. "I simply wanted the pleasure of meeting you again and taking a proper look at you. Time has been very kind to you, Jenny. You look as wonderful as ever."

"Thank you," she said, "but you should save your compliments for your wife."

"Araminta has more than her share of those, I can promise you. After all, I've paid her the greatest compliment that a man can pay a woman. I married her." He arched an eyebrow. "Instead of you."

"We both know why I broke off the engagement."

"It was a silly mistake on my part, Jenny. I've regretted it ever since."

"Then you'll have as much reason as I do to leave it buried in the past."

"But I don't," he said. "I feel that I owe you an apology. Anger has a cruel way of distorting the truth. In the heat of the moment, we both said things that were very unkind. I'm profoundly sorry about that."

"So am I, Nigel. It's not something I look back on with any pride."

"Then why can't we kiss to show that there are no hard feelings?"

"Because I don't wish to," Genevieve said crisply. "Put yourself in my position and you'll understand why." She took a deep breath and tried to sound calm. "We did have some happy times together—I'd be the first to concede that—but they were completely overshadowed by what happened later. I want to be left alone, Nigel. I can't put it any plainer than that."

"Won't you even tell me where you're going on the *Marmora*?"

"To Australia."

He was appalled. "Australia? Are you serious? It's a barbarous place. We used to send convicts there."

"That was a long time ago."

"You deserve better than that, Jenny," he said. "Much, much better. I expected you to have made a good marriage yourself by now. And how is it that you're traveling alone? You were never short of admirers before I came along."

"You came along and went, Nigel," she reminded him. "And you're on your honeymoon, which means—or *should* mean—that you're far too busy to pay any attention to someone from your distant past."

"It wasn't all that distant. When I look at you now, it seems like only yesterday."

"Yesterday, you snubbed me in the dining room for the second time."

"I thought that you'd prefer it if I kept my distance."

"I do, believe me."

"Then I began thinking about all the fun we had together," he said, "and I realized how stupid I was being. Yes, I'm married and I'm devoted to Araminta. But that doesn't mean I've turned my back on you, Jenny."

Their eyes locked and she felt a tremor of alarm. Nigel Wilmhurst had been furious when she had broken off their engagement, and he had vowed to get back at her at some point. Chance had now contrived to put her in a position where he could do just that. There was a lot of affection in his gaze but it was fringed with malice. She knew that he could be a dangerous enemy and did not wish to antagonize him. At the same time, she was not going to submit to any interrogation. Wounds that had healed some time ago now threatened to open again. Genevieve needed to get away.

"Excuse me, please," she said pointedly.

"Certainly," he said, politely stepping aside for her to pass.

"Good-bye, Nigel."

"Good-bye, Jenny," he said cheerily. "Until the next time."

Brian Kilhendry was seated at his desk when Dillman came into the office. The purser looked up from the letter he was writing. He was more hospitable than usual.

"Ah, good," he said. "I was hoping that you'd pop in to see me. Any progress?"

"A little, Mr. Kilhendry. We're still feeling our way into the case."

"Well, don't be too long about it."

"I came to look at those items that Mr. Dugdale left for safekeeping."

"Yes," said Kilhendry, opening a drawer to take out a small box.

"They're in here, Mr. Dillman. Unlike some of our passengers, Walter Dugdale was a sensible man. He put everything of value under lock and key."

"Thank you," said Dillman, taking the box from him to sift through its contents. "Now, then, what have we got here?"

"Some money, his passport, his return ticket, and a set of keys. Oh, and there's a gold watch that must have cost a pretty penny. His name is inscribed on the back."

Dillman examined the pocket watch first. It was large, expensive, and attached to a thick gold chain. On the back, beneath Dugdale's name, were the initials *C.P.C.*

"Is that some kind of academic qualification in your country?" said Kilhendry.

"No, I suspect that the initials stand for someone who gave him the watch."

"There are three letters. Some society or association, perhaps?"

"Not necessarily," said Dillman. "Americans tend to use their middle names more than anyone else. 'C.P.C.' could well be a person. A woman, possibly."

"Then she was not short of cash. Nor was Mr. Dugdale."

Dillman flicked through the wads of notes. Pounds sterling and U.S. dollars were there in equal amounts. Dugdale was taking a lot of money with him on his trip. A glance through his passport showed how well-traveled he had been. The pages had been stamped in well over a dozen different countries, some of which he had visited more than once. He was a man who, it appeared, had been in perpetual motion.

"What we don't yet know," said Kilhendry, indicating the sheet of stationery on his desk, "is his next of kin. I was drafting a letter of explanation to them when you came in. Was he married? He wore no wedding ring."

"He was married," said Dillman. "Twice, as it happens. But he had the air of a single man so I don't think he still has a wife. I fancy that the next of kin will be his daughter, Anna. I found an address for her in New York City."

"Let me have it, please."

"There was a photograph of her in his billfold. I'd say she is in her twenties but the photo could have been taken some time ago."

Kilhendry sighed. "There's no easy way to explain what happened," he said. "She'll be informed by telegraph first, of course, and that will be brutally short. I feel that she deserved a fuller account, though I'll omit the more gory details."

"That's very considerate of you, Mr. Kilhendry."

"It's the least I can do," said the purser. "I've been in touch with our agent in Marseilles. Preparations are in hand to unload the body there. All I told him was that we had a death on board. He can take over from there. It may well be that Mr. Dugdale's daughter wants the body sent back to America for burial. My letter can go with it."

"How did the captain react?"

"Badly," said the purser. "It's the worst thing that could happen at the very start of a voyage. He wants the murder solved as quickly as possible."

"So do the rest of us," said Dillman. "Where's the body now?"

"Locked securely away on a bed of ice. I'll be glad when we can smuggle it ashore in France." A note of rancor intruded. "Well," he continued, sitting back in his chair. "I suppose that this is what you were hoping for, Mr. Dillman: a chance to prove yourself as a detective."

"I certainly didn't hope for a murder, Mr. Kilhendry, and I resent the suggestion."

"Oh, come now. You and Miss Masefield wanted a case that you could get your teeth into. Then you could show us all the tricks of the trade you learned on the Cunard Line. You solved more than one murder for them."

"Not by using any tricks," said Dillman. "One of the reasons we had a degree of success was that we always enjoyed the full confidence of the purser."

Kilhendry glared. "That certainly isn't the case on the *Marmora*."

"I can't believe that even you would want us to fail."

"Of course not, Mr. Dillman. Nothing would please me more than if you and your partner were to find the killer and hand him over to us. Then I might actually believe some of the things that are said about you. As it is," said Kilhendry, "I dislike the way that you suddenly have to assume so much responsibility on my ship."

"Not from choice," said Dillman.

"Martin Grandage may have great faith in you, but I don't."

"All we ask is that you don't hinder the investigation, Mr. Kilhendry."

"I'd never do that," snapped the other. "I have a vested interest in getting this mess cleaned up. It's bad for the reputation of P and O."

"I thought you were more concerned with the reputation of Brian Kilhendry."

"The two go hand in hand."

"It could have been worse," Dillman pointed out. "We have the opportunity to get the body ashore in Marseilles and explain to the friends he made aboard that Mr. Dugdale is 'too ill' to continue the voyage. That's a major hurdle out of the way. Imagine how much more difficult it might have been if his death had occurred at some later stage when we were a long way from the next port of call."

"Whenever it happened," said Kilhendry, "it would have been a catastrophe."

"There are mitigating circumstances here. Supposing we had just left Marseilles when the crime took place. It's a long way to Port Said," Dillman argued. "Where else do we bunker on our way to Sydney?"

"Aden, Columbo, and Freemantle."

"There you are, then. We've got some lengthy stretches at sea ahead of us."

"Yes," the purser said sourly, "and I look to you and Miss Masefield to ensure that they're entirely free of trouble. We don't want to unload a murder victim every time we stop to take on coal. You'd better start to think of *your* reputation, Mr. Dillman."

When she heard the tap on the door of her cabin, Genevieve Masefield trembled with apprehension. Afraid that Nigel Wilmshurst might be calling on her, she decided to ignore the sound and finish dressing for dinner. But her visitor was too insistent to be put off by the silence from within the cabin. Knuckles were rapped harder on the timber and Genevieve eventually responded.

"Who is it?" she asked, standing by the door.

"It's me," said Lilian Cathcart. "Could I speak to you for a moment?"

Relieved that it was not her former fiancé, Genevieve opened the door and let Lilian in. She was pleased to see Lilian alone for once because it gave her the chance to gather some more details about a late-night discussion with Walter Dugdale that had taken place in the lounge. Wearing a pale green evening dress and an anxious expression, Lilian had come specifically to talk about the man.

"I feel so guilty about Mr. Dugdale," she said, eyes full of compassion. "There was I, wishing that he would go away, and he's struck down by a terrible illness. It's almost as if I wished it on him."

"That's ridiculous," Genevieve assured her. "You're not to blame."

"I was so unkind toward him."

"He meant you no harm."

"I can see that now," said Lilian. "I was very selfish earlier on."

"It's not a crime for a man to show fondness toward your mother. She has such vivacity; that will always turn heads. I was there when Mr. Dugdale first met her," said Genevieve, "and I could see that she'd made an impression."

"I know, Miss Masefield, and it was wrong of me to criticize her for that. Mother is so upset by what's happened to him. She's desperate to visit Mr. Dugdale."

"That won't be possible, I'm afraid."

"How long will this attack last?"

"You'd have to ask the doctor. All I know is that he's doing very poorly. Malaria is a cruel disease. One minute a patient is running a high fever; the next minute, he's shivering uncontrollably with cold. Nobody wants to be seen in that condition," said Genevieve. "Mr. Dugdale is best left alone."

"I do feel sorry for him," said Lilian, biting her lip. "He looked so healthy earlier on. This will ruin his holiday completely."

"Well, I hope that you won't let it ruin yours. Or your mother's."

"It was a blow for both of us, especially for Mother. I hadn't realized how much she cared for Mr. Dugdale. That's why I'm so full of remorse; Mother is very distraught."

"Try to offer her as much support as you can," suggested Genevieve.

"Oh, I will," said the other. "It's the one good thing to come out of this business. Mother and I were able to talk properly for the first time."

" 'Properly?' "

"Without arguing. I've been so silly and childish—I can see that now. Mother has been saintly with me, really, and so have you, Miss Masefield."

"Me?"

"Yes," said Lilian. "Both of you put up with me hanging on to you because I didn't feel able to stand on my own feet. I owe you an apology as well as Mother."

"No, you don't."

"It was very naughty of me to unload my worries on you."

"That's what friends are for," Genevieve said warmly. "I've enjoyed our time together. I'm just sad that you haven't been able to get into the spirit of things. Everyone else came aboard determined to have a good time, whereas you seemed resigned to suffer. There must be something about the *Marmora* that you like."

"Oh, there is," Lilian agreed with a show of enthusiasm. "Meeting you has been wonderful, of course, and there have been other people whose company has been very pleasant. Then there's the royal party," she added. "Every time they've come out on deck, I've been there to watch them."

"By the time you reach Port Said, you'll be bored by the sight of them."

"That could never happen."

Genevieve was touched by Lilian's honesty in admitting that she had been in the wrong and was delighted that her attitude toward the voyage was now more positive. The sudden disappearance of Walter Dugdale had brought mother and daughter closer and yet, paradoxically, it had also pushed them apart slightly. Genevieve could see that Lilian would no longer be so dependent on her mother or, indeed, on Genevieve herself. In a short space of time, Lilian Cathcart had visibly grown up.

"When did you last speak to Mr. Dugdale?" asked Genevieve.

"It must have been that night we finished up in the lounge with him," replied Lilian. "Mother was so cross about that. She wanted to stay and talk to him but I made her come away with me. Do you see what I mean about being selfish? Mother hated having to leave him alone with that German lady."

"Frau Zumpe?"

Lilian was surprised. "You know her?"

"Yes," Genevieve said casually, "I bumped into her one day. She's not a lady you can easily forget. How did she get on with Mr. Dugdale?"

"Very well, as it happens," said Lilian. "He somehow managed to charm her. I think that's what annoyed Mother. That and Herr Lenz, of course."

"What was he up to?"

"He kept speaking in German to Frau Lenz. It was very rude of him."

"You can hardly blame the man for wanting to use his own language."

"But it excluded the rest of us. Except Mr. Pountney, that is. He knew enough German to realize what they were talking about and he teased them a little. That stopped them." A smile touched her lips. "Mr. Pountney is a very nice man."

"I wondered when you'd notice that," said Genevieve.

"So cultured and assured."

"You should get to know him better."

"Oh, he's not interested in me," Lilian said wistfully. "Though he did ask me a lot of questions about our family business. He'd actually heard of Cathcart's Shoes. It turns out he's had business dealings in Leicester himself."

"There you are. You have something in common with him already."

"Not really. He didn't pay much attention to me. He was too busy telling the others about his investments in Egypt. Mr. Pountney said it is important to get a stake in the country," she recalled. "He told us he wished that he'd been around when the Suez Canal was being built. He'd have snapped up as many shares as he could. Apparently, that's what Mr. Disraeli did when he was prime minister."

"Yes, it was a brilliant investment. I was taught about it at school."

"I don't know anything about business," said Lilian, "but I was intrigued by what he told us. So was Frau Zumpe. She kept pressing him for more details. Mr. Pountney is such a marvelous talker. I could listen to him for hours."

"So why did you drag your mother away?"

"He'd left by then. So had Herr Lenz."

"So there were just the four of you."

"Three, really," confessed Lilian. "I might just as well have not been there because I didn't say a word. I just sat there and sulked while Mr. Dugdale talked to mother and Frau Zumpe. He made them laugh but I was seething with anger." She pulled a face. "That's why I feel so rotten about it now. I do hope I get the chance to make amends for it when he gets better."

"We'll have to wait and see," said Genevieve, knowing that it was a vain hope. "The main thing is that you recognize your mistakes. That's something to build on. And I don't think you should assume that Mr. Pountney has no interest in you. I've seen him give you admiring glances a number of times."

"I can't compete with the person who's really caught his attention."

"And who's that?"

"You, of course," said Lilian. "He talked about you a lot to Mother and wants to know all about you. Surely, you must have noticed. You've made a conquest."

Dillman had gone no more than a dozen yards from his cabin when he was ambushed. Polly Goss had been lying in wait for him. She was wearing a white satin evening dress, silver earrings, an Egyptian necklace, and far more cosmetics than before. Dillman caught a whiff of her perfume as she pounced on him.

"When are you going to listen to me playing the flute?" she asked.

"Whenever it is convenient," he replied.

"I have the feeling that you don't really want to, Mr. Dillman."

"That's not true at all. Suggest a time."

"Tomorrow morning? Ten o'clock?"

"I'll be in the first-class music room on the dot," he promised, "and I'm sure that I'll hear some first-class music. Have you decided what you're going to play?"

"Not yet."

Polly Goss showed her teeth in what she thought was an alluring smile but it only served to remind Dillman how young and immature she still was. He could see that she felt a trifle neglected by him so he offered her his arm to take her in to dinner. She took it at once and gave a little laugh of triumph.

"It doesn't have to be in the music room," she pointed out. "If you'd rather hear me in private, I could come to your cabin."

"The music room will be better. It has proper acoustics. Besides," he went on, "if you play in public, you'll have a larger audience. Other people will be attracted by the sound of your flute. You'll be like the Pied Piper of Hamelin."

"You're the only person I want to play for, Mr. Dillman."

"I'll certainly lead the applause, I know that."

"Thank you!"

She squeezed his arm then hung on to it tight until they reached the first-class dining room. There was a slight change in the seating arrangements. Dillman sat beside Polly and opposite her parents, but the face immediately next to Morton Goss had altered. The newcomer was Sir Alistair Longton, a distinguished-looking man in his sixties with a mop of white hair and bushy side whiskers. He wore a monocle through which he peered at the evening menu.

"Splendid fare!" he observed. "I can't fault the food on this ship."

"Then you'd better not meet Monsieur Vivet," said Goss. "He believes the only place that produces good chefs is France, and he's the self-appointed master of them."

"Yes," added Rebecca. "He made some very harsh remarks about the food on board. We don't think that's the case at all. What about you, Mr. Dillman?"

"I'm on your side, Mrs. Goss," replied Dillman. "We've had delicious meals."

"Delicious meals and delightful company," said Longton, with a chuckle.

There was a flurry of introductions and Polly was thrilled that she was dining with a member of the British peerage. It was, however, her father whom the old man had come to meet. Morton Goss had an admirer.

"I do believe that I may have read a book of yours, Professor Goss," Longton said.

"Really?" said Goss. "Which one?"

"*Treasures of Ancient Egypt.*"

"Oh, I wrote that years ago, Sir Alistair."

"It was years ago that I read it, old chap, but I do recall how it fired my imagination. Gave me the urge to visit Egypt as well. I couldn't believe my luck when Roland Pountney told me that you were actually on the same ship." He gave another chuckle. "Our paths were destined to cross."

"I'm glad that they have."

"I was determined to sit next to you at the earliest opportunity." He beamed at Rebecca and Polly. "And to meet your charming wife and daughter, of course. I'd better warn you that I've come to pick your brains, Professor Goss."

"I'll talk about ancient Egypt until the cows come home, Sir Alistair."

"Not to mention the camels, eh?"

Sir Alistair Longton chortled happily. He was a lively individual and kept the conversation bubbling throughout the meal. Though he wanted to know about the archaeological sites Goss had visited, he did not ignore the ladies. He was attentive to Rebecca and, by the time dessert was served, Polly had acquired another member of the audience for her flute recital. Dillman liked the buoyant old gentleman. Sir Alistair had none of the airs and graces that the detective had encountered in some members of the minor aristocracy. He was friendly, open, and ready to learn.

"You obviously like Egypt, Sir Alistair," noted Dillman.

"This is my fourth visit, Mr. Dillman," replied the other. "First two were with my late wife—God bless her!—but the last was on my own. I was surprised how much I enjoyed it. Won't be spending

Christmas alone, though. My son's joining me in Cairo."

"Where is he at the moment?"

"Somewhere in India, trying to work out how to get to Egypt."

"Is he in the army?"

"Yes, Mr. Dillman. My old regiment." He turned to Goss. "Do you know India?"

"I'm afraid not," said Goss. "Studying one ancient civilization is enough for me."

"India has its charms as well," said Longton. "When you have another lifetime to spare, I'd urge you to explore the subcontinent. Fascinating country!"

"So I believe, Sir Alistair."

"I miss it. But then, at my age, I've started to miss a lot of things!"

He chortled merrily again. Dillman bided his time until coffee was served. When there was a gap in the conversation, he did some gentle digging on his own account.

"You mentioned Mr. Pountney earlier on," he said.

"That's right," returned Longton. "Do you know the fellow?"

"I introduced him to Mr. Dillman in the smoke room," Goss explained. "He struck me as a thoroughly nice man."

"He is, he is," agreed Longton, "and surprisingly free from prejudice."

"In what way?" asked Dillman.

"Well, you know what we English are. Decent chaps, all of us, but inclined to snobbery. Even now, there's still a residual contempt for money made in trade. I don't share that contempt. Neither does Roland Pountney," he went on. "There aren't many Englishmen who'd give up their Christmas at home so that they could keep an eye on a commercial venture in Egypt. That's what he's doing."

"He told us that you were a prospective investor, Sir Alistair."

"I am, Mr. Dillman. It's something I'm seriously considering."

"What is the project?"

"A new hotel," said Longton, "right in the heart of Cairo. The land has been acquired and the architect commissioned. Pountney showed me an early sketch of the hotel. Took my breath away. It's going to be a veritable palace."

"Isn't the finance being raised from Egyptian sources?" said Dillman.

"Yes, but Pountney has a close link with them because of his other business interests there. He's a man with his finger on the pulse, I can tell you. Joy to meet him. And since I've also met the author of *Treasures of Ancient Egypt*," he added, "this trip is turning out to be the voyage of a lifetime for me."

Goss smiled modestly. "It's good to know that *someone* has read my work."

"Polly and I have read it," Rebecca said loyally.

"I tried to," admitted Polly, "but I couldn't understand most of it."

"All will become clear when you get to Egypt," said Longton. "And that flute of yours will come in useful, young lady. You can make some money as a snake charmer."

Polly shook with mirth and the rest of them joined in the laughter. Sir Alistair had made a favorable impact on the Goss family and they were sorry when he rose from the table and announced that he was meeting a friend over a postprandial cigar in the smoke room. Dillman made sure that he walked to the exit beside Longton.

"How sound an investment is this hotel, Sir Alistair?" he wondered.

"Sound as a bell. Pountney is going out to double-check but he has no doubts about its potential. We could stand to make a mint out of it. Why do you ask?" he said, one eye glinting through the monocle. "Are you the sort of man who's ready to risk a bit of capital?"

"Not really."

"If you were, I'd advise you to keep your money to yourself. Ordinarily, that is."

" 'Ordinarily,' Sir Alistair?"

"Yes, old chap," said the other. "If someone came up to me on a ship and said he had this brilliant scheme in the offing, I'd know, nine times out of ten, that I was talking to a confidence trickster. Not in this case."

"Are you sure?"

"Absolutely certain, Mr. Dillman. Roland Pountney is the exception to the rule. He's not pushing this project at anyone. He's simply doing them a favor by letting them get a slice of the cake. Don't worry," he continued, "I checked him out very carefully before I allowed myself to get interested. Pountney is as genuine as they come. Right school, right university, belongs to all the right clubs."

"I'm pleased to hear that you believe your money will be in safe hands."

"It will be," said Longton. "And the beauty of it is that, when it's built, I'll be able to stay at the hotel at a discount. I'll be popping to and from Cairo all the time. No, Mr. Dillman," he declared, "Roland Pountney is not a crook, I assure you. This is a P and O vessel. There are no criminals aboard the *Marmora*."

Creeping along the passage, the man paused outside a cabin and tapped on the door. When there was no response, he used a master key to open the door and went swiftly inside and crossed to the dresser. Pulling out each drawer in turn, he tipped the contents onto the floor without ceremony then searched quickly through the mound of clothing. The thief soon found what he was looking for. Slipping the jewelry into his pocket, he turned his attention to the rest of the cabin. He sensed that he would have a good haul.

ELEVEN

Vera Braddock was a tall, thin, angular woman in her sixties with a hooked nose and a mole on her right cheek that looked like a beauty spot. She wore a black evening dress with a series of elaborate taffeta flowers sewn around the neckline. In spite of her stately appearance, she was gentle and retiring by nature, with a soft voice that rarely went much above a whisper. She and her sister Elizabeth had returned to their cabin that evening to find that, to their horror, they had been robbed. When they were questioned by Genevieve Masefield, it was Vera who did most of the talking.

"We're traveling to Egypt for health reasons," she explained. "The English winter is far too harsh for Elizabeth. She's very delicate."

"I'm sorry to hear that, Miss Braddock."

"That was what frightened me about this crime. It was such a shock for Elizabeth, she had one of her attacks. We had to send for the doctor. He's given my sister some medicine and promised to call again in the morning."

"How do you feel now?" asked Genevieve, turning to the other woman.

Elizabeth smiled bravely. "Much better, thank you."

"My sister never complains," said Vera. "She's stoical."

Genevieve liked the two maiden ladies at once. She found them sweet, pleasant, and quintessentially English. The facial similarity was striking but they were otherwise very different to look at. Elizabeth Braddock was frail and almost bent double by a dramatic curvature of the spine. As she sat in a chair in their cabin, her breathing was labored. Vera, however, seemed to be in the best of health. The sisters were quite unlike the *Marmora's* other victims of theft. Where Mabel Prendergast had cried and Frau Zumpe had ranted, the Braddock sisters were ready to accept the consequences of their folly.

"We never should have kept the jewelry in here," admitted Vera. "We've been on P and O cruises before and there's never been the slightest problem of this kind. We got into the habit of keeping our valuables around us."

"I'll need a full list of what was taken," said Genevieve.

"Fortunately, our favorite pieces were not in the cabin. We were wearing them."

"Yes, Vera," said her sister, touching her ruby necklace. "They didn't get this—thank God—or my rings, of course."

She held up a skeletal hand that was covered in expensive rings. Vera, too, had an impressive battery of rings and a gold bracelet. By the sight of their jewelry, and from the fact that they could afford to spend so long in Egypt, it would be easy for a thief to deduce that they had wealth. Elizabeth's movement was so impaired, it would take her a long time to get back to her cabin from the first-class dining room. The walking stick that was propped up against the chair was like a fifth limb to her. When the meal was over, a nimble thief would be able to reach and search their cabin then make his escape before the two sisters even got down to the main deck.

"Most of our money was put in the safe," said Vera, "but we did keep rather a lot in reserve. That's all gone and so are some small woodcarvings that we like to take with us on our travels. They are very beautiful and quite expensive."

"Then the thief would hope to get a good price for them," said Genevieve. "He's clearly a professional and will know where he can sell everything that he's taken from the other two cabins."

Elizabeth was disturbed. "Two cabins? There's been another theft?"

"I'm afraid so, Miss Braddock. In fact, this is the third. In one case, only money was taken, but the first crime involved the theft of some jewelry that had great sentimental value to its owner."

"Dear me!" said Vera. "It sounds like an epidemic."

"We'll catch him," promised Genevieve. "Or *her*, of course. It may be a woman."

"A female thief? Surely not, Miss Masefield!"

"We've had to arrest more than one in the past, I fear."

"That's dreadful! What *is* the world coming to?"

"I work on instinct," said Genevieve, "and it tells me that the same person stole from all three victims. In each case, you see, the cabins in question were occupied by female passengers. It may well be that the thief is someone who has deliberately befriended you in order to win your confidence, and a woman might find it easier to do that than a man."

"But we've met so many people since we came aboard."

"I'll need a list of those who were at the same table as you tonight."

Vera was troubled. "You think that one of them is the culprit, Miss Masefield?" she said. "What sort of person would share a meal with you then slip away from the table to steal from your cabin?"

"One who had an idea that he'd find something worth taking."

"But how would he get such an idea?"

"From something you said, perhaps," Genevieve suggested.

"I'm sure you didn't volunteer the information that you kept valuables in your cabin, but you might inadvertently have let something slip."

"In what way?" asked Vera.

"Well, that gold brooch of yours is very eye-catching, Miss Braddock, and your sister's ruby necklace must have sparkled beautifully under the lights in the dining room." Genevieve glanced from one sister to the other. "Did anyone pass remarks about either of them?"

There was a long pause. Vera Braddock exchanged a worried look with her sister.

"Someone did admire Elizabeth's necklace," she recalled. "And he was very complimentary about my brooch as well. It's in the shape of a salamander, as you see. I told him that my sister had something very similar—from the same jeweler, in fact—except that it was in the shape of a dragon."

"Go on," said Genevieve.

"I may well have said that Elizabeth had the brooch back in our cabin," confessed Vera. "How could I be so stupid?"

"There's no guarantee this man *was* the thief."

"I'm certain that he wasn't, Miss Masefield. He was very personable."

"And he couldn't do enough to help me," added Elizabeth. "Passing me things at the table and so on. I'm rather restricted in how far I can reach."

"He helped Elizabeth up from her seat after the meal," said Vera.

"And then what did he do?" asked Genevieve.

"He told us that he had to meet someone in the lounge and he slipped away."

"That proves nothing. He might or might not be involved here. There would have been other people at the table who overheard your remark about the dragon brooch. I'll need to know the names of everyone in the vicinity."

"That's not difficult," said Vera. "I have a good memory for names."

Genevieve took out her notebook and pencil. "Then let's start with this man who expressed an interest in your jewelry," she said. "What was his name?"

"Mr. Pountney. Mr. Roland Pountney."

Polly Goss was more than a gifted amateur musician. She had real flair. Though Dillman would rather have been pursuing his investigation into the murder, he kept his promise to listen to her and, seated beside Rebecca Goss in the music room, he was very impressed by what he heard. As he had predicted, the mellifluous tone of her flute brought a number of curious passengers in to swell her audience and Polly was soon performing to almost twenty people. As far as she was concerned, however, the recital was aimed at only one of them and she looked at Dillman whenever she could. To that end, she began with some tunes she knew by heart, most of them composed by Stephen Foster. When she took up the more testing challenge of Scarlatti, she needed to follow her score but, even then, she kept flicking a glance in his direction to make sure that Dillman was listening.

The recital concluded with Dvořák's "Humoresque," adapted for the flute. It allowed Polly to show the full range of her talent, and her breath control was remarkable throughout. Warm applause followed, and Dillman clapped as loud as anyone, but the most enthusiastic listener was the man who had been standing at the back of the room. Claude Vivet surged forward to take Polly's hand and to kiss it with gratitude.

"Bravo!" he declared. "That was *magnifique!*"

"Thank you, Monsieur Vivet," said Polly, slightly overwhelmed.

"You are, I think, the true musician."

"I couldn't agree more," said Dillman, moving across to her.

"That was excellent, Miss Goss. A lovely program that was beautifully played."

Rebecca added her maternal congratulations and Polly basked in the praise. Dillman was glad of the opportunity to meet Vivet and, when Rebecca introduced them, he exchanged a handshake with the dapper Frenchman.

"You obviously enjoyed the recital," said Dillman.

"Very much," Vivet replied. "I have only one complaint to make."

"Complaint?" echoed Polly, bridling.

"Yes, you played nothing by a French composer. Debussy and Ravel, they both write for the flute, and there are others, too. Forgive me," he went on, "but I am a pianist, you see. When I am not in the kitchen, I am at the piano." His face lit up as an idea came into his head. "We must play together some time, Mademoiselle Goss," he said. "Flute and piano together make very nice sound. It is, for me, an honor to accompany you."

"Thank you," said Polly, flattered by his attention.

He turned to Rebecca. "You have no objection to this?"

"None at all, Monsieur Vivet," she replied. "But it's up to my daughter."

"It would save you practicing on your own," said Dillman, "and you couldn't have a more willing accompanist than Monsieur Vivet."

"Do not take me on the trust," warned Vivet, crossing to the piano. "You want to hear that I am worthy of you. Listen to this."

Lowering himself on to the stool, he lifted the lid and, without needing the music in front of him, played part of a mazurka by Chopin. It was a faultless performance. He broke off and turned to them with a dazzling smile.

"Chopin, he was Polish, maybe," he said, "but he *live* in France."

There was no doubting his skill at the keyboard, and the notion of having an accompanist appealed to Polly. She had disliked the man at their first meeting but his approval of her as a musician made her see him in a new light. After thinking it over, she consented to practice with him. He stood up and gave a little bow of gratitude.

"Today the *Marmora*," he said. "Tomorrow, the concert halls of Europe."

Polly laughed. "Oh, I don't pretend I'm that good, Monsieur Vivet."

"You will be."

Dillman was pleased with the arrangement. It would not only help Polly to improve as a musician, it would keep her preoccupied and less inclined to waylay him when his mind was on other things. While he did not wish to hurt her feelings, he knew that he would have to avoid her more assiduously in the future. Dillman turned to Vivet.

"I hear that you're a famous chef," he said.

"*Mais oui*," returned the other. "Claude Vivet, he is well known in France."

"How far are you going on the ship?"

"Only as far as Egypt. I have the invitation to cook in a restaurant there."

"French cuisine?"

"What other kind is there, *mon ami*?" Vivet asked with a laugh.

"Back home," said Dillman, "we prefer plain cooking."

"Then you miss one of the great pleasures in life. Eat a meal prepared by Claude Vivet and you would know what I mean. Soon," he boasted, thrusting out his chest, "I will cook for the Duke and Duchess."

"Onboard ship?"

"Of course. They accept my offer and I am allowed to use the kitchen."

"Won't that be dangerous?" said Rebecca.

"Why?"

"Well, the other day you had nothing but criticism for the food on board. Some of your comments may have got back to the chefs. You won't find many friends in the kitchen."

Vivet flicked a hand. "Who cares about friends?" he said. "All I want to do is to prepare the good meal. The chefs, they can learn from me."

"And will you really cook for the Princess Royal and her husband?" asked Polly.

He kissed the tips of his fingers. "The best food they ever taste!"

"I wish that I could be there."

"Maybe, we play a duet for them, eh?" he joked.

"A command performance," said Dillman, winking an eye at Polly. "Well, it's good to have met you, Monsieur Vivet," he continued. "I'll be interested to hear what the Duke and Duchess think of your cooking."

"They will beg me to work for them." Vivet became serious. "By the way," he said, turning to Rebecca, "I not see that friend of yours. The one who insulted me."

"That was Mr. Dugdale," said Rebecca, "but I'm sure that he didn't wish to insult you, Monsieur Vivet. He's such a gentleman."

"He not polite to me. He treat me like the dirt."

"You must have been mistaken," said Dillman. "I had the good fortune to meet Mr. Dugdale over breakfast one day. He struck me as a delightful man. I noticed he had not been around for a while. Someone said he'd been taken ill."

"Oh, I'm sorry to hear that," said Rebecca.

"I am not," snapped Vivet. "He deserve to be ill. That man, he deserve to die."

When the ship docked at Marseilles, everything went very smoothly. Tons of coal were taken on board and the body of Walter Dugdale was carried ashore with his luggage. Brian Kilhendry had organized the transfer carefully. The P&O agent came aboard and wheeled away the corpse, which was wrapped in a blanket and covered by a tarpaulin. Kilhendry stood at the top of the gangway to make sure there was no hitch. Dillman was part of the watching crowd at the rail on the main deck and he was certain that nobody would have guessed they had just seen a murder victim being unloaded. It was another example of how efficient and resourceful the purser was. Some passengers joined the vessel but none, apart from Dugdale, left. The killer remained on board.

When the ship set sail again, Roland Pountney was in the lounge with Myra and Lilian Cathcart, sipping a cup of tea. He demonstrated his skill in mental arithmetic.

"I'm told that the *Marmora* uses nine thousand tons of coal on a round trip."

"Goodness!" said Myra. "As much as that, Mr. Pountney?"

"According to the chief engineer," he confirmed. "It's a long voyage and those boilers need plenty of fuel. Now, then, if we say that an average ton of coal costs just under a pound—nineteen shillings and sixpence, to be exact—that will give us a total fuel bill of something of the order of 8,775 British pounds sterling." He grinned amiably. "No wonder they charge us so much."

Lilian was astonished. "How on earth did you work that out so quickly?"

"I have a good head for figures, Miss Cathcart."

"I'd have needed pencil and paper before I could have done it."

"But you don't eat, drink, and sleep in the financial world," said Pountney. "I do. That's why I always cost everything out. P and O is a good company. They know exactly how to set their profit margins. Fuel is only one of the overheads on a voyage like this. Imagine what the wages bill is for a ship's company of this size. There are so many factors to be taken into account. They've done a grand job," he concluded. "I take my hat off to P and O."

"So do I," said Myra. "I don't regret a penny we spent on this voyage."

"Nor do I, Mother," Lilian agreed, showing some real pleasure for the first time. "It's been an education in every way. And," she added, looking at Pountney, "we've met such nice people aboard."

He smiled in acknowledgment. "Thank you, Miss Cathcart. It's good to see that you're starting to enjoy the cruise at last. You've really blossomed today."

"That's what I told her," Myra said fondly. "Lilian has finally realized that we're on holiday. She's actually looking forward to setting her foot on Egyptian soil."

"Egyptian sand," corrected Lilian.

"Wearing a pair of Cathcart shoes, I trust," said Pountney.

"We'd never wear anything else."

They all laughed. Lilian's manner had changed radically. She was alert, happy, and interested. She was also growing steadily fonder of Roland Pountney. After the stern Midland businessmen she had met through her father, he was a refreshing change. What pleased her was that he had actually sought their company. Pountney liked her.

"Do you like living in Leicester, Miss Cathcart?" he asked.

"It gets rather dull sometimes," she confessed.

"You must come down to London and let me show you the sights."

It was a casual remark but it thrilled Lilian. The thought that her friendship with Pountney might develop further, brought a radiant smile to her face. Myra noticed it. Still upset by the disappearance of Walter Dugdale, she was consoled by the way Lilian was making such a conscious effort to support her. Myra no longer felt that she had an overgrown child on her hands.

"Where are you staying in Cairo?" said Pountney.

"At the Hotel Fez," replied Myra.

"Wait until the New Imperial is built. That will bring a touch of real grandeur to the city. It will be the only place to stay," he prophesied, "and I'll have a stake in it. If you'd like me to show you the site, I'd be happy to oblige."

"Oh, yes, please!" said Lilian.

"Who knows? When you see the potential, you'll want to buy shares in the scheme yourself. It's unwise to leave all your capital in Cathcart's Shoes, reliable and hard-wearing as they are."

He was about to discuss his project at greater length when Genevieve Masefield glided into the room. Pountney was on his feet at once to beckon her over. Lilian was a little crestfallen, feeling that she was now overshadowed.

"Have you heard the news about Mr. Dugdale?" said Myra. "Apparently, he was so ill that they took him ashore in Marseilles and transferred him to hospital. I spoke to Dr. Quaid about him. He said it was a distressing case."

"It must have been," said Genevieve. "Let's wish him a speedy recovery."

"Hear, hear!" said Pountney, sitting down again. "Damnable luck!"

Myra pursed her lips. "If only I could get in touch with him somehow." She brightened. "Walter knows our address in Cairo. Perhaps he'll make contact with us."

"It's possible," Genevieve lied, concealing the ugly truth from her. "You were very gallant yesterday evening, Mr. Pountney," she went on, smiling at him. "I saw you help that old lady up from her chair."

"That was Elizabeth Braddock," he explained. "A dear lady. So is her sister, mind you, but she's much steadier on her pins than poor Elizabeth. But she's a game old thing. Crippled with arthritis and heaven knows what else, but she still has the courage to sail all the way to Egypt."

He gave them a brief account of his evening with the Braddock sisters, speaking with affection of both. Watching him carefully, Genevieve could not accept that he was in any way involved in the theft from their cabin, yet he had monopolized them throughout dinner. She was still searching for a way to find out if he had an alibi for the time the crime must have taken place, and, as if reading her mind, he provided one.

"Yes," Pountney said. "Elizabeth Braddock was indomitable. I offered to help her back to her cabin but she wouldn't hear of it so I went off to the lounge instead. Had another long talk with Professor Goss. Anyone here met him?"

They had arranged to meet in his cabin and Dillman did not have to wait long. He was scrutinizing Dugdale's address book again when Genevieve arrived from her chat in the lounge. She told him about the latest theft and how she had just eliminated Pountney from the list of possible suspects.

"What about the other people sitting near the old ladies over dinner?" he said. "They could easily have picked up what was being said."

"Only if they had excellent hearing, George," she said. "Vera Braddock has a very soft voice. Besides, I've already checked on two of the men on the same table. One is even older than they are and the other was the ship's chaplain. I think that I was barking up the wrong tree."

"Somebody knew there was booty in their cabin."

"Clearly. But why pick on two harmless old dears like that? It's sickening."

"I know, Genevieve."

Dillman explained what he had been doing since they'd last met; he was irked by his lack of progress. Kilhendry's attitude was another irritant to him. When he talked about his latest confrontation with the purser, Genevieve was puzzled.

"You'd have thought he'd be grateful to have us on board," she remarked.

"I don't think we should look in his direction for gratitude."

"Why is he so antagonistic?"

"Martin Grandage says that Kilhendry resents the fact that we worked for Cunard. Also, of course, the purser dislikes Americans so he was not going to give me a twenty-one–gun salute. But I'll say this for Kilhendry," he conceded. "He's calm and effective in a crisis."

"Why can't he be pleasant as well? His deputy manages it without difficulty."

Dillman grinned. "More to the point, he likes Americans."

"So do I," said Genevieve, kissing him lightly on the cheek. She remembered something. "You mentioned an address book that you found in Mr. Dugdale's cabin."

"It's right here." He picked it up from the table. "It's a biography of Walter Dugdale. Unfortunately, some of it is in private code so I can't make out what it means." He passed it to her. "See for yourself."

She flicked through the pages, wondering why Dugdale had used so many abbreviations and what the tiny symbols represented. When Dillman drew her attention to a particular name, Genevieve was surprised.

"I didn't know that Myra Cathcart had given him her address," she said. "That's a bold thing to do on such a short acquaintance. And what does this exclamation mark stand for, George?"

"You tell me. You were the one who sat at the same table with them."

"Could it mean that he was smitten with her? And even considered a proposal?"

"I doubt it, Genevieve," he said. "I found six other names in there with an exclamation mark beside them. All were women. Only a Mormon would consider taking on that many wives. In any case," decided Dillman, "I have the feeling that he loved the freedom of the bachelor life too much. He'd survived two marriages. It would have taken a great deal to lure him into a third."

"Myra Cathcart is a very desirable woman."

"Then the exclamation mark might stand for something a little less flattering than a marriage proposal. Is that what he had in mind?"

"There was a definite twinkle in his eye."

"Judging by the contents of that book, his eye never stopped twinkling." He turned to the back page. "What do you make of those initials?"

"Could they stand for organizations of some sort?" she guessed.

"That's what I thought at first, Genevieve, then I noticed the circle around 'W.A.P.' If you look through the book, you'll find that some of the ladies have their names circled as well. Do you see what I'm driving at?"

"I think so. The exclamation mark could indicate a target."

"And the circle is a confirmation of success. 'W.A.P.' is one of his conquests."

"Or victims," she said. "Perhaps Monsieur Vivet was right about him and Walter Dugdale was not the benevolent character he appeared to be. He was a predator." Genevieve was reminded of someone. "I met another member of the breed."

"Who was that?"

"Nigel Wilmshurst."

"I thought he was pretending that you don't exist."

"Only when he's with his wife. He confronted me outside my cabin, so he obviously took the trouble to find out where it was. It was not a happy encounter."

"You called him a predator."

"That's what Nigel always was," she said. "He *used* people. He'd take them up with great enthusiasm then cast them aside when he tired of them. It was callous, George. It always embarrassed me."

"What did you ever see in the man?"

"The obvious things. Nigel is clever, good-looking, and rather dashing in his own way. Then there was the fact that he'll be the next Lord Wilmshurst," she admitted, "and I'm not immune to the glamour of a title. What I didn't know at the time, of course, was

161

how unscrupulous he could be. When he blocked the way to my cabin, I was scared."

"Did he threaten you in any way?" Dillman asked protectively.

"Not exactly, George. I just sensed trouble ahead."

"Of what kind?"

"That's the problem," she said. "I don't know. He's on his honeymoon with a beautiful young wife and he shouldn't even have time to notice me. But he did and it brought out that predatory streak in him. It was the way that he looked at me. I don't think I've seen the last of Nigel Wilmshurst."

The invitation to join the captain's table for dinner had excited Araminta Wilmshurst but her husband was more phlegmatic. It was something he expected as a right. Instead of feeling honored to sit at the captain's elbow, he thought that the man should be grateful to have him and his wife at the same table. When they joined the other privileged guests in the first-class dining room, Wilmshurst was allotted a seat that commanded a view of the whole assembly. He could see Genevieve clearly and he was amused at the way she winced when their gaze first met. Genevieve averted her eyes but he kept watching her, playing with old memories of their time together. Throughout the meal, he kept glancing up to check on her but she never looked in his direction again.

Seated opposite him, Araminta was aware that his attention kept wandering but she could not challenge him in front of their dinner companions. She waited until the meal was over before she stole a glance over her shoulder. When they got up from the table, she fell in beside her husband and gave him a sharp nudge.

"Who on earth were you looking at, Nigel?" she demanded.

"Nobody," he said with a smile. "Nobody at all."

Martin Grandage was gratified by the speed with which Dillman responded. Sitting in his office with a bottle of whisky and two glasses in front of him, the deputy purser looked tired. He gave his visitor a weary smile.

"Sorry to drag you away from your meal, Mr. Dillman," he said.

"Your note arrived as I finished my dessert. Perfect timing." Dillman took the chair opposite the desk. "My dinner companions were intrigued. A mysterious note arrives and I bow out. They must have thought I had an assignation."

"If you'd arrived earlier, that's exactly what you would have had."

"With whom?"

"Frau Zumpe."

He indicated the whisky but Dillman shook his head. Grandage poured himself a generous amount then took a first sip. It revived him at once. Dillman was curious.

"What was the lady doing in here?" he asked.

"Wielding a verbal cat-o'-nine-tails," said Grandage. "I thought at first that she was going to flay me alive. She demanded to know why we hadn't found her money yet."

"We do have a higher priority than that."

"Not in her book, Mr. Dillman. Frau Zumpe feels that we should have called in the gendarmerie and let them scour the ship for her missing cash. She'll ask us to put up WANTED posters next."

"Didn't you explain to her that we can achieve more by discreet inquiries?"

"I tried to—when she finally let me get a word in."

"Genevieve found her a real handful."

"So did I, until we got onto the subject of Walter Dugdale."

"Oh?"

"That was her main reason for coming here," said Grandage. "She'd only just discovered that he went ashore in Marseilles. Frau Zumpe was livid: Why wasn't she told that he was being taken to hospital? Why wasn't she allowed to see him before he left?"

"It's just as well that she doesn't know the truth."

"I think she'd have nailed me to the mast if I'd told her."

"Why was she so upset?" said Dillman. "She wasn't a close friend of his."

"She carried on as if she was. I think that she was using Mr. Dugdale as another stick with which to beat me. I was glad to get rid of her. However," he said, "that's not why I sent for you. There's been another odd coincidence."

"More money deposited in the safe?"

"Yes, Mr. Dillman. You've heard about the latest theft, I take it."

"Two old ladies with a cabin on the main deck. Jewelry was stolen."

"Along with the best part of a hundred pounds," said Grandage. "They're kicking themselves for leaving that amount of cash lying about. Anyway, that was last night. Earlier this evening, I was asked to put a slightly larger sum of money into the safe."

"In the same currency?"

"Oh, yes."

"I assume that the man who gave it to you was Roland Pountney."

"Not this time, Mr. Dillman."

"Then who was it?"

"The German photographer—Herr Lenz."

TWELVE

The Princess Royal and her family had settled into the rhythm of shipboard life but she still guarded her privacy. While she joined her husband and children in their daily walks on deck, she preferred to take most of her meals away from the public gaze. Over a midmorning cup of tea in her cabin, she studied a photograph of Gibraltar. Fife was looking at a second one, taken much closer to the Rock and from a different angle.

"This is even better," he said, passing it to her.

"Yes," she agreed, holding the two photographs side by side. "They're very good. I'm surprised that he got such excellent results in that rain."

"Herr Lenz is a professional, Louise."

"He certainly has the right name for a photographer. I should imagine that Herr Lenz spends most of his time staring through a lens."

"Except that the words are not the same in his language," he pointed out. "In German, it would be *Linse,* not 'lens.' Now, if he'd be called Herr Kamera, it would be very different." He chuckled. "I've just remembered that appalling pun that your father made on *my* name."

"You mean, when he called you Alexander the Great?"

"No, my dear. I got used to that particular gibe at school. It was when he created me Duke of Fife. He told that me that henceforth I'd have my own fifedom. I did my best to force a laugh. Even a king must be humored sometimes." He took the photographs from her. "Well, what do you think?"

"They're remarkable. So are the others," she said, indicating the pile beside her. "Whether he's photographing a person or a landscape, Herr Lenz is clearly an expert."

"You agree to the request, then?"

"I didn't say that, Alex."

"What harm can it do?"

"You know how shy I am of the camera."

"You've no need to be," he said with an affectionate smile. "The camera loves you. And the girls would appreciate a souvenir like that."

"I still feel that it's something of an imposition."

"I thought you liked the Wilmshursts."

"I did," she admitted. "They were a charming couple and so very much in love. That's why I agreed to dine with them, Alex, but I'm not sure that I want a photographer there as well."

"Only for a short time. He'd do his work before the meal, then disappear. It's not much to ask, Louise. After all, the Wilmshursts are on their honeymoon. They want to capture a special memory."

"It still feels a little intrusive. And it sets a precedent."

"Precedent?"

"If we agree to be photographed with two passengers, dozens of others will want to follow suit. We'll be besieged by requests. I couldn't endure that."

"You won't have to," he promised. "There's no reason why anyone else should even know about this arrangement. I'll make that clear to Lenz. This will be his only chance to point a camera at us." He tapped a photograph in front of him. "He's not asking us to stand on the Rock of Gibraltar in the pouring rain. All we have to do is to smile at him for a few seconds in here and that's it."

"Let me think it over, Alex."

"Why the delay?"

"Because I need time to get used to the notion," she said. "Herr Lenz may be a splendid photographer—as these examples of his work prove—but he's also the man who tried to take some pictures of us on deck. Mr. Jellings had to stop him."

"Herr Lenz has apologized for that. He was too impulsive. I don't think he realized that he needed permission. In any case," he said, "he's not the person who's making the request. It's Lord Wilmshurst's son."

"I know."

"You were happy enough to have photographs taken on *our* honeymoon."

"That was different, Alex."

"Not really," he argued. "You wanted to immortalize some precious moments on film. That's all that they want to do, Louise." He nudged her gently. "Have you forgotten what it was like to be a beautiful young bride?" She smiled and shook her head. "Think of Araminta Wilmshurst and put yourself in her shoes," he suggested. "Have you got the heart to disappoint her and her husband?"

His wife pondered, but her resistance to the idea was gradually weakening. She recalled the pleasure she had had looking at the wedding photographs in their album and at those taken on their honeymoon. Wonderful memories came flooding back.

"I promised to give Wilmshurst an answer today," said Fife.

"And all they want is one photograph?"

"Just one, Louise. It will all be over—literally—in a flash."

"Very well," she conceded. "Tell them that I agree."

Myra Cathcart was delighted with the confidence her daughter was now showing. Instead of trailing behind her mother all the time, Lilian felt able to go off on her own and talk to various acquaintances they had made. It enabled Myra to have some freedom of her own at last. The irony was that it had come far too late. It was a fine morning but it was still cold and so she wore her fur-collared coat when she went out on deck. Hands tucked inside a fur muff, she made her way to the stern of the ship and gazed wistfully back in the direction of France. She did not hear the footsteps behind her.

"I thought it was you," Genevieve Masefield said. "I recognized the hat."

Myra was startled. "Oh!" she exclaimed. "You surprised me, Genevieve."

"I didn't mean to creep up on you like that."

"To be honest, I'm glad of the company. It will stop me from brooding."

"Are you still missing Mr. Dugdale?"

"Very much," Myra confessed with a sad smile. "He is such a dear man. So different from my husband. Don't misunderstand me," she said quickly. "Herbert was a considerate man and we were extremely happy together but he was very provincial. Walter, on the other hand, is a man of the world. Talking to him just opened my eyes."

"It's a shame that your daughter didn't take kindly to him."

"I don't blame her for that. Lilian was only trying to protect me. When she heard that he was ill, she felt dreadful at the way she'd behaved toward him."

"Yes, I know," said Genevieve. "She told me."

"Lilian found the whole experience rather sobering."

"What about you, Myra?"

The older woman sighed. "I'm just left feeling terribly empty," she said. "It wouldn't have been so bad if I could have seen him before he went ashore. I wanted to say good-bye to him. Properly."

"That wasn't possible, I'm afraid."

"So the doctor told me. It was such a wrench for me when we left Marseilles. The thought of Walter, lying in hospital in a foreign country, really upset me."

"He'll be taken care of," said Genevieve. "In the circumstances, he could hardly remain on board. I think he's in the best place."

"You're probably right."

Genevieve felt a pang of conscience. She hated having to deceive her friend but she knew how much more distressing the truth would be for her. The fact that Myra had given her home address to a man she had only just met was significant. Dugdale was more than a casual acquaintance to her. Genevieve wondered how close their friendship really had been.

"At least you were able to spend *some* time together," she observed.

"Oh, yes, Genevieve. And I treasure every moment."

"Even though you never really had the chance to be alone with him?"

"But I did," said Myra. "That was the most wonderful thing of all. Lilian had a bath one morning and I sneaked off to see Walter in the lounge. Yes," she added guiltily, I know it's silly for a middle-aged woman to behave like that, and I was wrong to go behind my daughter's back but . . ." She gave a shrug. "Walter had asked me to meet him. It gave me such a thrill. I didn't know I could still have such emotions."

"There's no time limit on feelings like those, Myra."

"So I discovered. But there was a time limit on us. Walter knew that we wouldn't be left alone for long. That's why he apologized for rushing things."

"Rushing things?"

"Yes," said Myra. "He suggested nothing improper, mind you, but he told me how fond he'd become of me and asked a lot of personal questions that—if it had been anyone else but him—I'd have found rather impertinent. To start with, he wanted my address so that he could write to me. I gave it to him without hesitation. Then he said that he'd be returning to England next spring and asked if he could visit me in Leicester."

"What did you tell him?"

"I agreed, naturally."

"Did he suggest that you spend time alone with him again?"

"Yes, Genevieve. But he knew that it would be difficult with Lilian following me around. Walter said that we should wait until she'd started to relax and enjoy the voyage. He didn't want to compete for my attention with Lilian." A warm memory brought a blush to her cheeks. "And he didn't want us to meet in the lounge again."

"Why not?"

"It was far too public. He invited me to his cabin."

Genevieve was surprised. "And you said you'd go?"

"Why not?" asked Myra. "I trusted him implicitly. Oh, I know I was breaking all the social rules and doing something that would have horrified Lilian, but I didn't have the slightest qualm, Genevieve. I knew that it was the right thing to do." Her voice darkened. "Just as I knew that it would be the *wrong* thing to do with Herr Lenz."

"Did he ask you to go to his cabin as well?"

"No, but he tried to inveigle his way into ours. He offered to take photographs of me and I was vain enough to agree at first. I thought the sitting would be in one of the public rooms or even on deck." She rolled her eyes. "Herr Lenz had other ideas."

"What did he say when you refused?"

"He was angry," said Myra. "Herr Lenz is very proud of his work and he felt that he was being snubbed. He blamed Walter. He accused me of letting Walter talk me out of it but that wasn't the case at all. I simply felt uncomfortable about the whole idea."

"So did Lilian. I remember how worried she was."

"She was relieved when I called it off. The problem is," she explained, "that Herr Lenz hasn't given up. He keeps asking me to reconsider. He couldn't badger me so much when Walter was around to look after me, but I don't have his protection now. Herr Lenz is becoming a nuisance, Genevieve."

"I sympathize with you. Unwanted suitors can be very bothersome," she said, ruefully. "Just remember that there's safety in numbers. Make sure that Herr Lenz never catches you alone."

"I will." She removed a hand from her muff to grasp Genevieve. "Thank you!" she said. "Thank you so much."

"For what?"

"Listening to me. I've been able to get things off my chest."

"I'm only too pleased to be of help, Myra."

"Were you shocked by anything I told you? All my friends back in Leicester would be. They'd think I'd taken leave of my senses."

"I don't think that," said Genevieve kindly. "And I wasn't shocked in the least. I'm just glad to hear that you found a little happiness aboard."

"It was more than happiness, Genevieve."

Before she could elaborate, Myra heard her name being called and she turned to see a camera being pointed at her. Karl-Jurgen Lenz had set up his tripod while the two women were talking and he was now ready. Disappearing under a black cloth, he adjusted the focus slightly, then took the photograph. He emerged triumphantly from beneath the cloth and grinned at Myra.

"Thank you, Mrs. Cathcart," he said. "That was a pleasure for me."

Dillman knelt down to study the carpet more closely. He ran his fingertips over it.

"You've done a good job, Mr. Kilhendry," he said. "No sign of blood."

"Martin Grandage actually came in here to clean the place up. I didn't want any of the stewards to see those stains on the carpet. They might have started asking questions."

Dillman stood up. "That was very noble of your deputy."

"We're not afraid of dirty work on this ship, Mr. Dillman."

When Dillman asked for a master key to let himself into the cabin once occupied by Walter Dugdale, the purser decided to accompany him. He wanted to see the detective at work but his curiosity was tempered with disapproval. The detective stared at the floor, trying to remember the exact position in which the victim had been lying. He recalled the sight of the Norfolk jacket, soaked with blood that trickled onto the floor. It was an image he had locked in his mind so that it could be summoned up again.

Brian Kilhendry watched him with growing impatience. "Well?" he said, tapping a foot.

"Would you please stand behind the door?" asked Dillman.

"What?"

"Just for a moment, Mr. Kilhendry. Stand right here."

He eased the purser into the position behind the door then opened it. He shut it again at once and took a couple of steps into the middle of the cabin. Dillman shook his head then faced Kilhendry.

"That's not how it was done," he decided.

"What do you mean?"

"Nobody was hiding behind that door when Mr. Dugdale came in. There isn't really enough room. Besides," he said, pointing to the mirror on the far wall, "anyone entering the cabin could see the reflection of someone behind the door. I saw you clearly, Mr. Kilhendry."

"What if the place had been in darkness?"

"The spill of light from the passageway would still enable me to pick you out."

"So?"

"The killer was not in here when Mr. Dugdale let himself in."

"He could have been hiding in the bathroom," said Kilhendry.

"Hardly. That would have meant the victim was facing him when he came out of the bathroom. Mr. Dugdale was an obliging man but I don't think that even he would close his eyes while someone got into the right position to kill him. And we know that the attack didn't start in the bathroom itself," he said. "No blood, no sign of a struggle." He stood on the spot where the victim had fallen. "He was struck from behind and went down here. That leaves us with only one conclusion."

"And what's that, Mr. Dillman?"

"He let the attacker into his cabin of his own free will."

"Unless the man knocked on the door and forced his way in."

"That's highly unlikely," said Dillman. "Mr. Dugdale would have tried to fight him off. At the very least, he'd have put up his arms to defend himself. But there were no bruises on them. Dr. Quaid let me see the body when he'd cleaned it up. The only wounds were on the back of his skull."

"What does that tell you?"

"The murderer was someone he knew. Otherwise, he wouldn't have let him into the cabin or been ready to turn his back on him. That narrows the field a lot."

"He'd have let his steward in."

"We can forget him, Mr. Kilhendry. You told me how shaken he was when he reported what he found in here. No, it was someone else. Someone whom Mr. Dugdale had befriended on the voyage."

"From what you say, Mr. Dugdale was a very gregarious man."

"That was the impression I got, certainly," said Dillman, stroking his chin, "and Genevieve Masefield had the same opinion. She got to know him quite well."

Kilhendry was cynical. "Does that mean *she's* a suspect? Mr. Dugdale would have let her into his cabin with alacrity. Any red-blooded man would do that."

"It's a good point."

"I was trying to be droll."

"Yes," said Dillman, "but you raise an interesting possibility. One thing I do know about Walter Dugdale is that he'd be very willing to invite a woman in here. The viciousness of the attack suggests a man, but I'd not rule out a strong woman."

"That's good reasoning," admitted Kilhendry. "I'm sorry that I tried to joke about it. But why didn't you work all this out much earlier?"

"I did, for the most part. When I saw the body lying there, the first thing I did was to wonder how the killer had got in and out. I just wanted to double-check and to have a second look at the scene of the crime. Thanks for your help, Mr. Kilhendry."

"It was largely nosiness."

"Nosiness, or suspicion?"

"Well," said the purser, "there's an element of that, it's true."

"How can I dispel it?"

"By catching the murderer. I know that you have to move carefully but you don't seem to have made any advances at all."

"I think we have, Mr. Kilhendry."

"Oh?"

"We know when and how the killer got in," explained Dillman, "and we know that it was someone whom Mr. Dugdale became acquainted with on the ship. That takes us on to motive. What drives a man to commit a murder?"

"Envy? Hatred?"

"That gives us two suspects, immediately."

"Suspects?"

"I'm not saying that they're guilty, mark you," Dillman stressed, "but they were both known to the victim and they both had a score to settle. Even though he didn't like either of them, I fancy that he'd have invited them in if they said that they wanted a chat in private. Either man could fit the bill."

"Who are they, Mr. Dillman?"

"You mentioned envy. There's a German passenger called Herr Lenz who was positively consumed with envy. According to Genevieve, who sat opposite him over dinner, Herr Lenz developed a serious interest in an English lady who clearly favored Walter Dugdale. You know what usually happens in love triangles."

"Somebody ends up getting hurt."

"Then there's hatred," said Dillman. "Mr. Dugdale was a very likable man yet I believe I've met someone on board who hates him enough to want him killed. In fact, he'd glory in his death."

"What's the man's name?"

"Vivet. Claude Vivet."

They got off to a slow start. Polly Goss was nervous. She kept making mistakes and was feeling inadequate. Claude Vivet was surprisingly patient, taking her back over certain passages time and again until they got them right. He had brought a selection of French music with him and, while Polly recognized one or two of the more famous pieces, most of it was quite new and rather daunting. Rebecca Goss was the only member of their audience, hauled along at her daughter's insistence. Like Polly, she felt that she had misjudged the Frenchman earlier on. He was not merely a good musician, he had gifts as a teacher as well. Their instruments began to blend. Polly's confidence grew.

When the practice came to an end, she was full of apologies.

"I'm terribly sorry, Monsieur Vivet," she said. "I was hopeless today."

"No, no. You get better as we go along."

"I've worked so hard on my embouchure but you'd never have guessed it."

"I hear you play yesterday," he reminded her, "and I know what you can do. I think maybe you miss someone from the audience, no? The tall American gentleman. When you play for George Dillman, the flute sound like a bird singing."

"Thank you, Monsieur Vivet," said Rebecca, taking over when she saw her daughter's obvious discomfort at the mention of Dillman. "It's very kind of you to take an interest in her music."

"It's kind of her to put up with me on the piano."

"You helped her through that sticky patch at the start."

He grinned. "Maybe it was Polly who help *me,* eh?"

Polly gave a half-smile but she was still too embarrassed by the fact that the Frenchman had noticed her fondness for George Dillman to say anything. She turned away to put her flute back into its case. Vivet gathered up the sheet music.

"Why is your husband not here?" he said. "He does not like music?"

"He loves it," replied Rebecca.

"Yet he was not here yesterday to watch his daughter."

"Morton was working on his paper. He's giving a lecture in Cairo next week."

"A lecture?"

"Something to do with ancient Egypt," she said. "He's devoted the whole of his life to studying it. He assures me that I'll see why when we actually get to Egypt."

"Is a beautiful country." He kissed Polly's hand. "Thank you very much. I think we work well together. Tomorrow, I hope, I will be a little better."

Polly laughed. "You're very kind, Monsieur Vivet."

"I like to help any young musician, and is nice to practice with someone else. When we meet tomorrow, you try to bring your father. He will be proud of you."

"I asked him to come today," said Polly, "but he was too busy showing off those silly little stones that he's brought with him."

Vivet spread his arms and lifted his shoulders. "Silly little stones?"

"Relics from some Egyptian dynasty," explained Rebecca. "He's returning them to a museum in Cairo. No, I'm afraid that Polly will have to play on without her father. He's a true academic. His work will always come first."

Morton Goss wrapped the last fragment in cotton wool before putting it away in the box. They were in his cabin and he had just finished explaining what the relics were. His visitor was dressed

176

impeccably in a frock coat. Gray spats covered his shoes.

"This has been an absolute treat," said Sir Alistair Longton. "Thank you so much for letting me see them. I feel honored."

"I'm the one who's honored, Sir Alistair. You've read one of my books."

"So have thousands of other people, I daresay, but I was the one lucky enough to bump into you. It's a knack I have, you know. Chance encounters with people I've always wanted to meet."

"Really?"

"Yes," said Sir Alistair. "I once met the King at a regatta. He was Prince of Wales at the time, of course. Knew a lot about sailing, too. Then there was Thomas Hardy, the novelist—met him in London when we tried to get into the same taxi from opposite sides. I even crossed paths with Sir Henry Campbell-Bannerman, our last prime minister," he continued with a chortle, "though I'm not prepared to say in what circumstances."

"It sounds as if I'm in illustrious company," said Goss.

"It's where you belong."

"My wife thinks I belong at home and my daughter believes I ought to spend at least two hours a day listening to her as she practices on the flute."

"Women—God bless them! They never understand, do they?"

"No, Sir Alistair."

"What woman would keep relics of ancient Egypt beside her bed?"

"You won't mention this to anyone, will you?" asked Goss.

"No, old chap! Lips sealed and all that."

"There's only one other person who even knows that they're in here."

"The ghost of Rameses?"

Goss laughed. "Apart from him. No, I showed them to Mr. Dillman as well."

"Ah, that countryman of yours I met at dinner. Capital fellow. Struck me as a man who understood the meaning of discretion.

We invented it, of course," said Sir Alistair. "Discretion is our watchword. Been the basis of British diplomacy for donkey's years."

"Gerorge Dillman would have made a good diplomat. He's very tactful."

"But far too handsome. Can't have that in an embassy. Not a British one, anyway. Too distracting. Well," he said, "you have a perfect illustration of that in your family."

"Do I, Sir Alistair?"

"Don't say you haven't noticed the way that your daughter looks at Mr. Dillman. It's the same way you look at those relics of yours—covetously."

"Polly is still very young."

"Old enough to entertain a passion or two, Mr. Goss."

"Well, yes," the other said thoughtfully. "I suppose that she is."

"How old was your wife when you first met her?"

"Now that you come to mention it, not much above Polly's age."

"There you are, then," said Sir Alistair. "No need to worry about it. Calf-love, that's all. Mr. Dillman is a kind chap. Nothing untoward will happen. When you have features like that, you must be accustomed to that sort of unsolicited admiration. Never happened to me, alas," he went on with a ripe chuckle. "I had to work hard to get women to take notice of me."

"Perhaps I should have a word with my daughter."

"Fatal. Never forgive you, old chap. Least said, soonest mended."

"I knew that Polly had taken a liking to Mr. Dillman but I didn't realize it went deeper than that. The truth is, I don't pay enough attention to her."

"How many times have I heard a woman say that? Their national anthem."

"Yes," sighed Goss. "And my wife has written most of the verses."

"Thank you again, my friend," said Sir Alistair, shaking his hand. "Can't tell you what a thrill it's been, getting a glimpse inside the mind of an expert. Never an expert at anything myself, except looking smart in a military uniform. Time for a smoke?"

"I think that I do have. I like a pipe of tobacco at this hour."

"Then let's go and join the others, shall we? Promised to meet Roland Pountney there. Cigarette man, but I'm trying to convert him to cigars. By the way," he said, opening the door to lead the way out, "you really ought to think again about what Pountney told you. Even a small investment could bring you rich dividends."

"I won't say that I'm not tempted."

"Word to the wise: Think about it, Mr. Goss. Get a stake in this hotel while you can and you may end up being able to afford your own pyramid. Like that, eh?" he asked with a laugh. "I know that I would."

Dillman had to wait until late afternoon before he found the man on his own. Karl-Jurgen Lenz was standing at the rail on the promenade deck, gazing out to sea. A stiff breeze was plucking at the German's hat and coat. Dillman strolled across to him.

"I did warn you, my friend," he said pleasantly.

"*Warn* me?" asked Lenz, turning a hostile glare on him. "Who are you?"

"My name is George Dillman and I tried to tell you that taking photographs of the Duke and Duchess of Fife was not allowed. Someone came and stopped you."

"Ah, yes. I remember you now." He stood bolt upright to introduce himself. "Karl-Jurgen Lenz." There was no handshake. "I am a photographer. And you?"

"I'm just a passenger who's enjoying a round-trip to Australia."

"Oh, I see. Another rich American?"

"Far from it, Herr Lenz. We're not all millionaires, believe me."

"I speak to other Americans on the ship. They all have money, they all have time to go round the world. Me, I have to work for a living. It's a matter of honor."

"It's a matter of necessity with me," said Dillman, seeing an opportunity to introduce Dugdale's name. "I had to slave away for a long time to pay for this trip, so I'm determined to get my money's worth. But if you've met plenty of Americans, you may have come across a man called Walter Dugdale."

Lenz scowled. "Yes, I meet him."

"You don't sound as if you liked him very much."

"I didn't."

"Any particular reason?"

"No, Mr. Dillman. I just could not give him respect."

"I found him a delightful fellow," said Dillman. "Hoped I'd get to know him a little better but he seems to have disappeared. Haven't seen him for days."

"He left the ship at Marseilles."

"Oh? I thought he was going all the way to Perth."

"Someone say he was taken ill," explained Lenz. "The details I do not know, but he is no longer on the *Marmora*. That is good. I do not miss him."

"Well, I do. And I'm sorry to hear that he was too ill to stay with us. Mr. Dugdale was such a friendly character."

"He was not friendly to me. Let us forget him. He has gone for good."

There was a deep satisfaction in his voice. Dillman could see how much the German disliked Dugdale, but he did not press him on the subject. He remembered the money that Lenz had deposited with the deputy purser.

"That camera of yours looks like a very expensive one, Herr Lenz," he said.

"I only work with the best equipment."

"Does that include all the stuff you need to develop photographs?"

"Of course. When I travel, I take everything. Is in my cabin now."

"Isn't that rather dangerous?" suggested Dillman. "That equipment must have cost you a lot. Wouldn't it be safer to let the purser keep it locked up for you?"

"I need to use it every day."

"But there's always the risk that it could be stolen. I know it's unlikely but it's not a chance I'd like to take. What would happen if your camera disappeared?"

"It will not, Mr. Dillman. I have been on cruises before."

"Nevertheless, that equipment of yours is still a temptation."

"Only another photographer would want to steal it."

"Or destroy it," said Dillman. "Have you thought of that? If you had a rival on board—or someone you fell out with—he might take the camera out of spite so that he could toss it over the side of the ship. I think you should be more careful."

Lenz was angry. "Why you tell me this?" he demanded.

"I'm only offering you friendly advice."

"No, you have a reason. You wish to annoy me."

"Not at all," said Dillman, raising both hands in a conciliatory gesture. "Forgive me, Herr Lenz. I spoke out of turn. It's none of my business."

"I think you talk to Walter Dugdale about me. Is that it?"

"No, I assure you. Your name never even came into the conversation."

"Then why you say what he say?" pressed Lenz, jabbing him with a finger. "Why you talk about my equipment? Mr. Dugdale, he have an argument with me one day. He try to threaten me. He say what a shame it would be if my camera was dropped in the sea one day. I tell you what I tell him."

"And what was that, Herr Lenz."

"My camera is my livelihood," he declared, jabbing Dillman in the chest again. "It mean everything to me. I warn Mr. Dugdale that, if I catch anyone trying to steal it, I would kill him. You remember that."

THIRTEEN

Genevieve Masefield had an uncomfortable morning. It began, shortly after breakfast, with a bruising confrontation with Frau Zumpe, who was furious that her stolen money had not yet been recovered. When she heard there had been a third theft aboard, she was even more enraged, and accused Genevieve of being incompetent. It took almost half an hour to calm her down and persuade her to tell nobody else about the crimes that had been committed so that alarm would not spread. The woman was so tense and irascible, Genevieve had the feeling that something apart from the loss of her money was upsetting her, but she had no idea what it was.

After leaving her, Genevieve paid courtesy visits to Mabel Prendergast and to Vera and Elizabeth Braddock, assuring them she was still investigating their cases but unable to give them any hope of an early resolution. In its own way, the quiet despair of Mrs. Prendergast was as painful to Genevieve as the verbal assault by Frau Zumpe. The Englishwoman had less money and far less resilience than her German counterpart. She was suffering badly.

The extraordinary patience of the Braddock sisters came as a relief but Genevieve wished she could have brought more cheering news.

Late morning found her in the first-class lounge with a restorative cup of coffee. Though she had chosen a quiet corner where she could review the evidence she had gathered, she was soon spotted. Nigel Wilmshurst sauntered over to her with a grin.

"All alone and nowhere to go, Jenny?" he taunted.

She looked up with dismay. "What do you want?"

"The pleasure of seeing you again, of course. I told you I'd be back."

"Well, I don't have time to chat just now," she said briskly, about to rise from her chair. "You'll have to excuse me, Nigel."

"But you haven't even touched your coffee yet," he argued, pointing to her full cup. "Don't let me frighten you away. I won't stop." She settled slowly back in her chair. "How are you, anyway?"

"I'm fine, thank you. At least, I was until you arrived."

He smirked. "Am I such a bogeyman?"

"Of course not. I just feel that we don't need to pretend we're friends. It will be much easier for both of us if we simply keep out of each other's way."

"But I don't want to keep out of your way. I'm curious."

"Nigel—"

"Yes," he said, "I know that we parted on fairly hostile terms and I'll admit that I was hurt at the time, but that pain has faded away now. I found someone else and I couldn't be happier. I'm just rather sad that you haven't met someone who's willing to take you on."

Genevieve bristled. "I don't want to be 'taken on,'" she told him.

"Does that mean you're thinking of entering a convent?" he teased. "I wouldn't have thought you'd feel at home in that kind of environment, Jenny. Or are you simply trying to assert your independence? Good Lord!" he exclaimed with mock horror. "Don't tell me you've become a suffragette?"

"No," she replied, "though I sympathize with their aims."

"So what's been happening to you since we last met?"

"I've tried to choose my friends with far more care."

"Where have you been? What have you done?"

"That's my affair, Nigel."

"I'm genuinely interested," he claimed. "We were so close at one time, then you vanished into thin air. Did you go abroad or something?" He sat down opposite her and lowered his voice. "I was sorry to lose you, Jenny. You must know that. In your heart, I'm sure that you must have a few regrets."

"Yes, I do. I regret that I didn't find you out earlier."

"Now, that's a cruel thing to say."

"I'm only being honest."

"Don't you regret all those things that you lost?" he said. "An introduction to a world of glamour and privilege. Dinners at the Ritz. Parties, balls, opera, theater. Playing tennis on our private court. Swimming in our pool. I bet you do miss some of that, Jenny," he added, leaning toward her. "You turned your back on the chance to be the future Lady Wilmshurst. You must be green with envy at Araminta."

"No," said Genevieve, biting back a tart rejoinder. "I don't envy your wife in the least. I've told you, Nigel: I wish you both well. But I'd prefer to stay out of your life."

"Once we get to Egypt, you will be. We'll go off for a magical holiday in the sun while you sail on to that penal colony known as Australia. We'll probably never meet again," he said. "But since we *have* bumped into each other, can't we at least be civil toward one another?"

"I don't recall civility as being one of your major attributes."

He laughed. "You see. You haven't forgotten me at all!"

"Good-bye, Nigel."

"All right, all right," he said, getting up and raising both palms. "I'm going. But I daresay we'll meet up again before too long. You can't get off the ship, Jenny. There's no way to escape me."

"There's a very simple way."

"Is there?"

"Yes," replied Genevieve. "I introduce myself to your wife and ask her to keep a closer eye on you. I'm certain she'd oblige me."

"But you wouldn't do that. Your sense of decency would hold you back. You'd never try to inflict pain on another woman through me." He smiled confidently. "I know you better than you know yourself, Jenny. You have scruples. That's your weakness. I have very few. That's my strength."

Genevieve remained silent. There was an element of truth in what he said. She could never bring herself to use his wife as a means of getting rid of him. Araminta Wilmshurst was on her honeymoon with a man she adored. It would be vindictive to take away her happiness at such a moment. Genevieve had no defense. He was about to leave when a young man came into the lounge and waved cheerfully in their direction. Wilmshurst replied with a curt nod.

"Do you know Roland Pountney?" she asked.

"We were at Harrow together."

"Were you friends at school?"

"Certainly not!" Wilmshurst said with disdain. "Pountney was not in my year."

"You must have seen something of him."

"Only for the short time the little blighter was there."

"What do you mean?"

"Roland Pountney brought disgrace on himself. He was expelled."

Dillman was on his way to see the deputy purser when they came out of the music room together. Polly Goss had had a much more successful practice with Claude Vivet and she was in good spirits. When she spotted Dillman, her face glowed.

"You're too late," she said. "We've just finished."

"How did it go?" asked Dillman.

"Very well," replied Vivet. "Polly is a good musician. She learn very fast."

"Monsieur Vivet is teaching me how to play Debussy," she said excitedly. "We've been here for hours. You must come and listen to us sometime, Mr. Dillman."

"I will," said Dillman. "When you give another public performance."

He was pleased to see her looking so happy. The absence of her mother suggested that she had no qualms about being left alone with her accompanist, and she clearly liked the Frenchman now. Vivet had managed to win her over completely.

"The piano, I play only for pleasure," said Vivet. "It is in the kitchen that I perform best. The piano is only—how do you say it?—a second string to my bow."

"It's a pity you don't play the violin," remarked Dillman, "then you'd have even more strings to your bow."

Polly giggled but Vivet looked mystified.

"I'm sorry," Dillman said. "That was a rather silly joke. Tell me, Monsieur Vivet," he added, "why are all the best chefs male?"

"That is the wrong question, *mon ami*," said Vivet. "You should ask why the best chefs in the world are all Frenchmen. The answer, it is that we have a great tradition. We *care* about our food in France. In other countries, they simply eat it."

"Monsieur Vivet is going to cook for the Duke and Duchess of Fife," said Polly.

Vivet gave a little bow. "Is a real honor for me."

"I'm surprised to hear you say that," Dillman observed humorously. "France is a republican country, like ours. You don't believe in royal families anymore."

"Even a Duke and Duchess have to eat."

"I think it's very noble of Monsieur Vivet," said Polly. "He's supposed to be on vacation like the rest of us yet he's giving up his free time to work in a kitchen. That's so kind of him. Don't you think so, Mr. Dillman?"

"I do," he said. "And I'm sure that the Duke and Duchess are in for a banquet. But you must excuse me," he went on, moving away. "I have an appointment to keep."

Vivet gave another bow and Polly raised a hand in farewell. Dillman strode off and went down the steps to the next deck. When he reached the office, he was glad to find Martin Grandage on his own. The deputy purser was going through some papers. He glanced up with a bright smile.

"Come on in, Mr. Dillman," he said. "Take a pew."

Dillman lowered himself onto the chair. "You look less harassed this morning."

"That's an optical illusion. I feel as if I'm beleaguered."

"What's the problem?"

"A passenger named Claude Vivet."

"I've just been speaking to him," said Dillman. "He's a master chef."

"He's a master pain in the neck as well," said Grandage. "Because he has such a reputation, the royal party agreed to let him cook dinner one evening. That means he has to use our kitchen. It's caused an international incident, Mr. Dillman. Our chefs are Italian and they don't like the idea of someone trespassing on their territory."

"A case of too many cooks, eh?"

"It's more a case of France versus Italy, and it's all Monsieur Vivet's fault. Apparently, he's been pouring scorn on the quality of the food served on board. That really offended our chefs. They don't want him near them."

"Monsieur Vivet is not a man to hide his light under a bushel."

"I know; I've met him. He lets it blaze forth like the beam of a lighthouse." Grandage sat back with a grin. "This job will be the death of me. Thank goodness we're getting rid of that little Frenchman in Port Said!"

"Well," said Dillman, "at least you've had a little action. That's more than I can say. My work largely involves stealth. I stay in the shadows."

"Yet you managed to impress Brian Kilhendry."

"Did I?"

"Yes," said Grandage. "He told me about the visit you made to Mr. Dugdale's cabin. Brian went there to sneer and came away thinking he'd underestimated you."

"That's good to hear."

"It was only qualified approval, however. He still has reservations about you. But he liked your suggestion about instituting patrols."

"Obvious thing to do," said Dillman. "The thief strikes when he knows that his victims are distracted. Meals are the ideal time for him. When we have so many stewards on board, the sensible thing is to use them as auxiliary guards. Let them keep their eyes peeled during breakfast, luncheon, and dinner."

"The order went out to the chief steward," said Grandage. "He can't put his staff on sentry duty but he's promised to make sure that they're out and about during those critical times. Did you manage to speak to our photographer?"

"Yes, we had a chat on deck yesterday afternoon."

"Surly-looking individual."

"Herr Lenz is not a man who seeks popularity," said Dillman. "Except in one quarter, that is. He and Walter Dugdale vied for the affections of the same lady. Having met Lenz, I can see why Mrs. Cathcart preferred Mr. Dugdale, and it's reassuring to know that someone on this ship likes Americans."

Grandage laughed. "You'll win the heart of the purser yet," he said. "Brian is not as inflexible as he might look. But coming back to our jolly German, would you say that he's a man who's capable of murder?"

"More than capable. He had motive and means."

"It might take more than jealousy toward Mr. Dugdale over this lady."

"I think that Mr. Dugdale may have supplied it. He taunted Herr Lenz with the threat that he'd hurl his camera into the sea. Can you imagine how that must have rankled?" asked Dillman. "That camera is the most precious thing in the world to Lenz."

"What about that money he deposited with us?"

"I still haven't established where that came from, Mr. Grandage. I don't suppose you sniffed it before you put it away in the safe did you?"

"Sniffed it?"

"Yes," said Dillman. "If it came from the cabin belonging to the Misses Braddock, it might have smelled of lavender. According to Genevieve Masefield, the two old ladies use it by the bucketful. I doubt if the money would bear the scent, though. That's a pity," he decided. "If we could prove that Herr Lenz stole that cash— and that he battered Walter Dugdale to death—then my guess may be right."

" 'Guess?' "

"That the thief and the killer are one and the same person."

"How could that be?" asked Grandage with a look of disbelief. "Nothing was taken from Mr. Dugdale's cabin. You found his bill-fold still in his pocket."

"True," said Dillman, "and there was no visible sign that any-thing was missing. But, then, we don't know what he might have had that was worth stealing—and worth killing for in order to steal. Do you see what I'm driving at, Mr. Grandage? If we can link the murder with the thefts, then we'll have taken a big step forward."

"You said it was only a guess."

"It is at this stage. I may be wrong, of course, but it's a theory I'd like to pursue."

"You're the detective, Mr. Dillman. What does your partner say?"

"I haven't really had the chance to discuss it with her yet. We've been too busy gathering intelligence from various sources. But I've a feeling that she might agree."

Grandage scratched his head. "I'm not sure that I do," he said. "There's a big difference between robbing female passengers and committing a murder. What could Mr. Dugdale possibly have that would attract a thief who was prepared to stop at nothing? And how would the thief know it was there in the first place?"

"Good questions. I'll try to find the answers."

"I'll be interested to hear them, Mr. Dillman."

"Meanwhile, I'll attempt to impress the purser again."

"There's only one way to do that, I fear," said Grandage, with a chuckle. "You'll have to become a British citizen."

Brian Kilhendry understood the importance of visibility. He knew the sight of his uniform reassured passengers that everything was under control and his confident smile reinforced that message. Accordingly, he liked to stand outside the first-class dining room as the passengers filed in for their evening meal to exchange a few friendly words with them. He had mastered even more of their names by now and that always pleased the diners. It made them feel part of one large and privileged family. The purser waited until everyone was seated at the appropriate table then, when nobody was looking, he slipped quietly away.

He was doing it again. Nigel Wilmshurst was more careful this time but his wife still noticed. Every so often, he would toss a glance in the direction of a table on the other side of the room. Araminta pretended she had seen nothing. She was among friends and the conversation was lively. Like her husband, she tried to play a full part in it. When she had the opportunity between courses, however, she took a vanity mirror from her purse and held it up so that she could rearrange her hair in the reflection. By angling the mirror in the right direction, she at last discovered who had been causing the distraction.

Araminta delayed the interrogation until they returned to their cabin. After an excess of champagne, Wilmshurst was in an amorous mood. When he tried to slip his arm around his wife, however, she pushed him away.

"Who *is* she, Nigel?" she demanded.

"I don't know what you're talking about, darling."

"You were staring at her the other night and you did the same again tonight. Now don't lie to me. I saw you do it time and again."

"I was just looking around the room, that's all," said Wilmshurst.

"But your eyes always strayed to the same table—and I know why."

He lunged forward. "Araminta—"

"Don't touch me," she said, fending him off. "I mean to have this out with you. I saw her in my mirror, Nigel. I know how beautiful she was. Now, tell me her name."

"I don't know her name."

"But you intend to find out. Is that it?"

"No," he said vehemently. "You're my wife, Araminta. We're on honeymoon. You're the only woman in the world that I have eyes for at the moment."

"Apart from the lady in the blue silk dress. Who was she, Nigel?"

"Somebody who looked vaguely familiar. Somebody I thought I knew. But I was mistaken," he lied. "When we walked past her table on the way out, and I got a proper look, I realized that I'd never seen her before."

"Tell the truth," she insisted.

"That is the truth. I swear it."

"When we sat at the captain's table the other night, you couldn't stop looking at her. Why didn't you decide *then* whether you knew her or not?" She stared into his eyes. "So what is she, Nigel? Someone from your past or someone you'd like to get to know?"

"Neither, Araminta. This is ridiculous."

"I know what I saw in that dining room."

"And I know what I drank," he said, trying to end the marital inquisition. "Far too much. I can hardly stay on my feet. Look, why don't we talk about this in the morning when I can concentrate?"

She shook him with both hands. "Because I want to talk about it *now*."

"There's nothing to say."

"Oh, yes there is," she said. "We've still got a lot of time on this ship before we reach Port Said. How can I enjoy any of it when I know that my husband's mind is on someone else?"

"But it's not, darling. I've devoted every waking hour to you."

"Until we had that meal at the captain's table."

"Oh, for heaven's sake!" he exclaimed. "Don't keep on about it. Are you going to jump down my throat every time I so much as glance at another woman? I can't walk around wearing a pair of blinkers."

"A minute ago, you said that you only had eyes for me."

"You're starting to make me angry," he warned.

"We're married, Nigel. That gives me certain rights."

"It doesn't give you the right to cross-examine me like this, especially when I've done nothing wrong. Now, let's go to bed and try to forget the whole thing."

"That would suit you, wouldn't it?"

"Araminta—"

"I want to get to the bottom of this, Nigel."

"Then you can do it on your own," he barked at her, turning his back and starting to take off his things. "The matter's closed. Do you understand? It's closed."

Araminta Wilmshurst watched him with growing alarm. The

days they had spent on the *Marmora* had been the happiest days of her life but that happiness was suddenly threatened. She was torn between love and suspicion, wanting desperately to be reconciled with him yet fearing she was being cruelly deceived. As he continued to keep his back to her, a dreadful thought took root in her mind. She put a hand on his shoulder to spin him round.

"It's her, isn't it?" she said, voice icily calm. "It's that other woman."

Wilmshurst shook his head in denial but his eyes betrayed him yet again.

She was bitter. "And you told me that you'd run a mile if you saw her!"

There was a vulnerable side to Frau Zumpe. As she watched the woman in the lounge, Genevieve Masefield was astonished. The termagant who had chastised her that morning was now in a maudlin state, sitting alone in a corner with a glass in her hand, staring unseeing in front of her. Frau Zumpe looked lonely and morose. Genevieve felt sorry for her. Seated with Myra and Lilian Cathcart, she chatted inconsequentially until they decided it was time for bed. Myra was recovering slowly from the loss of Walter Dugdale, and it was largely because of the support and understanding that Lilian was offering. It was almost as if mother and daughter had exchanged their roles.

As soon as they had gone, Genevieve noticed that Frau Zumpe was trying to get to her feet. She obviously had been drinking heavily, and was unsteady. Genevieve went to her assistance at once.

"Let me help you," she said, taking her by the arm.

"I can manage." Frau Zumpe almost lost her footing. *"Mein Gott!"*

Genevieve held her tight and, in spite of the woman's protestations, insisted on helping her back to her cabin. Frau Zumpe soon had to admit that she might never have got there alone. She was

very grateful. When they reached her cabin, she asked Genevieve
to go in with her.

"I think that you're too tired for visitors," said Genevieve.

"Please come in. I want to say sorry to you."

"For what?"

"I tell you inside."

Genevieve helped her to a chair then shut the door behind
them. She glanced around the cabin. On the table was a small bottle of gin and an empty glass. Frau Zumpe had been drinking
before she even got to the dining room.

"Is there anything I can get you?" asked Genevieve.

"Sit down, please. I want to speak."

Genevieve took the other chair.

"I am sorry," said Frau Zumpe. "This morning, I was too
harsh."

"It's understandable. You were upset about the theft."

"That was not the only reason, Miss Masefield. I have other
worries."

"What sort of worries?"

"Nothing that you could help me with. It's too late now."

Frau Zumpe went off into a reverie that lasted minutes.
Genevieve sat there patiently and waited. The other woman suddenly blinked, as if waking up. She subjected Genevieve to a long
and searching stare. Genevieve thought that she might have to
suffer another bout of vituperation but Frau Zumpe was only trying to decide if she could confide in her.

"I did not tell you everything," she said at length.

"About that night when you talked to Mr. Dugdale?"

"Yes, Miss Masefield. We keep talking as the others leave us.
For a long time, we talk. The lounge was almost empty. We like
each other."

"There's no law against that."

"Walter—Mr. Dugdale—think that I am friends with Karl-Jurgen

Lenz because we are both German. But it is not so. Herr Lenz is not a nice man. We do not live in the same part of our country. He is from Bavaria and I am from Schleswig-Holstein. They are a long way apart. Herr Lenz has no interest in me. He like the English lady."

"Myra Cathcart. Yes, I know."

"We talk about our lives," said Frau Zumpe, a wistful expression upon her face. "Mr. Dugdale wonder what happen to my husband. I tell him. It is painful for me but I was able to tell him because he is a kind man." She swallowed hard. "I marry young, Miss Masefield," she explained. "We were happy together for six years, then Max, my husband, was killed at sea. He was sailing with a friend when they are caught in bad weather. The boat collapse and they are both drowned. The bodies, they did not find them for days."

"How dreadful for you!" said Genevieve.

"Max was a good sailor. He loved his boat."

"It must have been awful when you found out what happened, Frau Zumpe."

"It was," said the other. "For a year, I do nothing but cry. Then I see that my life, it must go on. So I force myself to get out, meet friends. What help me most is to travel. It take my mind off it." She gave a mirthless laugh. "It is strange. Max was killed at sea yet the place I like best is being on a ship. So I come on this voyage."

"I'm glad to know that it helped you in some way," said Genevieve. "Until your cabin was robbed, that is. That was another blow for you." Frau Zumpe nodded soulfully. "Go on telling me about Mr. Dugdale."

"He listened, he understood. He said I was very brave."

"I think that you are, Frau Zumpe."

"Not really. On the inside I am not brave at all."

"You told me that you talked with him until midnight."

"That was a lie," admitted the other. "We talked for much

longer. But we were not in the lounge, Miss Masefield."

Genevieve was amazed. "You invited Mr. Dugdale *here*?"

"No, we go to his cabin."

A faraway look came into her eye. Whatever had happened between her and Walter Dugdale was a cherished memory. Genevieve waited until she was ready to go on.

"They would not let me see him," Frau Zumpe complained. "When he was taken ill, they would not let me visit him. That was cruel. The doctor, he say that he is in no condition to receive visitors, but I am no visitor. I am his *friend*."

"I can understand why you were so upset."

"They did not even warn me that he was being moved to hospital in Marseilles. *Why?*" she asked. "Walter would have made them tell me. He would have asked for me."

"He was obviously too poorly to do that, Frau Zumpe."

"One minute, we are close, and then—he is gone."

"I was shocked by that myself," said Genevieve. "I had the pleasure of sitting at the same table with Mr. Dugdale. He was a man who enjoyed life so much."

"There had been tragedies for him as well. He tell me about them. But they do not make him bitter. He carry on with a smile." Frau Zumpe shook her head. "It make me feel ashamed."

"Of what?"

"Being so weak. Giving up when my husband died."

"But you didn't give up. You went through a period of mourning. That's only right and proper. It's only natural."

"That's what Walter told me. He help me so much, Miss Masefield."

"So it seems."

"Yet now he is gone out of my life."

Genevieve said nothing. When speaking about Walter Dugdale, she had found it very uncomfortable to lie to Myra Cathcart, but she suffered even more qualms with Frau Zumpe. The German woman had been drawn to Dugdale in a way that made light of the difference in their ages. Though she was appalled at his violent death, Genevieve saw there was a consolation in his disappearance from the ship. It would save Myra Cathcart from being badly hurt. If she discovered that Dugdale's friendship with Frau Zumpe had become close, she would be mortified. Genevieve wondered what further revelations there would be from her companion, but Frau Zumpe had said all that she could. Wearied by fatigue, befuddled by drink, and weighed down by unhappy memories, she closed her eyes and drifted off to sleep in the chair. The conversation was over.

As the *Marmora* sailed across the Mediterranean, the weather improved and the amount of daylight slowly lengthened. There was always something new to see. Corsica and Sardinia had been left behind and it was the island of Sicily that brought passengers on board now. Two of them were chatting at the rail on the main deck when Dillman came upon them. Morton Goss was smoking his pipe while Roland Pountney was holding forth about the advantages of seeking investments abroad. They both gave Dillman a cordial welcome.

"This is far more agreeable than sailing through the Bay of Biscay," said Pountney. "Have you been to the Mediterranean before, Mr. Dillman?'"

"No," replied Dillman. "It's a very pleasant experience."

"Mind you, they have their squalls and their gale-force winds here."

"I can vouch for that," said Goss. "There are endless accounts of Egyptian sailors being blown off course or destroyed at sea. Even the Phoenicians, who were master mariners, had problems in the Mediterranean."

"Yes," said Dillman, "but they weren't in a ship as large as the *Marmora.*"

"Or under the aegis of a company like P and O," added Pountney. "We've got a ship's company of over three hundred and fifty to look after our needs. In olden days, they didn't have such luxuries."

"They did have slaves to pull on the oars," Goss pointed out.

"They shovel coal into the boilers now. A vast amount of it, as well."

"Yes," said Dillman, "you have to be strong to be a stoker. They work shifts around the clock to keep the ship moving at this speed. That's the beauty of sail. If the winds are favorable, you can glide over the waves without anyone having to beaver away down in the engine room." He turned to Goss. "What would you have been in ancient Egypt? Master or slave?"

"I know what I'd *like* to have been," said Goss, exhaling a cloud of pipe smoke, "and that's the architect who designed some of their magnificent palaces."

"But you have a chance to fulfil that ambition right now," Pountney argued with a grin. "Invest in the project I've been describing and you can help to bring a wondrous new palace into being. That would make you an architect, of sorts."

"Let me think it over, Mr. Pountney."

"Of course, old chap. There's no hurry. Take all the time you want."

"I'd need to discuss it with my wife."

"You're under no pressure at all," said Pountney, touching him on the arm. "Take it or leave it, Mr. Goss. I only approached you because of your great interest in Egypt. Anyway," he continued, "I'll have to leave you in the capable hands of Mr. Dillman. I need to drop in on the purser."

There was an exchange of farewells before Pountney went marching jauntily off.

"Investing money is not really my field," confessed Goss. "It frightens me."

"You've done pretty well so far," said Dillman. "The biggest investment you've made is in your wife and family and it's obviously paid handsome dividends."

Goss needed a moment to agree. "Yes, yes. I never thought of it that way."

"I gather that your daughter has acquired an accompanist, Mr. Goss."

"That's right. Who'd have believed a French chef could play the piano so well?"

"Oh, I'd believe anything of Monsieur Vivet. He's very talented. The trouble is that he likes everyone to know it."

"Polly says that he's helped her a lot already," said Goss. "She didn't even like the man at first but now she can't wait to get to that music room with him." He opened his pipe and tapped it on the rail so that the tobacco fell out and blew away. "While we're on the subject of my daughter, I wanted to say something."

"Yes?"

"Well, I did tell you that she'd taken a liking to you."

"I'm fond of her as well, Mr. Goss."

"Look," said the other, licking his lips nervously, "I'm not good at talking about this kind of thing. My wife is always saying that I don't pay enough attention to Polly, and she's probably right. The thing is, Mr. Dillman, I hadn't really noticed how quickly she'd grown up."

"It's a habit young ladies seem to have."

"There's another habit as well," said Goss. "It was Sir Alistair Longton who pointed it out to me. I felt so stupid. I mean, I had seen it, of course, but I didn't recognize it for what it was."

"You don't need to tell me anything more," said Dillman, wanting to spare the man further embarrassment. "I understand the situation."

"Polly is infatuated with you."

"I certainly haven't given her any encouragement, Mr. Goss. Nor would I."

"She doesn't need any encouragement."

"I know. To be honest, I've tried to keep out of her way."

"That's very considerate of you."

"I don't want her to get hurt," said Dillman, "and I certainly don't want to cause any problems for you and your wife. It's been a delight to meet all three of you."

"And we've enjoyed meeting you, Mr. Dillman. Unfortunately, it looks as if my daughter has done rather more than that." He gave a pained smile. "I hope that you don't mind my mentioning it."

"On the contrary. I'm glad that you brought it up. Perhaps I should dine at another table this evening. It might ease the situation slightly."

"In one way," said Goss. "In another, it might make it worse."

"Worse?"

"Polly would feel that you were rejecting her."

"It's bound to come to that at some stage, Mr. Goss," Dillman reasoned. "Maybe I should tell you there's someone else in my life. If you could find a way to mention that to your daughter, I'd be grateful. I want to let her down lightly."

"I knew you'd understand."

"I'm sorry that you had to raise the topic."

"Well, I did," said Goss, "and I'm glad that it's over. I'm rather hoping that Monsieur Vivet has come to our rescue. He'll take Polly's eye off you and spare me from having to have this kind of awkward conversation."

"There's no need to feel awkward. It's one of the perils of fatherhood."

"There are ample rewards, as well. Polly has been a wonderful child."

"She's an exceptional musician," said Dillman. "I heard her play her flute."

"She won't be parted with it, Mr. Dillman. When we first

bought it, Polly used to sleep with it beside her." He gave a brittle laugh. "Considering how much it cost, maybe *I* should have slept with it."

"It's a fine instrument, Mr. Goss. You could tell that by its tone."

"It's the most important thing in Polly's life. She'd be lost without it."

The strongbox was in the middle of the cabin with its lid open to reveal the empty interior. Tufts of cotton wool lay all around it. Beside it, on the floor, was a long, black leather case that had once held an expensive silver flute.

FOURTEEN

The atmosphere in the purser's cabin was charged with tension. Brian Kilhendry was throbbing with anger and there was nothing his deputy could say to soothe him. Dillman stood there in silence, letting the others do all the talking. After managing to impress the purser, he could see that he had, albeit unjustly, now done the opposite.

"I blame you for this, Mr. Dillman," Kilhendry accused.

"That's unfair," said Martin Grandage. "This is nothing to do with Mr. Dillman. It could have happened just as easily if he'd not even been on board."

"Oh, no, it couldn't."

"Calm down, Brian."

"He's brought bad luck to the *Marmora* and it's the last thing we need. I've sailed on dozens of voyages in this ship and the worst crime we had to deal with was someone who cheated at cards. We've never even had a drunken brawl," Kilhendry said. "Cardsharps and petty theft, that's all."

"This particular thief is a bit more ambitious."

"Then there's the murder," Kilhendry reminded him. "Don't forget that, Martin. We still have a killer at large on the ship."

"Mr. Dillman has a theory about that."

"I'm not interested in his theories. I want arrests."

"So does he, Brian," said his deputy. "At least hear him out."

"I've had all that I can stand of his excuses."

Kilhendry flopped into his chair and glared at Dillman. News of the latest thefts had left him seething with rage. He pointed a finger at the detective. "And don't you dare say anything sarcastic about my nose," he warned.

"It's your ears that interest me at the moment," said Dillman quietly. "When they're available to listen to sound reason, I'd like to speak into them. Blame me, if you wish, Mr. Kilhendry, but you need me if we're to solve these crimes."

"We need you like a hole below the waterline!"

"Brian!" exclaimed Grandage. He turned to Dillman. "I'm sorry about this."

"Mr. Kilhendry is entitled to blow off steam," said Dillman.

"Tell him about your theory."

"I don't think he's in the right mood just now, Mr. Grandage."

"Then I'll do it," said the other, looking at Kilhendry. "Mr. Dillman believes that the killer and thief may be the same man. He feels there may be a connecting link between the crimes."

"He's right," growled the purser. "There it is, standing next to you. It goes by the name of George Dillman."

"Be serious for a moment."

"I *am* being serious, Martin. Look at his record so far—a vicious murder and four robberies. What's next, Mr. Dillman?" he taunted. "A mass suicide pact? A shipwreck?"

"What's next is for me to visit the latest victims," said Dillman. "I know the Goss family and they'll be overwhelmed by this. The relics that were stolen belong to a museum in Cairo and

Mr. Goss—Professor Goss, to give him his full title—has been looking after them as if they were the crown jewels. In its own way, the loss of her flute will be just as devastating to his daughter."

"Why should anyone steal a flute?" Grandage wondered.

"Because it's a costly item that can easily be sold."

"There's a more limited market for those stone fragments that were taken."

"But a much more lucrative one, Mr. Grandage," said Dillman. "And I don't think the thief would have stolen them if he didn't have a buyer in mind. They're heading back to Egypt, but not to any museum. They'll go into private hands. So will the jewelry that's been stolen. That's what we fall back on as a last resort."

"Last resort?" said the purser, listening to him at last.

"Yes, Mr. Kilhendry. He has quite a haul so far and may look to add to it. But the longer it stays on board, the greater the risk of detection. That means he intends to unload everything in Port Said. As a last resort, we search all baggage thoroughly before we allow passengers off, and we get our man."

"I want the bastard long before that!"

"We all do, Brian," said Grandage. "What do you advise, Mr. Dillman?"

Dillman was positive. "First of all, I'll speak to Mr. Goss and his family."

"On your own or with Miss Masefield in tow?"

"On my own. It means I'll have to break my cover, but that can't be helped. They're nice people and deserve all the help they can get. What puzzles me is how anyone knew that those relics were even there. Mr. Goss told nobody."

"The secret must have leaked out somehow."

"But how? He was extremely careful."

"Not careful enough," said Kilhendry. "The main items he was carrying were put in our safe, so he'll have something to deliver to the museum. But he's going to have egg all over his face when he admits that the rest of the stuff was stolen."

"Unless we can find it beforehand," noted Dillman.

"What hope is there of that?"

"Every hope. We're getting closer. I feel it."

Kilhendry was scornful. "You'll tell me next that you, too, have a nose for this kind of thing."

"Oh, no," said Dillman, meeting his stare. "That's your prerogative. I rely, for the most part, on my brain. It's the good, old-fashioned American variety. You'd be surprised how often it produces excellent results."

Araminta Wilmshurst kept her head in the book but she did not read a word of it. She was simply ignoring her husband as he paced restlessly up and down the cabin. When he glanced over at her, she kept her eyes fixed on the page before her. Wilmshurst stood directly in front of her but even that did not lift her eyes. He made an effort to control his rising temper and spoke as gently as he could manage.

"Araminta—" he began.

"Not now, Nigel. I'm trying to read."

"I need to talk to you."

"I'm not in the mood to hear any more of your lies."

"They were not lies. I was trying to spare your feelings, that's all."

"If you don't mind," she said pointedly, "I want to be left alone with my book."

"You've been gazing at the same page for ten minutes."

"It's more comforting than looking at you."

"We can't go on like this."

"You're standing in my light."

"Give that book here!" he said, snatching it from her hands.

"Nigel!"

"I'm not putting up with this any longer. We have to talk, Araminta. You must let me explain. When I've done that," he promised, "you can read as long as you wish." He put the book on the table and crouched down in front of her. "I'm sorry," he said. "I'm truly sorry that this has happened."

"I'm a lot more than sorry," she murmured.

"It's not my fault that she's on the same ship as us," he said earnestly. "The chance of that happening was so remote that it never even entered my mind. Heavens above! Do you think I *wanted* to see the damn woman again?"

"You loved her once. You got engaged to her."

"That was a ghastly mistake."

"You didn't think so at the time, Nigel," said his wife. "And neither did she. You told me how heartbroken she was when you broke off the engagement. For all I know, she may still be carrying a torch for you."

"That's absurd."

"Is it? She must have some feelings for you."

"I'm not interested in her or her feelings, Araminta. The only person I care about is you, and that's why I want to sort this out once and for all. We can't go on bickering like this. We're supposed to be dining with the Princess Royal and her family this evening," he said. "Have you forgotten that?"

"No, Nigel. I'm dreading it."

"But you begged me to invite them here. In fact, they prefer to dine in their own cabin so you'll get the opportunity to see inside it. Won't that be a nice treat?"

"I'd rather call the whole thing off."

"Araminta!"

"I would," she insisted. "How can I enjoy a dinner party when I've got this hanging over me? I wouldn't be able to eat a morsel of food."

"Yes, you will," he said. "If you'll just let me explain." She looked skeptical. "The reason I didn't tell you she was on board was that I was trying to keep it from you. That way, your feelings wouldn't have got hurt. Don't you see, darling? I wanted to protect you."

"Then why did you keep on shooting glances at her?"

"I wasn't conscious of doing that. It won't happen again, rely on it."

"Did she look at you?"

"No," he said firmly. "That's the other thing you never gave me the chance to tell you. She's obviously so shocked to see me that she daren't even turn her head in my direction. As for carrying a torch, there's no question of that. She has cause to hate me. I was the one who ended the engagement."

"Only because she did something that you couldn't tolerate."

"She may not see it that way, Araminta."

"But she was at fault," argued his wife. "Otherwise, she could have sued you for breach of promise. Nobody cancels his wedding lightly. She must have done something terrible for you to cast her aside like that."

"She did, Araminta."

"What exactly was it?"

"I'd rather not talk about," he said, getting up and turning away slightly. "It was very hurtful. Seeing her again brought it all back. Let's just say I discovered that she was involved with someone else. That was how much she loved *me*."

She got to her feet. "When did this all happen?"

"Don't make me go through it all again, Araminta. It was a nightmare."

"Then why didn't you cut her dead in the dining room?"

"I did," he said. "I treated her as if she wasn't there." He held her gently by the shoulders. "And that's what you must do, Araminta. Forget all about her. I apologize for what happened last night. We don't even need to eat in the dining room again or to visit any of the public rooms. Neither of us will ever see her again."

"But you'll think about her, Nigel. And so will I." She pouted at him. "I can see why you fell in love with her. She's very beautiful."

"So are you, my darling. Much more beautiful."

"Oh, I don't think so. No wonder you kept looking at her like that."

"I won't even leave the cabin again!" he affirmed. "We'll stay here."

"And let her frighten us away? No," she said with spirit, "I won't let anyone do that. We have as much right to be on this ship as she does. I'm not going to be imprisoned in here for the rest of the voyage."

"Then come with me this evening," he pleaded. "We're going to be guests of the Duke and Duchess of Fife. Most people would give their right arm for such an honor. Yes," he said, "and we'll have our photograph taken with them as well. Herr Lenz is going to give us a souvenir that nobody else on the *Marmora* will have." He kissed her softly on the forehead. "Say that you'll come."

"What was her name, Nigel?"

"Forget her, will you? She's dead and buried."

"I just want to know her name."

"Why? It will mean nothing to you."

"Oh, yes, it will. You said there'd be no secrets between us, yet you've never told me the full story of why you and she parted. At least, I want to know her name. Tell me that and I'll agree to go with you this evening." There was steel in her voice. "If you don't," she cautioned, "I'm not going anywhere with you."

There was a long pause as Wilmshurst wrestled with the possibilities. He was so used to getting his own way with her that he did not know how to cope with her resistance. Araminta had an unexpected streak of determination in her.

"Masefield," he said, capitulating. "Genevieve Masefield."

Genevieve Masefield was interested to hear about the special dinner for the royal party.

"What are you going to give them, Monsieur Vivet?" she asked.

He raised a finger to his lips. "That is a secret."

"How many people will be at the table?"

"Six. The Duke and Duchess, their children, and two guests." He rubbed his hands together. "They do not know what a feast they will enjoy this evening."

"I wish I could be there," she said.

"So do I." He took her hand and kissed it. "So do I, believe me."

Genevieve had been talking to Vera Braddock in the lounge when the Frenchman came up to her. The old lady had been introduced to him but she was rather nonplussed when he planted a kiss on her hand. Excusing herself, she went off to report the thrilling encounter to her sister. Vivet was more boastful than ever. He was telling everyone he met that he was about to cook for the royal party.

"It is a pity they do not let me play some music, as well," he said.

"That would be a case of gilding the lily," said Genevieve with a smile, "or of covering the food with too rich a sauce."

"My sauces, they are always just right."

"I'm sure that they are, Monsieur Vivet."

Though many passengers found him too ostentatious, Genevieve was rather amused by the Frenchman. He took himself far too seriously but she did not consider that to be a besetting vice. His effusive manner was a welcome change from the more restrained behavior of the majority of the passengers. Claude Vivet was a presence. Before she could question him further about the dinner party, they were interrupted by the arrival of Karl-Jurgen Lenz. Hands behind his back, he gave them a stiff bow.

"I have a present for you, Miss Masefield," he announced.

"A present?"

"When you see it, I hope that you forgive me, please."

Genevieve was wary. "What exactly is this present?"

"An example of my work," he said, bringing two photographs from behind his back and giving one to her. "A picture of the most remarkable woman on board the ship."

Genevieve was startled. It was the photograph he had taken of her when she was standing on deck with Myra Cathcart. Both women had been caught in an attitude of surprise that gave the photograph a peculiar life. Vivet looked over Genevieve's shoulder.

"You are right, my friend," he said. "Miss Masefield is the most remarkable lady on the *Marmora*. And the photograph, it is very good."

"Thank you," said Lenz. "But I did not take it because Miss Masefield was there. It is her friend, Mrs. Cathcart, who interests me. *She* is the lady I talk about. I apologize to both of them for taking the picture without warning them." He smiled at Genevieve. "I come to ask a favor."

"What sort of favor?"

"I have this other copy. Will you give it to Mrs. Cathcart for me?"

"Why don't you do it yourself, Herr Lenz?"

"Because you can tell her what I just said about her. I cannot do that."

"Very well," she agreed, taking the second photograph from him. "I'm sure that Mrs. Cathcart will be delighted to receive it."

"This lady," he said to Vivet, "has such an interesting face. That is what I look for with my camera: a face that has interest or a person who has the fame."

"Then you ought to take a photograph of Monsieur Vivet. He's a famous chef," Genevieve suggested.

"*Mais non*," said Vivet, holding up both hands.

"But Herr Lenz might want to take a picture of you cooking

this banquet for the Duke and Duchess. It would be a souvenir of a unique occasion."

"Why, yes," said Lenz, roused by the mention of the royal party. "You have the good face for a camera. I am happy to take this photograph."

Vivet was firm. "No, *mon ami*. I do not like to see myself in a picture. And when I am cooking, I will not allow anyone else to be there. It is my rule. I can only work alone. *Pardon*."

Clicking his heels together, he gave a little bow then walked away. Genevieve was baffled. Of all the passengers on board, she would have picked out Monsieur Claude Vivet as the one who would most readily stand in front of a camera. Yet he had refused to do so. She wondered why a man who deliberately courted attention would be so reluctant to have his photograph taken.

Morton Goss was in despair. He gazed down at the empty strongbox as if his life savings had been stolen. The padlocks had been levered open and tossed aside. The black leather case for the flute was also still lying where it had been found.

"Who on earth could have taken them, Mr. Dillman?" Goss wailed.

"A thief with some idea of their value."

"Where would he sell them?"

"I'm sure that Cairo has its share of antiques dealers who don't ask questions."

"This is a calamity. We must get them back."

"We'll do our best," said Dillman.

The loss of her flute had left Polly Goss inconsolable. Her mother was in Polly's cabin with the girl, trying in vain to comfort her. It left Dillman free to examine the scene of the crime and to question Goss.

"But nobody knew that I had them in my cabin."

"I did," said Dillman. "I don't think that anyone overheard us when you confided in me during a meal, but they may have. Did you tell anyone else about the relics?"

"Only one other person, and I trust him as much as you."

"Who was he?"

"Sir Alistair Longton."

"You explained that you had some of them in your cabin?"

"I actually showed him, Mr. Dillman," said Goss. "He has a genuine interest in ancient Egypt. Sir Alistair said that it was a privilege to see them."

"I'll need to speak to him."

"You surely don't think he's a suspect?"

"No, Mr. Goss," said Dillman, "and I certainly won't tell him they've been stolen. If I did that, he'd know I have an official position on board this ship, and I prefer to keep that secret. It enables me to work more effectively."

Goss looked at him with admiration. "You fooled me, Mr. Dillman," he admitted. "I'd never have believed that you were a detective. It came as a shock at first but I'm starting to see the advantages. You know us. You understand just how big a disaster this is for me."

"Don't forget your daughter. She's another victim of the thief."

"Polly was hysterical when she found out. I told you earlier how much she loved that flute. It was her pride and joy. She's absolutely brokenhearted."

"Then there's not much point in my speaking to her," said Dillman. "As long as you impress upon her—and upon Mrs. Goss—that I must remain under cover."

"Leave it to me." He looked down at the strongbox again and bit his lip. "How on earth could this have happened?"

"My fear is that Sir Alistair may have made an incautious remark."

"But he gave me his word."

"And I'm sure he intended to keep it," said Dillman, "but he's a gregarious man. I've seen him chatting to various people in the lounge. And he's fond of a glass of brandy as well. Who knows? He may have inadvertently let something slip over a drink with a friend. That's why I need to sound him out."

"Look at this," said Goss, bending down to pick up one of the broken padlocks. "Whoever got into this cabin knew what to expect. He brought something with him to break into the strongbox."

"A professional thief is always well prepared."

"How did he get in here, Mr. Dillman?"

"With a master key, I suspect," said the other. "There's no sign of forced entry."

"Where did he get such a key?"

"I wish I knew."

"If he can walk in here as easily as that, he can get into any cabin on the ship."

"Most of them don't have anything quite as valuable as those fragments of stone. This thief is very selective. He struck where he knew there'd be rich pickings."

"Why did he have to steal the flute as well?"

"That was an opportunistic theft," said Dillman. "When he got what he came for, he looked around to see what else was worth taking. In your daughter's cabin, he found the flute and realized how expensive it must be."

"Yet he didn't take the case with him."

"Here's the explanation for that." He retrieved the black leather case from the floor and pointed to the inscription. "Your daughter's name and address are on it in prominent letters. That means it could be traced to its owner."

"I see."

"Is the instrument insured?"

"Yes, Mr. Dillman," said Goss, "but we can't make a claim until we get back home to Boston. That's over a month. Besides, it's not the money that Polly wants. It's that particular flute."

"I understand. Well," said Dillman, "I'll make a start with my inquiries. I'm sorry this has happened. It reflects badly on us."

"No, it doesn't. It reflects badly on me. I was foolhardy. You did warn me."

"The relics were all insured."

"That's not the point," said Goss. "I was entrusted with their safekeeping and I let them get stolen. They'll never forgive me at the museum. It's a real tragedy. We'll never be able to have anything on loan from them again."

"Don't rule out the possibility that we'll recover them."

"What are the chances of that?"

"Pretty good, I reckon," said Dillman.

"We'd be so grateful to you."

"I do have a personal interest here, Mr. Goss."

"Personal interest?"

"Yes," said Dillman. "Apart from the fact that we're friends, that is. It's not all that long ago that you and I were chatting together up on deck. My guess is that's when the theft occurred. I unwittingly distracted you."

"It was Mr. Pountney who did that," said Goss. "Before you came along, we had a long talk together. In fact, it was he who suggested that we take a stroll on deck."

Myra Cathcart was not sure whether to be delighted or disturbed by the gift. As she examined it in the lounge, she had to admit it was a good photograph, but she wished that it had been taken by someone other than Karl-Jurgen Lenz.

"Why didn't he give it to me himself?" she asked.

"I think he was too shy," said Genevieve, seated beside her.

"He wasn't too shy to take it in the first place. The way he crept up on us was very unsettling. I'm still rather cross with him about that."

"I fancy that the photograph is a kind of peace offering, Myra."

"I don't want to make peace with Herr Lenz. He unnerves me."

"I can't say that he's endeared himself to me, either," observed Genevieve, "but he knows his work. It's a particularly good photo of you."

"Yes, it is, but it still worries me somehow."

"Show it to your daughter. See what she thinks about it."

"I will, Genevieve. That's good advice."

"What's this?" asked a cultured voice behind them. "Photographs?"

They turned to see Roland Pountney. After an exchange of niceties, he took a closer look at the photograph and agreed that it was good. He beamed at Genevieve.

"Splendid picture of you, Miss Masefield." he commented.

"I look startled," she said.

"That's what appeals to me about it. You're caught off-guard. It wasn't exactly the most gentlemanly thing for the photographer to do, but the result is well worth it. Do you know, I wouldn't mind a copy of that myself?"

"It's not for public sale, Mr. Pountney."

"Would you object to my having a photograph of you?"

"I think that I would," said Genevieve.

"Then, of course, I won't even consider the idea," he said obligingly. "I'll have to rely on my mental photograph of you, won't I? Incidentally, did I see you talking to Nigel Wilmshurst yesterday? I didn't realize that you were friends."

"We're not, Mr. Pountney."

"His manner toward you seemed very familiar." He turned to Myra. "This chap and I were at school together. Bit too arrogant for my liking. Not that I really knew him at Harrow. I was only there for a few years."

"Mr. Wilmshurst told me that you left the school."

Pountney laughed. "I didn't leave, Miss Masefield; I was kicked out. I'm rather proud of that little episode. It takes a lot to get expelled from Harrow but I managed it."

With a wave of farewell, he strode off across the lounge. Myra was bemused.

"Expelled?" she said in surprise. "I wouldn't have thought that was anything to be proud of, Genevieve. Would you?"

"No, Myra."

"I'd be too ashamed to admit such a thing."

"It was a long time ago," said Genevieve, "and Mr. Pountney has obviously put his youthful indiscretions behind him. All credit to him. Expulsion is a humiliation. Most pupils would be crushed by it. But not Mr. Pountney," she added, watching him as he chatted to some friends. "He appears to have thrived on it."

When Dillman had first seen the *Marmora,* he had thought that the ship was small, but it now seemed to have grown in size. There were too many places to hide. Identifying criminals was not easy when there were almost a thousand people to choose from. Most of them could be eliminated at once as suspects but there was still a daunting number left. Even with Genevieve's help, he could not hope to put all of them under scrutiny. The murder of Walter Dugdale was the most serious crime, but the thefts were creating unfortunate repercussions. Morton Goss and his family were only the latest victims. Dillman feared there would soon be more. Details of the crimes could not be kept secret indefinitely. They had to be solved quickly, before word leaked out.

Sir Alistair Longton was in the first-class smoke room when Dillman tracked him down. He was talking to an elderly man who wore pince-nez and who was just about the leave. Lighting a cigarette, Dillman waited until Longton was on his own before moving over to him. Longton drew on his cigar then inhaled the smoke.

"That was reassuring," he said with a chuckle. "Just met someone on this ship who's actually older than me. Bucked me up no end, that did."

"I fancy that you're younger than a lot of people aboard," said Dillman. "In spirit, that is. And that's what counts, Sir Alistair."

"Couldn't agree more. Interests, that's the secret."

"'Interests?'"

"Yes," said Longton, tapping his forehead. "Got to keep the mind active. Hobbies, projects, travel, meeting new people. Anything that stimulates. If you don't do that, the gray matter will ossify."

"There's no danger of that happening in your case."

"Bless me! No, Mr. Dillman. My problem is that I have too many interests. I'm always fascinated by specialist knowledge, you see." He chortled to himself. "When they try to nail me in my coffin, I'll probably sit up and ask them about the finer points of their trade. Born with an insatiable curiosity. That's me."

"I could see that from the way you talked to Mr. Goss."

"*Professor* Goss," corrected the other. "Give him his due."

"He's too modest to use that title outside university circles."

"He shouldn't be. Fellow's earned it. First-class brain."

"I agree, Sir Alistair. I've learned so much from him. I'm sorry that I'm not going to Egypt on this trip. He'd be an ideal guide."

"Given me a few pointers, I know that."

"Did he show you anything?" asked Dillman, watching for a reaction.

Longton looked blank. "Don't know what you mean, old chap."

"You were so intrigued by his work that I wondered if he let you see any of his prize exhibits. I was touched when he invited me to see them. But that pleasure still awaits you, obviously."

"Are we talking about the same thing, Mr. Dillman?" Longton said cautiously.

"I can't give details, I'm afraid. I promised Mr. Goss."

"Did you go to his cabin?"

"Yes, Sir Alistair."

"Then we *did* have the same experience," said Longton, relaxing visibly. "We're part of a charmed circle, Mr. Dillman. We'd never get the opportunity to handle them if they'd been on display in a museum. They'd be under glass."

"I was intrigued by the hieroglyphics. You can trace them with your finger."

"Oh, I did that, don't worry."

"How much do you think they're worth?"

"A small fortune, Mr. Dillman. That's why our friend was anxious that nobody else should know where they were." He exhaled more smoke and peered at Dillman through the fug. "I'm sure that you didn't breathe a word about this to anyone."

"No, Sir Alistair. Not a syllable."

"Neither did I. Even though I was asked to do just that."

"Oh?"

"Damn fellow pestered me like mad," said Longton. "Apparently, he saw me going off with Professor Goss and guessed that we were friends. Wanted to know if the professor kept any relics of ancient Egypt with him."

"Why?"

"Claimed that he'd liked to photograph them. Told me some cock-and-bull story about wanting to write a story for some German magazine and illustrating it with the pictures he took." Longton flicked his cigar ash away. "Let him know I didn't have a clue what he was on about. Sent him on his way."

"Was it a man called Karl-Jurgen Lenz?"

"That's the fellow," said Longton, removing his monocle. "Unsavory character. Never know what a man like that is thinking. Wouldn't trust him an inch, Mr. Dillman. He's far too shifty."

Genevieve Masefield needed some thinking time. She had gathered so much conflicting intelligence that she returned to her cabin so she could assimilate it in private. Pencil and paper were useful allies at such a time. Genevieve listed all the information she had gathered, beside the names of the people who had given it. Somewhere amid her scribbles, she believed, was a vital clue that needed to be teased out. She searched for it in vain. Dillman had taught her to look for a pattern at such times but that, too, eluded her. She was still seated at her table when there was a gentle tap on her door.

Genevieve was circumspect. It was unlikely to be Myra or Lilian Cathcart, both of whom she had spoken to earlier. That left Roland Pountney and Nigel Wilmshurst as the most likely visitors. Neither of them was welcome. The other possibility was Frau Zumpe, whom she had not seen since the latter's drunken confession on the previous night. When the tap on the door was repeated, she noted it was too soft for a man and too tentative for Frau Zumpe. Genevieve elected to open the door and was dumbfounded when she saw Araminta Wilmshurst standing there. They stared uneasily at each other for some while. It was the visitor who finally broke the silence.

"Miss Masefield?"

"Yes," said Genevieve.

"I'm Araminta Wilmshurst. I believe that you know my husband."

"Is that what he told you?"

"Eventually." She was almost shaking with nerves. "May I speak to you, please?"

"This is not really a convenient time, Mrs. Wilmshurst."

"It's very important to me. I'm sure you understand that."

Genevieve could see the effort it had taken her to pay the visit, and she felt sorry for her. At the same time, she sensed that any conversation between them would be awkward and possibly hurtful. Her instinct was to turn the woman politely away but she decided instead to confront a problem that she could not go on dodging.

"You'd better come in," she said.

"Thank you, Miss Masefield."

Araminta stepped into the cabin and gave it a cursory glance before turning to look at Genevieve, who closed the door after them. She had not realized that Genevieve was so much taller than she was. Araminta took a deep breath before speaking.

"I have to know the truth, Miss Masefield," she began.

"Truth?"

"About you and my husband."

"Then the person you should be asking is him and not me."

"I've heard what Nigel has to say. I'd very much like to believe him."

"Then that's what I'd advise you to do, Mrs. Wilmshurst," said Genevieve. "Our relationship was over some time ago and I haven't seen him since. It was pure accident that we happened to be on the same ship."

"I accept that. What I find much harder to accept—in spite of his denials—is that Nigel has lost all interest in you. He kept looking at you during dinner last night."

"Well, I didn't look at him, I can assure you."

"Yet there is still something between you."

"Not on my side, Mrs. Wilmshurst."

"It's the way his voice changes whenever he talks about you."

"I'm surprised that he even bothers to mention me," Genevieve said briskly. "What happened between us was over and done with long before you. We both have good reason to forget that period in our life."

"*You* do, I'm sure," said Araminta.

"What do you mean?"

"Well, you were the guilty party."

Genevieve blanched. "Is that what your husband said?"

"It's the truth, isn't it?"

Araminta Wilmshurst was in a highly vulnerable state. Only some deep anxiety could have brought her to Genevieve's cabin. She wanted a reassurance that Genevieve could not give her. Yet behind her tentative manner there was also a slight air of triumph, a conscious awareness that she had married the man to whom Genevieve had once been engaged. It put Genevieve in a difficult position. Wanting to spare her visitor any pain, she tried to bring the conversation to an end.

"Mrs. Wilmshurst," she said gently, "I appreciate why you came but I'm not able to help you in any way. Nigel—your husband—is the only person who can do that. I know that I pose a problem. Seeing me during your honeymoon must be like finding a specter at the feast. I apologize for that but it's not my doing."

Araminta was almost derisive. "Nigel said that you always had a glib answer."

"I am not being glib, believe me. I'm trying to show you some consideration."

"He told me that you'd try to patronize me, as well."

"Does he know that you're here?"

"No, of course not. This is between the two of us, Miss Masefield."

"Not when a third person is involved. Now, listen, Mrs. Wilmshurst. This may sound glib and patronizing but I don't care. I think that you should leave and forget you ever came here," said Genevieve, crossing to the door. "There's no reason why we should even see each other for the remainder of the voyage."

"You're not getting rid of me as easily as that," said Araminta, folding her arms. "I came for the truth and that's what I intend to get."

"Whose version do you want—mine or your husband's?"

"Yours. I need confirmation of what Nigel told me."

Genevieve was brusque. "I'm sorry, Mrs. Wilmshurst," she said, "but I don't want to come between the two of you. I suggest that you believe the version of events you've been given. Your life will be much happier that way."

"In other words, you deny that you were to blame."

"I didn't say that."

"Because you can't," said Araminta, becoming more strident. "You couldn't bear it when Nigel threw you over. It's quite obvious that you were only after his money and his title. And you might have got it if he had found out about your infidelity."

Genevieve gasped. "*My* infidelity?"

"I dragged the details out of Nigel earlier on."

"I see. And you believed him, of course."

"He's my husband!"

"Yes," said Genevieve, struggling for control. "He is, Mrs. Wilmshurst. That's what I'm forcing myself to remember, because it's the only thing that's keeping me from demanding that you get out of my cabin. I'll not be insulted like this."

"All I want is your admission that it's true."

"Then you'll have to wait a very long time."

Araminta pointed a finger. "Are you calling my husband a liar?"

"Let's just say that his memory may be slightly at fault on this particular subject."

"Why else would a man break an engagement?"

"Ask him," said Genevieve. "Jog his memory."

"You're patronizing me again," Araminta complained. "Do you know what I think? I think you've never really forgiven him for casting you off. That's why you want to cause trouble for him. That's why you're trying to distract him."

"I can't wait until he gets off this ship, Mrs. Wilmshurst."

"I know. It's because he reminds you of the terrible thing you did to him."

"He reminds me what a lucky escape I had."

"Now who's being insulting? Nigel is a wonderful man and he's *mine*."

"I don't envy you that, Mrs. Wilmshurst. I hope that you'll both be very happy."

"How can we be, when you've come out of his past to haunt him?"

"I'm not the one who's done the haunting," said Genevieve.

"What do you mean?"

"Ask your husband."

"Are you saying that you've met with him? You've *spoken* to him?"

"Not with any pleasure, I assure you."

"You're lying," challenged Araminta. "Nigel swore to me that he hasn't been anywhere near you. Why should he be? After the way you betrayed him, he ought to hate you. It was a shameful way to behave."

"I agree," Genevieve retorted, stung by the attack. "But I wasn't the person who was guilty of betrayal, Mrs. Wilmshurst. There was shameful behavior and it did bring an end to the engagement. I was the person to break it off and not your loving husband." She opened the door wide. "You asked for the truth," she said. "Now you know it. Good-bye, Mrs. Wilmshurst."

FIFTEEN

The photograph took much longer than they had expected. When Karl-Jurgen Lenz had set up his equipment, he arranged the group in different positions until he was satisfied that he had the best result. Fife was patient but his wife was increasingly restive. She regarded the camera as an intrusion into her privacy and wanted the photographic session to be over quickly. The children were always ready to face a camera, and they beamed obligingly until their mother pointed out that they should try to show more dignity. Nigel Wilmshurst, dressed, like Fife, in white tie and tails, was annoyed that his wife did not seem to be enjoying the occasion. He had used his father's name to secure the privilege of dining with the royal party and of having a photograph with them, yet Araminta now appeared to be strangely indifferent to both.

"Why is he taking so long?" asked Lady Maud.

"Herr Lenz will be ready in a moment," said Fife.

"We've been standing like this for ages."

"Be quiet, dear," suggested her mother.

"But I'm hungry."

"So am I," said Lady Alexandra.

Fife quelled them with a look. "It will be over very soon."

They were in the sitting room between the two cabins allotted to the royal party. A table had been set up in the middle of the room and six places had been laid. Candles burned in the silver candelabra at either end of the table.

"What is he *doing?*" murmured the Princess Royal.

"I think he's almost ready, Louise," said Fife.

Lenz waved a hand to indicate that Wilmshurst should move in closer to his wife then vanished under his black cloth to make final adjustments. The Duke and Duchess struck their familiar pose and their daughters tried to emulate them. Wilmshurst stole a quick glance at his wife, hoping for at least a sign of excitement from her, but Araminta's face was impassive and her gaze dull. The next moment, there was a sudden flash that was accompanied by a startling noise. Lenz gave them a formal bow.

"Thank you," he said. "It was an honor for me."

"We'll be interested to see the results," said Fife.

"You will not be disappointed, I think."

"Thank you, Herr Lenz."

Lenz turned to Wilmshurst. "Shall I take a photograph of you now, sir?"

"No," replied Wilmshurst.

"But you ask for one with your wife."

"Another time, Herr Lenz. I'll be in touch."

Wilmshurst was not just anxious to get rid of a man who was irritating all of them; he could see that his wife was in no mood to be photographed with her husband even though she had been thrilled by the notion when she first heard of it. Gathering up his equipment, Lenz thanked everyone again then left through the door that Wilmshurst held open for him. When the man had gone, Wilmshurst was deeply apologetic.

"I'm dreadfully sorry about that," he said, "I thought the whole thing would be over in a minute or so. Herr Lenz stayed long enough to paint our portraits, let alone take our photograph."

Fife was tolerant. "Perfection takes time. You cannot rush an artist."

"I do think there was a needless delay. He was enjoying the pleasure of being here so much that he couldn't drag himself away."

"Well, he's gone now. Perhaps we should all take our places."

"Yes, Father," Lady Maud said with alacrity. "What are we having for dinner?"

"Wait and see," advised Fife.

The Duke and Duchess sat at either end of the table. Their daughters sat on one side of it, with the Wilmshursts directly opposite them. The female members of the dinner party wore evening dresses. Araminta, in white satin, contrived a first smile.

"It's so kind of you to invite us," she said.

"In point of fact," Fife observed drily, "it was your husband who extended the invitation and we were grateful to receive it. I hope that you didn't mind changing the venue to our cabin?"

"Not at all," said Wilmshurst. "Araminta and I are delighted to be here."

"It's in the nature of an experiment, I fear," warned the Princess Royal. "There's a renowned French chef aboard and he insisted on cooking a meal especially for us."

"It was too tempting an offer to resist," said Fife.

"I'm glad that you accepted, my lord," said Wilmshurst. "It will make the occasion even more memorable. A German photographer, a French chef—what next? I wonder. A Chinese waiter, perhaps? It is taking shape as a truly international evening."

"With you and your wife as the guests of honor."

"Surely not!"

Fife beamed at them. "Honeymoon couples take precedence

over everyone else," he asserted, snapping his fingers. "That means there's only one way to begin."

Alerted by his signal, the waiter who had been lurking outside the door now entered with a tray that bore a bottle of champagne and six glasses. He set the tray down on a side table and, to the amusement of the two girls, opened the bottle with a resounding *pop!* They were delighted to be given a glass of champagne each. When everyone else had a glass in front of them, Fife raised his up in a toast.

"To the happy couple!" he announced.

His wife and children echoed the toast and sipped from their respective glasses, but the visitors looked far from happy. Wilmshurst responded with a smile but Araminta looked positively discomfited. When they looked at each other, there was a visible tension between them. It was not a good omen.

With so much information to exchange, Dillman and Genevieve met in his cabin before dinner. He was in formal attire and she wore a beautiful evening dress in ivory-colored taffeta, with elbow-length gloves of a slightly darker hue. Gold earrings and gold necklace completed the effect of unforced glamour. Dillman told her about the latest theft and about the biting criticism he had received from the purser.

"I'm glad I wasn't there, George," she said.

"So was I, though Mr. Kilhendry might have moderated his language in your presence. Fortunately, Mr. Grandage acted as a buffer between the two of us."

"He's turning out to be a real friend."

"He didn't think much of my theory, I'm afraid. Neither did the purser."

"What theory is that?"

"I've come around to the view that the thief and the killer may be the same person. Yes," he went on, seeing the doubt in her

227

eyes, "I know that it seems unlikely on the face of it. I just have this conviction that I'm right."

"But nothing was stolen from Mr. Dugdale's cabin," she argued.

"Nothing that we know of, Genevieve."

"Are you saying he disturbed a thief and that the man rounded on him?"

"No, it didn't happen that way, I'm certain of it. Mr. Dugdale let the man into his cabin because he had no reason to fear him. Until he turned his back, that is. The murder came *before* the theft."

"If indeed anything was actually taken."

"Yes, I could be way off-target here."

"That's unlikely, George. You have an uncanny knack of hitting the bull's-eye. But, wait a moment," she said, thinking it through. "If the thief wanted something in his cabin, why not simply steal it when Mr. Dugdale was not there? He had no need to commit murder at all."

"Oh, yes, he did. He was impelled to do so."

"By what?"

"I'm still trying to work that out, Genevieve," he confessed. "But this latest theft has convinced me that I'm on the right track."

Genevieve frowned. "I don't see how."

"It's part of the smoke screen. What better way to impede a murder investigation than by diverting the people who are carrying it out? You were diverted by the theft from the Braddock sisters," he said, "and I'm distracted by what happened to Mr. Goss. How can we concentrate fully on the murder when we have these other crimes dumped in our lap? Mr. Dugdale is dead. He's in no position to harry us. The other victims do exert pressure on us, Genevieve. Because they were charming old ladies, you want to do your very best for the Misses Braddock."

"I'd want to solve the crime even if I didn't like them."

"Yes," he continued, "but there's an added incentive for you.

It's the same in my case. I know the Goss family; I share their pain. The person who stole from their cabins was well aware of my friendship. He knew that I'd run to help them. There'll be more to come, I'm sure. The smoke screen will get thicker and thicker until the murder of Walter Dugdale is all but obscured. Do you follow my reasoning?"

"I do, George. But it's based on a troubling assumption."

"Someone knows who we are."

"Yes, we've been picked out as the ship's detectives. But *how*?"

"It wouldn't be difficult," he said. "When Mrs. Prendergast was robbed, all the thief had to do was to stay in the vicinity of her cabin until someone went to question her about the crime. You could have been seen going in and out."

"What about you?"

"I can fool the vast majority of passengers, but there'll always be one or two who can see through my disguise. Like us, professional criminals develop their instincts," he told her, "and the man we're after is extremely professional."

"Have you discussed this with the purser?"

"He didn't give me the chance, Genevieve. Nor did Mr. Grandage. All that they're concerned with is limiting the damage caused by the various crimes. They look to us to come up with solutions."

"We haven't managed to do that, so far."

"No," he admitted, "but we do have some suspects. Herr Lenz is one and Claude Vivet is definitely another. They both had good reason to hate Mr. Dugdale. I'll add a third name to the list: Sir Alistair Longton. He certainly knew that I was friendly with the Goss family because he joined us for dinner one evening. Sir Alistair also persuaded Mr. Goss to show him the very items that were later stolen."

"Have you had the chance to question him, George?"

"Yes, and he was very plausible. He claimed he'd never tell anyone about what he'd seen in that strongbox and I believed him at the time. Now," said Dillman, "I'm not so sure. It was almost as if he knew that there'd been a robbery and was protesting his innocence. Also, shortly after the Braddock sisters had money taken from their cabin, Sir Alistair deposited a sizable amount in the purser's safe."

"Would a professional criminal be so obvious?"

"Who would suspect someone like Sir Alistair Longton? He's a distinguished old gentleman who patently has enough money to travel in style. It's impossible to imagine him stealing from someone else's cabin or bludgeoning a man to death. You'd sooner accuse the captain of these crimes," said Dillman. "If Sir Alistair *is* involved—and it's by no means certain—then he must have an accomplice. A younger man."

"Roland Pountney."

"How did you know I was going to put him on the list?"

"Because he's definitely on mine, George."

She told him about her suspicions of Pountney and how he had been expelled from Harrow. His reaction to that expulsion surprised Dillman. It was a setback most people would try to conceal rather than celebrate with a laugh.

"Did he just volunteer the information?" asked Dillman.

"No," she said. "Nigel Wilmshurst told me. He has no time for Mr. Pountney. Nigel looked down his nose at him. Mind you, he does that to most people." She pulled a face. "And that brings me to another problem."

"Has he been bothering you?"

"His wife came to see me."

Genevieve explained what had happened and how guilty she felt about have to disillusion Araminta Wilmshurst, but her hand had been forced. Genevieve had her own pride. She was not going to be branded by anyone as a woman whose promiscuity had led to the breaking of an engagement. Dillman sympathized with her.

"It was the only thing you could do," he said. "You had to set the record straight."

"The poor woman looked as if she'd been poleaxed."

"Do you think she believed you?"

"Not entirely," she said, "but I planted a seed of doubt in her mind. By the time she left my cabin, she was starting to disbelieve her husband. There could be ructions. I fear that Nigel will turn on me."

Dillman took her by the shoulders. "I'm always here, if that happens."

"Thank you, George, but this is a battle I have to fight on my own."

"Not as long as I'm on this ship." He kissed her softly. "Remember that. At the slightest sign of trouble, just light a couple of distress flares."

Genevieve hugged him in gratitude.

"What state was his wife in when she left your cabin?"

"She was totally confused."

"Does she have enough strength to challenge her husband about this?"

"I couldn't say," replied Genevieve. "What I do know is this: If she does confront Nigel, I'd hate to be there when it happens."

Claude Vivet outdid himself. Working alone in the corner of the kitchen, ostracized by the other chefs, he produced a meal that was truly worthy of the royal party and their guests. It began with a plate of miniature savories, attractively cut into various shapes, to whet the appetite. A delicious bouillon, made from his own recipe, followed. Then came a choice of fish, meat, or game, all of it exquisitely cooked, carefully garnished, and served with a selection of vegetables so tender that all of the diners called for more. Before an array of desserts was offered, a salad was served, to clense the palate.

Wine had been selected by Vivet for each course of the meal and each bottle was the perfect complement to his delectable food.

231

Araminta Wilmshurst drank more heavily than her husband had ever seen her do before. Worried at first, he came to see it as bonus because his wife began to relax at last. Once or twice, when Fife told an anecdote, she even exploded into the characteristic giggle that had attracted Wilmshurst to her in the first place. Fife was a charming host and his daughters were supremely well behaved. What surprised the visitors was how hesitant the Princess Royal was. At no point did she initiate a conversation, restricting herself to an occasional comment yet listening intently to the remarks of others. Talk turned to the inclination of certain Englishmen to marry foreign wives. Fife reeled off a whole catalogue of them.

"Lord Esher married a Belgian lady," he said. "Her father was at one time the Belgian minister to the Court of St. James. Though she's spent her whole life in this country, the Marchioness of Tweeddale is of Italian extraction. Lady Sligo, widow of the third Marquis of Sligo, was a French lady. Countess Tolstoy, of course, is Russian," he went on, "and still calls herself by the name of her first husband even though she's been married to Philip Stanhope for well over twenty years."

"Then there's Mrs. Edward Stonor," said Wilmshurst, keen to include some names of his own. "We've seen her a great deal in London society. Mrs. Stonor is Greek. But, then, so is Sir Edward Law's wife. I had the good fortune to meet her, as well, before she and her husband moved to India. A handsome lady—very musical and passionately interested in literature."

Fife smiled. "My wife is passionately interested in salmon fishing."

"Alex!" she said in rebuke.

"It's true, Louise. You have a rare talent with a rod."

"And a practical one," Wilmshurst pointed out. "You can always eat what you catch. And if you can persuade Monsieur Vivet to cook it for you, then it will be irresistible."

"What are your interests, Mrs. Wilmshurst?" asked Fife. "Are you an angler?"

"Oh, no," said Araminta.

"Neither was my wife until she moved to Scotland."

"I dance a little, that's all."

"Nonsense!" Wilmshurst said proudly. "You dance superbly, Araminta. You're so light on your feet." He turned to the others. "At one time, she even considered training for the ballet."

"How wonderful!" exclaimed Lady Maud.

"Araminta has many talents. That's why I chose her as my wife."

Fife was quizzical. "Did your eye never stray to the Continent, then?"

"Not for a second, my lord," boasted Wilmshurst, resting an uxorious hand on Araminta's arm. "Why look abroad when you have something far better at home in England? I envy none of the gentlemen who've been mentioned so far. They chose foreign wives and have been blessed in those choices. But I'm the happiest of them all," he declared, raising a glass of the finest red wine. "To my wife!" he announced. "And to a long life of joy and togetherness!"

The Duke and Duchess lifted their glasses to toast the young bride but Araminta could take no more. Jumping to her feet, she burst into tears and fled the room. A deeply embarrassed Wilmshurst summoned up an apologetic smile.

"Araminta has not been feeling well today," he said.

Dillman shared a table with the Goss family that evening but he kept his eye on three of the men he had named as suspects. Each was at a different table. Karl-Jurgen Lenz was seated opposite Genevieve Masefield but his sole interest was in Myra Cathcart. Even from that distance, Dillman could see the intensity of his gaze and the single-mindedness that had made him so successful in his chosen field. Sir Alistair Longton was at the captain's table, seated between a Russian countess with a diamond tiara and an

Egyptian doctor who was sporting a thick black mustache. The Englishman was completely at ease, never short of a comment on any subject, but equally ready to listen to others. Longton was the sort of man whom Dillman had seen at a captain's table on dozens of voyages. He fitted in perfectly.

Roland Pountney was the interesting member of the trio. Deserting Genevieve's table, he instead chose to sit with Vera and Elizabeth Braddock, treating them with an affection he might be expected to reserve for his own maiden aunts. There was no hint of the loquacious businessman now. Pountney was taking care of two people he quite obviously liked, and they, in turn, were patently fond of him. Dillman had met some callous thieves before, but never one who would seek the friendship of the victims he had robbed. Of the three suspects, Pountney now seemed the least likely.

Dillman was soon reminded of the fourth name on his list. Polly Goss turned to him so that she could speak in private. Her eyes sparkled with renewed admiration.

"What do I tell Monsieur Vivet?" she whispered.

"Tell him?"

"We're supposed to be practicing again tomorrow, Mr. Dillman. But I can't do that without my flute. Yet you told us not to say anything about the theft."

"That's true," he agreed. "We have to keep this to ourselves."

"Monsieur Vivet will be expecting me."

"You'll have to invent an excuse."

"But he'll be so disappointed. He really enjoys working with me."

"And so he should," said Dillman. "You're a born musician."

"Not without an instrument."

Dillman could see the anxiety etched into her young face. Polly Goss was so perturbed by the loss of her flute that she would not be able to hide her feelings from the Frenchman. If pressed, Dillman feared, she would blurt out the truth.

"Would you like *me* to speak to Monsieur Vivet?" he offered.

"That would be such a relief!" she said. "What will you tell him?"

"I'll think of something. And I'll make sure I warn you in advance what it is so that you're not caught on the wrong foot." He gave her a kind smile. "You like Monsieur Vivet, don't you?"

"Yes, though not as much as he likes himself."

Dillman laughed. "He loves to blow his own trumpet—or, in this instance, to play his own piano. And he clearly plays it very well."

"He's a true musician. That's why he'd understand."

"About what?"

"How I feel now that someone's taken my flute. I wish I could tell him, Mr. Dillman. If I asked him, I'm sure that he'd keep it to himself."

"With respect to Monsieur Vivet," said Dillman, "I don't think he could keep anything to himself. The whole ship would know within hours, and that must never happen. It would make my job much more difficult. I work best by stealth."

She nodded vigorously. "I knew that you were somebody special," she said, "but I had no idea that it was this."

Dillman put a finger to his lips. "Let's not talk about it now."

"But it means that I'll get my flute back sooner or later."

"With luck."

"Oh, I trust you, Mr. Dillman," she said, eyes glistening with a mixture of awe and deference. "You can do *anything*."

It was a touching vote of confidence but it showed that the problem of Polly Goss had not gone away. Circumstances were such that it had become more complex. Before, she had been an impressionable young woman who was attracted to a handsome man. Now she was in love with the notion that he was a brilliant detective engaged in solving crimes. Dillman was determined not to let her down but he did not relish her veneration of him. Yet she had made an apt comment on the situation. Claude Vivet loved music as much as she did. He would never steal an instrument from someone with whom he enjoyed playing so much. As a suspect, Claude Vivet began to fade into the background.

Having given his services for free, Claude Vivet wanted only the reward of meeting the royal party. When the meal was over, he was escorted to their cabin by Martin Grandage so that he could receive their congratulations. Fife was full of praise for the exceptional quality of the dinner, and his daughters were equally complimentary. The Princess Royal confined herself to a nod of agreement at what was said by the others. Vivet bowed, grinned, and rubbed his hands gleefully together.

"You like my *Bavarois au chocolat*?" he asked.

"It was excellent, Monsieur Vivet," said Fife.

"We could eat it at every meal," added Lady Maud.

Vivet chuckled. "I think, maybe, it is too rich for that." He looked at the two empty chairs. "But where are the other guests? Did they not enjoy my meal?"

"Yes," said Fife. "Very much."

"I hope to meet them to hear what they have to say."

"Mrs. Wilmshurst was feeling unwell so they left early."

Vivet was alarmed. "Unwell? The lady eat something that she not like?"

"No, no," said Fife. "Nothing like that. She enjoyed every mouthful. I think that she was feeling a trifle off-color. Mrs. Wilmshurst will be fine after an early night."

"Look, this is ridiculous," Nigel Wilmshurst said angrily. "Open this door and let me in."

He was perplexed. When they had got back to their cabin, his wife had locked herself into the bedroom and refused to come out. She would not even speak to him. Wilmshurst had first reasoned with her, then pleaded, then offered all kinds of blandishments.

Nothing would coax her out. Pushed to the limit, he fell back on a threat.

"I could easily break this door down, you know," he warned. "Is that what you want me to do, Araminta? Do I have to force my way in?"

"Leave me alone," she said, sobbing quietly on the other side of the door. "Just go away, Nigel."

"But I'm your husband."

"I don't want to see you."

"Why?" he said, slapping the door. "At least give me an explanation."

"Stop hounding me," she implored.

"But I've a right to know what's going on. You've been in a peculiar mood all evening. I go to all the trouble of arranging a dinner with the Duke and Duchess, and what happens? My wife behaves appallingly." He pounded the door. "It's not good enough, Araminta. I demand to know what's going on. Are you ill or something?"

"No, I'm not ill."

"Then there's absolutely no excuse for what happened back there. We were their guests. What must they think of us? You put me in a most embarrassing situation."

"That makes two of us."

"You'll have to write a letter of apology to them." He then heard what she had just said. "'That makes two of us?'" he repeated. "What do you mean?"

"You lied to me, Nigel."

"No, I didn't."

"You misled me completely."

"About what?" He gritted his teeth. "Oh, no! We're not back to that, are we?"

"I wanted to know the truth."

"I *told* you the truth, Araminta."

"You told me what you wanted me to hear."

He was indignant. "Are you saying you doubt my word?"

There was a long pause. "I went to see her," she confessed.

"What?" he yelled.

"I went to see Genevieve Masefield."

"Whatever for?"

"Because I wanted to talk to her. I wanted to know what sort of person she was."

"I explained that to you, Araminta."

"But you didn't explain why you kept looking at her," she argued. "I wondered if she still had some hold over you. Yes," she went on as she heard him snort with disgust, "you may think it was stupid of me. But I needed to know that you were all mine."

"Of course I am," he said. "Genevieve Masefield means nothing to me."

"I think it may be the other way around."

"Why? What did she tell you?"

"That it was she who actually broke the engagement."

"That's a damn lie, Araminta!"

"But she had no reason to lie," said his wife. "If things had happened the way you told me, she'd have been ashamed. Yet she wasn't. Miss Masefield was dignified. She behaved as if she'd done nothing wrong."

"She's certainly done something wrong now," he asserted. "Can't you see what she's trying to do, Araminta? This is her revenge. She wants to drive a wedge between us. Because I threw her over, she wants to blight my happiness with another woman." There was another long pause. "Araminta? Why don't you say something?" More silence. "Listen, who are you going to believe? A scorned woman, or your husband?"

"I don't know what to believe," she admitted.

"Then open this door and let me tell you the full story."

"No, Nigel."

"You must. I can't stay out here all night."

"Genevieve Masefield was not 'a scorned woman,'" she said. "And she wasn't trying 'to drive a wedge between us.' She advised me time and again to leave before I heard something that I shouldn't. But I didn't, Nigel. I goaded her until she eventually told me the truth. It was Miss Masefield who broke off the engagement, wasn't it?"

"Don't be absurd!" he retorted. "Why on earth should she do that?"

"That's what I want you to tell me."

It was Wilmshurst who fell silent now. He was simmering with impotent rage.

Dillman elected to take a closer look at Roland Pountney, and there was no better way to do that than to express interest in the scheme he was trying to promote. When dinner was over, the two men sat together in the first-class lounge.

"It was Mr. Goss who aroused my curiosity," explained Dillman. "I don't think that he's ready to invest any money of his own in the venture, but I'd certainly like to hear more about it."

"Then you shall, Mr. Dillman," Pountney said with a warm smile. "You shall. How much do you know already?"

"Very little beyond the fact that it concerns a hotel in Cairo."

"The New Imperial Hotel. It's set to become the biggest and—though I do say it myself—the best of its kind in Egypt. Given the way the tourist trade has increased in recent years, it could turn out to be a gold mine."

"Then why don't you keep details of it to yourself?"

"Two reasons, old chap. First, I'm a generous fellow who likes to spread good news among selected friends. Second—and this is more important—I don't have sufficient capital to buy the stake that I'd really like. In short, I have to get funds from elsewhere. So I'm taking the hat around a series of small investors in order to increase the size of my stake. What the investors get is a guaranteed return on their money. All that I take from their dividend is a five-percent commission, which, in the circumstances, I feel is owed to me."

"I agree," said Dillman. "What are the precise details?"

Pountney gave a faultness presentation. He had details of the scheme at his fingertips and was able to meet every question with a convincing answer. It was his persuasive manner that alerted Dillman. The man's salesmanship was too smooth and well rehearsed. Pountney sensed his doubt.

"Yes, I know," he said. "It sounds too good to be true. If you wish to know more, I can show you the preliminary plans for the hotel and the forms relating to the share issue. Everything is in my cabin. Better still," he continued, "if you still think I'm trying to pull the wool over your eyes, speak to Sir Alistair Longton."

"I just might do that, Mr. Pountney."

"He was even more skeptical than you, at the start."

"But he has committed himself?"

"Oh, yes," said Pountney. "I told him that he could reserve his judgment until he actually saw the site but he insisted on pressing money upon me there and then. So did other people. I've already tucked away hundreds of pounds in the purser's safe."

Dillman was interested by the revelation. The money that Pountney had deposited had not been stolen from any of the passengers; they had willingly parted with it. Yet the detective still had lingering worries about Roland Pountney.

"What's the minimum investment?" he asked.

"Fifty pounds, Mr. Dillman."

"And the maximum?"

"I'd have to cap it at five hundred," said Pountney with a laugh, "or people will want to have a bigger slice of the cake than me. We can't have that, can we? Let's face it. I saw this opportunity first. I should reap the major rewards."

Dillman chatted with him for a few more minutes until they were joined by some other friends of Pountney's. The detective excused himself and headed for the door. On the way, he passed Genevieve Masefield, who was seated with Myra and Lilian Cathcart. By tugging at the cuffs of his shirt, Dillman signaled to Genevieve that he would meet her later in her cabin. He then went off toward the staircase.

The talk with Pountney had given him plenty to occupy his mind and he was still sifting through their conversation when he reached the main deck. There was a clicking noise at the far end of a passageway, then a head emerged furtively to check that nobody was about. Dillman stepped quickly into an alcove so that he would not be seen. The door opened fully, then shut. Footsteps could be heard departing. Dillman peeped out in time to see a uniformed figure disappearing around the corner.

It was Brian Kilhendry.

Myra Cathcart had handled the whole thing well. Schooled by Genevieve, she had returned the photograph to Herr Lenz over dinner and told him that she resented the sly way in which it had been taken. Lilian supported her mother, pointing out that other passengers who had been tricked into facing his camera might well have lodged an official complaint with the purser. Lenz could do nothing but apologize. Realizing that his pursuit of Myra Cathcart was now doomed, he tried to make amends with excessive politeness. Genevieve did her best to engage him in conversation, preventing him from causing Myra any more discomfort and probing for more information about his background. Of the suspects she had discussed with Dillman, the German photographer seemed to her to be the most likely. From the derisive laugh he had given when she'd mentioned the name of Walter Dugdale, she could see that his envy went deep.

When they adjourned to the lounge, Myra felt that she had

finally shaken off the attentions of the brooding Lenz, and she thanked Genevieve for her advice. Lilian, too, felt that—among the three of them—they had put him to flight. Myra did not expect to have another meal in Lenz's company. When Dillman walked past her, Genevieve talked with her friends for another ten minutes or so before excusing herself. She went swiftly back to her cabin and, once inside, removed her earrings and necklace before taking off her gloves.

Genevieve was pleased that she had been able to help Myra Cathcart dispose of an unwanted suitor, especially as he might have been the person who killed his rival. She was still trying to weigh the evidence against Lenz when there was a tap on the door. Expecting Dillman, she opened it immediately but she stared into the glowering face of Nigel Wilmshurst instead. He pushed her back into the cabin and followed her.

"Get out!" she demanded.

"Not until we've had a talk," he said, closing the door behind him. "Somebody has been telling tales to Araminta, haven't they?"

"Your wife forced her way in here as well. Does neither of you have any manners?"

"What did you tell her, Jenny?"

"That's between the two of us."

"Not when it concerns me," he warned, advancing slowly toward her. "Now, tell me. I want to know everything that was said."

"Then why don't you ask your wife?"

"I need to hear it from you."

Genevieve tried to push past him in order to reach the door but he grabbed her wrist and held it tight. Wilmshurst was smoldering. She started to become alarmed.

"Let me go," she cried. "You're hurting my wrist."

"I'll do more than that if you try to play games with me." He forced her down into a chair before releasing his grip. "For the last time," he said, "what did you tell her?"

"I simply defended my name."

"What name?" he sneered. "You don't *have* a name, Jenny. You have no position at all in English society. But I do, and I'll fight tooth and nail to retain it. Your family were nonentities," he said. "They made their money in trade. I was foolish even to get involved with someone like you, from the lower orders."

"I'd like you to go, Nigel," she said calmly, "before this gets out of hand."

"It already *is* out of hand."

"I didn't ask your wife to come here."

"Maybe not, but you didn't turn her away, either."

"I made every effort to do so. I had no reason to cause her harm."

"No," he said, looming over her. "I was the real target, wasn't I? You probably couldn't believe your luck. You finally had a chance to strike back at me."

"I've never had the slightest desire to do that."

"Well, that's what you've done, whether you intended to or not. Araminta is in a terrible state. And all because of the poison that you poured into her ear."

"I told her nothing that was untrue, Nigel," she said, trying hard to maintain her composure. "Unlike you, I didn't willfully mislead her. You weren't the person to break off our engagement— I was. And we both know why."

"Did you tell her?" he pressed. "Did you go into details?"

"No. I didn't need to do that."

"If I find out that you explained what—"

"I explained nothing," she said, interrupting him. "Beyond the fact that you were the guilty party and not me. But it's only a matter of time before she finds out your little secret, Nigel. I hope, for her sake, that she doesn't do so in the way I did."

"Be quiet!"

"No woman wants to share her husband with other men."

"I told you to be quiet!" he howled, threatening to strike her.

Genevieve put up her hands to protect herself. "Well, you must be so pleased with yourself," he taunted. "You've hit back at me and wounded Araminta in the bargain. I always took you for a person of discretion but you've obviously coarsened since I last saw you."

"There's no need to insult me, Nigel."

"*I'm* the one who's been insulted—by you!"

"Yes, I suppose that the truth is pretty insulting. No wonder your wife looks at you through new eyes. She can't trust you any longer, Nigel. You told her a pack of lies."

"We were very happy until you came along."

"And so was I," she said.

"Who cares about your happiness?"

"I do, Nigel."

"Well, I don't," he said with contempt. "And I'm not going to let you do this to me. For heaven's sake, I'm supposed to be on my honeymoon."

"You conveniently forgot that when you started harassing me."

"I did nothing of the kind."

"You sought me out, Nigel. Admit it," she challenged. "So did your wife. I had no reason to get near either of you. If there's friction between you—as is obviously the case—then you brought it on yourself. Don't try to blame me."

"But you're the one who stuck the knife into me, Jenny."

"Only after you'd stabbed me in the back. How do you think it feels to be accused like that by your wife? She looked at me as if I were some kind of harlot. And all because you told her that I'd been unfaithful to you. That was cruel of you, Nigel," she said. "It was cruel, hurtful, and unjust."

"What about the things you told Araminta?"

"She forced them out of me."

"Well, I'm going to force them back into you," he promised, grabbing her by the arms to haul her upright. He shook her hard. "You can begin by apologizing to me," he insisted. "Then you can come and say how sorry you are to Araminta for misleading her. You can explain that what you told her was a pack of lies."

"But it wasn't."

"Don't argue with me!"

"Let go, Nigel," she said, struggling to break free. "Let go of me."

"Promise that you'll do what I say, first."

"Never!"

"Promise!" he ordered, slapping her across the face.

The shock of being hit was far worse than the pain. It took Genevieve a moment to realize what had happened. When she did, she fought hard to push him away. But he was far too strong for her. Crazed by anger and stung by his wife's rejection of him, Wilmshurst would not be denied. He wrestled with Genevieve until the two of them fell to the floor and rolled across the carpet. He pinned her to the ground and put his face an inch from hers. She could see the mingled hate and disgust in his eyes. What frightened her was a strange glint as lust stirred. Lying on top of her, Wilmshurst had her at his mercy. Genevieve put all her energy into an attempt to force him off.

"No!" she shouted. "Leave me alone, Nigel. Get off!"

SIXTEEN

When he walked along the passageway, Dillman first made sure that he was unobserved before he approached her cabin. He gave a sharp tap on the door and expected a fairly quick response. Instead, there was a protracted silence. Convinced that Genevieve was inside, he put his ear to the door and heard muffled sounds. It was almost as if someone were drumming their heels on the floor. Dillman then heard a man's voice, yelling in pain, followed by the sound of a scream from Genevieve. He did not hesitate. Putting his shoulder against the door, he gave a concerted shove. The lock rattled. When he heard further noises of a struggle from within, Dillman took a step back before hurling himself at the door with full force. This time, the lock gave way and the door burst open.

The scene that confronted him made Dillman blink in astonishment. Sitting astride her, Nigel Wilmshurst was holding Genevieve down with one hand while using the other to muzzle her. She was resisting fiercely but unable to escape. Spurred into action, Dillman was on the attacker in an instant, grabbing him by the shoulders to drag him off her, then hauling him to his feet so that he could pound him with a relay of punches. Wilmshurst tried to defend himself but he was no match for the detective. Having drawn blood and subdued him, Dillman helped Genevieve up from the floor and across to the chair. She was badly shaken.

Wilmshurst saw an opportunity to slink away but Dillman was too quick for him, reaching the door first and closing it before standing with his back to it. He had to control the urge to pummel Wilmshurst even more. Blood dribbling from his nose, the other man tried to summon up a note of authority.

"Who the hell are you?" he demanded, using a handkerchief to stem the flow of blood. "And what do you mean by barging in here like that?"

"My name is George Dillman and I'm a ship's detective."

"That doesn't give you the right to attack me."

"It gives me every right," said Dillman, putting a hand on his arm. "I'm placing you under arrest, sir. You'll have to come with me."

"Arrest?" echoed Wilmshurst in disbelief. "On what charges?"

"Assault, for a start. Did you invite this man into your cabin, Miss Masefield?"

"No," she said, still panting from her ordeal.

"Then he must have forced his way in here. That's a second charge."

"Get your hand off me," said Wilmshurst, trying in vain to brush him away. "Have you any idea who I am?"

"Yes, Mr. Wilmshurst," said Dillman, tightening his grip. "You're someone who's in a great deal of trouble. I'm just hoping that you'll resist arrest so that I'll have an excuse to finish what I just started. Don't tempt me, sir."

"The captain will hear about this."

"He certainly will, Mr. Wilmshurst. He's a stickler when it comes to behavior aboard his vessel. He'll not condone what I just saw." He turned to Genevieve. "How are you feeling now?"

"I'm fine," she said, rubbing a bruised arm. "Thank goodness you came."

"I heard someone yell."

"He had his hand over my mouth. I bit it."

"Look," said Wilmshurst, realizing the difficulty of his position and trying to ease the situation, "there's no need to take all this so seriously. Jenny and I are old friends. We were just indulging in a little horseplay, weren't we, Jenny?"

"No, Nigel. That was not horseplay."

"Tell this fellow that you've no intention of pressing charges."

"But I have," she affirmed. "Believe me."

"Let's go, Mr. Wilmshurst," said Dillman.

"Wait. You've got hold of the wrong end of the stick. All right," said Wilmshurst, adopting a conciliatory tone, "I did get carried away, I confess that freely. We dined with the Duke and Duchess this evening and the wine was rather heady. I obviously had too much. I'm sorry, Jenny, I really am. I swear it. Let's forget the whole thing, shall we?" he suggested. "For the sake of old times."

"No," she said. "What you did was unforgivable."

"That's the view I take," said Dillman.

"Who asked for your opinion?" snapped Wilmshurst.

"I'm a witness, sir. I know what I saw."

"This is between Jenny and me."

Genevieve turned away in disgust. "I never want to see you again."

"It was all a dreadful misunderstanding."

"Yes," agreed Dillman. "You misunderstood the basic courtesies. Men are not supposed to force their way into a lady's cabin in order to attack her. It's considered impolite. Now," he said, "are you going to come quietly or do I have to drag you out?"

"Where are you taking me?"

"To the master-at-arms. You'll spend the night in a cell."

"That's monstrous!"

"So was your assault on Miss Masefield."

"Jenny," he pleaded. "You can't let this happen to me. I can't be locked up."

"It's the best place for you, Nigel," she said.

"What about my wife?"

"What about her?" said Dillman.

"She'll be expecting me."

"She may be expecting a husband, sir, but I doubt if she'd welcome back a man who's just committed the offenses that you did. Out we go," said Dillman, twisting Wilmshurst's arm behind his back. He turned to Genevieve. "I'll be back as soon as I've put him where he belongs. Come on, sir."

Protesting wildly, Wilmshurst was forced out of the cabin without ceremony.

Brian Kilhendry was astounded. He could not believe what his deputy had just told him. The two men were in the purser's cabin later that night. The atmosphere was heated.

"Mr. Dillman *arrested* him?" he said.

"Yes, Brian. Mr. Wilmshurst is cooling his heels in one of our cells."

"Does Mr. Dillman realize *who* Mr. Wilmshurst is?"

"I think that he knows only too well," said Martin Grandage.

"His father is Lord Wilmshurst."

"Mr. Dillman doesn't care if his father is the emperor of China. He put Mr. Wilmshurst under arrest and, from what I heard, had every reason to do so. I applaud what he did."

"Well, I don't, Martin. There'll be repercussions."

"Our duty is to support the ship's detective."

"Ordinarily, I'd agree," said Kilhendry, "but this is a special case. Mr. Wilmshurst is very well connected. He and his wife dined with the royal party last night."

"I'm well aware of that. I was the one who had to keep our chefs from trying to lynch Monsieur Vivet. He prepared a meal for six people but, when we got to the cabin, Mr. and Mrs. Wilmshurst had left." He gave a shrug. "They could at least have stayed long enough to compliment the chef. Monsieur Vivet was put-out."

"I'm put-out as well, Martin. This business is very worrying. We need an extremely good reason before we put anyone under lock and key."

"Mr. Dillman had a good reason," said Grandage.

"I disagree."

"He attacked Miss Masefield. Do you condone assaults on our staff?"

"Of course not. But then, Mr. Wilmshurst probably doesn't know that she's employed by P and O. He believes she's just another passenger. From what you tell me, they're old friends."

"They were engaged to be married at one stage."

"There you are, then," said the purser. "This is a domestic dispute that shouldn't involve us at all. Mr. Dillman exceeded his authority. He should have released Mr. Wilmshurst with a warning and let him return to his own cabin."

"Why?" Grandage said waspishly. "Was his wife waiting to be assaulted as well?"

"Martin!"

"It's a fair point. Damn it all, they're supposed to be on their honeymoon. What sort of husband deserts a beautiful young wife to wrestle on the floor with another woman? There's no way you can whitewash this, Brian."

"That's not what I'm trying to do."

"Then stop blaming Mr. Dillman. I think that he acted correctly."

"Well, I don't. Tomorrow morning, there'll be hell to pay."

"Only if you side with Mr. Wilmshurst."

"Passengers have certain rights. We can't simply arrest them on impulse."

"There was strong provocation in this case," argued Grandage. "Lord knows what would have happened if Mr. Dillman hadn't arrived when he did. I think it's time you stopped riding him, Brian."

Kilhendry bridled. "What do you mean?"

"You know quite well. You've been on his back since he joined the ship."

"Only because I wanted to make sure that he did his job."

"There's more to it than that," said Grandage. "You've resented him because he used to work for Cunard. Don't you think it's time you got rid of that particular chip from your shoulder? Just because you were rejected by Cunard when you applied for a purser's job, you don't have to carry out a vendetta against their former employees."

"That's not what I'm doing."

"Yes it is, Brian."

"You know nothing about it."

"I know more than you think. You have a phobia about people who worked for Cunard. In George Dillman's case, of course, he committed a second unforgivable sin in your eyes: He was born in America."

"Don't remind me."

"Then don't punish him for something that wasn't his fault."

"Shut up, Martin."

"It happened years ago," Grandage said reasonably. "Don't you think it's time to forgive and forget? You can't tar a whole nation with the same brush. All right, you had a hellish time. I can see that. You were treated abysmally. Does that mean you have to behave so badly toward Mr. Dillman? Grow up, man. Shrug it off."

"It's nothing to do with you," Kilhendry said defensively.

"It is if it affects the running of this ship."

"Mr. Dillman was too hasty. He should have used more discretion."

Grandage was sarcastic: "What was he supposed to have done?"

he asked. "Wait politely outside the door until Genevieve Masefield was raped?"

Dillman held her in his arms for a long time before he spoke.
When he had arrived back at her cabin, Genevieve was still thoroughly jangled by the experience. All that she wanted was the
comfort of his arms and the reassurance of his presence. There had
been no tears. She was too annoyed with herself, wondering why
she had been foolish enough to open the door of her cabin without
first checking to see who the caller was. Profoundly grateful for the
timely arrival of Dillman, she looked up at him with a wan smile.

"Is there anything I can get you?" he said.

"No, thank you, George."

"Some brandy, perhaps?"

"I feel fine, now that it's over."

"Do you feel up to telling me what happened?"

"I think so," she said, gently breaking away from him. "Though
it all went so fast, it's something of a blur. . . . After you gave me a
signal in the lounge, I waited for ten minutes before coming back
here. Almost immediately, there was a knock on the door."

"And you assumed that it was me."

"Yes, George. Unfortunately, it wasn't. It was Nigel. I'd never
have expected him to call on me at that hour," she explained. "He
and his wife had been dining with the Duke and Duchess. I
thought they'd all still be together."

"Why weren't they?"

"Because of what I said, apparently."

"What—to Mrs. Wilmshurst?"

"That's right. At least, that was the accusation he hurled at me.
Nigel claimed that I was trying to wreck his marriage by telling
lies to his wife."

"But you only told her the truth."

"Part of the truth," she said, "and I only did that because she goaded me into it. Why on earth did she have to come here in the first place? Why not simply ignore me?"

"I can answer that, Genevieve," he said fondly. "You're a gorgeous woman. Any wife would feel threatened by you if she knew that you'd been close at one time to the man she'd married. What brought her here was a mixture of curiosity and fear."

"And a certain amount of arrogance," recalled Genevieve. "She treated me with such disdain, as if I belonged to a lower order of creation. I wasn't standing for that," she said, with spirit, "and I let her know it."

"Quite rightly."

Genevieve pondered. "I wonder," she said at length.

"You couldn't let Mrs. Wilmshurst talk to you like that."

"Perhaps not, George, but I took no pleasure in hurting her. When I told her that I was the one who'd broken off the engagement, she was rocked. Mrs. Wilmshurst left here in a daze. I felt almost sorry for her." Her voice hardened. "Then she had a row with Nigel and he came here in search of revenge. I've never seen him so angry. He blamed me for everything. He demanded that I apologize to him and to his wife."

Dillman was shocked. "He wanted you to admit that *you* were in the wrong?"

"He ordered me to lie about what happened between us. To pretend I was the guilty party. Nothing could make me do that," she said. "Since I knew that you'd be coming soon, I tried to keep him talking as long as possible. But Nigel lost his temper. He just threw himself at me. You know the rest."

"Not quite, Genevieve."

She shook her head. "I don't know," she said, reading the question in his eyes. "I don't know if that's what he would have done. There was a moment when I feared that might happen, but I don't think that even Nigel was capable of that. He'd have been too worried about the consequences," she decided. "Even in that

253

state, he'd have realized that he'd have lost his wife for good if he'd gone any further."

"He went well beyond the limit, as it is," said Dillman.

"I can't tell you how thankful I am, George." She went back into his arms and he hugged her. Genevieve looked up at him. "Where is he now?"

"Locked up safely in a cell."

"What about his wife?"

"That's no concern of yours, Genevieve."

"But it is," she said, easing herself apart from him. "Lord knows, I don't approve of what he did, but he is her husband. Mrs. Wilmshurst will be wondering where he is. If he's away all night, she's bound to get terribly upset."

"I thought of that," explained Dillman. "That's why I asked Mr. Grandage to slip a note under the door of her cabin. It won't give any details of what happened in here. It will just say that her husband is being detained because of drunken behavior."

Genevieve was rueful. "If only that's all it was!"

"It was a factor, there's no doubt about that. In the cold light of day, of course," he went on, "Mrs. Wilmshurst is going to learn the ugly truth."

"Only if I press charges."

"But you must, Genevieve. He assaulted you."

"Let me sleep on it."

"He deserves to be punished."

"To some extent, he already has been," she pointed out. "You beat him black-and-blue, George. I could see how much you hurt him. And a night behind bars will be a real humiliation for someone like Nigel."

"So it should be," he said. "Show him no mercy."

"It's his wife that I keep thinking about. She'll suffer as well."

"The decision is up to you, Genevieve. But you know my feelings."

254

"I do. I'm still very confused by it all. Give me time."

"Of course."

"Thank you." She kissed him on the cheek then lowered herself into a chair. "Well," she said, "this has all been a distraction. When you came here this evening, you weren't expecting to have to rescue me like that."

"No, I came to talk about the other crimes that have been committed."

"Then let's do that, shall we? I saw you in the lounge with Roland Pountney."

"Yes," he said. "Mr. Pountney troubles me. When I'm listening to him, I feel as if I'm acting in a play with someone who's taken a role so often that he knows the lines perfectly. All I had to do was to provide him with his cue."

"Could he be our man, George?"

"He'll certainly bear more scrutiny."

"I wonder why he was expelled from Harrow."

"I have a feeling that we'll find out in due course," said Dillman. "I also think that there's one avenue we haven't fully explored. If, as I believe, something was stolen from Mr. Dugdale's cabin after he was killed, there may be a way of finding out what it was."

"How?"

"By asking a person he invited in there."

"Frau Zumpe?"

"She may have seen something, Genevieve, or he may have mentioned a valuable item that he kept in his cabin. I know it will be tricky," he said, "asking a woman what happened during a tender moment, but it's the only option we have."

"I agree. I'll be happy to speak to Frau Zumpe."

"Good. It may give us the break we need."

"While we're on the subject of German passengers," she said, "I still think we should keep Herr Lenz under observation. There's something very odd about that man."

"I'm glad that you mentioned him."

"Why?"

"Because of something that happened when I left the lounge," he said. "The thief has been able to get in and out of cabins at will. That means either he can pick a lock very easily or—much more likely—he has a master key. Only two people have master keys to all the cabins."

"The purser and the chief steward."

"Exactly. Imagine my surprise, then, when I saw Mr. Kilhendry sneaking out of a cabin on the main deck earlier on. He looked so furtive. I made a note of the cabin number and checked it against my list. Who do you think it belongs to, Genevieve?"

"Karl-Jurgen Lenz?"

"The very same," he said. "Now, why should the purser be calling on him?"

Araminta Wilmshurst spent a sleepless night alone. After she heard her husband storm out of the cabin and slam the door behind him, she began to have misgivings about the way she had locked him out of the bedroom. She waited for him to return but he never came. Instead, a note from the deputy purser was slipped under the door. Araminta was appalled to learn that her husband had been arrested because of drunken behavior.

When he had walked out on her, she decided, he had turned to alcohol for solace—and had far too much of it. Araminta felt that she was partly to blame. Overcome with guilt, she wanted to go to her husband but she knew that he would hate to be seen in such circumstances. All that she could do was to lie on the bed and brood about the way their honeymoon had suddenly turned sour.

Next morning, when she heard a knock on the door, she bounded over to it.

"Nigel?" she asked.

"No," said a guttural voice. "It is Karl-Jurgen Lenz."

"Oh, I see."

"I wish to arrange a time for the photograph, Mrs. Wilmshurst."

"Not now, Herr Lenz."

"I can speak with your husband, please?"

"This is not a convenient moment," she said, anxious to send him on his way. "My husband is not here, I'm afraid. He'll get in touch with you when we've made a decision. Good-bye, Herr Lenz."

"Good-bye."

There was a long pause before she heard his heavy footsteps retreat down the passageway. Araminta was consumed with embarrassment. How could she and her husband even contemplate having their photograph taken when there was so much unresolved hostility between them? What would people think of the couple when they discovered that he had been locked up in a cell for the night? Araminta felt lost, lonely, and utterly bewildered. The cruise was turning into a nightmare.

She went back into the other room and sat disconsolately on the bed. It was all her fault, she decided. If she had not been impelled to confront Genevieve Masefield, none of these unpleasant consequences would have happened. Thanks to her, a rift had opened in the marriage and she had no idea how to close it. She heard a key being inserted in the lock and rushed into the sitting room. Nigel Wilmshurst let himself into the cabin and stood despondently before her. His face was bruised, his eye black, and his shirt stained with blood. There was a hangdog expression on his face.

"Nigel!" she cried, embracing him. "What happened to you?"

George Porter Dillman had never enjoyed any of his visits to the purser's office but the one he paid this morning was particularly uncomfortable. Without even consulting him, Brian Kilhendry had gone over his head.

"You released Mr. Wilmshurst?" Dillman said angrily.

"I'd never have locked him up in the first place."

"He assaulted Genevieve Masefield."

"Then he needed to be cautioned and sent back to his cabin," said the purser. "That's what I did this earlier this morning. You can thank your lucky stars he's not going to sue you for grievous bodily harm."

"I only used necessary force."

"He claims that you beat him to a pulp."

"The man was attacking Genevieve," retorted Dillman. "I couldn't let him do that. Don't you care if a member of your staff is set on like that?"

"Of course. I take it very seriously."

"Then why do you side with the attacker and not the victim?"

"I side with nobody until I've heard the full facts of the case."

"But you already have, Mr. Kilhendry. I was a witness."

"Yes," said the other, "but your version of events doesn't quite accord with the one I had from Mr. Wilmshurst. What I really need to hear is Miss Masefield's account. It's up to her whether or not charges are pressed."

"The man deserves to be locked up for the rest of the voyage."

Kilhendry was offhand. "That may be how you did things on Cunard, Mr. Dillman," he said, "but we try to handle things with more tact on the P and O. And there's another consideration. Mr. Wilmshurst has friends in high places. The last thing we want is bad publicity."

"Are you telling me that you're *afraid* of him?" Dillman challenged.

"Not at all. I just prefer to tread carefully. You should do the same."

Dillman was fuming. "If I hadn't intervened last night, my partner might have been seriously injured and perhaps even sexually assaulted. I witnessed the attack," he emphasized. "How was I supposed to 'tread carefully' in that situation—ask Mr. Wilmshurst if he needed some help?"

"There's no call for sarcasm," said Kilhendry.

"You should have talked to me before you even thought of releasing him."

"I make the decisions on my ship, Mr. Dillman."

"Does Mr. Grandage approve of what you've done?"

"Leave him out of this."

"In other words," concluded Dillman, "he doesn't. He has some notion of loyalty to his staff. Follow your code and we'd let people like Mr. Wilmshurst run riot at will. What does he have to do before you sanction his arrest—assassinate the Princess Royal?"

"A night in the cell sobered him in every sense," said Kilhendry. "He's deeply sorry for what happened and is prepared to make a full apology to Miss Masefield."

"He committed a criminal act against her."

"Then it's up to her to take the matter further, Mr. Dillman. You can huff and puff all you like. Until I've spoken with her, the sensible thing is to release Mr. Wilmshurst so that he can go and explain things to his wife. Have you considered her?"

"Yes," said Dillman. "I asked Mr. Grandage to put a note under her door."

The purser was offended. "Why wasn't I told?"

"Perhaps he felt that you'd overrule him."

Kilhendry stared at him with undisguised dislike. He was quite unrepentant about what he had done. Dillman met his gaze without flinching. Ever since they had met, the purser had put a series of obstacles in his way. Though Kilhendry exhorted the two detectives to solve the crimes that had been committed, he did nothing to help them. Now that someone had actually been arrested, Kilhendry had seen fit to release the man.

"There's something else, isn't there?" Dillman said quietly.

"I don't know what you mean."

"Oh, I think you do, Mr. Kilhendry. It's not just the fact that we used to work for Cunard. For some reason, that puts us in your bad books straightaway. But there's something else as well. It's to do with me."

"I warned you that I don't have the highest opinion of your nation."

"That's unfortunate," said Dillman, "because I have great respect for the Irish. At least, I did until I met you. Most of the Irishmen I've encountered have been friendly, outgoing people. You're the opposite. Why is that?"

"I can be friendly and outgoing with people I care about."

"That seems to cover almost everyone on board except Genevieve Masefield and me. I've even seen you being nice to the other Americans on board," noted Dillman. "You turn on that Irish charm of yours like a faucet. Why do we never see it?"

"Because you've done nothing to deserve it yet," said Kilhendry.

"I made an arrest. That's what I'm paid to do."

"But this case is not as simple as it looks. It transpires that there's some history between Mr. Wilmshurst and your colleague. At one time, it seems, they were engaged to be married. According to him, some provocation was involved."

"He forced his way into her cabin."

"So did you, Mr. Dillman. There's a broken lock to prove it." He turned his back. "So why don't you leave it to me to sort out this mess? You should be out there hunting the real criminals we have on board." Kilhendry faced him again. "What are you waiting for?"

Genevieve Masefield was still undecided about whether or not to press charges. Though she had been frightened at the time by the assault, she had recovered quickly and no longer felt as vengeful as she did at first. If she had been dealing with Nigel Wilmshurst in isolation, she would have had no qualms about demanding formal action against him, but there *was* his wife to consider. Even though Araminta had made some scathing comments about her,

Genevieve felt sympathy for the woman. Araminta would have been mortified to hear of her husband's arrest. Wilmshurst himself would have been thoroughly chastened. When she gave her statement to the purser, therefore, Genevieve said that she needed more time for reflection before she reached a decision. During the course of the morning, she devoted a lot of thought to the problem but no easy solution presented itself.

Hoping to speak to Frau Zumpe, she was unable to find the woman until luncheon and by then it was too late. Dillman had assigned her another task. Genevieve was to sit beside Roland Pountney throughout the meal and keep him distracted while her partner searched the man's cabin. Both detectives agreed that Pountney had to be considered a major suspect. When she sat opposite him, Genevieve knew that she might be looking into the eyes of a killer.

"How nice to see you again, Miss Masefield," he began. "I had the feeling you were dodging me."

"Whatever gave you that idea?" she asked.

"Oh, this and that. One senses things."

"I've no reason to keep out of your way, Mr. Pountney. As you see, here I am."

"And very welcome, at that!"

They shared a table with the Cheritons and the Braddock sisters. Genevieve was happy to be part of a wholly British contingent though she was disconcerted by the hopeful smiles that Elizabeth Braddock kept shooting in her direction. She was desperate to give the two sisters some good news about the theft from their cabin but she was not yet in a position to do so. Genevieve concentrated on her main purpose.

"How did you get into the business world, Mr. Pountney?" she asked.

"By accident, I suppose," he replied. "When I left Oxford, I suddenly found myself without any immediate means of supporting myself. I was sent down, you see," he confided with a grin. "Expelled from Harrow, sent down from university. Not the most promising start to a career, is it? But we Pountneys are made of stern stuff."

"What happened?"

"An uncle of mine came to the rescue. He had a thriving business, selling antiques in London, and took me under his wing. That was it, really," he said. "I turned out to have a flair for the work. He taught me about how and when to invest, how to set profit margins, and how to recognize a situation where you can make a real killing. After a couple of years, I felt able to branch out on my own."

"Into antiques?"

"No, I moved into another field. If you can sell one thing, you can sell them all."

"You've done remarkably well for someone of your age."

"I had plenty of incentive," he said. "My father despaired of me when I was kicked out of university. He'd funded me for so long, I felt that I owed him a reward of some kind so I turned over a new leaf. And here I am," he announced, spreading his arms. "No blotches on the family escutcheon for a decade. I'm proud of that."

"When did you first start traveling abroad?"

"Ah, that was the real stroke of fortune, Miss Masefield."

"Why was that?" asked Genevieve.

"Because it taught me that I was being too parochial in my outlook."

"You're one of the least parochial people I've ever met."

"Thank you," he said. "I take that as a compliment. And now, I suppose, you'd like to hear exactly how that stroke of luck came about."

"Only if you wish to tell me, Mr. Pountney."

He laughed. "I'm afraid that you wouldn't be able to stop me."

Dillman forsook his own meal in order to search the cabin. Worried that Genevieve was uncertain about pressing charges against Nigel Wilmshurst, he tried to put the whole matter out of his mind while he concentrated on the task at hand. Instead of asking the purser for a master key, he had gone straight to the chief steward, who, aware that Dillman was investigating a murder, gave him the key without hesitation. The detective was grateful. Kilhendry would have been far less cooperative and, since the purser was now under suspicion himself, Dillman wanted to keep clear of him.

He did not waste any time. After making sure that Pountney was in the dining room, he went to the man's cabin and let himself in with the master key. The place was impeccably tidy. Whenever Dillman touched anything, therefore, he took care to replace it exactly as he had found it. Pountney was an enigma. Though the latter had a plausible explanation for the money he had deposited in the purser's safe, Dillman was not entirely sure he should believe him. What would not have been handed over to Kilhendry was any of the jewelry that had been stolen, not to mention the Egyptian relics and the silver flute. If Pountney was the thief, the booty would be hidden in the cabin.

The search was swift and methodical. He went through the closet, the bedside cabinet and the drawers in the dresser. He even lifted up the mattress to see if anything was concealed beneath it. Dillman found nothing incriminating. Pountney's briefcase also yielded no proof of actual wrongdoing. The documents relating to the New Imperial Hotel appeared to be in order and there was the map of Cairo with the exact location marked on it. Dillman put it all back in the briefcase before replacing it on the spot from where he had taken it. He was coming to accept that his instinct had let him down for once, when he stepped into the bathroom. He opened the cabinet then checked every item arrayed on a shelf above the washbasin. None of it was in any way suspicious.

As a last resort, Dillman lay flat on the floor and peered under the bathtub. His hopes soared. Something had been wrapped in a piece of waterproof material and stuffed into the far corner. He had to extend his arm fully in order to retrieve it. When he unrolled the package, the first thing he saw was a passport.

"Now, then," he said, picking it up, "what do we have here?"

Genevieve was forced to wait in order to speak to Frau Zumpe. For some time after luncheon was over, Sir Alistair Longton monopolized the German woman, talking to her in the corner of the lounge and showing her some paperwork. As soon as he departed, Genevieve went across to Frau Zumpe. The latter was blunt.

"You have found my money yet?" she asked.

"No," admitted Genevieve, "but we are very close to retrieving it, along with other things that were stolen. All that we need are a few more tiny pieces of evidence. I'm hoping that you can provide one of them."

"Me?"

"I want to ask you something about Mr. Dugdale."

"Oh," said Frau Zumpe, her face softening into a smile. "You were good to me, Miss Masefield. You let me talk about him. Thank you."

"I'd like you to talk a little more, please."

"Is very painful."

"I understand that, Frau Zumpe, but this is very important."

The other woman glanced around the lounge. It was too full of people to allow a really private conversation. Frau Zumpe suggested that they go back to her cabin, where there was no danger of being overheard. They set off together.

"You put me in the difficult position, Miss Masefield," she said.

"Did I?"

"Yes, I talk to Sir Alistair Longton. He tells me that he has invested a lot of money in this new hotel in Cairo. He calls it a golden opportunity. I would like to buy some shares myself," explained Frau Zumpe, "but how can I when I have no money to pay for them?"

"Is that what you told Sir Alistair?"

"No, I remember what you say. I do not mention the theft."

"Thank you, Frau Zumpe. I appreciate that."

"But I will not go on lying about it forever."

"I don't think that you'll need to," said Genevieve.

They reached the cabin and Frau Zumpe let her in. The last time Genevieve had been there, the other woman had been in a sentimental and confiding mood. She might not be quite so forthcoming now. Genevieve resolved to proceed with care.

"Do you still miss him?" she said.

"Yes, I do. I think of Walter every day."

"At least you had some time together, Frau Zumpe."

"It was too short," the other said resentfully. "He was snatched away from me."

"I know."

"We understand each other, you see. Lots of men, they have no interest in a woman like me, but he was different. Walter was my friend. I never meet him before, yet I feel I know him a long time."

"That was the effect he had on me as well," said Genevieve.

"So what you wish to ask about him?"

"Did he discuss his business with you at all?"

"Not really," said Frau Zumpe. "He wanted to talk about me."

"Yes, but earlier that night, Mr. Pountney was talking to both of you about his venture in Egypt. Mr. Dugdale was a businessman. He must have offered an opinion on the scheme," said Genevieve. "Did he encourage you to invest?"

"He said that I should find out a lot more details first."

"Did he have any reservations?"

"Walter tell me that he has doubts about Mr. Pountney, that is all. When we were alone, we did not give him or his hotel a second thought. We had too much to talk about."

"In his cabin?"

"Yes, Miss Masefield."

"Did you notice anything when you were there?"

Frau Zumpe was baffled. "What you mean?"

"Was there anything unusual in the cabin?" asked Genevieve. "Anything that was very special and worth a lot of money? Think hard, please. I need to know."

"I was not there to search his cabin."

"I understand that."

"We just wanted to be alone," said Frau Zumpe. "Walter is very dear to me. He make me feel like a woman for the first time in years. Do not laugh at me for that."

"I wouldn't dream of it."

"He liked me. He trusted me."

"I can see that, Frau Zumpe."

"Walter proved it," the other said proudly. "I am the only person on the ship who knows about it. He did not show it to anyone else but me."

"What did he show you?"

"His album, Miss Masefield. He collected stamps. He tells me that he has one of the finest collections in the world. That was what I see," she said. "His stamp album."

Though they took care to leave the lounge separately, Sir Alistair Longton and Roland Pountney met up on the staircase to the main deck. Longton was cheerfully optimistic.

"Brought her to water," he said. "All she has to do now is drink."

"Don't waste too much time on Frau Zumpe. I think she has cold feet."

"Have to warm them up for her, Roland."

"What about Mr. Goss?"

"Oh, I think we can forget about him. Not interested in money."

"Silly man!" said Pountney, as they reached the deck and walked along the passageway. "By the way, had George Dillman been in touch with you?"

"Not yet. Why?"

"He could be a possible. I told him to sound you out."

Longton smiled. "He's an American. They all have money."

"Mr. Dillman may be good for a couple of hundred, at least." They stopped outside a door. "I could see that he was interested so I gave him the full treatment."

"Even *I* would fall for that, Roland." Longton chuckled merrily as he inserted his key into the lock. "Just imagine the look on their faces when they find out the truth!"

He opened the door and they stepped into the cabin. Both of them came to a halt when they saw that someone was already there, lounging nonchalantly in a chair.

"Come on in, gentlemen," said Dillman. "I've been waiting for you."

SEVENTEEN

Warmer latitudes not only brought passengers out on deck for longer periods, it enticed them to shed some of the winter garments with which they had set out. Heavy overcoats, fur hats, fur muffs, thick scarves, and woolen gloves gave way to lighter wear. With the coast of North Africa now visible from the starboard side of the *Marmora,* people had the idea that they were slowly closing in on their destination. Most of them had never been to this part of the Mediterranean before, so it had an exotic appeal for them. The royal party was also much more in evidence, moving freely around the deck and no longer the object of intense scrutiny by others. With a hot sun hanging in a cloudless sky, few passengers were troubled by nostalgia for the cold, damp, windswept British Isles that they had abandoned to spend Christmas in milder climes.

Two of the passengers were unable to share in the pleasure of watching the distant coastline and feeling some warmth on their faces at last. They were seated in the deputy purser's office with

Dillman standing behind them. Unlike most apprehended criminals, Roland Pountney and Sir Alistair Longton did not seem at all disturbed. They were as relaxed and affable as if they were resting in the lounge. Martin Grandage could not understand their attitude.

"Aren't you ashamed of what you did?" he said.

"Not in the least," Pountney replied airily. "We have to make a living."

"But not by preying on innocent people. You sold shares in a company that doesn't even exist. People trusted you."

"That was the beauty of it, Mr. Grandage. I knew that they'd need more than my word to convince them so I referred them to someone who had complete faith in the scheme. And so he should," he said, smiling at his companion, "because he helped to dream it up."

"Confidence tricksters often work in pairs," noted Dillman.

"Yes," said Grandage, looking at Sir Alistair, "but it's rare to find that one of them is a member of the British peerage."

"He's not. This is what put me on to him." Dillman handed over a passport. "As you'll see, Sir Alistair Longton's real name is Alistair Pountney. He's been traveling on a false passport so that's another offense to take into account. In other words, Mr. Grandage, you have a father and son sitting in front of you."

Pountney grinned. "A family enterprise," he explained.

"Not any longer," said Grandage.

"We had a good run. It was bound to end sooner or later."

"Yes," added his father. "In this business, you must always be prepared for the tap on the shoulder. I'm delighted that it was administered by Mr. Dillman. He's a man with style. The last time we were caught it was by some heavy-handed London constables. It was a relief to be arrested by a gentleman."

"I'm glad you weren't foolish enough to resist arrest," said Dillman.

"What would have been the point?" asked Pountney. "There

was nowhere for Father and me to hide. Once you'd found our little cache, we were doomed."

Dillman's search of his cabin had been a revelation. Apart from the passport, which had disclosed the older man's true identity, Dillman had found documents relating to another bogus scheme, and clear evidence of complicity between the two men. Startled when they found him waiting for them, they had chortled happily when told that their run was over. The hundreds of pounds that had been charmed out of various billfolds could be returned to their rightful owners, who would realize that the paperwork issued by Pountney was utterly worthless. Dillman had exposed a clever fraud.

"I had my doubts about Mr. Pountney from the start," Dillman admitted, "but the name of his accomplice came as a surprise. Sir Alistair—Mr. Pountney Senior—had persuaded me that he really did see military service in India."

"And so I did," the old man said proudly. "I spent three years on the North-West Frontier with the rank of major. What I omitted to tell you, however, is that I was cashiered." He chuckled to himself. "They finally discovered why the funds from the officers' mess were being drained. Arrest by the army. Not a pleasant experience. You were much more courteous, Mr. Dillman."

"Thank you," said the detective.

"We applaud you," said Pountney. "You beat us at our own game. Neither of us suspected that the debonair George Dillman was actually a detective. Well done!" It was a sincere compliment. "Now you can see why I had to keep up the tradition," he continued. "Father was booted out of the army for stealing. I was expelled from Harrow for selling things that did not actually belong to me, then sent down from Oxford over a betting coup that I devised during Eights Week." He laughed at the memory. "The master of my college was rather upset when he realized that I'd tricked ten guineas out of him."

"You won't be tricking money out of anyone else for a long

time," warned Grandage, "and I'm sorry that you treat the whole thing as a huge joke."

"We enjoy our work, old chap."

"Well, I enjoy mine as well. Especially when I can hand over two criminals to the master-at-arms." Grandage opened the door and spoke to the burly sailor outside. "Take these gentlemen to the cells, please, Mr. Dyer," he said. "They are expected."

Roland Pountney and his father rose from their seats and insisted on shaking Dillman's hand before they left. Imprisonment seemed to hold no fears for them. They went off cheerfully. The deputy purser closed the door behind them.

"What did you make of that, Mr. Dillman?"

"I've never met anyone before who actually enjoyed being arrested."

"What was the idea?" asked Grandage. "Did they intend to pay for their holiday in Egypt by cheating our passengers out of a large amount of money?"

"No," said Dillman, handing him the package he had found under the bathtub, "when you have time to sift through this, you'll find that they had return tickets to England on another P and O ship. On the way back, they'd intended to sell shares in a nonexistent British company."

"But for you, they'd probably have got away with it. This is a real feather in your cap, Mr. Dillman. When he hears about this, the purser will be mightily impressed."

"He wasn't too impressed by my last arrest."

"Ah, yes," said the other. "Mr. Wilmshurst. I'm bound to say that I think Brian took the wrong action there."

"Does he often do that?"

"No, he doesn't. In fact, the two of us rarely disagree on things like that. Because I'm his deputy," said Grandage, "I have to back him to the hilt. Most of the time, I'm happy to do that. Brian Kilhendry rarely makes a mistake."

"He certainly made one where Nigel Wilmshurst was concerned."

"Miss Masefield can still press charges against him. What has she decided?"

"Genevieve is still mulling it over," said Dillman. "She knows where I stand on the issue but it's not up to me. What's holding her back from taking the matter any further is concern for Mrs. Wilmshurst."

"Yes, I feel sorry for her as well," said Grandage. "She's a young bride on her first trip abroad. How is she going to cope with all this?"

"That depends on what her husband tells her. I doubt if it will be the truth."

The Duke and Duchess of Fife examined the photograph in their cabin. It was a striking group portrait. Karl-Jurgen Lenz had delivered it but he was peeved when he was not allowed to hand it over in person. Instead, Mr. Jellings had thanked him, taken it from him, then given it to his employers. Even the Princess Royal was pleased.

"It's a lovely photograph of the girls," she observed.

"And an even better one of their mother," said Fife. "I know that Herr Lenz was a nuisance but he's produced a remarkable result. It was worth all that delay."

"For us, maybe, Alex."

"What's that?"

"I don't think that Mr. and Mrs. Wilmshurst will want a copy of this."

"Why not?" Peering more closely at the photograph, he clicked his tongue. "Dear me! I see what you mean, Louise."

"Mr. Wilmshurst looks so strained."

"What about his wife? She could be facing a firing squad, not a camera."

"It was their idea to invite Herr Lenz in the first place."

"Yes," said Fife. "Wilmshurst will regret it when he sees this photograph. They're on their honeymoon," he reminded her, "yet the curious thing is that they don't look as if they're together. Why is that?" He stroked his mustache. "I wouldn't mind being a fly on the wall in their cabin just now."

Nigel Wilmshurst was in a sorry state. Even though he had washed and shaved, his face still bore the marks from the fight with Dillman. His pride was even more wounded. It was afternoon yet he was still in his dressing gown. Neither he nor his wife had ventured outside their cabin all day, having had their meals served in private. Given his battered appearance, Wilmshurst was not willing to be photographed by anybody, and Lenz was dispatched for the second time when he called again. All Wilmshurst wanted to do was to lie low and avoid all company.

Araminta was more bewildered than ever. Prompted by feelings of guilt, shame, anger, relief, and betrayal, she was not sure how she ought to react. What she also felt was an overwhelming sympathy for her husband. In the past, his confidence had always been unassailable, yet now he seemed wary and hesitant. She decided that the kindest thing she could do was to wait until he was ready to tell her the full story of what had occurred. If she pressed him for details, it would only add to his discomfort. Most of the time was therefore spent in a hurt silence. It was eventually broken by Wilmshurst. Slumped in a chair, he glanced across at his wife.

"I'm sorry," he said. "I'm so dreadfully sorry, Araminta."

"It was partly my fault."

"No, it wasn't. I brought this on myself. If I'd told you the truth at the start, none of this would have happened. We'd have been able to enjoy our honeymoon."

"We *did* enjoy it, Nigel," she said. "For a time, anyway."

"I lost control," he confessed. "When you locked me out of the bedroom last night, I was seized with a desire for revenge. *She* was responsible for it. She was the person who'd come between us. I had to confront her."

Araminta was aghast. "You went to Miss Masefield's cabin?"

"Only to warn her to stop spreading lies about me."

"Did she let you in?"

"I made her," said Wilmshurst, adjusting the facts to present himself in a more favorable light. "I told her how unhappy she'd made you and demanded an apology."

"And did you get one?"

"Not exactly."

"You shouldn't have gone to see Miss Masefield like that," she said, "especially when you'd lost your temper. Anything could have happened. And why tell her that we were having difficulties? That was entirely our affair. Nobody else need have known."

"They already did, Araminta. Have you forgotten how you brought the dinner party to a sudden end?" he asked. "When you charged out like that, the Duke and Duchess must have thought you'd gone mad. They certainly won't have any illusions about us."

"It was the last straw, Nigel," she said, shaking her head in dismay. "When you raised your glass to toast me, I felt something snap inside me. I simply had to get out of there. But I did as you said," she continued. "I sent them a note of apology."

"It will take rather more than that to clear the air, I'm afraid."

"Go on telling me about Miss Masefield."

"There's not much more to tell."

"You still haven't explained how you got those injuries to your face. In that note from Mr. Grandage, it said that you'd been involved in drunken behavior. Did you fall and hurt yourself?"

"Not quite," he replied. "Jenny—Miss Masefield—took exception to my demand and sent for the ship's detective. He tried to hustle me out. I'm not used to that kind of treatment so I resisted strongly. That's when I got these bruises."

"You should complain to the purser."

"I've already done so, Araminta."

She became thoughtful. "You say that Miss Masefield sent for this man. Why was that, Nigel? Why didn't she just ask you to leave?"

"I told you. I was in a state. I was determined to get what I wanted."

"So you refused to go from her cabin?"

"In effect."

"That was a terrible thing to do, Nigel. Wasn't she frightened?"

"Of course," he said, "and rightly so. I let her see just how angry I was."

"You must have upset her a great deal if she had to call in a detective to have you removed. It was wrong of you to stay," she said. "I know how I'd feel if someone forced his way in here when I was on my own. It would be terrifying."

"I only went to reason with her, Araminta."

"Refusing to leave is not very reasonable behavior."

"I hoped that you'd be on my side!" he cried in exasperation.

There was a long pause. She looked at his battered face again and felt a surge of sympathy. Remorse displaced all other feelings. She could not blame him for rushing off to confront Genevieve Masefield when she had done exactly the same herself. Araminta was not deceived. She knew that he was not giving a full account of what had happened, but that did not matter. Nigel Wilmshurst was still her husband. The vows she had made at the altar bonded them indissolubly together. What he needed most at that particular moment was love and support. Crouching beside him, she put an arm around his shoulders. He responded with a weak smile.

"Araminta," he said tentatively, "I need to ask a very big favor of you."

Claude Vivet was in an irrepressible mood. He was still basking in the praise from the royal party. After giving himself the pleasure of criticizing the luncheon fare, he spent half an hour at the piano in the music room. Genevieve Masefield met him as he was leaving. She had to submit to the inevitable kiss on the hand.

"I have lost my friend with her flute," he complained. "Miss Goss, she had the sore throat and it hurts her to play."

"I'm sorry to hear that, Monsieur Vivet."

"So am I, Miss Masefield, but I am not surprised. The food on this ship is getting worse. That is what gave her the pain in the throat. Those Italian chefs, ha!"

"Everyone else seems to enjoy the meals," said Genevieve.

"Only because they have not tasted one prepared by me." He gave a bow. "Last night, I cook for the Duke and Duchess. They tell me they have never eaten so well. I show them how a dinner should be prepared."

"I'm glad that they were duly appreciative."

"If I was English," he boasted, "I would be knighted for my services in the kitchen. But then," he added with a grin, "if I was English, I would be a very poor chef."

"That's unkind, Monsieur Vivet."

"Honesty often is unkind."

"There's a difference between honesty and opinion," she argued.

"But my opinions are *always* honest."

"That doesn't mean that you're right."

He gave a teasing laugh then put his head to one side as he appraised her. "Ah!" he sighed, "it is such a pity that you will not be staying in Egypt. I would love to show you all of the sights, Miss Masefield."

"But you'll be working at a restaurant, Monsieur Vivet."

"I would find time for you," he said. "Have no fear."

"I'll have to explore Egypt another time," she said. "My ticket is taking me all the way to Australia. What sort of cuisine shall I expect there?"

"Nothing but the kangaroos, cooked over an open fire."

Genevieve laughed. "I don't think it's quite that primitive."

"Beside France," he declared, "everywhere in the world is primitive."

"Then why did you agree to leave Paris?" The question seemed to catch him off-guard and he was lost for an answer. "Why go to Egypt when you have such a following in France?"

"Because I need the new challenge. I will not stay there long."

"Are you going back to Paris afterward?"

"Maybe, maybe not. I have to see." He grinned broadly. "The one place I will not go is Australia. When they want the meal there, they have to go out and shoot it. You would be better off in Cairo with me."

"Thank you for the offer."

He kissed her hand, clicked his heels, and departed. Genevieve reminded herself of the fierce row the little Frenchman had had with Walter Dugdale. What rankled with Vivet was that the American had vilified both his country and his culinary skills. The chef was deeply patriotic. Such insults would have cut deep. Genevieve considered the possibility that it was Vivet who had cornered the murder victim in his cabin but she soon dismissed the notion. Dugdale never would have let him in, much less turned his back on the angry Frenchman. They had to look elsewhere for their killer.

She returned to her cabin with some trepidation. To get to her door, she had to go past the cabin occupied by the Wilmshursts and she feared that one or both of them would emerge in time to see her. Her fears were groundless. She reached her cabin without incident and, since the lock had now been repaired, used her key to let herself in. A sealed envelope lay on the floor. Pushed under her door, it bore her name in a neat hand. Genevieve picked it up and tore open the envelope. When she took it out, she was astonished to see who had written the letter. It was from Araminta Wilmshurst.

Polly Goss grew tired of promenading around the deck with her mother. Vexed by the loss of her flute, she was also fascinated to see what Dillman was doing to recover it. The revelation that he was a detective had made him even more appealing to her. Now that she had a legitimate excuse to go in search of him, she decided to do so.

"I'm going in, Mother," she said.

"Then I'll come with you," offered Rebecca.

"No, no. You stay out here. You're enjoying the fresh air. I want to read."

"As long as you don't disturb your father."

"He won't even know I'm there."

"He's still working on those lectures of his," said Rebecca, "and wondering what on earth he's going to say to the museum about those stolen artifacts."

"But he'll have them back by then," insisted Polly.

"How do you know?"

"Mr. Dillman will find them—and my flute. I'm certain of it."

Her mother wagged a finger. "Now, I don't want you bothering Mr. Dillman."

"I wouldn't dream of it, Mother."

"He has enough on his plate without you getting under his feet."

"I won't go anywhere near him," said Polly, moving away. "Good-bye."

But she did not go in the direction of her cabin at all. In spite of her denial, she wanted to find Dillman, to see if he had made any progress. A search of the public rooms would come first, then she would scour the other decks. If necessary, she told herself, she might even have to go to his cabin. The prospect was exhilarating.

They met in the passageway not far from the first-class smoking room. Since there was nobody else about, it seemed safe to have a private conversation. Brian Kilhendry gave a grudging smile.

"I believe that congratulations are in order, Mr. Dillman," he said. "Because of you, a pair of dangerous confidence tricksters are behind bars."

"Until you release them, that is," Dillman said wryly.

"They'll only be released into police custody."

"Then Nigel Wilmshurst should be with them."

"That matter's been resolved," explained the purser. "Miss Masefield came to see me a short while ago and said that she'd decided not to press any charges against him." He saw Dillman's surprise. "She didn't discuss it with you, I see. Perhaps she doesn't value your opinion as much as I thought. The main thing is that we can close the file on the whole business."

"If you say so, Mr. Kilhendry."

"You don't agree, obviously."

"Let's just say that I'm preoccupied with other things at the moment."

"Arresting those two men was an excellent start," said Kilhendry. "Now we have to find the thief and the killer. I'm certain that they're different people."

"And I'm equally certain that the crimes are linked."

"Are you any closer to catching this mystery man, Mr. Dillman?"

"A lot closer," said the detective. "I'm slowly eliminating suspects until only one is left. Roland Pountney was on my list at one time but he wouldn't stoop to something as obvious as stealing from other people's cabins. To him and his father, crime was a form of art. They reveled in their work."

"They're reveling in separate cells at the moment."

"I'll have another prisoner for the master-at-arms soon."

"As long as it isn't Mr. Wilmshurst."

"No," said Dillman, "it will be one of three men."

"Who is the prime suspect?"

"Someone I think you know, Mr. Kilhendry."

"And who's that?"

"Karl-Jurgen Lenz." Dillman saw his eyes flicker with embarrassment. "Yes," Dillman said. "I didn't realize that you were on such familiar terms with him."

"I'm not."

"Then why did I see you sneaking out of his cabin?"

Kilhendry gulped.

"Maybe you were right. Maybe I am looking for two people, after all. One to steal and one to provide the master key to a cabin."

The purser was defiant. "Are you accusing *me*?"

"When you stepped out of Herr Lenz's cabin, you more or less accused yourself."

"I didn't go there to see him," said Kilhendry.

"Then why did you go?"

"To show you up, Mr. Dillman. A murder had been committed. Day after day went by with no sign of progress, so I thought I'd take a hand in the investigation. You'd told me that Herr Lenz was a possible suspect," he said, "so I used a master key to get in, and searched his cabin. I was hoping to find enough evidence to have him arrested. Then, I must admit, I was going to crow over you."

"But you didn't find any evidence?"

"None at all. His cabin is full of photographic equipment. There's nowhere he could have hidden the stolen items." He shrugged. "The cupboard was bare."

"Why didn't you tell me this?" asked Dillman.

"Frankly, I was too embarrassed. How would you have felt if you knew I was trying to beat you at your own game?"

"I think I'd have been rather amused. You pitted your nose against my brain. It could be a close contest, Mr. Kilhendry. But, seriously," Dillman went on, "you could have saved me the trouble of keeping Herr Lenz under scrutiny. He could have been crossed off the list much sooner."

"I know," conceded the purser. "I should have owned up."

"I'm glad that you've now done so. I can cross you off the list as well."

Kilhendry was hurt. "Did you really think me capable of theft and murder?"

"For a time," said Dillman. "Then I remembered how wedded you are to your job. You wouldn't risk losing it by robbing your passengers. You're too professional. And don't ask me who else is under suspicion," he added as the purser was about to speak, "because I'm not saying. You'd only try to get to him first."

"Oh, no. I learned my lesson. I won't try to compete with you again."

"Does that mean you'll support me for a change?"

"I'll do more than that," said Kilhendry. "If you find out who's behind all these crimes, I won't simply be the first to pat you on the back—I may even be forced to look at Americans in a more friendly light."

He flashed a grin and walked off, leaving Dillman to wonder if he was indeed finally starting to win the purser's respect. Without it, the rest of the voyage would continue to be punctuated by arguments between the two men.

Dillman was due to meet Genevieve soon so he walked toward his cabin. Disappointed to hear that she had elected not to press any charges against Wilmshurst, he hoped it might not be too late to change her mind. When he got to his cabin, he was alarmed to see that Polly Goss was waiting outside the door like a sentry. She rushed up to him.

"I knew that you'd come here eventually," she said. "Any news, Mr. Dillman?"

"No," he said, "but the trail is getting warmer."

"When can I expect to get my flute back?"

"When I find it. Now, you must let me get on with my work, Miss Goss," he said, crossing to the door of his cabin. "If I track it down, you'll be the first to know. For the moment, you'll have to excuse me."

"But I came to tell you something," she said. "About my father's Egyptian relics."

His ears pricked up. "Go on."

"Well, when you first talked to him about the theft, I was too busy crying in my own cabin. I never had the chance to speak to you. My father tells me that you wanted the names of anyone who knew that those little stones were in his cabin."

"That's right. Apart from myself, the only other person in whom he confided was Sir Alistair Longton," he said, concealing the man's real identity from her, "and I can give you a categorical assurance that he was not the thief."

"But he wasn't the only person who knew the relics were there, Mr. Dillman."

"Who else was there?"

"To be honest, I'd forgotten we'd even mentioned it. It was only a remark in passing and I thought no more of it. Mother was there, as well," she said, "so it was as much her fault. We should have told you earlier."

"Told me what?"

"Someone else did know that Father had those things in his cabin."

"It was your accompanist, wasn't it?" guessed Dillman.

"That's right," she confirmed. "Monsieur Vivet."

Nigel and Araminta Wilmshurst were drinking tea in their cabin when the deputy purser called. Though he had some reservations about the decision that had been made, Martin Grandage passed on the news with an easy smile.

"I thought you'd like to know that Miss Masefield is not pressing charges, sir."

Wilmshurst rallied. "Are you sure?"

"Absolutely, sir," said Grandage. "You're off the hook."

As soon as he had gone, Wilmshurst turned to his wife and smiled for the first time that day. Araminta was as relieved as he was, but she had not forgotten the supreme effort of will it had cost her to write a letter of abject apology to Genevieve Masefield. While it may have achieved the desired effect, it had left her feeling slightly degraded. There was little sympathy in her voice.

"Now," she said, fixing her husband with a stare, "I think I'm entitled to hear the whole truth. Why exactly *did* Miss Masefield break off her engagement to you?"

She was punctual. When he let her into his cabin, Dillman gave her a welcoming kiss.

"Under the circumstances," he said, "I thought it would be safer to meet here."

"I don't think that Nigel will dare to cross my threshold again," said Genevieve. "I had a letter from his wife, apologizing for the way that both of them behaved toward me. He'd obviously made her write it."

"Is that why you dropped the charges?"

"Yes, George. I want to put the whole thing completely behind me."

"But he attacked you."

"I survived. He didn't go unpunished," she argued. "Nigel spent a night in solitary confinement and I daresay he has a lot of bruises to nurse. You hit him very hard."

"I intended to, Genevieve," he said. "Is there no chance you'll reconsider?"

"None."

"Fair enough."

"Don't look so downhearted," she said. "Mr. Kilhendry told me that you made two arrests: Mr. Pountney and his father. I'd never have guessed they were working together. Sir Alistair seemed so genuine."

"A genuine scoundrel," he said. "However, we've got more important things to discuss. *They* may be out of action but the killer is still at liberty. I want him *today,* Genevieve. Did you manage to question Frau Zumpe?"

Genevieve nodded. She told him about her chat with the woman and the discovery that Walter Dugdale was a keen philatelist. As well as building up his own collection of stamps, he had established such a reputation in the field, that he had been invited to lecture to other enthusiasts.

"He showed Frau Zumpe his watch," she said. "It was presented to him by the Chicago Philatelic Association. The initials were on the back: 'C.P.A.' Mr. Dugdale also told her that he was going to speak to a couple of associations in Perth. That will explain the initials you found in his address book. One was 'W.A.P.' That stands for 'Western Australia Philatelists.'"

"In that case, P.B.S. must stand for Perth's Best Stamps."

"You're close, George," she said. "I made a point of asking Frau Zumpe about the initials. P.B.S. is short for 'the Penny Black Society.' They're extremely rare stamps and Mr. Dugdale had two of them in his collection. Frau Zumpe saw them. Did you know that the first adhesive stamps were issued in Britain, in May 1840?"

"No, Genevieve, I didn't"

"The older the stamp, the more expensive it is to buy."

Dillman snapped his fingers. "I *knew* he had something worth stealing in that cabin," he said. "I'm just surprised he didn't keep his album in the safe."

"But he did. That's the interesting thing," she said. "Mr. Dugdale took it out during the day so that he could enjoy looking at it, then had it locked up again last thing at night. On the night in question, apparently, it remained in his cabin."

"And so did Frau Zumpe."

"I didn't press her on that point."

"I suspect that Mr. Dugdale may have done so," said Dillman.

"It's quite clear from his address book that stamps were not the only things he collected. I think it's time we retrieved that album, don't you?"

She was astonished. "You know where it is, George?"

"I think so." He opened the door. "Let's go and ask for it back."

Claude Vivet read the letter several times before putting it on the table to smooth out the fold in the stationery. Written in the Princess Royal's own hand, it thanked him for the superb meal he had cooked and wished him well in his future career. The Frenchman was content. His work had won royal approval and he could use the letter as a reference. He was so busy staring at the elegant calligraphy that he did not hear the first tap on the door. A louder knock sent him across to open it. Vivet was taken aback when he saw Dillman and Genevieve outside.

"May we come in, Monsieur Vivet?" Dillman asked politely.

The Frenchman was defensive. "Why?"

"Because we need to speak to you. Miss Masefield and I work for P and O as detectives and we've reason to believe that you can help us with our inquiries." Dillman raised an eyebrow. "It's not a request, sir."

"You wish to talk to me?" Vivet said with a look of injured innocence. "What am I supposed to have done?"

"We'll tell you inside," said Genevieve.

Vivet stepped back so that they could enter the cabin then he closed the door behind them. He offered them a seat but they preferred to remain on their feet. While Dillman did the talking, Genevieve looked around for possible hiding places.

"Certain items have been stolen on the ship," said Dillman, "and, taken together, they're of considerable value. In addition to money, a quantity of jewelry was taken, along with some Egyptian artifacts and a silver flute."

"A flute?" he repeated.

"Belonging to Miss Polly Goss."

"But I play the piano with her in the music room," Vivet protested. "I love music. Why would I wish to take her flute away from her?"

"Because it can be easily sold," said Dillman. "Also, of course, since you did show an interest in Miss Goss, you would be the last person we'd even consider as the thief. You could take the flute with impunity."

"And these other things—what do you call them?"

"Egyptian artifacts, Monsieur Vivet. Relics of an ancient civilization. The sort of thing that antiques dealers in Cairo would pay a lot of money for. We believe that's where you intend to dispose of them."

"I am no thief, Mr. Dillman," pleaded Vivet. "I am only a chef."

"You're much more than that, I fancy," suggested Genevieve. "You're a pianist, a raconteur, and a talented actor. You took great care to attract attention to yourself so that we would all dismiss you as a ridiculous egotist. But that was only a mask."

"This is very insulting to me, Miss Masefield."

"Don't stand on your dignity, sir," said Dillman. "It's not only the thefts that we've come to discuss with you. There's the murder of Walter Dugdale as well."

"Murder?" Vivet slapped his thigh. "Someone did me a favor and killed him?"

"Don't pretend that it's the first time you've heard about it."

"But it is, Mr. Dillman. First I am a thief. Now, I am a murderer also." He spread his arms. "What else do you wish to accuse me of?"

"We need to search your cabin," said Dillman.

"I insist," Vivet said angrily, opening the door of the closet and pulling out the drawers in the dresser. "Look anywhere you wish. Take the cabin to pieces. And when you do not find anything, I will expect you to apologize to me on your bended knees."

Dillman looked hard into his eyes. The injured innocence had been replaced by a calculating stare. Vivet was urging them on so that he could humiliate them. Dillman's eye fell on the letter on the table. Vivet snatched it up.

"Here, look at this," he cried, thrusting it at Dillman. "It is a letter of thanks from the Princess Royal. She knows my true worth. She does not call me a thief or a murderer. She respects me."

"Excuse us, Monsieur Vivet," said Dillman, backing to the door. "I can see that we don't need to search your cabin, after all."

"Why not?" asked Genevieve.

"Because he's much too cunning to hide anything in here, Genevieve. Come on."

"Where are we going?"

"To the place where Monsieur Vivet *has* stored his booty."

Most of the passengers on the *Marmora* had taken luggage with them that was not wanted on the voyage itself. Marked as such, it was stored in the hold. The royal party had a special arrangement. A large storeroom on the main deck was set aside solely for their luggage, so that they could have access to it at any time. Having borrowed the key from Mr. Jellings, the two detectives let themselves into the room. It was packed with trunks, valises, and assorted bags. All of them were ticketed as belonging to the Duke and Duchess of Fife.

Genevieve was puzzled. "Why have we come here, George?"

"Because it's the only way he could get the stuff safely off the ship," said Dillman. "Monsieur Vivet knows that his bags will be searched at Port Said so he's taking no chances. The only people whose luggage will not be touched are the Duke and Duchess. It has the same immunity as diplomatic baggage," he explained, starting to search among the trunks. "All that Monsieur Vivet has to do is to reclaim his haul once it's been waved through customs."

"I hope that you're right about this, George," she said, still unconvinced.

"No wonder he was ready to cook a meal for them. They're

doing Monsieur Vivet a much bigger favor. They're taking his stolen goods ashore."

"Unless we can find them."

"Oh, they're here, all right, Genevieve. I feel it in my bones. Help me search."

They moved trunks, lifted valises, and shifted the various other items the royal family had felt were necessary on their vacation in Egypt. Dillman looked for a bag that was different in color and type from the others. When he finally found it, it was tucked away behind the largest of the trunks. He hauled it out. Protruding through the top of the bag was a long object that was wrapped in a piece of thick cloth.

"I'll bet that's Polly Goss's flute," he said.

"What about Mrs. Prendergast's money?" asked Genevieve.

"That will be here. So will everything stolen from Frau Zumpe and the Braddock sisters. Then there's Mr. Dugdale's stamp album— that is worth a small fortune. My guess is that the haul would have been even bigger by the time we reached Port Said." He felt inside the bag. "Ah, this is what I was expecting to find."

"The Egyptian relics?"

"Still in their cotton wool, Genevieve. All safe and sound."

"That's more than I can say for you, Mr. Dillman," said a voice from behind them. "And don't think I'm afraid to use this gun, because I've already done so once."

They had not heard Martin Grandage coming into the room, closing the door gently behind him. Holding a revolver on them, he took a few paces forward. His voice was cold and peremptory.

"Now, take your hand out of the bag, Mr. Dillman," he ordered. "That's stealing."

"You'd know all about that," said the detective, removing his hand but keeping a few of the stone fragments in his palm. "You and Monsieur Vivet made an excellent team. You let him into the cabins and he did the rest. Then you hid everything in here."

"You should have let us get away with it."

"We couldn't do that, Mr. Grandage. We have standards."

"That was your trouble, Mr. Dillman," said the other. "You and Miss Masefield were too tenacious. I thought we could shake you off, but you wouldn't give up, would you?"

"Now I see why you pretended to be so helpful to us," said Genevieve. "It meant you could keep an eye on everything we did. You only asked us to act as unofficial bodyguards for the royal party because it would keep us distracted from you and your accomplice."

Grandage smiled. "The plan worked beautifully, at first."

"Did it have to involve killing Mr. Dugdale?"

"No, Miss Masefield. That was forced upon me, I'm afraid. Mr. Dugdale found out something that threatened the whole scheme, so he had to be removed. Also, he'd insulted my partner and I couldn't allow that. When I took him his precious stamp album one day, I also took this," he said, holding up the gun. "All I had to do was to club him from behind when he turned his back. If I'd let you take out the album, Mr. Dillman, you'd have seen that it had bloodstains on it."

"So do you, Mr. Grandage," said Dillman. "All over your hands."

"I'm not in the mood for metaphors."

"You must have thought you had the perfect system. As deputy purser, you had knowledge of where best to strike, and a master key to get into the cabins. What let you down was Monsieur Vivet's vanity," said Dillman. "He simply *had* to show off by cooking that meal for the royal party."

"I arranged it for him," said Grandage. "The evening was a great success."

"Not really. Your accomplice had a letter of thanks from the Princess Royal. He waved it in my face. It was then I realized how he'd get the stolen items off the ship. In short, Mr. Grandage," he said, "that meal was a mistake. Indirectly, it gave the game away."

His palm tightened around the stone fragments. "What do you intend to do with us?" he asked.

"Silence you, of course," said Grandage, with venom. "Like this."

He moved quickly forward, raising the gun to dash it down against Dillman's skull, but the detective had anticipated the attack. He hurled the stones into the other man's face and caused a momentary distraction. It gave Dillman the chance to grab the wrist that was holding the gun. The two men grappled fiercely. Grandage still held the weapon but Dillman managed to twist the barrel upward and away from him. Genevieve did not stand idle. Snatching up a large valise, she swung it hard and struck Grandage on the back of the head. The gun went off with a deafening *bang* in the confined space but the bullet lodged harmlessly in the ceiling.

Dazed by the blow from behind, Grandage was soon overpowered by Dillman. Though he tried to fight back, the deputy purser was at a disadvantage. The detective was bigger, stronger, and fueled by anger. Dillman disarmed him, punched him until he begged for mercy, then stood over him.

"You're a disgrace to that uniform, Mr. Grandage," Dillman said with contempt. "I'm glad that you'll never get the chance to wear it again."

Everyone was delighted to have their property restored to them. Mrs. Prendergast sobbed with relief, the Braddock sisters were overjoyed, and Frau Zumpe was so pleased that she gave Genevieve an impromptu kiss of thanks. When he visited the Goss family, Dillman chose to take his partner with him, explaining that Genevieve had been working covertly with him to solve the theft. It was also a polite way of telling Polly Goss that he was not, after all, traveling alone on the ship. Happy to have her flute back, she was saddened to realize that her fantasies about Dillman had no hope of fulfillment. It was Morton Goss who was the most grateful.

"A thousand thanks, Mr. Dillman," he said, nursing his stone fragments. "And to you as well, Miss Masefield. I can't tell you what it means to have these relics back. You've saved my professional life."

"Then it's a fair exchange," said Dillman, "because they helped to save our lives."

Brian Kilhendry was both shocked and humbled. Having boasted about his ability to sniff out criminals, he was compelled to admit that he had been working alongside one without having the slightest suspicion. The arrest of Martin Grandage, and the revelation that his deputy was a killer, had badly shaken him. He watched with deep embarrassment as Grandage and Claude Vivet were locked in separate cells. His discomfort was even greater when he gave a full report to the captain. By the time he summoned the detectives to his office, he was feeling very jaded but he was prepared to give credit where it was due. The purser insisted on shaking them both by the hand to congratulate them.

"You were right and I was wrong, Mr. Dillman," he confessed.

"Your deputy hoodwinked us as well as you, Mr. Kilhendry," said Dillman. "He never even crept onto the edge of my list of suspects."

"Unlike me."

"I had a feeling that someone in a uniform was involved."

"What I can't understand is why a man like Monsieur Vivet needed to steal," said Kilhendry. "He's a respected chef with a huge reputation in France."

"That's not quite true," explained Genevieve. "Though he gave people his card to impress them, he was no longer employed by that hotel. He'd been sacked for stealing, and his reputation was in ruins. It struck me as odd that he was going to Egypt to work. When I asked him if he'd go back to France, he was very defensive."

"We got the full story out of him when we arrested him," Dillman added. "He left France in disgrace, went to England, and met up at some stage with your deputy. Apparently, Mr. Grandage was

291

nursing a grudge against P and O because he had not been promoted to the rank of purser."

"Yes," said Kilhendry, "Martin was passed over several times."

"It obviously hurt him. When he came across Monsieur Vivet, he realized that they had a lot in common. They were two disappointed men, looking for a chance to make good. The scheme they dreamed up was almost foolproof."

"Until they came up against you and Miss Masefield."

"We had some luck along the way," said Genevieve.

"I'm the one who had the luck," conceded Kilhendry, "and I was too boneheaded to acknowledge it. Having you two on board was my salvation. Yet all I did was to hinder you." He gave a soulful smile. "I can understand how Martin felt. I was rejected by Cunard and never forgave them. Some of my bile spilled over onto you. I'm sorry about that. It was vindictive of me."

"In a way," said Dillman, "it helped. You were so antagonistic toward us that we were determined to prove ourselves. Your attitude spurred us on."

"You deserve a special apology, Mr. Dillman," said the purser. "I had a bad experience with some of your fellow Americans and I regret to say that I let it sour me. You suffered as a result. It's too painful to go into details," he explained. "Let's just say that I once met a young lady in New York and thought I'd found the person I wanted to share my life with. She felt the same about me," he said wistfully. "But, unfortunately, her family didn't. They were wealthy and I was not. They told me that I wasn't good enough for her. So they set out to break us apart in the most brutal way." He waved a hand. "It's all in the past and I should have outgrown it by now. Having met you, Mr. Dillman," he went on, managing a grin, "I can see all Americans are not like that."

"No," replied Dillman. "I'm certainly not wealthy. You know the rates of pay for P and O crew, Mr. Kilhendry. None of us will be able to retire on our riches. We do the job because we happen to like it."

"And it gives us the opportunity to travel," said Genevieve.

"You'll always be welcome on any ship of mine," promised Kilhendry. "In fact, I'll go out of my way to ask for the pair of you. We have four people in custody and the stink of crime is finally starting to clear. Captain Langbourne is very grateful to you. We haven't even reached Port Said yet and you've swept the ship clean of villains."

"Not necessarily," Genevieve pointed out. "We may still have a few criminals aboard. It's a long way to Australia. Anything can happen between now and then, Mr. Kilhendry. The two of us will have to stay on guard."

"The *three* of us," corrected Dillman. "Isn't that right, Mr. Kilhendry?"

"Yes," the purser said with enthusiasm. "The three of us."

Port Said was a bustling harbor, teeming with people and full of tumult. So much was going on that it was difficult to take it all in at once. The royal party was the first to disembark, given a formal welcome on shore before being conducted to waiting cars. Other passengers then began to go down the gangway. The Goss family was among them, relieved that their stolen property had been found, though still stunned by the news that the Frenchman who had accompanied Polly Goss on the piano had been the thief. Myra and Lilian Cathcart were also eager to go ashore. Sorry to leave friends like Genevieve Masefield, they were excited by the thought of the vacation that lay ahead.

Frau Zumpe, Mabel Prendergast, and the Braddock sisters all insisted on thanking Genevieve once again before they left the ship. Karl-Jurgen Lenz merely gave her a curt bow as he took his farewell. The four prisoners were escorted off the ship under armed guard. Knowing the charges they faced, Martin Grandage and Claude Vivet looked grim, but there was no trace of discomfort about Roland Pountney and his father. They tripped down the gangway as if they were still on vacation. Nigel and Araminta Wilmshurst moved with less certainty. Though she held her husband's arm, the young bride did not have the appearance of someone on honeymoon. She had an air of resignation about her.

George Porter Dillman was glad when they set sail again. He felt that the *Marmora* had unloaded a large amount of unwanted baggage. Other passengers had joined the ship in Port Said but none, he suspected, would pose the problems they had already encountered. It might actually be possible to enjoy the voyage to Australia from that point on. There was one certain way of ensuring that. Dillman waited until they were halfway down the Suez Canal before he broached the subject.

After dining at the captain's table, he and Genevieve came up on deck. It was a warm evening, the ship glided smoothly through the water, and the sounds of the distant orchestra drifted into their ears. As the two of them stood at the rail, the stars cast a romantic glow.

"Captain Langbourne was in a buoyant mood this evening," said Dillman.

"So he should be, George. We solved all the crimes for him."

"He couldn't thank me enough."

"No," said Genevieve. "I heard him. You had him eating out of your hand. He's so impressed that I think he'd do absolutely anything for us."

Dillman turned to look at her. "Anything at all?"

"Yes, George."

"Do you think that he'd perform a wedding ceremony?"

He smiled fondly at her. Taken by surprise, Genevieve was too thrilled even to speak. Instead, she flung herself into his arms and gave him his answer in the only way that occurred to her. The orchestra played on and the *Marmora* surged forward, a moving beacon of light in a long corridor of darkness.

POSTSCRIPT

At the outbreak of the First World War, the Marmora *became an auxiliary cruiser in the Royal Navy Tenth Cruiser Squadron. On July 23, 1918, she was torpedoed off the Irish coast by a German submarine. Ten members of the crew were killed.*

In December 1911, the Princess Royal and her family were on their way to Egypt on the P&O liner Delhi, *when the vessel was wrecked on the coast of Morocco. All were rescued, but the Duke of Fife caught pleurisy as a result of immersion in the sea and died on January 29, 1912.*